From Kitchen To Garret
Hints For Young Householders

By

J. E. Panton

From Kitchen To Garret
Hints For Young Householders
by J. E. Panton

Copyright © 2024

All Rights reserved.

No part of this publication may be reproduced, stored in a retrieval system, or transmitted in any form or by any means, electronic, mechanical, photocopying or Otherwise, without the written permission of the publisher.
The author/editor asserts the moral right to be identified as the author/editor of this work.

ISBN: 978-93-61424-31-1

Published by

DOUBLE 9 BOOKS

2/13-B, Ansari Road
Daryaganj, New Delhi – 110002
info@double9books.com
www.double9books.com
Tel. 011-40042856

This book is under public domain

ABOUT THE AUTHOR

Jane Ellen Panton (or Jane Ellen Frith Panton) was an English writer. Panton was born as Jane Ellen Frith in Regent's Park in 1847. Her father, William Powell Frith, was a successful painter, and Panton claims he had little interest in his children. After her mother, Isabelle Jane, died in 1880, she discovered her father had a lover and more children. At this point, her father marries his old mistress. Panton appears as a model in Augustus Egg's 1859 painting trilogy Past and Present, which dealt with an unfaithful husband. She also appeared in two further paintings, one by her father and the other by Alfred Elmore. She married James Albert Panton at All Saints' Church in Kensington on August 10, 1869. Her husband was a partner in a family brewery, and his brother's widow bought him out in 1882. During that time, she lived in the Dorset market town of Wareham, which was featured in her 1909 memoir, Fresh Leaves And Green Pastures, the domestic print run of which was destroyed in settlement of a libel action brought by local squire Guy Marston, who contested the claim that he had willfully destroyed records of the Rempstone estate upon his inheritance. The memoir, however, was published in the United States.

CONTENTS

PREFACE 7

CHAPTER I
CHOOSING A HOUSE 9

CHAPTER II
THE KITCHEN ARRANGEMENTS 18

CHAPTER III
MEALS AND MONEY 28

CHAPTER IV
THE HOUSEMAID'S CLOSET,
AND GLASS AND CHINA 39

CHAPTER V
FIRST SHOPPING 46

CHAPTER VI
THE HALL 51

CHAPTER VII
THE DINING-ROOM 59

CHAPTER VIII
THE MORNING-ROOM 76

CHAPTER IX
THE DRAWING-ROOM 85

CHAPTER X
CURTAINS, CARPETS, AND LIGHTING 98

CHAPTER XI
BEDROOMS 110

CHAPTER XII
DRESSING-ROOM 140

CHAPTER XIII
SPARE ROOMS 145

CHAPTER XIV
   THE SERVANTS' ROOMS 158

CHAPTER XV
   THE NURSERIES..167

CHAPTER XVI
   IN RETIREMENT 188

CHAPTER XVII
   THE SCHOOLROOM 200

CHAPTER XVIII
   BOYS AND GIRLS...210

CHAPTER XIX
   ENTERTAINING ONE'S FRIENDS...218

CHAPTER XX
   THE SUMMING-UP..233

INDEX..245

PREFACE

In presenting this book in a completed and augmented form to the public, I think a few words of explanation are necessary, lest the way in which the chapters are written may lay me open to a charge of egotism.

About two years ago I began writing a series of short articles in the pages of the 'Lady's Pictorial' on the absorbing subject of housekeeping, meaning to confine myself strictly to the house and home of the British matron who begins life with little money and less experience, never thinking anything more would come of them than a mere temporary access of work for a few weeks; but I had not begun them for more than a month when, through the office of the paper, a regular and increasing mass of correspondence began to reach me, asking questions on every subject under the sun, from the proper management of a house and the feeding of a baby to the fearful inquiry whether I thought a wife should leave her husband or not when she discovered all too late she liked somebody else better than she did her lord and master. Since then I have become a species of 'mother confessor' to hundreds of unknown and valued friends in all parts of the world. I have correspondents in New Zealand, India, America, and in all parts of the Continent, and they have demanded of me that I shall produce a book evolved from my articles and from the pages of 'Answers to Correspondents,' which have been my work and my great pleasure since the articles on the home began; and as they persist in asking for my experience and my opinions I am obliged to give them, though knowing and fearing I shall be accused of speaking everlastingly about myself; still I have never mentioned a thing I have not tried or experienced, nor spoken of a single chair, table, or, in fact, anything that I have not honestly and truly tried myself.

From my correspondence I have evolved quite a new profession, which I commend to any lady who has taste and may wish to earn her living, I go to people's houses and advise them about their decorations, and tell them the best places to go to for different things; I buy things for country ladies, and write them long letters on every subject under the sun for a set fee, and have made some of the nicest friends possible through this means; and I feel sure that any lady who cares to take up the 'profession,' and is of *sufficient social status to be above the suspicion of taking commission or bribes from tradespeople to advertise their wares,* and who above all possesses a quick eye and a certain amount of taste, can make a good and steady income in a remarkably pleasant way, while a great future would be before any gentleman possessed of the same qualifications, for he could see to estimates for painting, repairing, &c., and could act as a buffer between the purchaser and the workman, and, being thoroughly acquainted with his business, would soon become the boon and benefactor, to the ordinary person who requires his house done up and furnished, who is much wanted, and that no lady can be, because of the necessary fighting powers and technical knowledge.

In connection with my work, we have now started a society for the employment of ladies who will either decorate a house entirely, make the chair-covers and curtains I recommend, or work at ladies' houses at dressmaking and upholstering, so that I may justly pride myself on the fact that at least my particular column in the 'Lady's Pictorial' has been of some small practical good already. The address of the 'Workers' Guild' is 11 Kensington Square, W.

I may mention, in conclusion, that I have revised and rewritten the whole of the articles which appeared in the 'Lady's Pictorial,' and in some cases entirely evolved new matter out of my inner consciousness; and if only the public extends to my book half the sympathy and appreciation I have received from my thousands of correspondents for my articles, I shall never regret the day when, at my editor's request, I seized the sceptre and became the ruling genius of many and many an unknown home.

J. E. Panton.

The Manor House, Watford, Herts.

CHAPTER I
CHOOSING A HOUSE

In the following chapters I propose to give young housekeepers, just launching their bark on the troubled seas of domesticity, the benefit of the experience that has been bought by me, occasionally rather dearly, in the course of some eighteen or twenty years; for I have often been struck with amazement at discovering how few really practical guides there are that even profess to help newly married girls past those first shoals and quicksands that so often wreck the little vessel, or that spoil and waste so much that could have been usefully employed had knowledge stood at the helm, and experience served as a lighthouse to point out the rocks and narrows. Naturally, no one ever uses another's experience entirely: to do so would make life too near perfection and too monotonous to be pleasant. Still, there are a hundred little hints that I have constantly been asked to give, a great many helps to household arrangement that I have bestowed on many of my young friends starting in life; and I trust I may not be considered unduly egotistical if I lay before my readers the result of some years of life, and a good deal of experience obtained by looking about me generally.

I shall propose in the first two or three chapters to sketch out some 'notions,' as our American cousins would say, about the questions of house-choosing and house-furnishing, I shall then pass on to the question of servants; then babies will have their turn; education, more especially of girls, will not be forgotten; and I shall endeavour to do my utmost to state plainly and describe accurately, not only how a house should be furnished, but how it should be managed and kept going, literally from garret to basement.

As very rich people can place themselves unreservedly in the hands of a professional decorator, and can moreover depend on their housekeepers afterwards for all details of domestic management, I shall begin by supposing the model couple who wish to choose a house and furnish it are not rich; if they were they need not come to me for hints, for they would be able to gratify every one of their own tastes, and need only discover the best and most expensive shops, where skilled assistants would be ready to hang expensive papers and brocades, and to fit up all the thousand and one things that fashion calls necessary, without any of my assistance. But neither are they very poor: they are young, happy, and have taste, and are rather disheartened at finding out what a very little way their money seems able to go. They have looked longingly at Persian and Turkey carpets, at beautifully designed paper and exquisite hangings, and have come home from a long day's investigation of shop-windows that has almost made Edwin forswear matrimony altogether, and that has plunged Angelina into an abyss of despair that makes her snappish to her brothers and sisters, and brings a sad look into her mother's eyes, who seems to see the first shadow 'of the prison-house' close in around her child, and yet is powerless to help her escape, because, poor dear soul, she has no means of doing so herself; being as she is the victim of the old *régime* of flock papers and moreen curtains and heavy mahogany, and being conscious, too, of the vast sums it cost her to start in housekeeping. However, I refuse to hear any grumblings at all, and demand calmly enough to know if I may see the house that our young folks mean to inhabit. Ten chances to one that they do not even know where it is likely to be: how then, I ask, can they possibly know what they will want, or what is likely to suit the house or the locality, or, indeed, any of the many things that are positively necessary to know, before as much as a roll of wall-paper can be bought or a chair or table purchased?

Here is hint number one. It is from not knowing and understanding the house in which one has to live, and through purchasing furniture simply because we like it, and not because it suits us or our domicile, that such mistakes are made. First know your house; then, and not until then, can you proceed to furnish it in a manner that will result in pleasure to you and your friends for as long as you live in it.

To young people like my couple, I would strongly recommend a house some little way out of London. Rents are less; smuts and blacks are conspicuous by their absence; a small garden, or even a tiny conservatory (the joys and management of which ought to have a chapter all to themselves), is not an impossibility; and if Edwin have to pay for his season-ticket, that is nothing in comparison with his being able to sleep in fresh air, to have a game of tennis in summer, or a friendly evening of music, chess, or games in the winter, without expense; and with Angelina's absence from the temptations of shop-windows in town, where, if she does not know of anything she wants when she goes out for her aimless walk, she soon sees something that she cannot resist, which she buys just because she has the money in her pocket, and likes the look of an article she would never have thought of had she been outside the range of temptation.

Another reason for choosing the suburbs at the commencement of married life is that in this case the rival mothers-in-law and the rival families will not be running in and out perpetually; and neither will Angelina be always contrasting the old ease, plenty, and amusements in her sisters' lives, and which used to be hers, with the somewhat straitened and monotonous existence that she must put up with until Edwin has made a mark in the world, and is able to keep his carriage and live in style. Granted, then, that the suburbs have been selected, the first few months of the engagement can be advantageously spent in running down on Saturday afternoons to divers 'Parks' to look at houses that sound so beautiful on paper, and are too often the very reverse in the reality, in sauntering in the neighbourhood of each 'eligible residence' and in endeavouring to discover what are the *pros* and *cons* of each, and in finding out the soil and the aspect, and if there are or are not any pretty walks to be found in the country round. Avoid clay; let no persuasions, no arguments, persuade you that clay—at all events suburban clay—can ever be anything save depressing and rheumatic. You may drain, you may dig, but clay is like a ghost that will not be laid, and that sooner or later asserts itself in the most unpleasant and decided manner possible.

One of the prettiest suburbs we know of is utterly spoiled by its clay soil. In warm days it depresses, in damp it chills; and in an east wind the soil looks so dreary, so parched, that the mere sight of it is wretched, while fog and mist hang over it all the winter, and sour the tempers and warp the minds of the inhabitants until there is a lack of hospitality and an amount of work for the doctors that is wonderful, if unpleasant to contemplate.

Of course, all the S. or S.W. and S.E. suburbs are the most fashionable and the most sought after; and although, to my mind, Penge and Dulwich are dreary and damp, they are evidently well supported and much lived in, but the higher parts of Sydenham are to be preferred; while Forest Hill, the higher parts of Lordship Lane, Elmer's End—where there are some extremely pretty and convenient villas—and the best parts of Bromley, Kent, are all they should be. Still, to those who do not mind the north side of London, Finchley, Bush Hill Park—where the houses are nice to look at and excellently arranged—and Enfield are all worthy of consideration.

Edwin's work and its locality must, after all give the casting vote, for, if it be at the West End, Liverpool Street Station is out of the question, and Victoria, is a *sine quâ non*, and, of course, he may choose to live in town. If he does, I should strongly persuade him not to be guided by fashion, and to prefer a good-sized, old, well-built house in an unfashionable locality, to a small, heated, stuffy, badly put together residence in one of the parts of town that are inhabited by those with whom he can never hope to associate.

Indeed, when I have seen the tiny hovels in Mayfair where ladies and gentlemen crowd together, and where their servants herd under tiles or in the damp, dark cellars, I have thought that Fashion and Folly were two names for one thing, and have had but a small opinion of those who could condemn themselves and their poor domestics to such an unhealthy and miserable existence, just because Park Lane is close by and it is fashionable!

Doubtless the great thing that strikes us when we are house-hunting is that if women architects could get employment houses would be far better planned than they are now. In each bedroom, it seems to me, that I have inspected—and their name is legion—the male mind that designed the rooms never took into consideration that a bed should not stand between the windows and the door; which, by the way, is always put so that the moment it opens the occupant of the bed has a full view of the passage or landing; he has given us no recesses in which we can put shelves, and by a judicious curtain arrangement do away with the necessity of buying large and expensive wardrobes; he puts the fireplaces where, if we are ill, we could not possibly enjoy ourselves with sitting over the fire and warming ourselves; and he gives us far too many windows as a rule, and almost ruins us in blinds and curtains, to prevent the neighbours from gazing at us when we are dressing.

He forgets cupboards, and in fact insists on producing month after month an excellent shell, but one that requires altering considerably by a lady before it really can be lived in at all; and I would strongly suggest that female architects for domestic architecture solely would be a great help to all who have to live in houses planned and executed by men who have no idea of comfort, and but small appreciation for the trifles light as air that make all the difference between that and great discomfort.

If Edwin be at all handy at carpentering he could do a great deal to make even a builder's design much better—he could rehang doors and extemporise screens; but I look forward to a time when it shall be necessary for houses to be passed by a sanitary commission before they are allowed to be let at all; when all these discomforts will be minimised, and when dust-bin refuse and bad drainage shall be penal if used for foundations and put into houses; when the lesser evils of badly placed doors, windows, and fireplaces will be looked after, as making parts of what should be a perfect whole.

Before taking his house in the suburbs, Edwin must see he holds it on a lease that does not include structural repairs. He must give a properly authorised inspector, *from a distance*, a fee to inspect all the drains; he must examine the foundations and look to soil, see that the doors and windows really fit, and that the skirting board has not shrunk away from the flooring. He must look to the roof and the chimneys, and, if possible, get a character for it from the last tenant; and then, and then only, need he and Angelina come to me and say, 'We have settled on our Paradise; now please come and see it and tell us what we had better buy first, and what we must do to furnish it and make it look as pretty as we intend it to do.'

And yet, even when Edwin and Angelina have at last settled on their house, and have sensibly inspected it from top to bottom, I should, long before buying any furniture, decide definitely which room was to be dining-room, which bedroom, and which drawing-room, and, being guided by the sunshine obtainable in each, rather than the builder's plan, utterly refuse to enter a shop until I had made up my mind how the rooms are to be appropriated.

Sunshine is the very first necessary of life; without it sickness comes, low spirits are one's portion, and a thousand and one tiny ailments hang about us, until we sum up a tremendous doctor's bill, utterly ignorant that we could have cured ourselves comfortably had we had any sense, and dispensed with our blinds, regardless of the fading of our carpets and curtains; or moved our morning-room into the sacred precincts of the drawing-room, which obtains all the early sunshine, and has none at all during the hours when we should be sitting there. But the possession of a large and hideous, white marble mantelpiece and a tiled hearth to the ugly, wasteful grate says 'drawing-room' too plainly for the ordinary mind to rise above the builder's dictum; and so a cheerful breakfast table is sacrificed, for conventionalities that I, for one, never see without longing to disregard, simply because of their family likeness to every one else's possessions, and gloom and low spirits seize their victim, and work their wicked will, sending off the husband to town with an aching head, and causing the wife a long, laborious morning of snapping at servants and children, simply because she had not begun her day with a proper amount of sunshine. I could fill a whole chapter with praises of the life-giver, the mighty, beautiful sun; and whenever I see blinds hardly raised, or carefully adjusted to save the furniture, I know that I shall find inside those guarded windows faded cheeks, even if the chairs are fresh, and weary, tired people, who are hardly aware what sort of a day it is outside, and who are shivering over a fire that would not be wanted were the fire nature has given us allowed to do its work. Therefore, do not be guided in your choice of rooms by the fact that the builder has made a sunless, dark-looking room the dining-room, and a cheerful, light, and pretty chamber the drawing-room. The white marble mantelpiece does not matter one bit.

I can soon alter that, and a tiled hearth is not such a dear or precious luxury that one cannot afford to put in another in the drawing-room, and it is extremely nice to have a hearth where we can put down our plates and dishes to keep hot should any one be late; and the other details are generally so small in their differences that I am sure there is no reason why we should not have strength of mind to be different to our next-door neighbour, who most probably has taken things as she found them, and in consequence is rarely, if ever, without a headache.

Even in the smallest houses in these days there is generally a third room, and this I should advise being kept entirely to sit in. I cannot imagine anything nastier than to sit in a room in which one has one's meals; the mere worry of seeing them laid would annoy me so that I don't think I should be able to enjoy them afterwards; and then nothing seems to me to quite clear away the terrible sensation, and smell of meals, that appear to saturate the walls of any room where food is constantly served, while the additional fire that seems the only reason that compels people to remain all day in one atmosphere is paid for over and over again by the extra warmth of the house itself, and the satisfactory manner in which damps and draughts are exorcised, while no one can tell the advantage it is to health to have a change of rooms, and to sit in a place where food and the evil odours attending meals never can come.

And here let me impress upon you, my readers, always to be guided by common sense, not by fashion and conventionalities; to do a thing because it is healthy and sensible, not because Mrs. Jones next door and Mrs. Smith over the way do it; to buy a thing because it is required, because it is pretty and suitable to your house and your means, not because it is 'so very expensive,' and so can never become 'common,' or because it is the 'very last thing out'; and, above all, do not mind taking advice and using your eyes, being quite sure that older folks, even if they are stupid and slow-going, have probably seen more and know more than you do, simply because their lives have been longer by a great many years than yours are at present. And do not be above letting other people have the use of your talents, for the world would be much nicer and happier altogether if we were not all so profoundly selfish and exclusive, and were not so desperately afraid of soiling ourselves and our garments by rubbing shoulders against anything or any one to whom we can apply the word 'common.'

I myself should like to see every beautiful thing common. I should love to know that all the world saw, possessed, and cared for art colours and art furniture, and had nice tastes, and I look forward to a time when even our poor brethren will appreciate all the inexpensive lovelinesses that are to be had now by those who know where to get them, and I trust that some day free art exhibitions and lectures may teach them what real beauty is, and so enlighten and enliven lives that at present are of the dullest and most sober description.

In stating that life itself may be changed by sunshine and by cheerful surroundings, and that even the bitter lot of the poor would be bettered by art, I am aware I lay myself open to the same jeers that greeted the Kyrle Society—that blessed society that, regardless of cold water, goes on its way, giving of its talents to the sick and needy; but I maintain my position for all that, and regardless of the ridicule levelled at them, anent sunflowers and dadoes taking the place of bread and clothes, I point to the hospital wards, transformed from bare whitewashed prisons into artistic, charming, home-like rooms, and I should like to have the statistics given me of all who have recovered there, and the time they took to recover in, in the two different aspects of the walls, being perfectly certain that there would be more and quicker recoveries in the reign of the Kyrle Society than when the wearied, suffering creatures had nothing to look at or think about save their own painful, cruel lot.

Or if you wish another example still, take the well-known famous description of the sour tempers and hard days possessed and lived by Thomas Carlyle and his wife, and then go and inspect the house in which they lived together for some thirty-eight years. The house itself is delightful—an old-world place, full of beautiful corners—and could be made charming with a little money and taste, but the hideous paper and paint still lingering behind them, the dark windows, in some cases half-filled with ground glass to keep out the view of a building that looks singularly like a workhouse—all accounted to me for a great deal of Mrs. Carlyle's ill-health and low spirits, and for a vast quantity of Mr. Carlyle's dyspepsia and ill-tempered behaviour; for he could be nothing else in sunless rooms and with walls papered in the ugly, depressing manner in which he doubtless considered them satisfactory, or, still more likely, thought that any paper did as long as the walls were covered.

Therefore, in selecting house and furniture, and choosing your rooms and appropriating them, remember the first thing is to be cheerful. Dark days will come in life to us all, but they will not be hopeless and too dreadful to be endured if we cultivate a cheerful, contented spirit, and insist on having cheerful surroundings.

Do you recollect, I wonder, the orthodox dining-rooms of twenty-five years ago?—the heavy, thick curtains of red or green cloth or moreen damask; the tremendous mahogany sideboard, generally with a cellarette underneath it, which, I recollect, made an admirable tomb in which to bury one's dolls or obnoxious books, generally triumphantly taken from the schoolroom; the chairs that required two people to lift them; the carpet that seemed immovable, and that was too heavy to be shaken more than once a year; and the woolly-bear hearthrug that always smelt of dust, and that was a receptacle for all sorts of cinders, toy-bricks, leaden soldiers, and bones dragged in and buried there by a delinquent dog or cat? Why, the mere shaking of that rug once a week resulted in the discovery of all sorts of treasures that had been lost, and the dust that came out was enough to choke the neighbourhood, and doubtless would have done so had the other inhabitants not all been engaged with their own. Ah! if you do not all of you remember the dining-room of the past, I do; but never without a shudder, or a wonder how we managed to live in such a dark and dusty atmosphere, where work, reading, drawing, and writing all had to be hustled out of sight and out of the way of the parlour-maid, who came to 'lay the cloth,' and renew the foul odours, which had only just been exorcised, which breakfast had left behind it to poison the morning with. I should think that domestic furniture was at its very lowest depths of despair then; but that is thirty years ago, or perhaps forty, and nothing turned the tide for quite twenty years!

In the beginning of those evil days the graceful furniture of Chippendale and Sheraton was pushed away and consigned to attics, or sold cheaply at country auctions to fit up inn parlours or rooms behind shops; and the heavy 'handsome' furniture of mahogany and damask bore down upon us, and made us for a time the most depressed of people, heavy with our ugly furnishings, and the mock of all nations that had better taste and lighter hearts than we were possessed of.

It would take too long to trace the gradual development of taste and cheerfulness since then, neither do I know to whom is due our present state of emancipation and love of pretty things, but even sixteen years ago light was only just beginning to be vouchsafed to us. Now it is impossible to buy an ugly thing in good shops, and each person's house is no longer the reflection of one particular upholsterer's shop or of one particular style; but it is a carefully arranged shrine, cared for and looked after, and judiciously managed by the owner, who, if she have not taste herself, is now shamed into using some one else's, by the contrast she cannot help seeing her home presents to all the others into which she enters; and one of the most hopeless people I know, who began life with gilt legs to her chairs and a collection of family plate (plated) on her sideboard, has become unobtrusive, even if she can never be tasteful, simply by seeing how different her own notions were to those of the cleverer people with whom circumstances brought her into contact!

However, this chapter will become too long if I relate any more 'fearful examples,' and, impressing on my readers the great necessity of sunshine and cheerfulness in their scheme of furnishing, I will pass on to the subject of the house itself, which must be most carefully chosen after long and deliberate inspection thereof, as I remarked before; one of the most necessary of all mottoes to be recollected in starting in life being, 'Do nothing in a hurry. More haste, less speed.'

CHAPTER II
THE KITCHEN ARRANGEMENTS

The other day I was asked, as I so often am by young couples, to go with them to look over a house they had just taken, and to give them some advice on the decoration and management generally thereof; and when we had thought about all the pretty colours and graceful draperies we considered suitable, I asked to look at the kitchen department, and I was truly horrified to discern that my young folks had only been into the kitchen once, and had no idea of its capabilities.

I at once departed to look at it, and found all the accommodation for the unfortunate maids consisted of a square box, one half stove, the other half door, a couple of shelves for all the bridal glass and china, and a larder in which one could have placed the meat, butter, and bread without moving from the fireside, and which, useless enough in winter, would be doubly so when summer came, and added another trial to those of the already overburdened cook. However, the agreement was signed and the house taken for five years, during which, I am quite certain, no servant would remain a moment over her month, and in consequence of which that establishment will, I know, be in a continual state of misery and turmoil.

Of course one can hardly expect young people to think of these prosaic and disagreeable details for themselves, but they are most necessary details for persons to consider. Personally I would much rather regard life as a smooth chariot gliding along a rose-embowered road, propelled by some mysterious and wonderful power called Love, who is, of course, entirely ignorant of anything save kisses and blisses. I do not want in the very least really to know how dinner is cooked, how houses are managed, and the very names of chairs and dusters are properly obnoxious to me—or rather would be if we could only do without them. But, alas! we cannot; we must be clean, we should be healthy, and it is imperative that we should have kitchens and be warmed and fed; and, as fairies are extinct and brownies no longer appear and do work mysteriously and pleasantly before we are up in the morning, even a bride must be told about these unpleasant localities, and must learn to take an interest even in her scullery and the position of her dust-bin. Therefore, on the principle of getting rid of our disagreeable duties first, we will begin with hints for kitchen management before thinking about the purchase of the rest of the furniture; for it is a very good rule to buy what we must have first, and then keep any surplus we may have to spend afterwards; and we will begin with the kitchen, for that department is always the most uninteresting to the young housekeeper, for she has only a certain amount of money to spend on everything, and she grudges, I am sure, every pound she has to spend on pots and pans, that she thinks would be so useful if added to the small sum she has at her disposal, for extras and ornaments in the other rooms in her house.

If their household consist of two maids and Edwin and Angelina alone, their *batterie de cuisine* need be neither an extensive nor expensive one, for after a lengthy experience of maidens and their ways I have come to the conclusion that the fewer things they have the fewer they will spoil, and that we are far more likely to have clean saucepans and pots if there are none to put aside and no others to use, if, as the maid thinks, she has not time at her disposal for the moment in which to clean them. Now if she have only the saucepans in actual use they must be cleaned as soon as they have been used, or the food will most certainly tell tales of her.

The position of the kitchen in a house makes an immense amount of difference in the work, for if it be situated underground it makes quite one servant's work difference. Fortunately builders are more and more inclined to think of this, and it is now rare to find in a new house the unpleasant and unhealthy arrangement that exists in most London houses. First of all, the staircase to the kitchen is always a dreadful source of worry. We must cover the stairs to deaden the noise, and the wear and tear is so great that the covering has to be renewed well-nigh yearly if we are in any way to preserve a tidy appearance. The best material to use on these stairs is a species of harshly woven Dutch carpeting. It is made in art colours, and is about 1s. 6d. a yard; or Treloar's pretty crimson cocoanut matting, which is a trifle less in price, and lasts more time, when, if it should show signs of wear, it can once more be covered with oilcloth, and then I think the stairs will look as nice and keep as tidy as long as possible.

If there be any passages in and round the kitchen and servants' apartments generally, I have discovered that a most excellent plan here is to have a high dado of oilcloth, headed by a real dado-rail painted black, and then papered above with one of the blue and white washable papers that resemble tiles, are moderately inexpensive, and always clean and bright. At one time my passages in those regions were my despair; they were narrow, and bits and corners—paper, plaster, and all—were continually knocked out in the most depressing way, especially at the back door, where, moreover, every boy who came for orders or with parcels solaced himself while waiting by leaning his greasy head or putting his dirty hands on the wall-paper, until the whole place looked disgraceful almost before the paste was well dry. I was at my wits' end. Cretonne and matting were decidedly out of place. At last the idea of oilcloth came into my head, and for six years it has now been up, and is as good as the day it was purchased. I continued this up the back staircase, with very favourable results as regards wear and tear, for a box knocking against it does not hurt it in the least, and any marks can be rubbed off at once with a dry duster. The oilcloth is not stretched too tight, and it is nailed top and bottom, then secured at the top with the dado-rail, which, being made of what is technically called 'scantling,' is most inexpensive; a neat pattern is chosen in oak-browns.

The oilcloth made like an old Roman mosaic would of course be preferable as far as appearance goes, but this costs double, and therefore I was obliged to have an ordinary and commonplace-looking one instead; but should the æsthetic eye revolt against the ugly colours of cheap oilcloth, I may mention it can be painted any colour easily, and this can make it at once pretty to look at.

I am of opinion that such a dado would be a great thing in the kitchen itself, where the walls so speedily become soiled by the heat from the hot-water pipes that the kitchen soon becomes dismal for the servants to sit in. I do wish it would enter into the plan of even quite a small house to have a tiny room where the servants could sit and work, or have their meals, out of the kitchen atmosphere; and then perhaps I should not mind the look of the kitchen quite so much; but even in a large house there is seldom a room one can set aside for this purpose, and often enough the only place a maid has to live in is the one in which all the cooking is done, and where, winter and summer alike, a large fire has to be kept going from morning until night.

But until that happy day arrives we can make the orthodox kitchen almost a model one, with a dado of oilcloth as high as we can get it, and a light varnished paper above the dado; the varnishing allows of constant washing, and though this is, of course, an expensive process, it insures cleanliness, and, the first outlay once made, it does not require renewing for some years. The ceiling, however, should be whitewashed, with the scullery walls and ceiling, and those of the cellars, &c., regularly once a year—about May. Nothing should be thought more necessary than this; and once a year, when this is done, the mistress should overlook every single possession she has, comparing them with a list made at the time she entered the house, which she should never let out of her own possession, and which she should alter from time to time, as things are broken or lost or bought.

The most important thing now to consider is the grate, and nowhere, I think, does the ordinary landlord or builder 'skimp' more than in this; and let me ask any young bride to put her pride in her pocket here, and to consult her mother, or the last bride but four, or any one who has had a grate in her own possession, before she passes the grate that the landlord has provided her with. Of course I can only *hope* any new householder will take advice; the dear things always know so much better from theory than we do from practice, and are never going to make the mistakes we did, and from which sprang the knowledge we are as anxious to give them as they are unwilling to take, that I can only humbly ask them to see about the grate before they really put themselves in its power, and I beg them to insist on having a new one; for on no other portion of the house does so much of our comfort depend, a bad grate spoiling the cook's temper and wasting the food horribly, while a good one is an endless treasure, of which we really cannot make too much.

If our young folks are too proud to ask advice, let them go to Steel and Garland's, on the Holborn Viaduct, where I have seen some most picturesque kitcheners, which I must confess to hanker after in a manner that perhaps is not right; but I cannot help it, they look so charming, and are, I believe, so satisfactory in their working. They have blue-tiled backs, and have also delightful ovens and a broad expanse over the fire that would heat any amount of saucepans at the same time; and if Angelina goes to live in her own house, I should certainly recommend her to see these before buying any other kitchen grate. They are most economical as regards coal; and if Angelina be wise enough so to manage her cook as to impress upon her what an excellent fire can be made and kept up in a kitchener using the small coal almost like dust, that is so very inexpensive, and that the best Wallsend need not be taken for the purpose, she will soon save the cost of her stove over and over again in the difference in the price of the material she uses to keep it going.

Of course this small coal can be burned in a kitchener that has not blue tiles, and is a simple, ugly thing; but these are not as reliable as a good stove is, and the ovens burn and spoil so much, owing to the inferior iron of which they are made, that an effort is worth making to secure a good and *reliable* grate, else Edwin's dinner may occasionally not be quite as nice as could be wished for him to come home to. But, cheap grate or dear grate, never allow for one moment that an odour therefrom should pervade the house. This may require a battle; but it is one to be won by the mistress if she exhibit firmness, and, above all, a due knowledge of her business as manager of the household. The terrible and sickening smell that so often has been known to fill a house simply comes from grease having been allowed to fall on the oven plates inside. This waxes hot, and then is followed by the odour, which there is nothing like anywhere besides. To obviate this, a cook should always carefully look after any spot or drop of grease, and if by any chance the oven has become foul, it must be cleansed by burning some hay or straw in it; but this need not occur at all if the cook be commonly careful, any more than that green-water need smell, if a small crust of bread be placed in the water while it is boiling, and then the water should at once be emptied away into a corner of the garden, or down the sink if there be no garden, when a little carbolic acid should be added, which would take away the odour at once. These may appear very trivial matters to write about, but a great deal of our comfort and, in consequence, of our happiness depends upon these trifles. I know nothing more disagreeable and trying than a bad smell, and if Edwin comes home to a house reeking of dinner and the oven, what wonder that he flies to his pipe and wishes himself back in his club; while his wife cannot possibly smile and look pleased to see him, when she is suffering untold miseries from the refractory grate, and a cook who would be only too glad to save her the odours if only she knew how.

I am no advocate for mistresses spending their lives in a perpetual harassment of their unfortunate servants, but there is one thing that should never be left to the tender mercies even of the best servant that ever lived; and that is the sink, or, in fact, any drain that may be in the kitchen regions. I cannot tell how it is, but a domestic appears to me to be born into the world bereft of any sense of smell. They never can smell anything. You will go into the kitchen and discover an odour enough to appal you, and you will say, 'What is this terrible smell, I wonder?' but your cook will reply, 'Smell, mum? Oh, I don't smell anything; perhaps it have drifted in at the window.' But do not be daunted by that. Do not for one moment think you are wrong and she is right, but persevere, and hunt that smell down, and ten chances to one you will find something that requires your immediate attention in the sink line, or else that, despite most stringent orders, cook has started a private dust-bin, and has put away and forgotten something that is breeding a fever under your very nose.

Insist upon a regular flushing of every drain or sink every week, as a matter of course; and I should advise you to see this done for yourself, and, furthermore, that you should yourself supplement the flushing by using liberally some disinfectant. If you do this yourself, keeping the disinfectant locked up and labelled 'Poison,' there will be supplied to your servant's mind a reason why you should personally superintend the flushing part of the business, and she will not then have the idea in her mind that is so often in the mind of the ordinary servant, that you are spying after her because you cannot trust her. The drains are far too important a matter, you can tell her, to leave to any one, and therefore you must see after them yourself. Sanitas in saucers is a very good disinfectant, and smells most pleasantly; and permanganate of potass diluted largely with water is excellent to put down the sinks and drains themselves; but there is no smell about this, so I, personally, prefer carbolic or chloride of lime, because then I know for certain that something of the kind has been used, and the rather pleasant odour from the disinfectant also seems to send away at once any disagreeable smell that may have been hanging about. In the sinks themselves should be kept a large lump of soda; this should weigh half a pound or more, and be renewed every day or two; this prevents the grease from the saucepans clogging the pipes, as such a large piece dissolves very slowly, and all the water that passes over the soda serves to cleanse the pipe in a most satisfactory way. It is always an excellent thing to set aside particular days and hours for different duties. They are not half so likely to be slurred or omitted as they are in a house where *any time* does for *anything*. Therefore Saturday, immediately after the orders have been given, is an excellent time for seeing to the drains. Saturday morning most people are at home, and a quarter of an hour takes little out of the morning, while a good deed has been done, and the house has been purified for Sunday.

And here let me just for one instant dwell on the great necessity of regularity, order, and, above all, early rising, in a small household. If you lie in bed, *Sundays* or weekdays, things cannot possibly prosper with you; you cannot possibly either keep beforehand with life if you live in a muddle or breakfast late; and should you be late on Sundays you not only hurry to church yourself, or stay away altogether—a wretched habit—but you prevent your servants attending, or allow them to go when the service has begun, and they are too hurried and worried to properly appreciate the weekly rest that should be such a help to them. Every member of the household and every visitor should be punctual at the breakfast table, and nothing save real illness should excuse a breakfast in bed. A headache is more often cured by getting up than by remaining in the bedroom atmosphere; and be sure of this, lying in bed upstairs means waste, laziness, and unsatisfactory behaviour generally in the regions of the kitchen. Hence I feel I cannot say too much against it, or in favour of regularity, punctuality, and early rising, without which excellent qualities no household can get along practically or become anything save a place of hopeless muddle.

Though it would be waste of space to write out an exact list of kitchen utensils in these days, when every respectable firm publishes one at the end of their catalogue, and which, by the way, may generally be halved as regards the quantities with advantage, it may not be out of place here to give a few general hints on the subject. And we may begin by stating that 'plenty makes waste,' and that 'enough is as good as a feast,' and then we will make up our minds to purchase only just sufficient kitchen articles for the cook's use, at all events until we know our cook and learn if she be to be trusted; though even then I see no reason why she should have more material at her command than she can use; for I believe this idea of superfluity has done more harm in the kitchen than enough, no servant being sufficiently strong-minded to resolutely put aside anything she can do without.

In a small and, shall I say, impecunious household it is not so much what we want as what we can do without that has to be considered; and it is really astonishing on how little we can 'get along,' as far as mere existence is concerned, if we resolutely turn our back on all that is not positively necessary for us, although I must confess that under such circumstances life is certainly not worth living, and has to be a very bare and barren matter altogether; and I hope that Angelina, at all events, will not have to live quite such a Spartan existence as this; still, great care must be exercised, especially in the kitchen, if she be to have a pleasant time of it among nice and pretty things.

In the first place, Angelina must show her cook that she really does know her duties as mistress of a household, and she must be able to hold her own when cook demands extravagant supplies; while at the same time she must not expect a quart of milk a day to suffice for a household consisting of a baby, two servants, the master and mistress, and last, but not least, two cats, as a friend of mine did; but she must diligently study beforehand quantities of divers things, so that she may be ready when called upon to prove she really does know what she is talking of; and a judicious selection of kitchen utensils will point out to her cook at starting that her mistress has ideas of her own on the subject of household management.

Now six saucepans must suffice, and this is really a most liberal allowance, as four might be made to do; two must be nicely lined with enamel, and must be kept entirely for milk and white sauces, such as melted butter, for nothing else should ever be cooked in a saucepan that is required for delicate cookery. After a long experience, I must confess that no one's kitchen utensils please me as much as Whiteley's do; they are good and reasonable, and can be relied on to be as cheap and wear as long as any one else's. Indeed, for these things he is really cheaper than any one I know of, and I now buy all there that I require for kitchen use. He supplies a list of goods suitable for different-sized houses; but no one requires, I think, all that he considers necessary, and a little weeding should be done from even his smallest list, according to the number of the rooms in the house. Still, these lists are a great assistance, and Angelina would do well to write for one before she finally makes up her mind what to order.

There are generally three or four prices quoted for nearly all domestic articles, such as fryingpans, gridirons, saucepans, &c., and it is safe to make it a rule to take a medium quality. At a shop you can trust, the very best, no doubt, must always be best, but '*good enough*' for use and wear is to be our rule, and when you have discovered that such-and-such an establishment really tells you the truth, you may depend that for your purpose the medium quality will answer as well as anything, while even in some cases the lowest will occasionally be good enough for the purpose for which you require it. There are certain things no housekeeper should ever be without, and one is a bread-pan with a cover, and this is sometimes quite a difficult thing to procure. No one seems now to have time to put their bread in pans, and the milk in those nice white-lipped basins I can never see without longing to buy, but these two things should be insisted on in Angelina's kitchen. The bread taken in to-day should not be used until to-morrow, and when received from the baker should be immediately put into the pan in the larder and covered over. This keeps it moist and fresh, and, without having the evil properties of new bread, is as pleasant to eat, which it could never be if left to dry in the hot kitchen, or to become dusty and dry, or may be even damp, on the larder shelf. The pan should be wiped out every morning with a clean cloth, and on no account should pieces be allowed to accumulate.

There is, I think, more bread wasted in an ordinary household than is quite pleasant to contemplate. Crusts are cut off and put on one side in the dining-room, and of course no one in the kitchen will look at them after that; or double the quantity is cut at luncheon and dinner that is required, and once more this is put on one side. Now, it is quite easy to calculate how much bread should be used in a small household, but it is very difficult to find out where the waste is when the establishment increases. Still it is possible, and I do hope Angelina will begin by impressing on her cook that she will not allow waste, nor what makes sometimes a fearful amount of waste, i.e. the calling at the back door of those dreadful people with carts, who want to buy bottles, or rags, or bones, or such like trifles; for these men often tempt young servants to thieve, and often enough, too, snatch up a spoon or fork, should one be lying about, while the servant's back is turned, and she is searching for her hoard of things, none of which really belongs to her at all.

I recollect quite well one year, when I was at Bournemouth seeing these carts going about regularly to different houses morning after morning, and as my window faced the road, I had the curiosity to watch what they received, more than once. Opposite to me lived a family, the mistress of which had often enough lamented to me the fearful appetites possessed by her servants, and one day, about 8.15, just when I was going down to breakfast, I saw the cart arrive, and saw also half loaves of bread, 'chunks' of meat, and pieces of butter and bacon, all brought out in an unappetising manner together, and shunted into the cart. My friend's breakfast-hour was half-past nine, so the cart had merrily gone on its way long before her blinds were drawn up; but the very next time she spoke of her servants' gigantic capacities for putting away food, I 'up and spake' of what I had seen in such a way that the cart never called there again, and her bills were reduced to one-half in less time than it takes to tell of them.

The driver of that cart once stopped at my door and descended into the kitchen. Luckily for me, I was, as usual, writing at the window at my desk, and, seeing him come in, I waited a few moments, and then descended into the lower regions too, and found him eloquently persuading my good little cook to sell bones &c. to him, but she was refusing staunchly; and then I appeared, and though, I confess honestly, I was shaking with fright, and was only sustained by the knowledge that the gardener was cleaning the boots near by, I gave that man a 'piece of my mind,' and, informing him that it was he and his fellows who made young servants thieves, bade him begone, telling him that if ever I found him on my premises again I would give him in charge; which so alarmed him that he fled at once to other houses, doubtless vituperating me in his mind all the time; but that I did not mind, as long as he transferred himself and his kindly attentions somewhere else.

In a well-regulated household every morsel of food should be used; the bones always are useful for soup, and a 'digester' should be one of Angelina's most indispensable possessions. This should always be at hand for stock; and excellent soups, than which nothing is nicer on which to begin one's dinner, can be procured by aid of the digester, if Angelina has a thoughtful cook, who uses every morsel to advantage, and never throws away a bone, even a fish bone, all of which aid the soup, and save buying other provisions.

Care and thought are centred in the kitchen, and once Angelina has carefully trained her maid into nice ways, the house will go like clockwork, and that is why I should advise any young housekeeper to take young girls as household servants (*not on any account, by the way, as nurses; no young nurse is worth her keep save as an under-servant*); an 'experienced cook' quotes her experience, and Angelina, having none to fall back upon, trembles and is conquered; but with a bright, intelligent girl, Mrs. Beeton's most excellent book on household management (as regards food), a little common-sense, and a mother who has brought her daughter up sensibly, Angelina can start on her way, quite certain that she and her maidens will work together in a pleasant and satisfactory manner, and that she will never be exposed to domestic earthquakes such as occur with 'experienced servants,' who, having brought themselves up in a big establishment where nobody cared for them, go into Angelina's small one in order to get as much out of it as they can, regarding all mistresses as their natural enemies!

One more subject as regards the kitchen. Never allow, on any pretext, that a dust-bin or a 'wash-tub' is ever needed. With a kitchener every morsel of *débris* should be burned in the close grate; and a dust-bin is never a necessity to any one who knows her business, and is determined never to allow of the smallest waste. There is nothing a kitchener will not burn—remember that, please! and flatly refuse to allow a dust-bin in any part of the house; it only means that waste will go on *ad libitum*, and that dirt and untidiness are favoured by one's cook.

CHAPTER III
MEALS AND MONEY

I am going to devote this chapter entirely to the matter of money—that is to say, to indicating how the income should be apportioned, and what it costs to feed a small family who are content with nice plain food, and who do not hanker after elaborate cooking and out-of-the-way dishes; in which case they must not come to me for advice, as I have really no information to give them; and to further indicate as far as I can—outside the limits of a cookery book—some of the meals that can be managed without either much fuss and worry and an undue expenditure of money and time.

If Angelina really intends to marry on an income varying between 300*l.* and 500*l.* a year, she must sit down and weigh the *pros* and *cons* most carefully. Dress and house-rent are the two items that have risen considerably during the last few years; otherwise everything is much cheaper and nicer than it used to be before New Zealand meat came to the front, and sugar, tea, cheese, all the thousand and one items one requires in a house, became lower than ever they had been before; and therefore, if she be clever and willing to put her shoulder to the domestic wheel, she can most certainly get along much more comfortably in the way of food than she used to do. For example, when I was married, sugar was 6*d.* a pound, and now it is 2*d.*; and instead of paying 1*s.* 1*d.* a pound for legs of mutton, I give 7½*d.* for New Zealand meat, which is as good as the best English mutton that one can buy. Bread, too, is 5½*d.*—and ought to be considerably lower—as against the 8*d.* and 9*d.* of seventeen years ago; and, besides this, there are a thousand-and-one small things to be bought that one never used to see, and fish and game are also infinitely less expensive, for in the season salmon is no longer a luxury, thanks to Frank Buckland, while prime cod at 4*d.* a pound can hardly be looked upon as a sinful luxury, and this is the price we paid in the season in the Central Fish Market, where fish is always to be obtained fresh, cheap, and in as great a variety as at any West End shop; while of course those detestable Stores, much as I personally dislike them, have done much for us in lowering the prices of grocers, who are always willing to give ready-money purchasers every advantage, the while they are civil, send the purchased articles home, make out their own bills, and take care their customers are not worried to death, as they are at the Stores by supercilious youths, who make the place a rendezvous, and simper with girls who have been sent to do shopping, and combine it with large instalments of flirtation. No, I must say I have not one good word for the Stores; and, furthermore, I detest them because, living as I do a little way out of town, I am persecuted on my return journeys with enormous parcels, of all sorts and descriptions, that jam one's elbows, fall down incontinently on one's best bonnet, and are pushed under one's feet, until the twenty minutes' travel are rendered purgatorial by people who will shop at the Stores, and are in consequence turned completely for the nonce into beasts of burden, all to save a very problematic shilling or two; but as cabs to and from the station have to be added to the fare to town, I venture to state they would be far better served by a local grocer, or by either Whiteley or Shoolbred, whose prices are the same as at the Stores, and whose carts come to one's door. But these little points are just where the ordinary woman's finance comes utterly to an end. She can readily comprehend that sugar at 2*d*. a pound is cheaper than sugar at 3*d*.; but tell her to add to the cost of this the fare to town, wear and tear of temper, gloves, and clothes, odd cabs, and the necessary luncheon, and she is floored at once. She recognises the 2*d*. as against the 3*d*. immediately, but she cannot grasp the rest; besides which, at the Stores she sees one hundred and one things that she buys simply because they are cheap, and not because she requires them in the very least; so if Angelina values her peace of mind let her eschew the Stores, and, instead, talk to her nearest grocer on the subject, and see what can be done with him before she goes elsewhere.

Now, I think, that 2*l*., or, at the most, 2*l*. 10*s*., should keep Angelina, Edwin, and the model maid per week in comfort, and yet allow of no scrimping; but in this case Angelina must put a good deal of common-sense in her purse as well as money. Meat for three people need not be more than 12*s*., 4*s*. for bread and flour, 2*s*. for eggs, 4*s*. for milk, half a pound of tea at 2*s*. 6*d*. — if they will drink tea — 1lb. of coffee made of equal proportions of East India, Mocha, and Plantation, comes to about 1*s*. 7*d*., sugar 6*d*., butter (2lbs., enough for three people) 3*s*., and the rest can be kept in hand for fruit, fish, chickens, washing; and the thousand and one odds and ends that are always turning up at the most unpropitious moments; such as stamps, boot-mending (two items that have largely assisted in turning my hair grey), ink, paper, string, and, in fact, all those things that an unmarried girl rather fancies grow in the house, and that she is very much surprised to find have to be purchased.

In any case, let me implore Angelina to pay her books every week herself, and never on any account to run up bills anywhere for anything. Let her never be tempted to have any single thing that she cannot pay for on the spot; and she will live happily, and be able to 'speak with her enemies'—if she have any—'in the gate'; that is to say, she can boldly interview her tradespeople, knowing she owes them nothing, and coming cash in hand can demand the best article in the market, which is, after all, the due of those who go and buy for ready money and should never be given to those who will have credit. There is nothing so dear as credit—please remember that, my readers, and start as you mean to go on by paying for everything as you have it; and, above all, know from your husband what he can give you, and have this regularly once a month. If you are fit to be his wife at all, you are fit to spend his money, and to spend it, moreover, without the haggling and worrying over each item that is considered necessary by some men to show their superiority over their women folk, but which should never be allowed for a moment; and should our bride have a small income of her own, this should be retained for her dress, personal expenses, &c., and should not be put into the common fund, for the man should keep the house and be the bread-winner; but, alas! middle-class brides have seldom anything to call their own, their parents thinking they have done all they need for them, should they find them a husband and a certain amount of clothes.

I very much myself disapprove of the way middle-class parents have of marrying off their daughters and giving them nothing beyond their trousseaux; and I do hope that soon fathers and mothers will copy the French more in this matter of a dowry than they do now. I maintain that they are bound to give their daughters, beyond and over such an education as shall allow them to keep themselves, the same sum when married as they received when unmarried, so shall they be to a certain extent independent and have a little something to call their own. Why, in most cases, if Angelina wants to give Edwin a present she has to buy it out of his own money! Can there be a more unenviable position for a young wife, to whom very often the mere asking for money is as painful as it is degrading? It would not hurt any father to give his daughter 50*l*. a year, and the difference it would make in that daughter's comfort and position is unspeakable; and would not be more than half what she would cost him were she to remain on his hands a sour old maid.

Another thing I disapprove of is placing the household books week by week or month by month under the husband's inspection; it leads to endless jars and frets, and discussions; therefore, having talked matters over once and for all, discuss money no more until you require additions to your allowance as the family increases; or can do with less; only know always how matters are going in business, so as to increase or retrench in a manner suitable, should circumstances alter.

Domestic matters must, of course, be discussed now and again between husband and wife; but a sensible woman keeps these subjects in the background, and no more troubles her husband with the price of butter, or the cook's delinquencies, than he does his wife over the more intimate details of his office, which he keeps for his clerks and his partners generally; while the day's papers, the book on hand, people one has seen, are all far more interesting things than Maria's temper, Jane's breakages, or than the grocer's bill, which, if higher than it ought to be, is Angelina's own fault, and can only be altered by herself, and not by worrying Edwin.

Common-sense housekeeping can only be done if the eyes be constantly open to see and the ears to hear. Waste must never be allowed. No servant should be kept who wastes, and if there be no dust-bin, save for cinders, no pig's tub, no man calling at the door for bottles, and, above all, if there be a mistress who is always on the alert to use anyone else's experience, housekeeping need be nothing of a bugbear, and can be done at one quarter the price that it usually costs. But most girls marry in perfect ignorance of everything save the plot of the last novel, the music of the last opera, the fashion of the last dress, and undertake duties they neither care for nor mean to understand, seeing nothing beyond the wedding finery, which is far too often an occasion of almost criminal display, and that must indeed appear a mockery to the poor bride, who contemplates her foolish wedding dress and wishes profoundly she had the money it cost her.

The great curse now of English households is this seeming to be what you are not, this wretched pretending of 400*l.* to be 800*l.*; the shirking of work, domestic details, and common-sense housekeeping that characterises the bride of this day, who only wants to enjoy herself and spend a little more, see a little more gaiety than the last bride did, and who sees nothing holy in the name of wife, only a mere emancipation from the schoolroom; who wants to decorate a house, not make a home; and who sees in her children, not human souls to train for time and for eternity, but pretty dolls to dress, to attract attention, or tiresome objects to be got rid of at school at the earliest opportunity.

That marriage means much more than this is gradually borne in upon the butterfly, who either sobers down in the course of years, and becomes faded and worn and peevish; or else, impatient of control, she breaks all bounds, and the whole family is disgraced by an *esclandre* that is as terrible as it is preventible. With such women as this we have nothing to do; but many of these poor creatures would have been saved had they been brought up properly, so I trust, after all, my words on the subject of common-sense housekeeping will not be considered out of place.

Though they are certainly a little discursive, still they have to do with money emphatically, and that was the first part of the subject I proposed to treat of in this chapter, so before I leave it let me say just a few words on the best system of keeping accounts, a most necessary portion of any woman's business as mistress of a household.

The best authority I know on the subject of accounts is a personal friend who began housekeeping many years ago on a very small and uncertain income. Her husband was a literary man, and had of course that most tiresome and extravagance-encouraging income—a fluctuating one; yet she told me only the other day she could tell to a sixpence what she had spent ever since she was married; that at the end of the year she always sat down, first with her husband, then with her grown-up daughters, and carefully went over each month's expenditure, and in this way she was enabled to manage well, for a glance would show her, if she had spent too much, where she could retrench, or where, if the income had increased, she could best 'launch out' in order to insure more comforts and less forethought and worry: in consequence of her arrangements she was always beforehand with the world, and never owed a sixpence she could not pay. A young housekeeper is often bewildered between account books. She buys one, of course, and then is bothered by detail, or begins to find 'sundries' a most convenient entry—and so, alas! it is. But our model housekeeper shrinks from sundries, or any of these somewhat mean subterfuges, and boldly discovers how she has spent her money, although I must confess I myself am such a bad hand at this sort of thing that, could I be seen, I feel convinced I should be found to be blushing violently at giving advice which I far too often do not follow; indeed, I always feel inclined to imitate the old woman-servant whose balance sheet consisted of so many 'foggets,' among other items, that her master (of course he was a bachelor), confused with the idea of having so much firewood, begged her for an explanation, when she remarked, ' 'Taint faggots, master; *'tis forgets*.' Fortunately her honesty had been tried by many a long year's service, or she might have got into serious trouble; and I think when we too have 'forgets' we are not unlikely to get into trouble when at last we have to face boldly a day of reckoning, which must come sooner or later.

But if I am not a good hand at accounts my friend is, and I here append a leaf from her account book, which, ruled and written by herself, is to me a model of what it should be. Of course the columns can be added to, to any extent, but this will show at once how to keep one's bills before one: in such a manner, that one sees at once how and where the money has gone, and I can but hope this capital system will be adopted at once by all those who are starting in life with the best resolve of all, that nothing shall persuade them to get into debt.

1887	Butcher, Fishmonger £ s. d.	Baker £ s. d.	Grocer £ s. d.	Greengrocer £ s. d.	Coal, Gas, & Lighting £ s. d.	Rent, Rates and Taxes £ s. d.	Wages £ s. d.	Dress £ s. d.	Washing £ s. d.	Total £ s. d.
Jan. 1 Messrs. Slater & Co.	5 0 0	—	—	—	—	—	—	—	—	5 0 0
" 5 Smith	—	1 0 0	—	—	—	—	—	—	—	1 0 0
" 6 Whiteley's account	—	—	1 1 0 0	—	5 0 0	—	—	—	—	6 1 0 0
" 7 Income Tax	—	—	—	—	—	10 0 0	—	—	—	10 0 0
" 8 Water Rate	—	—	—	—	—	2 4 0	—	—	—	2 4 0
" 9 Poor Rate	—	—	—	—	—	5 0 0	—	—	—	5 0 0
" 10 Christmas Rent	—	—	—	—	—	25 0 0	—	—	—	25 0 0
" 11 One quarter Gas, due Christmas	—	—	—	—	5 0 0	—	—	—	—	5 0 0
" 15 Housemaid	—	—	—	—	—	—	5 0 0	—	—	5 0 0
" 16 Parlourmaid	—	—	—	—	—	—	6 0 0	—	—	6 0 0
" 17 Cook	—	—	—	—	—	—	7 10 0	—	—	7 10 0
" 18 Worth	—	—	—	—	—	—	—	20 0 0	—	20 0 0
" 19 Mrs. Jones	—	—	—	—	—	—	—	—	2 0 0	2 0 0
" 20 Potatoes	—	—	—	0 1 0 0	—	—	—	—	—	0 1 0 0
" 25 Fish account	3 0 0	—	—	—	—	—	—	—	—	3 0 0
" 27 Sundry Groceries	—	—	2 0 0	—	—	—	—	—	—	2 0 0
" 28 Coal	—	—	—	—	5 0 0	—	—	—	—	5 0 0
Total	8 0 0	1 0 0	3 10 0	0 1 0 0	15 0 0	42 4 0	18 10 0	20 0 0	2 0 0	110 14 0

And here let me say that there should always be a special column for medical attendance; and without doubting the medical profession in the least, let me impress upon all who have to call in a physician to note his visits in the column set apart for the purpose. I always note a doctor's visits in my diary, as this often checks his accounts, for, without meaning to be dishonest, a doctor often makes the most astounding mistakes. For example, not long ago I saved myself 7*l*. on a doctor's bill by sending an exorbitant account back to my then doctor, drawing his attention to the fact that by my diary only so many visits had been paid, whereas so many had evidently been charged for; when the clerk wrote back to say the error had been made in the addition, and that of course this would have been rectified next time! I can't say if it would have been; all I know is, I was saved the money by always putting down the visits; so I most strongly advise Angelina to put the column in her account book as a reminder, even if she cannot put down in that the exact sum; and I must say I do most heartily wish it were etiquette for doctors to send in their bills made out in items, instead of that business way of 'To medical attendance, &c.,' for I cannot see why they should not. Even a lawyer gives items of his detestable; and what should we say to a modiste who sent in her bill, 'To dress and draperies to date,' without items? I like to know what I am paying for; and why should not my case, mentioned above, be the case of many? One word before I leave the doctor—pay his bill at once; no one is kept waiting longer than a doctor; no one *usually* deserves his money more; it is a disagreeable bill to keep about, and should be always settled as soon as possible.

Now for one hint more, as applying both to meals and money. If you want to save begin with the butcher and the brewer—not that I for one moment want to run down beer—my husband being a brewer, I should not be likely to do so; and I mention this fact to show I cannot be a rabid teetotaler—but I do say and maintain that beer is not necessary for women and for women servants, that young people especially do not require stimulants—I, for one, never took either wine or beer until I had passed the pleasant age of thirty-one or thirty-two—and that milk is far better for both servants and children, youths and maidens, than malt liquor of any sort or description, and that therefore milk should be a somewhat large item in the housekeeping accounts. Angelina should have milk for luncheon and milk instead of that odious tea after dinner; Mary Jane should be encouraged to drink milk with her supper, and a proportionate save is at once made in the accounts, though, after all, one can only give general ideas on this subject, as, of course, individual tastes have to be studied, and no one person's expenditure is quite a guide for another's. Many people dislike milk, and this subject of a pleasant beverage is one that often harasses me mentally a good bit, for I don't honestly think filtered boiled water pleasant (unfiltered unboiled water is unsafe drinking), and unless we fall back on milk and home-made lemonade, we are rather hopeless, for beer is out of the question, as far as I am concerned, in kitchen and schoolroom, and if some genius would invent something cheap, healthy, palatable, and without alcohol in it, I for one will patronise him largely, and give him honourable mention, if not a medal, all to himself.

Still, until that is done I strongly advise Angelina to pay the milkman rather than the brewer, and by drinking milk herself to set an example which will speak louder than any amount of argument. And general ideas, too, can only be given on the subject of meals. Yet general ideas are most useful as a species of foundation on which to raise the rest of the fabric, so I will shortly sketch out now a foundation scheme that should be of great assistance to those girls who are beginning housekeeping on small means, and less knowledge of the subject on which depends so much of their welfare and happiness.

It maybe of some little assistance to Angelina if I begin my short dissertation on meals by giving her one or two hints as to what to have for breakfast, before passing on to other subjects, as in some small households this always appears to me to be somewhat of a stumbling-block to a young mistress, accustomed to see a large amount of variety, prepared for a grown-up family.

What is eaten for breakfast depends, naturally, a great deal on individual tastes, and there are endless little dishes that require the attention of a first-rate cook; but Angelina and Edwin must rise superior to this, for they will not be able to afford such things even if they desire them, and I do hope they do not, for I do not know a more despicable way of spending one's time or one's money than in squandering it over food and expensive cooks. If things are nice and are nicely sent to table, that should suffice, and I think perhaps a few simple hints on the subject would not be out of place, for while Angelina should, of course, order carefully all that is required, I see no reason why she should rack her brain and harass her cook, particularly when that damsel will have to do a great deal besides merely cooking the breakfast.

Whatever else there is not, there should be a little fruit. Oranges, pears, apples, and grapes are cheap enough if purchased with sense, and as 'dessert,' as a rule, is unnecessary save for appearances—and we are too sensible to think only of these—I should advise the fruit that nobody appears to grudge the money for then; appearing at breakfast, where it makes the table look pretty, and where it is really good for both young and old folks, too. Then, if possible, have either honey or marmalade, it is much healthier and cheaper than butter, and generally try to have either a tongue (3s. 6d.) or a nice ham (8s. 6d.) in cut, it is such a useful thing to have in the house; as also are sardines (1s. a box, large size, 6½d. small), as if unexpected folk drop in to luncheon, or supper be required instead of dinner, they are there to 'fall back upon'; and if they appear at breakfast some really fresh eggs, nicely fried bacon, curried kidneys or plain kidneys, mushrooms, a most healthy dish, and not too expensive at some times of the year; curried eggs and rice, bloaters, and bloater-toast, occasionally a fresh sole, a mackerel split open, peppered, and salted and grilled, a cutlet of cod, an occasional sausage (and ever since I can remember we always have had sausages for breakfast on Sundays), form a list from which a single dish can be chosen, and which should suffice, more especially when we consider the honey and fruit, both of which look nice on the table, are more wholesome, and save the butter and meat bill. And once the cook is trained into our ways, and she knows what to do, there is no need to order breakfast, a great comfort for those who have much domestic routine of food to think of before beginning the day. Do not have hot buttered toast or hot bread. Those two items make the butter bill into a nightmare, and are also most unhealthy, but have nice fresh brown bread, Nevill's hot-water bread, the nicest bread made, oat-cake (2s. a large tin at any good grocer's), and fresh, crisp, dry toast, and then I think neither Edwin nor Angelina can complain, more especially if a nice white cloth (freshly taken from the press, in which all cloths should be put folded the moment they are taken from the table), with a pretty red border, and nicely folded napkins, each in its own ring and each embroidered with initials in red, be used, and I think that I shall not be suspected of being a fussy old maid, if I suggest that the crumbs should be brushed off by the maid and the cloth folded with Angelina's assistance, in which case it will last twice as long as it would if, as usual, it is crumpled up and shaken out at the back door in a manner much affected by careless servants. But these trifles save the washing bill, which in these days is no light consideration.

At first another meal that will trouble our bride is that most necessary of all meals—luncheon. By-and-bye, when little folks have to be thought of, this midday dinner becomes a very easy business, but I must own that luncheon and the servant's dinner combined is a terrible trouble during the first year or two of married life.

I think it was Shirley Brooks who used to say he believed that were women left to themselves they would never have dinner at all, and that they would either keep something in a cupboard and eat from it when positively driven to do so by the pangs of hunger, or else they would have a tray brought up with tea, bread-and-butter, and an egg, and think they had done well; and I confess freely that my first idea when I hear that the lord and master of my establishment is going out to dine is, 'Thank goodness, there will be no dinner to order;' but this is all very well occasionally, albeit I don't see why we women should not have the same amount of food alone as when in company, but it becomes serious if it goes on for long; therefore I once more impress upon Angelina to be sure and have her proper luncheon, just as she used to do at home with her sisters and mother before she was married. Another reason for the midday meal is that no servant will ever grumble at the food prepared for them if it has first been into the dining-room, and a good deal of trouble of this kind would be saved. It is, I own, very difficult to find food for three women that is economical as well as satisfactory, but a fair arrangement would be as follows:—Of course there will be a small piece of beef on Sunday; for a small household about 6 lbs. of the ribs of beef is best. This should be boned (the bones coming in for Monday night's soup) and rolled, and sent to table with horse-radish, placed on the meat; Yorkshire pudding, which should be cooked *under the meat*, and sent in on a separate very hot dish, and appropriate vegetables according to the time of year. For a large hungry family a piece of 12 lbs. of the top side of the round should be chosen. There is only very little bone here, and not too much fat, and besides being cheaper than any other joint it is most economical, and as nice as anything else. But more of this anon.

The beef can be cold for Angelina and the maids on Monday, with, say, a lemon pudding. On Tuesday 'dormers' can be made, with rice and cold beef, and sent in very hot, with nice gravy, and simple pudding; a mould of cornflour and jam is delicious. Wednesday, a small amount of fish could be purchased, and cold beef used if desired. Rice pudding, made with a méringue crust, is very good indeed. Thursday, if no more beef be left, a nice boiled rabbit could be had, with some bacon round, and a custard pudding. Friday, 1½ lb. of the lean part of the neck of mutton would make a delicious stew, and pancakes could follow. Saturday, about three pounds of pork could be roasted, and sent in with a savoury pudding and apple-sauce, and a sago pudding to conclude the repast. This could be finished cold at Sunday's supper. Here is variety and economy combined. One great thing I find in housekeeping on a larger scale is to have one or two good-sized joints, and to fill in the corners with fish, poultry, and rabbits. Fish can always be contracted for cheaply. I pay 2s. a day, and get an ample supply for dinner and breakfast, and sometimes enough for the schoolroom tea too; and poultry and rabbits can often be bought at the London markets very inexpensively, while I procure my chickens from delightful people in Liverpool, Messrs. Hasson and Co., 12 Dawson Street, who sell them to me at prices varying from 4s. 6d. to 5s. 6d. the couple, according to the time of year.

Edwin's dinner requires, of course, more consideration, and he may have very pronounced tastes that require special studying, but in any case I say it is well and economical to have soup and fish before the meat. Soup made from bones and vegetables is as cheap and as nice as anything I know, and sixpence or a shilling a day will keep you in fish, if you set about this properly; but the great thing about all meals is to have what you may like sent to table looking nice, and to have none of the accessories forgotten, an elaborate and expensive meal ungracefully served on ugly china, or without flowers, and with half the condiments forgotten, being often enough to spoil any one's temper, when a cheap, well-cooked dinner, prettily and tastefully put before Edwin, will satisfy him, more especially when the household books are equally satisfactory when pay-day comes.

Let me conclude this chapter by once more impressing on our young housekeepers never to allow jars and squabbles about money. At first starting know everything about your income, and settle exactly what is to suffice for dress and food, and have a settled day, once a month is best, on which to receive that allowance. Should Edwin have a fixed income this is a comparatively easy matter to settle between husband and wife; but should it fluctuate, as the income does of a man who lives by his pen, pencil, or even by stockbroking (a manner of living that would drive me mad) or by rents from land, it is safe to arrange expenditure on the basis of the *least* sum obtained by these means, drawing an average for the last three years, any surplus going on joyfully towards the second year, towards procuring books, taking a holiday, or bringing something home for the house; there being no pleasure like that of spending money we can feel is thoroughly our own, and that may actually be wasted if we like on something delightful, because it is not required to pay some odious bill or replace some ugly and necessary article.

CHAPTER IV
THE HOUSEMAID'S CLOSET, AND GLASS AND CHINA

One of the very first things to be recollected, either in the kitchen or housemaid's pantry, is that there should be a place for everything, and yet no holes or corners where dilapidated dusters, old glass-cloths, bottles, and other *débris* could be stuffed away; and another axiom to remember is that every glass, tumbler, cup, saucer—in fact, every possession one has—should be neatly scheduled and kept in a book, which should be inspected and gone through twice a year, or when any change takes place in the establishment. That disagreeable remark, that so often completely floors a mistress, ' 'Twasn't here when I came,' would in this case never be heard, as the sight of the list, duly signed and dated by both mistress and maid, would of course be a complete answer to any such statement; and seeing at stated intervals what glass and china had fallen victims to the housemaid is a wonderful deterrent, and also saves any large and sudden call upon the purse, which always comes at a time when the exchequer is at its lowest, but which need never occur in an appreciable manner should each article be replaced the moment it is broken. I am no advocate for having what is called best things, holding that one's everyday existence should be as refined and cultured as when one has 'company,' yet it is necessary in most of our households to have best glass and a best dinner-service, and these should be kept in a proper glass closet, under lock and key, as indeed should all spare glass and china; for, if the most trustworthy housemaid has an unlimited supply at her command, she will never tell of each separate smash, and reserves the grand total for the bi-annual day of reckoning with the book, when the mistress has often to make an outlay that is most disheartening to her, as regards not only the cost, but the blow it is to her to discover the carelessness and deception of, perhaps, a favourite maid, who would have been neither careless nor deceiving had she had to come to her mistress for every single glass over and above the few she had at her command.

Nothing has altered more in the last twenty years, both in character and price, than glass and china, and nothing shows the taste of the mistress of the house more than her plates and tumblers. No one has now any excuse for having ugly things, because good glass is as cheap as bad, and good china can be had by any one who has the taste to choose it, and the knowledge where to go and buy each separate thing. Granted that we have selected our saucepans, our basins, and other necessary things known to any one, and to be chosen from a list either sent for from Maple or Whiteley—for Maple, I have discovered, issues these lists too—and which, it seems to me, would only be waste of paper and time for me to enumerate here, we must, of course, now proceed to think about our dinner set. The best everyday one I know of is a species of plain white china supplied by Maple, and which has the owner's monogram on the edge of the dish. These plates and dishes are so extremely cheap that when I say they are 2s. a dozen I scarcely expect to be believed, and even now I cannot help thinking there must be a mistake; but the rest of the service was equally inexpensive, and I really do not think I am making an error in giving this as the price. I invariably have my soup-tureens, sauceboats, and vegetable dishes made without handles—a pretty, rather oval shape, with the monogram on the side and on the top of the cover. There is nothing makes a table look worse than chipped or mended crockery; and how often has quite a nice service been spoiled by the fact that either the handles were knocked off and smashed, or else they were riveted on. Now if we have no handles or ornamental knobs to be knocked off, the service lasts three times as long as it otherwise would. The plain white service also insures cleanliness and absence of greasy or black finger-marks, and one never tires of this as one does of the elaborate patterns and colours some people prefer, and which are extremely difficult to match once the manufacturers have broken up the design.

I remember some friends of mine who had a service with a whole flight of red storks on, flying over each plate, and anything more ugly and incongruous it is difficult to think of. I never dined there without remembering the storks, whereas a plain service would not have been noticed in any way. For a best dinner service we should have something better, for of course the china I have been speaking of is not china really; that is to say, I would not see my fingers through it if I held it up to the strongest light that was ever made, and young people who are asked what they would like in the shape of a wedding present should remember that Mortlock, in Oxford Street, has quite charming designs, but even here I should distinctly advise, buy the plain ware, with either monogram or crest, for of this one never tires.

I once saw a charming dinner set that had been made by Mortlock; it was a beautiful pale buff ground, with a black monogram, and the china was of a delicious feel and touch, and as light as possible. Each vegetable dish was an artistic shape, and, in fact, if ever my ship comes home I shall have one like it; at present I have plain white china with a pink and gold band, and the crest and monogram in the centre of each plate, &c.; of course, this was a gift, and the nuisance it is is dreadful, for when a plate is broken I have to send the bits to Staffordshire to be copied, where they keep me waiting months for it, and charge me so highly that I am beginning to detest the whole thing.

The glass for everyday wear and tear should be as inexpensive as possible. I like quite plain glass; tumblers cost about 6s. a dozen, and the glasses for wine are equally cheap; but for best glass Salviati ware is lovely, and really, if bought judiciously, is not so very expensive after all. Besides which, it allows one to have a different set of glasses for each person. I have a dozen different sets of three each, so that if one be broken and cannot be replaced exactly like its predecessor it is not a set of thirty-six that is done for, but only a set of three, which after all need not be spoiled quite, as having odd glasses one still more odd does not make the blot on the table that it otherwise would.

The finger-glasses should also be Salviati ware. Another suggestion for Angelina, should she be asked to write down a list of things she is most anxious to receive as presents—a good plan, by the way, for birthdays and Christmas, and one we always follow, as then one is sure of receiving something one requires, and not the endless rubbish that accumulates when well-meaning friends send gifts *quâ* gifts to rid themselves of an obligation; and who crack their brains pondering what you would like, and at last send you something you not only don't want but think hideous, albeit it may have cost pounds. Water bottles should invariable be coloured. The Bohemian ware—a lovely green hue—is particularly useful for this purpose, and there is a charming shop in Piccadilly where all sorts of coloured glasses and bottles are to be procured—opposite Burlington House—Douglas and Co.— and nowhere else is this charming glass as cheap and pretty as it is there. I got a sweet blue bottle and glass for a bedroom for 9*d*., and another, quite a beauty, for 1*s*. 6*d*. At these prices one can well remain 'mistress of oneself though China fall.' The teacups and saucers can also be white or pale buff, but my favourite ware is Minton's ivy patterned china. We used to have it at home, and I have it still, as it is one of those delightful things that one can always match. It is a little expensive, but then it is so pretty! The cups are all white, but the handles represent a bit of ivy, the leaves of which are in relief round the handle, and just give a pleasant, fresh look to the breakfast table. The plates have a wreath of ivy also in relief on them, and breakfast dishes, cruets, and plates that stand heat are made to match; so that all can be *en suite*, except the hot-water dishes. These are plain white, with a double dish holding hot water, that keeps bacon &c. hot, *not* for late comers—these lazy people should never be considered—but for those who may prefer fish first, or like to have a second helping. This tea ware is good enough for best as well as everyday wear; but be sure and avoid the species that is not raised and has a gilt edge, for no one who has not seen the two sets together could understand how different they can be. I do not like gilt on anything; it is always vulgar, always suggestive of *nouveaux riches*, and on china has a way of washing off that is most trying, unless it happens to be burnished, when it costs a young fortune, and one's heart is broken every time a cup or plate receives a jar. A very good way in schoolrooms or nurseries, of which more anon, to secure the smallest amount of breakages is to give each child its own cup, plate, and saucer, each set to be of a different pattern. There are some lovely specimen cups, the set of which costs about 7*s*. 6*d*.—not a bad birthday present, especially if a silver teaspoon is added, with pale yellow, marguerite, and brown foliage depicted upon them. The same style of cup has also a beautiful design of blackberries, and I have also seen a pale pink daisy that was perhaps the most charming of the lot. If a child's own plate &c. get broken one hears of it at once, and they are at once replaced. The governess has her own set too, and it is a good plan to have two or three extra sets for schoolroom visitors, for in well-regulated houses, where the governess makes herself pleasant, schoolroom tea is a delightful meal, and, if shared by intimate friends, makes a pleasant break for the governess, and gives the children an opportunity of seeing outsiders, and learning how to behave when company is present.

    The best dessert service that I know of is to be bought at Hewett's Baker Street Bazaar. It is Oriental-looking and most uncommon. It has a green ground, and a raised pattern of flowers, butterflies, &c., and looks so good, no one has any idea of its cheapness; for example, a man who set up to be a great judge of china once was dining with us, and taking up one of my dessert plates, he began to expatiate to the lady on his left hand on the beauty and rarity thereof. I let him go on for some time, and at last I told him the price—2*s*. each plate; and, though he was silent and appeared to believe me, I am certain he did nothing of the kind. The dishes are dearer, but not too dear, and are all low and nice shapes, and tiny plates can be obtained to match for preserved fruits or French bonbons, all of which look nice upon a dinner-table.

    Mortlock has also a plain white dessert service, of which the edges of the plate are pierced, and the dishes are like baskets, which are charming, and not too expensive; but these are rather colourless on a table unless a great deal of scarlet is used too in the flowers, and I prefer a little colour introduced myself. Still, if we avoid those terrible swans on sham ponds, with holes in their backs, like the Elle women, to hold flowers, that used to be sold with the white service, we might do worse than have this one. Of course, real china, Crown Derby, and Worcester are all nice for this purpose; but we who cannot afford this style of property can be consoled with the idea that there are other things quite as pretty within our reach, although, maybe, they are neither as costly nor as precious, nor as liable to be broken.

While we are on the subject of glass and china I should like to say a few words more about the arrangement of the glass and china, and especially about the everyday dinner and breakfast table management, as in a small establishment it entirely rests upon the shoulders of the mistress whether the table presents a charming appearance or whether it does not. I will not suppose that Angelina burdens herself with experienced maidens, but I will think she has taken my advice and secured a couple of bright pleasant girls, of whom she can make friends, and who are not already spoiled for her use in some large establishment, and this being so, she will no doubt at first have to lay her table herself. This may be considered a hardship by our bride, but I am quite sure she will soon cease to regard it as one. Anyhow, I beg she will try my nice girls, and if they fail, why, she can but fall back on her 'experienced' ones after all, but she must not take them haphazard, but must select them as she does her personal friends, because then she will, knowing something about their family, their inherited tendencies and their dispositions, be able to know how to manage them. We do not 'make friends' with strangers unless we know something of their forbears, and this rule should apply to strange servants quite as much as it does to acquaintances who do not live with us, and only come in now and then, and are easily dropped should they prove uncongenial and disagreeable.

It is so easy to get your maiden into nice ways if she have no bad ones of her own, out of which you have to take her first, and, beginning at once to show her how you like things, you will soon be able to rely on her, and she will take a pride in copying you, and you will soon have your reward in service that is real, because it comes from the heart and not from the eye.

I am a great advocate for white china, because the washing of this cannot be scamped, and as far as possible all breakfast china should be white, with just a pattern of ivy or daisies, as described above; and the breakfast-table could be laid something as follows, putting the mistress at the head of the table if she wishes, and the master *at the side*, not at the foot—a most dreary arrangement, unless the breakfast table is filled by others besides the host and hostess, which in Angelina's case is most unlikely. In front of Angelina is arranged the breakfast equipage, and I strongly advise her to have either cocoa or nicely made coffee, and to taboo that wretched tea that destroys so many digestions and unstrings so many nerves. Coffee is not more expensive, and a charming drink is made from equal parts of Mocha, East Indian, and Plantation coffee at 1s. 5½d. a pound and 1s. 4½d. It should be bought in the berry, and ground each morning; but as this is too much labour in our small household, I should suggest buying half a dozen pounds, two of each kind at a time, mixing them carefully and keeping them in a tin biscuit-box, filling up a smaller canister that holds a pound as required. I always do this, and the coffee is as fragrant and good the last day I use from it as on the first. This should be made for two people in one of Ash's kaffee kanns, purchasable in Oxford Street, the best coffee machine I know of anywhere, and, being furnished with a spirit-lamp, it has always means of keeping the coffee hot, and the cheerful song of the little lamp is very pleasant when we come down on a cold wet morning. Of course the milk must be boiled, and sent in very hot in a china jug to match the china, and Barbadoes raw sugar is better with it than the ordinary lump. Very pretty basins, both for moist and lump sugar, can be bought at the Baker Street Bazaar, in Oriental china, for 1s. or 2s.; butter-dishes at 6d., in blue and white china, also marmalade and honey pots, for about 2s.; and as the blue harmonises with green, these pots can be used quite well with my favourite ivy service, of which I spoke before.

In the centre of the table there should always be an art pot with a plant in. Of course I know people *will* consider that expensive, and will sometimes even put another enemy of mine (a worse enemy even than that terrible hat-stand!) in this place of honour—I mean a cruet-stand. But let me tell you what this expensive item has cost me since this time last year—just five shillings. I had my pot for years, naturally, and this is not included in the outlay, but this some years ago cost 3s., so no one can object on the score of expense. In this pot I had planted a cocos palm, 3s. 6d., a most graceful plant, and the other 1s. 6d. went for three tiny ferns, all of which are flourishing mightily, and will soon have to be transplanted and make room for smaller ones again. Any lady fond of gardening could have planted these herself, and, naturally, cheaper plants are to be had; but the fine, graceful foliage of the cocos is so pretty, and the plant lasts so long, that I can heartily recommend it from long experience.

Of course, round the centre plant can be arranged three or four specimen glasses of flowers; but this I have never time to do except on special occasions, yet it adds much to the effect of a breakfast-table, and no young housekeeper who has not a settled occupation, such as keeps me employed from nine until one, should ever allow her table to be flowerless or ugly. In front of Edwin should be placed any hot food provided for breakfast, on nice china hot-water dishes; the bread should be placed on a wooden bread platter, that has neither a text nor a moral reflection carved on it—two things that always seem to me singularly out of place on a bread-stand; and the knife should be one of those very nice ivory-handled ones, made on purpose by Mappin and Webb, I believe, that cost 7s. 6d., but that last years.

At the corner of the table, between Edwin and Angelina, should be neatly arranged salt, pepper, and mustard. A tiny set of cruets for breakfast can be bought to match the ivy festooned ware, and is as pretty as can be. Very pretty white china salt-cellars &c. can be also purchased, with white china spoons to serve with; and Doulton makes charming sets also, which go with any service, and are very strong, but these have plated mounts; and I am not nearly as fond of them as I am of plain china, as these always look and are clean; and either plated ware or silver tarnish very soon, and make a great deal of work for our one pair of hands; which is one very strong reason why Angelina should put away all the pretty silver salt-cellars she is sure to receive when she is married; reserving these and other handsome possessions until she can afford a butler, or until she has trained her maidens well, and is justified in taking extra help, under the housemaid, when, if she likes, she can bring it out and use it daily.

As in every other department, in the housemaid's department should rules and regulations be found. She should clean certain rooms on certain days; she should never leave her silver in greasy, or her knives in hot water; she should keep soda in her sink just as the cook does; and she should be instructed how to keep her glass clean and bright, a smeared glass or plate being at once returned to her for alteration should she bring it up to table.

Let the housemaid, moreover, have two or three coarse dust-sheets for covering the furniture when she is sweeping and dusting (and see she uses them), a large piece of 'crash' to place in front of the fireplace, when she is cleaning the grate, and a housemaid's box and gloves. She must, furthermore, have three dusters, three glass-cloths, a good chamois leather, a set of brushes and plate-brushes, a decanter-drainer, a wooden bowl for washing up in, which must be kept free from grease of any kind, and she must wash out her dusters for herself. This makes them last much longer than they otherwise would, and if she has only a certain number she cannot waste and spoil them. Little things like these are what almost ruin a young housekeeper, because she does not know how to manage, and because she is too proud, as a rule, to ask any one why dusters vanish into thin air, and why the washing bill adds up so mysteriously.

Silver can be kept beautifully clean if washed in clean soda water daily, and then cleaned with a little whitening; which glass should be always rubbed bright with a leather.

These items appear insignificant, but I am sure they will be useful hints to many of my less experienced readers.

CHAPTER V
FIRST SHOPPING

In life, as in everything else, it is extremely difficult to draw the line anywhere. I want both my young people to care about their house, and know every detail of its management, but they must not become domestic dummies, and think of nothing save how to make a shilling do the work of two, and how to circumvent that terrible butcher, or that still more awful laundry-woman. Once started, the details that seem so ugly and wearisome on paper need never be gone into again, but it is necessary to have some plan and stick to it, else the jarring of the wheels of the domestic car will always be heard, and life will indeed be stale, dull, and unprofitable. People provide their own poetry, my young friends, and life is a very good thing if you do not expect too much from it, or if you will not refuse to accept other folks' experience, for she has nothing new to give you, nothing to show you she has not shown us all before you. You are not the only young people who have started on a diet of roses and cream, and not the only ones either who have found this disagree with them. So buckle too manfully, and work your way onwards, being quite sure that every fresh home started and kept going on excellent sound principles of health and beauty does a work little known of, less understood about, perhaps, by those who inhabit it, but none the less beneficial to all those who come within its influence.

But I do not mean to preach a sermon, much as I should like to do so, but only to preface my remarks on the subject of our first shopping and how we should begin our scheme of decoration.

It is usual for the landlord to allow a certain sum for the decoration of a house; but rarely, if ever, does that sum allow of anything like really artistic papering and painting. Yet, I maintain, artistic surroundings are far more important than handsome furniture or even an elaborate wedding dress; and I think if we have common sense, and find a good journeyman carpenter and painter, who will work himself with his men under our directions, we shall manage very well indeed.

Could we afford it, of course, I would employ Morris, or Smee's people, or Collinson and Lock, with their delicious arrangement of 'fittings'; but we cannot, and our first business is to find some inexpensive man who will do as he is told. Then we can buy our papers and set to work. There is no saving like that we can make in this first work, if we can only put our hand on our man. And when this is done our next step is to describe the work we shall require to be done and to ask him to send in a contract, which is to be for everything, and is not to be departed from on any account whatever.

The great advantage to me in employing our own man is that we buy our own wall-papers &c. just wherever we like, and can, moreover, obtain a large discount on them if we pay cash, and insinuate that we expect the aforesaid discount as a matter of course. Then we can start on our shopping and to enjoy ourselves, though I question much if shopping be quite as charming an occupation as one expects it to be. Certainly, unless one starts with a clear conception of one's needs, a long day's shopping can result in nothing save great confusion of ideas, and a fearful consciousness that one has bought the very things one ought not to have purchased, and entirely forgotten the very articles of which we were most in want.

To avoid this disagreeable termination to our day, we must never start in a hurry, never be obliged to hasten over our purchases; and once our minds are made up on the subject of colours, we must not allow a 'sweetly pretty' pattern or beautiful hue to tempt us. Having made up our minds what we want, let us buy that, and nothing else.

Therefore, before going out really to purchase, we must settle definitely what are our requirements; and after really making the acquaintance of our house, the next thing to do is to find out what pretty things can be bought, at which shops, and at the most reasonable rate; and this is only to be done by a painstaking inspection of what the different establishments have to offer us, and by not disdaining to look in at shop windows, keeping both ears and eyes open, and using our senses and, if possible, other people's experiences, as much as we can. This is a long and tedious process, but one worth going through, if we really want our house to be a home, and the experience we purchase with our furniture will go a long way towards helping us to solve the problem set before so many of us: how to live pleasantly on small means. One axiom we can undoubtedly lay to heart and remember, and that is that no one establishment should be resorted to for everything. Long experience teaches me that each shop has its specialties; it may supply everything from beds to food, from saucepans to grand pianos, still there is always some one thing that another shop has better and cheaper, and it is as well to find this out before we start away to buy our furniture, for I have often been made very angry by seeing exactly the same thing I gave 5*s.* for in one shop sold at 2*s.* 6*d.* in a less fashionable but equally accessible neighbourhood, while nothing varies as much as the price of wall-papers. I have known the self-same paper sold at 2*s.* 6*d.*, 3*s.* 6*d.*, and 4*s.* a piece by three different firms, all within a stone's throw of each other; and, naturally, patterns alter from year to year, and we can scarcely ever match a paper unless we purchase one designed by some well-known designer, such as Morris, Jeffreys, Shufferey, Collinson and Lock, and Mr. E. Pither, of Mortimer Street, W., for whose cheap artistic papers I for one can never be too profoundly grateful.

But even more important than to find where to get the cheapest things is it to consult the house itself on what will suit it best in the way of furniture, and we should never allow ourselves to buy a single thing until we have taken our house into our confidence, and discovered all about its likes and dislikes. This sounds ridiculous, I know; but I am convinced a house is a sentient thing, and becomes part and parcel of those who live in it in a most mysterious way. Anyhow, to put it on the most prosaic grounds, what would be the use of buying a corner cupboard that would not fit into any corner, or in purchasing a sofa for which there was no place to be found once it was bought?

It is, therefore, far better to know our house thoroughly before we really begin to furnish; and I cannot too strongly advise all ladies to buy merely the bare necessaries of life before they go into their houses to live, reserving the rest of their money until they are quite sure what the house really wants most. But here let me whisper a little hint to our bride: a man before he is married is apt to be far more generously minded than he is once he has his prize safe; therefore, there should be a clear understanding that so much is to be spent really and positively; otherwise the bridegroom may think, as many men do, that, as things have 'done' for a while, they can 'do' for ever, and he may button up his pockets and refuse to buy anything more than he has already done. I have known more than one man do this; and even the best man that ever lived—by which every woman means her own husband, of course—never can understand either that things wear out or women require any money to spend.

When starting out on our shopping, we should put down first of all what we wish to buy, and then what we wish to spend, and we should never be persuaded to spend more on one thing than the outside price we have put down for it in our own schedule. If we do, something will have to go short, and that may be something very important both for health and comfort.

You know individually what you can afford, so make a note of that, and keep to it firmly, never allowing yourself to spend any more on that particular thing, thinking you can save elsewhere, for your list should be so exact that you cannot possibly spare anything you have set down in it.

And now another axiom to be remembered when shopping: never allow an upholsterer to direct your taste or to tell you what to buy, neither allow him to talk you out of anything on which you have settled after mature consideration.

The best of upholsterers has only an upholsterer's notions, and naturally rather wishes to sell what he has, rather more than he desires to procure you what you want. He spots an *ingénue* the moment she enters his shop, and he cannot help remembering that here is the person likely to buy his venerable 'shop-keepers,' and he brings them forward until, bewildered by the quantity and ashamed not to buy after all the trouble she thinks she has given, Miss Innocence spends her money, and regrets her stupidity for the rest of her life.

All young people starting in life are so very certain that they are going to do better than any one else, that they invariably scoff at the idea of an upholsterer being able to direct them, but let them start prepared for this by my hint, and let them keep their eyes open; and if they do not see things that have not been brought to the light of day for ages at first, and before the man has realised he has a forewarned damsel and no *ingénue* to deal with, they need never believe a word I say for the future. But I have seen and watched this little comedy too often not to know I am really stating a fact.

Start on your shopping armed with this caution, your list, and a determination to be content with what you can afford, and a determination to get the prettiest things you can for your money, and you will do well; and above all remember that your lines have fallen on days when beauty and cheapness go hand in hand, and don't hanker after Turkey carpets, when the price of one would go far indeed to furnish the whole of the room for which you would so like it, regardless of the fact that if you purchase such an expensive luxury you will have nothing whatever left with which to buy suitable chairs, tables, and plenishing to match a carpet which is only fit to go where expense is no object.

And please mark carefully the word 'suitable,' for there is no word so absolutely set on one side in our English language. Do not be guided by fashion, or by what some one else has done or means to do, or by anything at all, save the length of your purse and the house where you are to live; and recollect cheap things are easily replaced, while expensive ones wear one to death in taking care of them, and in marking sorrowfully how much sooner they fade or go into holes than we can afford to replace them.

If all this is remembered, laid to heart, and well thought over, the first shopping can be commenced at any time, and should consist of a careful selection of wall-papers and paints for at least the hall, dining-room, and staircase.

CHAPTER VI
THE HALL

Perhaps the most difficult part of a house to really make look nice is the hall, especially in one of the small houses of the period, where that tiresome man, the builder, appears to consider either that an entrance to the house is not necessary at all, or that the smaller it is, and the more the stairs are in evidence, the better and more appropriate it is to Angelina's lowly station in life; indeed, this idiosyncrasy is not confined to small houses, for I know of more than one good-sized domicile that is entirely spoiled by the manner in which the staircase rises from the front door, scarcely allowing that room enough to open, or which has not space even for the hat-stand and hall-table to which the British matron is as a rule so very fondly attached. However, there is now a distinct advance in the matter of the hall in many of the new houses; and we will take it for granted that we have a small space at all events that we can make the very best of, for nothing adds so much to the appearance of a house as a nicely arranged hall. Indeed, were I now beginning housekeeping, nothing should induce me to take a house where there was not an appreciable distance between the sitting-rooms and the front door, for if this latter opens direct on them it is impossible to avoid draughts and constant catching of cold; a nicely warmed sitting-room becoming well-nigh uninhabitable when the front door is opened on a cold or windy night: a chill and cutting draught enters, and in a moment a bad cold is caught. I know nothing more important, therefore, than to consider the position of a front door in choosing a house, as not only one's comfort but much of one's health depends upon this. I have had this 'borne in upon me,' as the Shakers would say, often and often, when I have been staying in a house where there is literally not a square yard of hall, where the stairs and the front door seem all one, and where the drawing-room literally opens out into the place where the front door is. Even in not particularly cold weather, nothing keeps such a house even warm, and the sudden changes of temperature caused by this arrangement are so great that I have had to live in a shawl and yet could not rise above freezing point; and, of course, what it must be in the depth of winter I must leave my readers to imagine.

The first thing to look at, then, is what we can do with our hall, when we have it. If the front door is very near us, we must hang over it a good thick curtain. I should advise a double curtain of serge or felt. This could be arranged on one of those delightful rods that are, I believe, only to be purchased of Maple, and that move with the door itself in some mysterious way, with a bracket arrangement, and that prevents the necessity of drawing the curtain itself when the door is opened. Of course this would only be for winter use and for when the delightful east wind was blowing; but over all the doors in my hall I have curtains which remain up all the year round, because they look so nice, and are really of a great deal of use in more ways than one. As the doors open inwards, these are only put up on the ordinary narrow brass poles with rings, and are tied back with Liberty silk handkerchiefs, or in several instances looped high with cords, as in Illustration No. 1. This allows of the curtain being dropped in one moment should more warmth be desired. These cords and tassels are procurable at Smee's, while the handkerchiefs are Liberty's. A 3*s*. 6*d*. handkerchief, cut in half and hemmed, is the proper size to use for this purpose, should they be preferred to the cords. Some of the curtains are made of stamped velveteen at 2*s*. 3*d*. and 2*s*. 6*d*. the yard, edged round the bottom and one side with a ball fringe to match, and others are made of serge; but I prefer the velveteen—it wears beautifully, and can be made to look as good as new by being re-dipped by Pullar the dyer, who lives at Perth, who is very well known, and has agents all over the kingdom, so there is no expense, incurred in sending the things to him. The curtains over the doorways of the sitting-rooms are always kept tied back, and I furthermore put in tintacks down the sides nearest the wall to keep them in place, and to keep out the draught. This does not harm the curtains in the least if very small bits of tape are sewn on the material, and the nail inserted in these, not in the curtains themselves. Over the door that leads into the kitchen departments the curtains should be in one piece, capable of being drawn; to keep this in place it is well to put the last ring over the end of the pole, so that it cannot be drawn on more than one side. This saves it from looking like a rag, which it would do could it be drawn with equal ease both sides, and also secures that it shall remain drawn over a door that would be always revealing all sorts of domestic secrets were it not for the friendly shield of the concealing curtain, in the praise of which I feel I cannot really say too much.

Fig. 1.—Suggestion for draping arch in hall.

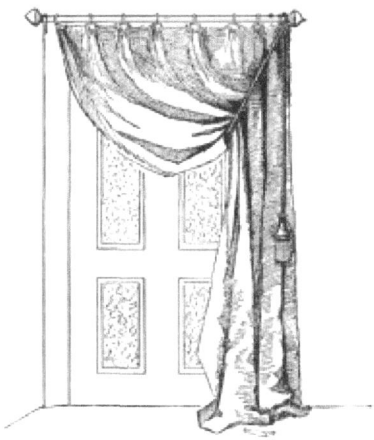

Fig. 2.—Suggestion for draping door in hall.

The flooring of the hall is our next consideration. If we have tiles, and very many houses have tiles nowadays, I think I should be inclined to say, leave the floor just as it is. If you put down a nice rug, dirty boots soon reduce it to a state of dirt and squalor; and nicely washed tiles really look as well as anything. Of course a good thick mat must be placed at the front door. This is best purchased at Treloar's, in Ludgate Hill, for I really do believe his mats never wear out. I have had one for years with 'Salve' on in red letters, and that mat is as good now as the day on which I purchased it, and it has had the wear of boys to contend with, to say nothing of, first, an extremely chalky soil, and then a clay one. Behind the door I should put a brass stand, just to hold the wet umbrellas. Maple has very pretty brass stands indeed for about 25s. 6d.; but when dry each member of the family should be made to take his or her umbrella into their own room, and put them in a corner there *not* rolled up. The life of an umbrella is quite doubled in length if this simple rule is remembered, and, indeed, if there be a room where the umbrella can be allowed to dry, I should advise its being put there at once open, for umbrella stands wear out one's umbrella quicker than any amount of wear. Very pretty stands are now made from drain-pipes, which are painted, and in some cases embellished with flowers made from clay in imitation of Barbotine ware; but these are easily broken, and I think a brass one much the best for all purposes.

Now, on no account allow any one to hang up a coat or wrap in the hall. First of all, a collection of coats and hats tempts a thief; and, secondly, I cannot imagine anything more untidy-looking. The men of the household can be easily trained to take their own especial property at once into their own rooms, where there should be accommodation for them; and visitors' hats and coats can be taken possession of by the maid, and hung up in the passage behind the curtained door that leads to the kitchen, where they are out of sight at all events, and can be given back to their owners quite as easily as if they were making our hall like an old clothes shop, or filling it with water from outside. On no account, therefore, buy a hall stand, brass hooks or a row of pegs in some unobtrusive corner answering every purpose, as far as I can see. Of course if the master comes in wet his garments must go straight to the kitchen fire, anyhow; if he be dry, why should he not take his hat and coat into his own dressing-room? We do not put on our bonnets and jackets in the hall, or keep them there either, and I cannot myself see why he should. But it is all a matter of management and use, and if he be asked to begin properly by taking his property upstairs, I am quite sure there will be no trouble about that detestable piece of furniture, a hat-stand.

Of course, nowadays no one thinks of having imitation marble-paper in the hall—that monstrosity is at last never now to be met with; but the hall paper is rather a difficult business, and must be chosen especially to suit *the* hall for which it is intended. A soft green paper makes almost any hall and staircase look cheerful, but my pet paper is undoubtedly Pither's 'blue blossom,' at 1s. 6d. a piece, and I especially recommend a dado here, but not a paper one—this soon gets shabby. Children's little paws, boxes going up and down, a thousand things inseparable from a staircase, in the shape of wear and tear, all have to be considered. Therefore, either a dado of matting, with a real wooden rail, painted the colour of the paper or else a wooden dado, or one of really pretty cretonne, are all to be preferred, because they stand a good many hard knocks, and remain unspoiled to the last. A matting dado, I think myself, is the very best, and, if desired, the stair-carpets can be saved much wear by covering them in their turn with narrow matting too. I really think a blue hall is as pretty as any, and then old-gold curtains over the doors look charming; but a sage-green hall looks extremely well, and I have seen a terra-cotta paper, with a chintz dado, using Liberty's Mysore chintz, that had a very pretty effect indeed. If the banisters end in a round, a good effect is procured by placing a plant in a pot there. I had one that never got knocked over; but, for fear of a catastrophe, a brass pot with an aspidistra should be selected, as, if this falls, it cannot be utterly and entirely done for, as a china one would be containing a fragile fern or a delicate palm, neither of which, by the way, would stand the draught as the long-suffering aspidistra invariably does. I like pictures up the staircase, and, should there be a staircase window, artistic jugs and pots, more especially the Bournemouth and Rebecca ware, sold by Mr. Elliot (who lives at the top of the Queen's Road, Bayswater, No. 18), should stand all along the window-ledge; and if the outlook be ugly, the entire window should be covered by a fluted muslin curtain in art colours, using either Madras, which does not wash well, and must always be new here, or Liberty's artistic muslins at 1s. a yard, with the appearance of which I am delighted, either for window blinds or summer quilts, or material for throwing over sofas, instead of guipure and muslin. It is sold in all colours, and is one of the best things I have seen for some time.

  How we furnish our hall must of course entirely depend on the room we have. Liberty has some charming bamboo settees in black, and arm-chairs to match. These are especially suitable for a hall, while an oak chest with an oaken back is a most valuable possession; the chest holds comfortably the year's accumulation of papers and magazines until it is time for them to go to the binder, and the top and back are charming with heavy jugs on, made too heavy to be blown over by filling them with sand, in which, when flowers are plentiful, blossoms can be put, and when they are scarce, leaves and berries and pampas grasses show to great advantage. If any small tables are about, have plants and books on them, and above all avoid any appearance of a passage or hall—nothing makes a house look so miserable. A good thing to hang in the hall is a nicely illuminated card saying when the post goes out, with a box underneath for the letters, and the time-table and a hat-brush should be in some unobtrusive corner, whence they should never be moved on any pretext whatever; a fixed matchbox, that should always be full, is another institution, and a candlestick in good order should be put on one of the tables when the hall gas is lighted. The painted artistic-looking candlesticks sold by Liberty at 2s. 9d. are very pretty, but a brass candlestick does not get shabby quite so soon, and is not much if any dearer. One more axiom: never have loose mats at the room doors outside; they only turn over with the ladies' dresses, and get untidy, while a piece of indiarubber tubing at the bottom of the door keeps out far more draught than any mat possibly can. If the hall be not tiled, I recommend it to be covered with Pither's capital hard-wearing drugget over felt, with one or two dhurries about, put down carelessly, for sake of the colour; these wash beautifully and wear excellently, and begin at 1s. 6d. each, rising in price according to size, while one or two of the Kurd or Scinde rugs would be even better than these, as they stand a very great deal of wear and tear.

Before passing away from the hall, I will just mention two or three schemes of decoration that are absolutely certain to be a success, and therefore can be adopted without any chance of a failure: No. 1 is Pither's invaluable red and white 'berry' paper at 1s. 6d. a piece; a dado of red and white matting—Treloar, Ludgate Hill, has a capital one at about 1s. a yard, and varnished paint the exact colour of the red on the flower; blue hard wearing drugget on the floor, and red, white, and blue striped dhurries for *portières*. No. 2.—Paper of a good sage-green, with dado of Japanese leather paper in sage-green, and gold all the paint varnished sage-green and Pither's terra-cotta hard-wearing drugget on the floor and stairs; terra-cotta and grey-blue serge curtains would be safe here, and if there be a back staircase and no boys in the house, the dado may be replaced by a frieze of Maple's grey-gold Japanese leather paper; this resembles a flight of birds among palm branches, and this arrangement is simply a perfect hall, but not suitable for one where there is much traffic. All the paint, on doors, wainscot, and frieze or picture-rail alike, must be one shade of green only, and I most strongly deprecate for any place the odious habit of picking out styles and wainscoting with another shade of paint; this is never needed, only adds to the work, and draws attention to the paint, at which we do not want to look, and which would only serve as a pleasant background to oneself and one's belongings. The sides of the stairs and the balustrading should all be painted to match, though the mahogany handrail should be left alone.

Scheme No. 3 would only do where expense was no object, but would undoubtedly make a most lovely hall. This would be in cream-coloured varnished paint, with a high wooden dado painted cream colour, and then embellished with sketches of birds and flowers by Mrs. McClelland's clever fingers; the paper could be a good gold-coloured Japanese leather paper, and the carpets could be Oriental rugs sewn together, while the hall should have a handsome Oriental square of carpet, and one or two divans placed about it; the draperies could be Liberty's beautiful chenille material in Oriental colours too, and great care should be taken with their arrangement. In all cases I strongly advise the ceilings to be papered, no one who has once indulged in a coloured or decorated ceiling ever going back to the cold, ugly whitewash, with which we have all been so contented so long. It is generally safe to put a blue and white ceiling paper with a yellow or red wall paper, a terra-cotta and white with green walls, and a yellow and white with blue walls, taking care to carry out this combination of colouring in the carpets, draperies, &c.

Much as I dislike gas, it is a necessity in any hall, and I here produce two sketches of beaten iron gas-lamps that would be suitable for almost any style of decoration; these are from the designs of Messrs. Strode, 48 Osnaburgh Street, Regent's Park, and cost respectively 5*l*. 15*s*. and 1*l*. 4*s*. each; quite simple hanging lamps are to be had from Mr. Smee at 35*s*., in beaten iron, but these are not quite large enough by themselves to light a hall, and two at least would be required.

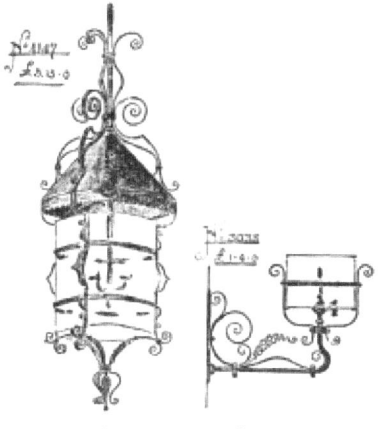

Fig. 3.   Fig. 4.

On no account, by the way, allow your front door to be disfigured with the terrible 'graining,' against which I am always waging war. Painters always beg to be allowed to 'embellish' at least the front door with the hideous but orthodox arrangement of yellows and browns, scraped mysteriously and agonisedly with a comb, or some such instrument, in a faint and feeble attempt to deceive callers into believing that the door is made of some highly polished wood, veined by nature, in a way that could not deceive the veriest ignoramus; but I stoutly set my face against such an idea, and denounce graining as the hideous and palpable sham it undoubtedly is, advising all who come to me to have some good deep self-colour for their front door, and generally suggesting a very dark peacock-blue door for a 'blue blossom' hall, a very dark Indian red for the red berry, and a dark sage-green for the sage-green hall, adding brass handles and furniture; this stamps the house at once as an artistic one, and one in which 'graining' will not be allowed at any price.

And here I will pause for a moment to beg any one who may need these words of mine to refuse to allow any graining whatever in their houses; it is a barbarism that should be allowed to die out as quickly as may be; it is always ugly, always inartistic, and, being an undoubted attempt to seem what it is not, I set my face against it always. I would rather have deal, rubbed over with boiled oil, than the most 'artistically' imitated piece of walnut or mahogany ever produced by the grainer's tools; the one is neat, the other a vulgar sham—vulgar because it is always vulgar to seem to be what one is not, and to pretend to be what can be contradicted by the tiniest scratch, rather than to be confessedly of a cheap material, and therefore graining cannot be too strongly condemned.

Many people cling to it who dislike it as much as I do, because they are told nothing can be done to it, unless all the paint is burned off; there never was a greater fallacy! To paint over graining all one has to do is to have the paint washed thoroughly with strong soda and water, and then rubbed down with glass-paper, then apply one coat of Aspinall's water-paint and one coat of his enamel, and you can possess at once all the colour you require, without any trouble at all. Of course a perfect 'job' is only made by burning off the paint, but no one could ever tell this had not been done, and very particular people can themselves apply first of all Carson's 'detergent,' sold at Carson's paint works, La Belle Sauvage Yard, for 5*s.* a tin; this brings off the old paint in flakes, and leaves the bare wood ready for the painter's brush. Still this is not necessary, and people who have kept to graining because they dread the burning-off process need do so no longer, unless they positively cannot afford the new paint required to cover it over.

A stone hall in the country looks much better if the stones are painted a good red or blue, instead of being whitened daily, and Treloar's scarlet cocoanut matting is invaluable in back passages and on kitchen stairs; and above all we must recollect that the hall gives the first welcome to our guests, and that therefore the more it resembles a cosy, comfortable, artistic room, the more likely is the rest of the house to be a charming and successfully designed and furnished home.

CHAPTER VII
THE DINING-ROOM

In my first chapter I laid just a little stress on the word 'suitable'; but in looking back at it, I find I did not say half what I intended to on the subject of making that most suggestive tri-syllable our guiding star, as it were, in our whole scheme of life, and it may not be out of place just to dwell upon it a little, before proceeding to lay out any money, because if we calmly and dispassionately regulate our desires by their appropriateness to our purse, and our standing in the social scale, we shall find our requirements diminish sensibly, and our purchasing powers increased in the most pleasing and comfortable way.

Therefore, in starting to buy the furniture for our modest dining-room, let us consider not what is handsome or effective or taking to the eye, but what is suitable to Edwin's position, and what will be pleasant for Angelina to possess, without having unduly to agitate herself and worry herself to death in nervously protecting her goods and chattels from wear and tear, which often enough is reflected on her, and wears and tears her nerves, and takes up her time in a manner that would be pathetic, if it were not so ridiculous and so extremely unsuitable to her position as a British matron. Therefore, with a small income it is the reverse of suitable to make purchases that can never be replaced without months of anxious striving and saving; for though, of course, incomes may increase, they seldom increase in proportion to the wants of the household; and it is better to buy strong plain furniture, to purchase cheap and pretty carpets and draperies that can be replaced without a serious drain on our income, than to revel in expensive chairs and tables which, should they be scratched and broken, can never be matched without much more sacrifice than they are worth; and if we march along manfully, determined to act suitably, not fashionably, we shall enjoy life a thousand times better, and have at the same time the pleasing consciousness that we are doing good to our fellow-creatures, without knowing it perhaps, but most satisfactorily; for example is worth a thousand precepts, and practising is more than a million sermons, all the world over.

How often a well-managed house, an income carefully (not meanly, not lavishly, but *carefully*) administered, or a pretty idea pleasantly carried out, has shone like a bright light in this naughty world—other people have seen our strivings, may be have noted our cheerful bright house, and seen our small but comfortable *ménage*, and have gone on their way cheered and refreshed by our example, and in copying it have influenced some one else in quite another part of London or the suburbs; and, alas! how many may we not have helped on the downward path of extravagance and foolish lavishness by our foolishness or our needless display, which we have repented of, most likely, long before all the bills were paid.

Taking into consideration the fact that no one can live to themselves, even in the purchase of chairs and tables, we may, perhaps, be forgiven our sermon; but lest Angelina tires of our prating, and shrinks appalled from the serious manner in which we cannot help regarding the starting of any new home, we will leave off preaching on unsuitability, and proceed on our journey in search of nice and suitable furniture for our small dining-room.

Fig. 5.

Great care must be taken in selecting our dining-room chairs, and we earnestly advise all intending purchasers of these necessary articles of furniture to look not so much at the appearance as to their capabilities for affording a resting-place to a weary back; for I have often endured a silent martyrdom at many a dinner-party, in the houses of those amiable but mistaken people who go in for Chippendale chairs, embellished by carvings just where one leans back, or for those other still more agonising seats which have a round gap or space, and through which one almost falls should one try to lean against them and so obtain rest; and I am naturally anxious to save others from the sufferings I have endured, either on the chairs just spoken of, or seated on one the seat of which was so high from the ground that my legs have refused to reach it, and I have hung suspended in mid-air, until I have hardly known how to sit out the long and elaborate meal I was enduring, certainly not enjoying.

Fig. 6.

Now here are five chairs illustrated, any one of which would be quite safe to have. No. 5 is the most expensive of all, and would cost about 3*l.* 10*s.* each. These are ebonised New Zealand pine, and are upholstered in a dull brown morocco, which has worn splendidly. Nos. 6, 7, and 8 are Mr. Smee's designs, and are made with a peculiar curve in the backs, which just takes one's shoulders, and gives one a comfortable resting-place without appearing to be in the least a lounge. These chairs can be had for about 32*s.* and 42*s.* respectively, No. 6 being upholstered in a species of woollen tapestry, which wears well, and would be singularly suitable for a small *ménage*, and is, therefore, not out of the reach of most of us; while for folks who require something much less expensive than even the cheapest chairs just spoken of, there are the 3*s.* 6*d.* rush-seated black-framed chairs, sold by Messrs. Harding Bros., Beaconsfield, Bucks, which are strong, artistic in appearance, and infinitely to be preferred to the chairs in the terrible 'suites,' that are such a temptation to the unwary, and to those who make that most fatal of all mistakes, and do their shopping in a hurry—than which there cannot be a greater error.

Fig. 7.

From Kitchen To Garret | 61

In a small room I am much inclined to a round table; these are much more cosy, and much more easily arranged to look nice; but, in any case, the table need only be stained deal, with fairly good legs, for in these days the table is always kept covered by a tablecloth, and is never shown as it used to be in the old times, when half the occupation of the servants, and often enough of the unfortunate mistress too, was to polish the mahogany incubus, and bring it up to a state of perfection. We have other and better occupations now than this constant 'furniture tending,' I am glad to say; and, oh! how much prettier our houses are, to be sure, than they used to be.

Fig. 8.

There are two of these species of tablecloths especially to be recommended, both for their artistic and their inexpensive merits, and are far to be preferred to the tapestry cloths kept ready made in most shops. Self-coloured felt or serge makes an admirable cover, especially if a border is added of some contrasting colour. Peacock-blue serge looks well with an old-gold border, about six inches wide; each side of the border has a gimp combining the two colours, and the cloth itself is edged with a tufted fringe. Two shades of red look well too; but, of course, the cloth must be chosen to harmonise with the room in which it is to be used, and not bought, as Englishmen all too often make their purchases, because the thing is pretty in itself, forgetting that it ceases to have even a claim on the score of beauty when placed among incongruous surroundings. I may mention, now I am on the subject of tablecloths, that I much dislike the custom of leaving the white tablecloth on all day long; this invariably makes the room look like an eating-house, and causes the cloth to appear messed, for dust from the fire settles upon it; and I always insist on the white cloth being brushed, *folded in its folds on the table by the two maids,* and then placed at once in the press, a cloth managed like that lasting twice as long and looking much better than the one that is left on for two or three days at a time; for few if any of us can now afford a clean tablecloth every day, not only on the score of the washing, but because the washing process too often applied ruins our cloths, and results in nothing save a series of holes, worn by chemicals and careless mangling; therefore the white cloth must be removed, and replaced by a good art serge or felt, made up, as suggested above, with a band of some contrasting hue. This cloth careful people remove during meals, for no one can be sure whether gravy or wine will not be upset; and teacups and saucers have been known to be turned over bodily even in the best-regulated families. These accidents do no positive damage if the good cloth is removed; and, after all, this is a small thing to recollect, and may save expenditure both of money and temper too.

These tiny hints are of course meant for people who are not well off, but may not be out of place even to those richer people who are lucky enough not to be obliged to worry after every trifle. A penny saved is a penny gained; and even the richest among us has need to be careful. What he saves can after all be given to some poor brother.

But however rich you are do not be persuaded to buy that ugly, expensive, and tremendous thing a sideboard; neither waste your substance on dinner-wagons, they spoil the appearance of everything; but get some obliging and clever upholsterer to make you a cabinet or two, one for each side of the fireplace, if you have recesses there, and take care they are pretty, for much of the look of your home depends upon what you have in the shape of armoires. I have two made in ebonised wood from a design given me by a Royal Academician, which are illustrated here. They have three shelves, then a broad space where are deep cupboards, and then again an empty space, where books can be kept, or great jars put to decorate it. On the three shelves I arrange china, which is also arranged on the top of the part that has three cupboards. These have brass hinges and good locks, and hold wine, dessert, dinner napkins, and trifles, such as string, nails, and other necessary articles, and answer every purpose of a sideboard, and, instead of being ordinary, ugly things, are so

decorative that no one ever enters my room without noticing them and asking me where they are to be procured. I have had mine some years now, but extremely nice ones are made by Mr. Smee, the prices beginning at 6*l*. 6*s*. in plain deal ready for painting any special hue to suit any room, to 10*l*. 10*s*. each in oak or walnut; and I very strongly recommend them to people who really wish their home to be artistic, and not a mere warehouse for necessary furniture, for while they answer the same purpose as a sideboard, they are pretty to look at, and would not be out of place in an ordinary sitting-room.

Up to this present moment I have said nothing about the colour or arrangement of the walls of the dining-room, and so, before proceeding to dilate on the rest of the furniture, I will here give my readers a few hints on this subject. In the first place, then, let all people about to furnish determine that their dining-room shall be cheerful somehow, and let them eschew anything like dark colours or dingy papers, refusing to listen to the voice of the charmer, who has his 'appropriate' designs to sell, and does not care in the least for your ideas on the subject; and, having mentally selected the colour that appeals to their taste, let them refuse manfully to be talked out of their purpose by a man who has no ideas beyond the conventional ones of dark colours for a dining and light ones for a drawing-room.

For those people who can afford it, I advise invariably a plain gold Japanese leather paper, with a bold red and gold leather paper as a dado. The plain paper is 4*s*. 6*d*. a piece of nine yards, *French* or narrow width; the dado paper is 1*s*. 6*d*. a yard. All the paint in the room should be the exact shade of the *red* of the ground of the paper, and the painter should be instructed to keep entirely to one shade of paint, to do no 'picking out' or embellishments at all, but to paint wainscot, shutters, dado rail, and doors alike in one uniform shade of a good red, mixing the last coat with varnish, or else giving one coat of Mr. Aspinall's invaluable enamel paint, which gives a smooth and polished appearance, particularly suitable for this special tint of red. The dado rail is sold by Maple ready to put up at 2¼*d*. a foot; thus it would be easy for any one to calculate exactly how much such a scheme of decoration would cost. Then the ceiling should be papered in pale yellow and white. The cornice should in no case be outlined or 'picked out' with colours, but should be a uniform shade of cream, thus just shading into the paper without calling attention to itself.

Fig. 10.—Dining-room at Gable-end, Shortlands.

Here let me pause for one moment to impress emphatically on my readers the great necessity of recollecting that paint and paper are after all only a background to oneself and one's belongings, and therefore are not to be brought unduly forward. The paint must always be kept one shade of one colour; the cornice must always be coloured a deep cream, and the necessary relief in doors and shutters is obtained by filling the panels thereof with a good Japanese leather paper, which at once causes the proper decorative effect with the expenditure of a very little money, the effect being heightened by the addition of brass locks and handles, which cost very little, and yet just add the finishing touches to the room.

Should the Japanese paper be too expensive, the red effect could be obtained by one of Pither's papers with a bold frieze in a good floral design. This is united to the paper by a frieze or picture rail, sold by Maple at 2¼d. a foot unpainted, and from this frieze the pictures hang on brass hooks made on purpose; these are about 2s. 6d. a dozen; and the pictures are suspended from them on copper wires; this, however, only answers where there is no gas, as gas corrodes the wire rather quickly, and then cords must be used; but where there is no gas the copper answers perfectly, and looks far better than anything else can possibly do.

Should red be objected to altogether—and I hope it may not be—here is another scheme of decoration; a dark sage-green paper, with a very little gold in it; a gold and green Japanese leather dado; all the paint one shade of sage-green, and a terra-cotta and white ceiling paper; terra-cotta serge or damask curtains edged with ball fringe, and a sage-green tablecloth with pale terra-cotta border. With the red decoration the curtains &c. can be a rather faint pinky terra-cotta; this produces an excellent effect, while in some rooms a dull blue would harmonise most excellently with the red. Let me mention one other trifle: always insist on that ghastly round in the centre of the ceiling, above the gaselier, being removed. Workmen always say this is impossible, just as they generally declare they cannot paint over graining; but it is quite an easy business, and makes an immense difference in the appearance of any room, and is another 'little-thing' the forgetting of which always annoys one, and spoils what might otherwise be a perfect whole.

I generally advise a dado in the dining-room, because of the rubbing the paper always receives from the backs of the chairs; but this said rubbing can be obviated by putting all round the room on the floor against the wainscot a two-inch border of wood. This does not show if painted to match the wainscot, and always keeps off a great deal of the wear and tear the wall receives. Yet sometimes, when the paper is a really handsome one, a dado can be dispensed with for some time; the placing of one when the paper itself has been up a few years having the effect often of making a new room of it, and doing away with the re-papering process; which is always such a terror by reason of the dilatoriness and utter worthlessness of many of the British workmen we are forced to employ, painters, as a rule, being the most unsatisfactory of all; and I am quite sure many young men who now starve genteelly as clerks, either in or out of place, could earn much more money, and be constantly employed too, if they would take to honest papering and painting, and carry out our ideas in our houses for us, giving us honest, *sober* work in return for honest pay. However, we must not sermonise more than we can help; and having suggested a few ideas for covering the walls and buying the most necessary articles of furniture, I now proceed to dwell upon those small extras which will make the room comfortable, should Edwin have to sit in it when he is at home and has letters to write; or should the bride-elect be obliged sometimes to make it her morning room, to save the fire, or the extra work caused by a third room to a servant. A simple window-seat, as in sketch 11, can often be placed in a suburban bow-windowed villa, and at once makes a cosy seat. This frame costs 7s., and can be made by a local carpenter.

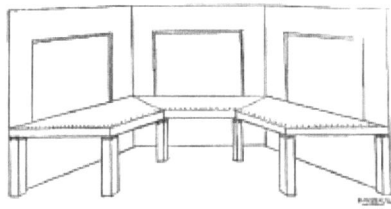

Fig. 11.

The top is made of sacking, and takes four yards at about 1s. a yard; the front is made from a deep frill of cretonne lined with unbleached calico, and is sewn on rings (fig. 12). These are suspended on nails, and the whole of the top is cushioned with cretonne, cretonne cushions being sewn on rings and hung on the wall to make a back for these seats. The description of arrangement of curtains suitable for this will be found in the chapter on curtains; and I maintain that no girl or woman either need consider it a hardship if she have to spend her morning sewing or reading here, while she could write her necessary letters at the desk prepared for her husband, and which is a necessity in any house for a man who has accounts to keep and letters to write. Still, if Edwin is not a very much better specimen of a husband than the ordinary smoker of the period makes, Angelina will have to sit in her third room sometimes, for there is nothing more trying than an atmosphere of stale smoke, and I look forward to a time when men of the rising generation will be a little less selfish than they are at present in their indulgence in a habit that, so far as I can perceive, has not one merit to recommend it.

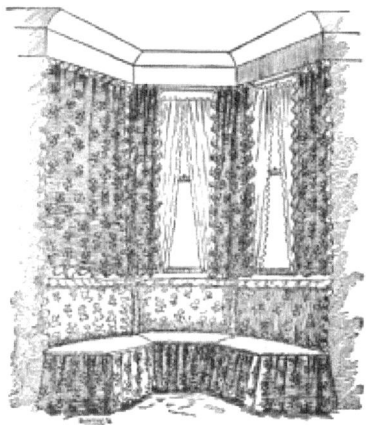

Fig. 12.

How often am I asked by girls how they can get rid of the disagreeable effects of smoke after dinner! They say—and very rightly too—that they really dread breakfast-time, and that their morning is poisoned for them by the indescribable odour that greets them when they come down refreshed from their night's rest to take up their day's work cheerfully; that it would be worse if Edwin smoked in the drawing-room, and they have no small room where they could allow him and his friends to work their wicked will, and that therefore they feel hopeless. And I cannot keep from wondering why men should smoke as they do; and thinking over this, and remembering how terrible it has been to me to come down to stale smoke, I should like to beg Edwin seriously to consider whether he need indulge in this habit in his own domicile, and whether the save of his after-dinner cigar would not conduce to his happiness as well as to Angelina's comfort; and really I have small heart to describe how Edwin can have a comfortable corner in his dining-room when I feel convinced the more comfortable he is made the worse effect it will have on everything in any pretty room.

I often wonder if men ever reflect on what their smoke costs them—how many delightful books, pleasant journeys, pretty engravings and photographs, and, in fact, all sorts of pleasant and permanent belongings, fly off into thin air by means of those pipes and cigars that really seem part of a man at present, and, in fact, are far too often their first thoughts.

I am not speaking for myself, gentle reader. The atmosphere of smoke is absent from my own especial domicile, and is reserved for my atom of a conservatory, should an occasional spoiled friend come down and look miserable without his pipe or cigarette—for cigars I cannot have even there; but I am writing for all the young people who are beginning life, and who think they make their husbands happy by giving them *carte blanche* to do just 'as they like in their own house.'

My dear girls, you cannot make a greater mistake with your husbands, and later on with your sons, than to wait upon them and give in to all their little lazinesses and selfishnesses at home. It may sound ridiculous, but it is a fact that old coats and slippers in the home circle mean manners to correspond; that bad manners often show a bad heart; and that a man is far more likely to care for the wife who exacts the small attentions that would have been lavished on the bride, than for her who opens the door for herself, rings the bell when he is in the room, and fetches things for him to save him steps that ought to be taken for her and not by her; and that boys who are allowed to bully and 'fag' their sisters and their mother are sure to make the selfish, inconsiderate husbands of which we hear so much nowadays.

And this great smoke question means a great deal too. It is a selfish, disagreeable habit, verily; and I can but hope that Edwin will think of this when in his pretty dining-room, and confine himself to the garden or conservatory with the door shut, even if he does not seriously consider how many pleasures for both vanish into smoke with the fumes of his post-prandial cigar; while the odours in which he condemns Angelina to begin her day would be done away with, and cheerfulness reign instead of dulness and a sense of nausea that are most trying to any one who does not like cigars.

Hoping that these words may have due effect, we will contemplate allowing our bridegroom to have a comfortable armchair in one corner of the room, and a big desk in another. The armchair, of course, is rather a serious item, and should really be made for the person who intends to sit in it. This naturally means an expenditure of from 8*l*. to 10*l*., according to the covering; so this may be done without until Edwin is older, if he cannot afford it. Now, in that case, I should recommend his buying one of those delightful low wicker-work chairs, which can be bought anywhere for 5*s*. or 6*s*. This can be painted to match the room, or ebonised with Aspinall's lovely and invaluable enamel paints—paints that have a glaze upon them and wear beautifully, and can be applied at home, and it can be cushioned by any local upholsterer, or even by Angelina herself, if she be clever with her fingers. The best material for covering these chairs is undoubtedly a strong tapestry at about 5*s*. 6*d*. a yard. Maple has the best-designed tapestries for the money in London, and one should be carefully chosen to harmonise with the room; the cushion should be tied in its place, or sewn in its place, with very strong tapes or thread, and should be buttoned down. It takes two and a quarter yards double width material and four and a half single width to make a cushion for the sides and seat, and the seat cushion should be finished off with a frill two inches wide. The comfort of these chairs is much enhanced by the addition of a small square soft cushion to fill up the hollow in the centre and stuff into one's back. These can be easily made either out of paper torn up and rolled into strips and then put into a piece of twilled cotton for a case, and a second case made from the material saved out of the chair covering itself, or small down cushions can be bought at Whiteley's in Turkey-pattern materials which can be hidden in a covering like the chair, as suggested above, or—whisper this, please—the hair-cushions placed in the back of ladies' skirts now can be utilised for stuffing these cushions to far more advantage than if they were retained in the position suggested by the dressmaker; and then the appearance of the chair is complete, with the addition of a Turkish embroidered antimacassar at 2*s*., which always makes any chair look nice, and even expensive (see Illustration 13). These chairs can be bought, enamelled any colour and cushioned complete, for 31*s*. 9*d*. at Colbourne's, 82 Regent Street, W., made to my pattern.

If you have a more expensive chair, do not buy one with a straight back; comfortable as they look, they are no use in practice, and every chair should be rounded for comfort, even if our grandmothers would shake their heads over the decadence of a generation that requires round backs to their chairs. Then there should be solid square arms on which books can be placed, if we like to put one down for a few moments, or even a cup of tea allowed to stand there, should it be necessary. Mr. Smee made me such a chair—it was 8*l*. 18*s*. 6*d*., I think—and I would not part with it on any consideration. It is covered with a very beautifully designed tapestry, and is trimmed with a deep woollen fringe, knotted and headed with broad gimp, and is simply perfect; but he took an immense amount of trouble about it, and made it to suit me, going on the same plan as that on which the wicker chairs are formed, only making mine higher from the ground, the lowness of the wicker chairs being their only failing; and even this, of course, is no failing in the eyes of a great many of our younger brothers and sisters.

Fig. 13.

Edwin's desk should be wide and strong, and should have good deep drawers. This can be bought ready made for about 12*l*., but I can provide a similarly convenient article for 2*l*. 15*s*.; that is to say, I can provide Edwin with ideas on the subject that any small carpenter can carry out. I have had for years a writing-table made by our own carpenter which cost me 2*l*. 5*s*., and is now doing honourable service as a dressing-table in a boy's room. It was made simply in deal, had three very deep drawers on each side, and one flat long drawer at the top; and the top was covered neatly with a piece of Japanese leather paper, which was quite as serviceable as good leather. I then had it nicely painted to match the room, added brass handles and locks, and had an extremely pretty desk or dressing-table for very little money. It is now painted a very beautiful blue, Aspinall's hedge-sparrow's-egg blue, and is most useful; deep drawers in a desk or dressing-table meaning comfort, for there is nothing more uncomfortable than having nowhere to put one's things. Good inkstands—indeed, the best I know is the deep blue-and-white china one to be bought at the Baker Street Bazaar for sixpence—should never be forgotten. Two should be bought, one for red and one for black (there is no ink, by the way, like Stephens' blue-black fluid; I cannot write without it, and always take it with me wherever I go); a box for string, filled, a post-card case, a letter-weigher, and a date-card and candlestick, and also a tray for sealing-wax, pens, ink-eraser, &c., all should find places on the desk, and above it, or on one side, should hang something to hold letters—a basket at 4½*d*. does beautifully; beneath it should be a wastepaper basket, and if Angelina be wise she will have a sack in a cupboard from some paper works, into which all pieces of wastepaper should be put. The sack soon fills, and from disposing of the contents there are seven shillings, which come in handily for plants, or flowers, or any of the many trifles that seem nothing to buy, but that run away somehow with so very much money—trifles making up life after all. If possible, keep a bunch of flowers on the desk. I am never without one winter or summer, and there is ample room on the desk I describe for this and also for dictionaries, two plants, and three brass pigs taking a walk, which I always use as a letter-weight.

The dining-room desk should always be looked after by the mistress herself, who should also take care that fresh ink, pens that will write, a blotting-book, and wastepaper basket are in every room in the house that is used, including the spare bedroom. Seeing to this often saves a good deal of time and temper too; for I know of nothing more irritating than to have to write a note in a hurry and have nothing handy to do it with.

The dining-room, or, indeed, any room, would not be complete without a few words on the subject of the mantelpiece, which is always rather a difficult matter to arrange; for one must have a clock there, and that means expense, unless we are content with a very charming specimen Oetzmann, of the Hampstead Road, used to sell for 25s. I have had one three, nay, four, years in my drawing-room, and it still goes excellently. It is blue, and in a tall slender black case. It is called the Chippendale clock. I dare say he keeps them still. Then there should be candles in blue and white china candlesticks, and any pretty ornaments Angelina may have, and, if none are given her, why, 1l. judiciously laid out at Liberty's or the Baker Street Bazaar will furnish more than one mantelshelf delightfully. I could make my readers smile over my hunt sixteen years ago for some nice candlesticks if I had the time, and could contrast my difficulties then with the *embarras de richesse* now. But space does not allow of these digressions. Still, whatever else is done without, let us be sure to have a couple of well-filled spillcases, and a matchbox with matches in it fixed to the wall; though, if we have the ordinary marble incubus of the orthodox suburban residence to deal with, we shall have to think over the mantelpiece question most seriously, for this is indeed a burning question, and one that would daunt the stoutest heart to answer satisfactorily, and I look forward hopefully to a time when builders will eschew the expensive and ugly marble in favour of wooden mantelpieces, which are, to my mind, all they ought to be.

In the first place, a wooden mantelpiece continues, as it were, the scheme of decoration of the room, and, without being unduly prominent, makes the necessary unobtrusive frame for the fireplace that a staring white marble erection can never be. And, in the second, any stain from smoke can be washed off the painted mantelpiece, while a few days' carelessness, a smoky chimney, or a housemaid's unclean paws can ruin a marble mantelpiece beyond the hope of redemption; therefore on all accounts I think a wooden one is to be preferred.

Of course, some people, even in a small house, regard the possession of the marble in the light of a patent of nobility—it is so handsome (odious word), so genteel; but these belong to the hopeless class, for whom little or nothing can be done. As an illustration of what I mean, I may tell you I once was asked by one of these individuals to come down to her country house and give my opinion on the subject of some wall-papers she was hesitating between; and when I entered her drawing-room, where my lady was not, but was heard scouring about upstairs, hastily changing her dress to be fit to be seen at four o'clock in the afternoon, I saw just such a gorgeous marble erection, and, in a species of compromise between the taste of the day and the sense of proud possession given by the marble, there was a valance hung round the edge of the shelf, supported, or rather tied on, with tapes, so that the fact of the material of which the shelf was made was visible to the eye of the visitor. I could not take my eyes off it, and on learning that my opinion was asked in reference to the room in which I was, I asked about the valance, suggesting how ridiculous it looked suspended, poor thing, in mid-air, and hinting that a board would give it a reason for its existence; but this was received with so much surprise that I could not recognise how beautiful the marble was, that I got out of the room as soon as I could, knowing that here any advice I could give would be utterly thrown away. In a great house where gorgeousness, not prettiness, reigns, marble is, of course, more in place than it is with us, but I do not like it at all in our cold native land, where our grey skies and dark atmosphere cry out for colour, and I would relegate it to Italy, where it contrasts charmingly with the ardent skies and glowing air inseparable from that land of sun and flowers. I do hope some builder, who is intent on building houses for the Edwins and Angelinas of the day, may read my humble words, and, turning his back on the marble, may put up in the pretty residences that are now the rule and not the exception the simple wooden mantelpiece that lends itself so kindly to decoration, and does not assert itself like the 'handsomer' one does in a small house—in a manner that resembles a rich relation come to call, and reduce the poor connection to a sense of his position and utter lowliness.

The mantelpiece of wood can have one or two little shelves in the comers under the shelf itself; here can be placed cups or vases for flowers. Then comes the shelf itself, and finally the over-mantel. In one of my rooms where the slate mantelpiece is hopeless, I have covered the top with a plain board, painted turquoise blue, the colour of the room. This is edged by a goffered frill of cretonne, like the curtains, about a foot deep. It is nailed on the front of the board, and the nails hidden by a moulding, also painted blue. Over this I have a glass about two feet wide with a bevelled edge, and framed in plain deal, painted blue, and surmounted by a shelf about four inches wide, supported by two small blue brackets. Of course the frame of the fireplace ought to be blue too, and it is a sore subject, I can tell you, that it is not; but being of black slate it is not so trying as it might be—not so trying, for example, as another room would have been had I not boldly painted its odious yellow and white marble mantelpiece black, to match my paint, and so removed an eyesore that looked like nothing so much as poached eggs very badly cooked and sent to table. I did go through the farce of asking my good and indulgent landlord, who, fortunately for me, was artistic, and gave his consent freely; but I am afraid, even if he had not, I should have painted it quite as boldly, and trusted to 'luck' to have escaped any fearful penalty when my lease was up, and I left my decorations behind me for some one else—decorations that include another painted mantelpiece, this time a dull grey stone thing, that is quite lovely in a terra-cotta coat of paint, and its top covered, as I have just described the blue covering, with a terra-cotta painted board, and a frill of blue and white Mysore chintz.

I am always being reminded of how much a fireplace is in a room by going into quite charming chambers where nothing is wanting save and excepting a nice arrangement there. The whole room is spoiled, and the ugliness there contrasts so forcibly with the rest of the room that I can never avoid mentioning it, and begging the owner to call at Shuffery's, in Welbeck Street, whose cheap wooden mantelpieces and tiled hearths cannot possibly be too widely known, and are cheaper than those of any other firm: though, of course, a clever draughtsman can make his own designs, and a wooden mantelpiece could be made by an ordinary carpenter, but the 'stuff' must be well seasoned and carefully put up, so as to have no risk of fire.

Always, if possible, have a tiled hearth and a very simple fender. A gorgeous fender is a mistake; if a tiled hearth is provided all one requires is a black frame to enclose the hearth, with two brass knobs just to brighten it up; then get some brass fire-irons and two standards at Maple's or else at Hampton's, where brass things are very good and cheap, and, if in any way obtainable, see your grates are Barnard's. They save their cost in coal in a very short time, and are very pretty and simple. I have one that cost a little over 4*l.*; it has a simple black frame, enclosing some pretty blue and white tiles, and has firebrick sides and bottom, and is as low as the hearthstone. The fire in this grate keeps alight from about 11 A.M. until 2 P.M. in the coldest winter weather, and I have never once during that time to ring for coals. Another ordinary stove during the same hours has to be continually watched and replenished, and while the blue and white room is always hot, the other room, possessed of the all-devouring grate, is never even warm, and sometimes one end thereof is hardly above freezing point. I have an equally good grate in the drawing-room, and here a fire made up at eight burns steadily until eleven at night, and often is quite a gorgeous fire at bedtime. I believe these grates are made at Norwich, but Shuffery sends them or similar grates equally satisfactory with his wooden mantelpieces; which, by the way, are supplied with Doulton ware fenders like the tiled hearths. These save needless trouble to the servants, as they only require dusting and an occasional wash-over to be always clean.

While we are on the subject of fires, I can tell my readers of a comfortable manner to keep in a fire in a bedroom or drawing-room, when a fire is wanted, but not a 'regular blazer.' To insure there being a fire, line the bottom and front of the grate with a newspaper, then fill it up, nearly to the top of the fireplace, with quite small coal, on the top of this lay an ordinary fire, with nice lumps of bright coal, wood, &c., and set light to it; this fire will burn downwards steadily, and can be left to take care of itself; and then, when the room is required for use, all that is wanted is a judicious poke, and a pretty cheerful blaze rewards you, while you have the satisfaction of knowing your fire is in, and no waste of fuel to any appreciable extent is going on, should the room not be in occupation.

Before I end this chapter I may just give some few hints as to what to do with our fireplaces when a fire is not necessary though, in my own case, an open Japanese umbrella suffices, because the temperature in England changes so quickly and so often that I scarcely can feel fires are an impossibility; but quite a pretty change in the room can be made by placing the sofa or the grand piano straight across the fireplace, of course removing fender, &c., and so making it appear as if it had vanished; while another nice effect is made with putting a fender made of virgin cork instead of the ordinary one, and filling up the grate with great ferns and flowering plants or cut flowers, frequently changed, for nothing save the ubiquitous aspidistra lives comfortably in this lowly and draughty situation. The cork fender should be filled with moss, and then jam pots sunk in it full of water; in these arrange your flowers: put a hand-basin in the grate itself, and bend large leaves of the *Filix mas*. fern over the edges; these completely cover the bars of the grate; then large peonies can be arranged in the basin, and the whole looks like a bank of flowers. This can only be managed in a country room, where flowers are plentiful; but not a bad fire-screen is made from a wire frame with a deep flower trough in front; ivy should be trained all over the frame, and then flowers and ferns can be arranged in the trough at it small cost. Let this, however, be done only in one room in the house.

Never put it out of your power to have a fire whenever you feel cold. No one knows how much illness is saved by this small precaution.

One or two things must also be remembered before we leave the dining-room altogether. Footstools must be provided, and by the side of the grate should hang a bass brush to keep the hearth tidy, a pair of bellows to coax a lazy fire, and a fan to screen any one who should dislike the blaze in their eyes; and the wall-paper will last all the longer if a Japanese paper fan is nailed in such a manner that the bristles of the brush rest on it and not on the wall; just as the carpet will last longer if the coalscuttle stands on its own small linoleum mat, which can be painted any colour with Aspinall's paint, and will always wash clean, cheerfully every day.

CHAPTER VIII
THE MORNING-ROOM

Even in a small house I very strongly advise the third room to be set aside emphatically for the mistress's own room—sacred to her own pursuits, and far too sacred to be smoked in on any occasion whatever. And this room can hardly be made too pretty in my eyes, for undoubtedly here will be struck the key-note of the house, for the chamber set aside for the mistress of the house is unconsciously a great revealer of secrets. Is she dreamy, lazy, and untidy?—her room tells of her. Is she careful, neat, energetic?—her room brightens up and bears witness to her own character. Does she write?—these are her pens, and her dirty little inkstand, looking like business; or work, or paint? Well, ask the room sacred to her use; it will tell you of her much better than I can, and if she be only an honest English girl, anxious to rule her house well, and to really make it 'home,' her room will disclose all this, and will be always ready for her, and for any one else who will come to her there for the help, pleasure, or counsel she in her turn will be so happy to give once she has bought her own little experience.

Or should it happen that Angelina has no pronounced tastes, and does not intend to plunge head-first among the bread-winners with pen or pencil, she will have all the easier task in arranging her tiny room. On the walls we may hang a pretty sage-green paper, taking great care there is no arsenic in it. In the recesses of the walls beside the fireplace I should put shelves, painted sage-green, the colour of the paint, and edged with narrow frills of cretonne similar to that used on the mantel-board; these are sewn on tapes, and the tapes nailed to the shelves, and hidden by a moulding similar to the one on the board. And should Angelina desire a cheap, useful species of cupboard, one of these shelf-fitted recesses can be draped by a cretonne curtain, which would look pretty, the while it hid any baskets or boxes or odds and ends wished out of sight yet close at hand at the same time. These shelves are put in to the height of the mantelpiece, and, the tops being wide, hold a nice quantity of decorative china, and, being backed by fans or large blue and white plates, bought very cheaply at almost any glass and china warehouse, add immensely to the artistic appearance of the room, the walls of which will, I hope, be hung with pretty photographs or engravings, or sketches of home friends, or places, done by friends or even by our bride herself.

If she can paint, or has any girl friend who can do so, she should now embellish her door panels with graceful pale pink flowers, remembering never to fall into that fatal and ugly mistake of drawing or representing flowers in the colours that nature herself never uses for them. There is my favourite pink flower, the flowering rush, to be remembered, and this pictured among its own surroundings, marguerite daisies and long grasses, would be admirable on the sage-green paint, and doing this will occupy Angelina nicely during those long hours that are hers when the honeymoon is over, and Edwin has once more to put his neck into the collar and set to work to keep the little house going.

I should also like Angelina to keep round her in this her own room as many reminiscences as she can procure of her old home. If she have a prudent, loving mother, I think many a little imprudence may be avoided, if a photograph of the dear face is always looking down upon her; and if she have an honoured father, his precepts will be recalled in a similar manner, and insensibly she will be helped on her way, as she was in her girlhood, by the loving counsel she can never be too old to require, live as long as ever she may.

Then there should always be something here in the shape of a desk, for Angelina will have to write letters, if only to answer invitations, though I trust sincerely she may have something better to do with her time than that. And if she can copy Edwin's writing table, she will find it a great comfort to her, for the deep drawers will hold paper, envelopes, and the thousand and one things she should never be without; such as string, untied, *not cut* off parcels, and neatly rolled up in lengths, half-sheets of letters to be used for notes to *familiar* friends or for tradesmen's orders, paid bills—no *un*paid ones, please—and brown papers also saved from parcels, elastic bands, and answered and unanswered letters; which, if important or private, should never be left on a desk in a letter-rack, for 'maidens' are but mortals, and an open epistle is too tempting a thing for most servants to leave untouched and unread. Be sure and have a wastepaper basket, and somewhere in a cupboard the sack I mentioned before, in which to put the contents of the basket *at once*, as soon as it is full; and do not keep any letters about in your possession once they are replied to, especially if they are chatty letters about people and their sayings and doings, but destroy them at once. They are safe in the wastepaper bag; but a letter is like a ghost, and turns up when least expected, often working irreparable mischief; in fact, in these days of penny postage, a letter is only written for the moment, and should be put beyond the power of doing harm by any honourable person the moment it has answered its purpose. Remember how often one's opinion changes. One makes friends or quarrels with an acquaintance, and writes to one's intimates about these tiny circumstances, and no harm is done if the letter be immediately destroyed, besides which there is always the chance that death may pounce upon one, and leave one's hoards defenceless, and our friend's confidences at the mercy of our successors. Who re-reads old letters? Life is too rapid now for this. Once answered, tear up these amusing, compromising epistles, and beg your correspondents to do the same, and then not very much harm will be done by them after all.

In Angelina's room there should always be some sort of a sofa. Maple has beautiful deep sofas, I think for 8*l.* 8*s.*; these can be covered with serge, or else velveteen or corduroy velvet, in a good sage-green colour or peacock blue, and finished at either end with a square pillow or cushion covered with the same; the velveteen is 2*s.* 6*d.* a yard, and wears beautifully; it is preserved too, when not in use, by throwing over it a large cover made of either guipure and muslin, costing 30*s.*—rather a large item—or by two or three of the striped curtains, joined. These cost 1*s.* 6*d.* each at Liberty's, but I personally prefer the guipure, or else a large square of Madras muslin, edged with a goffered frill, or else a cheap lace. This should be folded back, should you require to lie down much on the sofa, as otherwise it soon crushes and becomes dirty and untidy. Remember, young people, I am no advocate for lying about on sofas, and I abhor idleness, but a proper amount of rest and care often saves a long illness, and there will be times in all your lives when a sofa is not a luxury but a positive necessity. A book can always be read, or work be done, for, properly pushed down at the back, the cushions support the shoulders, the while the legs are supported too, and so proper rest is obtained; and if the sofa be in Angelina's own room, she will use it when she would think twice before going solemnly into the drawing-room, where she may be disturbed by visitors, or be, perhaps, fireless, to take the repose she may possibly have been ordered.

There should be two firm little tables, or even three, according to space. The floor should be stained about two feet all the way round, and the square of carpet should be as pretty as possible. Flowers and pot-ferns should be as much used us the money will permit, as nothing makes a room look so nice. The curtains should be cretonne and muslin underneath, arranged as I shall describe in the chapter set apart for curtains. There should be a work-table, a stand for newspapers with a paper-knife attached—tied on, in fact, and re-tied when not in use, for no possession takes quicker to its heel than does a paper-knife—and plenty of books and magazines, obtainable from a library; or by judicious exchanges among friends or acquaintances made by advertising; for it is astonishing how many papers can be seen by a clever person, who can manage to exchange the one or two she takes in for one or two more, that in their turn go on again in exchange for others; and this is neither extravagance nor waste of time, for every one should be as well read in the events of the day, as most people are in the events of bygone years; for one's own times are, I think, quite as amusing and far more instructive than even the events of those days when there were no newspapers and nothing very much happened.

Let me beg of you all to remember two things: one is, that on *no* account is this little room to have gas, or to be smoked in under any pretext whatever, and that here all must be to hand that Angelina is likely to want; she must have her own duster, her sticking-plaster, her little remedies for tiny hurts, her cotton, needles, thimble, her string, her stamps, her pins, her gum, her glue, and be able to put her hand on brandy, the one spirit that I would allow inside the house, and which is a most invaluable necessary medicine; and if she be wise and her servants are tired, she will be able to give a sister or very intimate friend her cup of afternoon tea without ringing, should they come in on a busy day and require refreshment, when it would be unkind to take Jane off her work to provide it. No lady was ever the worse for making her own tea, or even washing her own teacups, and a little thought for Jane will insure Jane thinking of and for you, in a time when you may be *very* dependent on her for this care and thought.

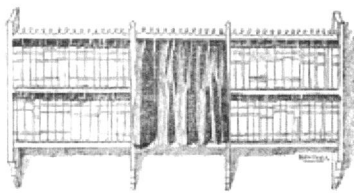

Fig. 14.

The tea-things can be kept 'handy' behind one of the curtained recesses, and a small brass kettle can also be concealed there; but there are some rooms, alas! so evilly constructed as to be positively without recesses for the shelves, and in this case the books that Angelina will require in her own room must have a bookcase made especially for them, and the recess for the teacups must be made as in the drawing of the bookcase on this page. The best bookcases are undoubtedly the revolving American bookcases, first introduced by Messrs. Trübner, the well-known publishers, of Ludgate Hill. These hold a great many volumes, take up small room, and on the top of them china can also be placed; but they are expensive, a good-sized one costing 5*l.* 5*s.*, and so, if this be out of the question, I recommend a long plain oak bookcase that I have had made for me from the design of a relative, for they hold a vast quantity of literature, and only cost the comparatively small sum of 1*l*. 18*s*. 6*d*. This bookcase is about eight or nine feet long, and consists of two rows of shelves, each wide enough to hold books the size of a bound volume of 'Good Words.' The top of the last shelf has a narrow battlement of oak just cut out in scallops to relieve the plainness and to serve as a rail to support the china that stands on the top of the bookcase; and the shelves are all edged with a two-inch frill of velveteen or cretonne to harmonise with the rest of the room. The shelves are divided into three parts, and the centre part looks very well with a velveteen curtain over it, nailed to the top shelf, and hanging in a straight line from top to bottom. Behind this curtain can be placed all sorts and conditions of things, from paper-backed shilling books, that are not in the least bit decorative, to string or gum, or the cups and saucers spoken of above, if we have no other place to use as a cupboard in the room. The shelves are hung on the wall, just resting on the dado rail, and are supported with nails driven into the wall and by the dado rail itself. On the top the big blue jugs and coarse rod pottery Rebecca jars sold by Mr. Elliot, in the Queen's Road, Bayswater, should be placed, as then the bookcase is not only useful but remarkably ornamental.

To supplement the ordinary lack of cupboard room, it is occasionally better to have one or two low square black cupboards about. Against the wall, where a table may be put sometimes, they look very nice, and are of incalculable use. They cost very little, and if the panels are filled in, either with Japanese paper or imitation tapestry, and the top covered with a cloth and used for books, plants, or pieces of china, scarcely any one would see they were cupboards, and so you have a useful piece of furniture doing double duty, as cupboard and table, for the expense of one. I have in one corner of my especial room a most beautiful cabinet which holds all my odds and ends comfortably, and is such a success that I cannot help describing it here, although Angelina may not of course care to go to the expense, but it is so pretty and withal so inexpensive, as compared to the usual run of cabinets, that I think I may venture to recommend it to her. It fits into one corner, and is of deal, painted sparrow's-egg-blue to match the room. It stands about five feet eight. The under part is a cupboard. Then come three deep drawers, flanked by two little shelves—two each side of the drawers. The top shelf is hidden by a small curtain of old-gold coloured velveteen, and in the under shelf stands a blue pot that cost sixpence. There is a flat shelf forming the top of the cabinet with china on, and at the back, which goes into an angle to fit the corner, is another shelf about three inches wide on which more china stands. The drawers and cupboard have brass handles and locks, and the whole thing complete, made to order and measure by Mr. Smee, cost me 8*l*. 8*s*., and I often look at it and wonder how I existed, or where I put all my papers and things generally, before I saved up money enough to buy it for myself. The chairs here can be all the deep, low, basket-work chairs, and these need not cost much, but these chairs must be bought with great care and circumspection, they are all such different shapes, and should never be purchased in a hurry—that fatal hurry that is at the bottom of so much waste and extravagance in the world; for, remember this, a thing obtained quickly and hastily seldom is the thing one really requires, and then a double outlay is necessary, or else perpetual discomfort is our portion, just because we were not judicious enough in our behaviour to take enough time over our purchases; and nowhere is hurry more fatal than in choosing one's chairs. You young people are apt to think only for the day, and do not care to remember that a time will come when legs and backs will ache; but I know this, and this is why I want you to be quite sure that you do not get the basket-chairs that go back too far, or are too low, or too high, but that the medium chairs are chosen, in which you can rest thoroughly when they are cushioned; and furthermore supplied with an extra cushion to fill up the gap in the back, and that are not high enough to require a footstool, but yet are not low enough to send one's feet to sleep, because of the manner in which they leave no room for the length of limb possessed by the unfortunate person who sinks into their comfortable-looking depths to rest, and cannot understand why he is so very uncomfortable when he has been there so short a time. Cretonne makes pretty covers for the cushions, which should be stuffed with wool and a little flock—all wool would make these cushions too expensive; but cretonne is not heavy enough for a man's wear, and either tapestry or woollen brocade or serge should be used for cushions for Edwin's accommodation. If a sofa be afforded, three of these chairs, or four at the outside, will amply furnish the little room; and they can have over their backs, as a finishing touch, an embroidered Oriental antimacassar, arranged to show both embroidered ends one above the other, and not tied in bows—a most inartistic and ugly arrangement in my eyes, and one quite useless and untidy too; for there is no doubt that a properly arranged antimacassar saves the chair cushion a great deal of the wear and tear and the rub of dusty shoulders, and need not be any trouble if a little thought is given to their arrangement, both in sitting down and rising from the chair.

If other chairs are required, higher and squarer, although I cannot think they are necessary myself in this small room, those painted blue, red, or black, and with cane seats, costing about 12s., are the best. The cane seat should be provided with a square cushion, covered in any odd pieces of damask or cretonne, and trimmed with a frill, and tied to the chair by four pairs of stout black tape strings, so that the cushion cannot slip about, as it otherwise would. These chairs would also do for the extra chairs in the drawing-room, if even the rush-seated Beaconsfield chairs at 3*s*. 6*d*. each are not pronounced quite good enough.

A very good, useful table, called the Queen Anne table, can be obtained from Oetzmann or Maple for about 25*s*. It is square, with square legs, and has two useful shelves, and the whole is covered in art-coloured velveteens. I have had one in very hard wear for seven or eight years, and it is now as good as the day when I bought it. I had some charming square stools made on the same plan for 7*s*. 6*d*. each, to hold large blue and yellow pots purchased at Whiteley's for 2*s*. 11*d*. each, and filled with palms, and these standing about in odd corners or in the centre of a bow-window add very much to the appearance of any room, for nothing gives so Oriental or artistic an appearance as plenty of plants, ferns, and palms; and these need not be out of the reach of any one who cares for pretty things, because with care they last and flourish for years; while cut flowers and flowering plants are out of the reach of any of those for whom I am especially writing these papers—that is to say, unless they keep their eyes very wide open, and utilise every morsel they can beg, or pick from the hedges and fields; that even in the suburbs are not swept quite clear of daisies, grasses, and even occasionally primroses and anemones.

Footstools must be a *sine quâ non* in each room, and more than one or two should, if possible, be provided. The square Oriental-looking ones, at 4*s*. 6*d*., purchasable at Shoolbred's, are very nice, but big, square, old-fashioned ones, made by the carpenter, or, better still, by Edwin, are the best of all; they do not run away from you when you put your feet on them, and their wear is everlasting. They are square frames of wood, rather heavy, and stuffed a little with flock on the top, and covered with a good stout woollen tapestry; they are quite half a yard across each way, and serve for two people if necessary. Then there are the ordinary round hassocks for 1*s*. 6*d*., covered in odds and ends of old carpets. These are soon made artistic by covering them over the carpet with artistic serges embroidered in crewels; white narcissus, or oranges and the blossoms looking very nice indeed on a terracotta serge; and yellow daisies or pomegranates on a peacock-blue serge being also quite charming to behold. Brackets are very useful for corners, and I especially recommend the bamboo brackets to be bought at the Baker Street Bazaar and at Liberty's. They are so cheap and light-looking, and hold odds and ends of china so nicely, and if many pictures or photographs do not adorn Angelina's walls, quite a grand effect can be obtained by making a bracket the centre of a scheme of decoration; elaborated from Japanese fans, that can surround the bracket like a halo, sending out branches or beams of colour from such a centre in all directions, in a manner invaluable to those who have no other means of decorating their walls.

Were I Angelina I should sit here in this tiny room, and do my work here all the morning, having every meal in the dining-room, and resolutely spending my evenings in the drawing-room. There is, of course, rather more firing required, but not more than is necessary to warm the house thoroughly, and this will save in health and spirits far more than the house coal costs. Quite a different current to one's thoughts is given by a change of room, and a really dull feeling often disappears when one's surroundings are changed, and one goes into a fresh pure atmosphere; for whatever the weather is, I do hope Angelina has her windows open top and bottom, and, in fact, sleeps with them open too; but this I shall say more about when I reach the bedrooms, and talk about health, which will be later on; though before I describe the papering &c. of this little room I must beg Angelina not to fall into the habit of so many young wives, of having nothing between breakfast and dinner save perhaps cake or a cup of tea, but to have a properly cooked chop or morsel of meat at the orthodox hour for luncheon. For while I know how difficult it is to do this because eating by oneself is so dull, and it does not appear worth while to have cooking done for oneself alone, I cannot too much impress upon my bride that she must remember health is the first consideration, and that very bad effects are often caused by the manner in which proper food is forgotten or gone without in the middle of the day, a matter far too many girls never think about at all.

It is almost impossible to lay down any hard-and-fast rules for the decoration of a morning-room without seeing the room itself, but I am sure no colour is so entirely satisfactory as the blue which is the exact shade of a sparrow's egg or an old turquoise. Mr. Smee, at my express desire, keeps this blue paper, at 4s. a piece, always in stock, and a perfect room can be made by using this paper, Aspinall's enamel paint, the exact shade of the ground of the paper, and a frieze of dead gold Japanese paper at 3s. 6d. the piece of nine yards; a frieze or picture rail painted blue unites the frieze to the 'filling,' and the panels of the doors, shutters, &c., should be panelled with red and gold Japanese leather paper. The painter must not be allowed to pick out or embellish the paint at all (I cannot repeat this too often), and the cornice must be one uniform cream colour. The ceiling of this room should be papered yellow and white, and curtains could be made from the yellow printed linen sold by Mr. Pither, 38 Mortimer Street, Regent Street, at 1s. a yard, and edged by ball fringe sold by Mr. Smee at 6½d. a yard.

Another arrangement for a room which had much sun could be from a sage-green paper, with a broad frieze of one of the many beautiful floral papers to be purchased nowadays, with a good deal of pink in; or better still would it be to go to Mrs. McClelland, of 33 Warwick Road, Maida Hill, W., and get her to paint a frieze of pale pink and dark red roses on American cloth; this is put up with drawing pins and taken down like a picture, and would make a most admirable wedding present; it would certainly be a joy to any bride for all her life long, and should therefore be considered by those who are about to make a marriage gift.

In this case all the paint must be sage-green, and we must get as much pink—really pink—and *peacock* blue with it as we can muster. Therefore, on the mantelpiece we can have a cretonne with pale pink flowers; our over-mantel and board being painted sage-green, with, if possible, sprays of pale pink chrysanthemums or roses on. And then place on the mantelshelf first a candlestick, choosing the pretty small embossed brass ones that Maple used to have at 2*s.* 6*d.* each; then a spill-case in blue and white china, always remembering to keep them full of spills—they save a great deal of waste in winter both of matches and temper; then a photograph frame, holding a *home* photograph of mother, father, or sisters in an oak frame (the plush and leather ones soon soil and look tawdry); then a vase for flowers—a low shape; then one of the tall sixpenny Baker Street vases, that look beautiful with a single rose or two; marguerites or fuchsias in summer; and with grasses and ferns in winter; and then the clock, continuing the same arrangement the other side; and, despite the sneers levelled at them, use Japanese fans as a background as often as you can; the colour is so invaluable a help, and, being excellently managed, goes with anything.

The doors should be painted to match the frieze, and the over-mantel should also be decorated in a similar manner, and the ceiling should be papered with a good terra-cotta and white paper. Some terra-cotta or pink should be introduced into the chair coverings, &c., but the exact shades must be carefully chosen by some one whose eye for colour can be trusted emphatically.

This room should be under the care of the housemaid, who should dust and sweep it before breakfast, and should also see to the hall. The cook will have quite enough to do with the dining-room and her own kitchen, while the drawing-room can be left to be looked after, when the bedrooms are done and the breakfast things washed up; though the ornaments and flowers must be entirely looked after by the mistress, should she only be able to begin life with two servants.

CHAPTER IX
THE DRAWING-ROOM

It is quite useless to attempt to have a pretty drawing-room, unless the owner really means to have it in constant use, and intends to sit in it regularly. I am quite convinced that rooms resent neglect like human beings do, and that they become morose and sulky-looking if they are kept closed, or only opened when strangers are expected.

It is no use then to bustle about to arrange this antimacassar, or to put yonder chair just a little bit out of its constrained position, to put flowers in the vases and books on the tables, in a spasmodic attempt to give an air of life to the dead chamber. Something will betray you, the chill atmosphere will inevitably chill your friends, your constraint in an unaccustomed room will communicate itself to them, and you will infallibly all be as stiff and unhappy as you can be, without perhaps being able to define the cause.

Therefore, as your room is to be lived in, let me beg of you to buy nothing for it that you cannot replace easily, to have nothing gorgeous, or that will not stand a certain amount of careful wear and tear, for as sure as your room is too grand to be lived in every day, so sure will your acquaintances find you out, and put you down at once upon the list of dull folks to be avoided, that we all of us keep somewhere mentally or otherwise.

A light hue for a drawing-room has been found to be a necessity ever since the days—those awful days—of white papers covered with gilt stars. There is always something a little depressing about the evening. One is tired with the day's work, worried by domestic duties, or disappointed at the very little fruit the long twelve hours have given us; and therefore we should be careful to arrange our evening-room with the intention of having cheerful surroundings, if we can have nothing else, and that is why I should like to have our drawing-room in blue, or else in yellows and whites.

I must say I still hanker after a dado, because in the drawing-room I like to hang all sorts of odds and ends upon it, which give an original air to the room, and also insures favourite photographs, fans, or pretty hanging baskets with flowers in being close to one's chair, or near one's eyes, should we wish to look at them. A very pretty effect is obtained by stretching a cretonne material round the base of the wall for a dado, hiding the nails with a dado rail of bamboo. Liberty's blue and white cretonnes are invaluable for this, but then it is rather difficult to

Fig. 15.—Drawing-room at Gable-end, Shortlands.

obtain a blue paper to match. Still it is to be done and we are repaid for the trouble, I think, by the effect when it is up. A yellow-and-white paper looks charming with a blue dado, also a terra-cotta paper and paint are not amiss, though I confess myself rather disappointed with this effect in a drawing-room I once had; but then the paint was put on in my absence, and I feel convinced it was not the shade ordered. If people are really tired of dados, and will have none of them, the walls can be papered blue to within about two feet of the top; then a frieze of pale yellow and white can be put on either of paper or cretonne, the join hidden by a rail, on which are placed hooks which hold pictures. These then are brought down to the proper level for light, and are not suspended out of vision, as are so many paintings and engravings in houses of people who are artistic enough by birth and education to know better; then, too, by using these hooks the great expense of picture-rods going all round the rooms is saved, without damaging the walls either by hammering in brass-headed nails.

I think a panelled room painted blue for a drawing-room is perfect; but unless the house that Angelina takes is panelled already, this is no use for her, as panelling is expensive work, and would be the landlord's property, too, when the lease is up, so that is out of the question. Still, I know of panelled rooms yet existent whose owners look at their grained walls and wonder how they can make them less hideous, and perhaps some of them may see this book, and may resolve to do away with that terrible eyesore, a grained device, and set to work to paint the walls a delicate sparrow's-egg-blue, furthermore embellished by long designs of rushes and grasses, either stencilled or painted on by some one of the many girls who can paint, and who can be found always at Mrs. McClelland's studio, should we number not one of those useful damsels among our acquaintances. Whatever style of decoration is adopted, I hope we may have a blue wooden mantelpiece and over-mantel; brass bells, brass locks and handles to the doors, and finger-plates must replace the china abominations provided by the landlord; but these must be carefully marked down as belonging to the tenant, and the china ones must be put away carefully too, to replace the brass ones again when Angelina's lease is up, or she will have to feel that her money has gone into the landlord's pocket, which is never a cheerful subject for contemplation.

Now for the carpet, the style and price of which can range from 35s. 6d. to almost any amount that you like to spend. The cheapest ones are the Kidderminster squares, which can be purchased at Mr. Treloar's, on Ludgate Hill, or at Shoolbred's or Maple's. In fact, at the risk of being vituperated by these gentlemen, I say, in low tones of caution, go to all of these establishments, and, taking as usual plenty of time over your choice, see all the blue carpets they have: at one or other of the shops you will be sure to see exactly what you want. I do not think the cheap squares are ever really artistic; but they are inoffensive, and most wonderfully inexpensive, and wear beautifully. Still, the colours and patterns are not quite my beau-ideal of a carpet design, but beggars cannot, alas! be choosers, and if we must really be very economical we can but be thankful for these carpets, because they replace the hideous Dutch carpeting and frightful 'Kidderminsters' that used to be the portion of such of our ancestors as could not afford Turkey or Axminster, and had to fall back on these, and on the 'best Brussels,' the crude and frightful greens and reds of which haunt my dreams sometimes, when I am meditating on furniture and remember the days that are no more; being duly and sincerely thankful that they are no more, as far as carpets and furniture in general are concerned.

Rising above the 'squares,' we ascend to the delightful blue carpets, also in Kidderminster, that are sold by the yard. I once possessed one which was the joy of my heart, which I bought at Shoolbred's. But I took a friend there the other day, having roused her to enthusiasm over mine, to find no more were made; 'for customers,' said the polite man who served us, 'will insist on novelties, and grumble frightfully do they see the same goods on show as they saw some years ago, whether or not that they were as pretty as they can be. No, the cry is always for some new thing.' And so we could not buy any more of my blue carpet, and I look at the one I have apprehensively, and cannot bear any one to walk upon it, because I know, once gone, I can never replace it. It was about 4s. 6d. a yard, and wears beautifully. However, we were shown another that quite put my poor carpet out of court, both in colour and design; but then it was 5s. 6d. a yard, and though that did not matter to my friend, fortunately, it mattered to me; and so I was left carpetless, until I saw some beautiful self-coloured felt, which looks very well with rugs on, but shows dirt, and what housemaids call 'bits,' in rather a depressing manner. However, blue carpets are to be bought, I feel convinced, and they are certainly worth the search.[1] If money is forthcoming for a really good carpet, I should propose, first, the blue Kidderminster, at 5s. 6d. a yard, made into a square, and edged with woollen fringe, put down over, first of all, brown paper, and then a carpet-felt. This insures warmth, and trebles the chances of wear. Secondly, a really good Oriental carpet with a good deal of white in it. Mr. Smee has a charming one, that harmonises beautifully with blue, and that costs about 10*l.* for rather a small room. Thirdly, one could have a nice matting (putting this down over the brown paper) at about 1s. 6d. to 2s. a yard, with good rugs scattered about. These are expensive items, and would cost 8*l.* or 9*l.* to provide enough, and of the right sort; but the wear of really good rugs is marvellous. I have two large ones I bought at Treloar's nearly ten years ago; they are in the dining-room, where there is a great deal of wear and tear, and they are as good now in appearance as the day I bought them, but I think they cost me a little over 2*l.* 10s. each.

> [1] Since writing the above I have found my blue carpet at Messrs. Colbourne's, 82 Regent Street, where it can always be procured.

Of course, if we spend on our carpets we must be prepared to save elsewhere; our curtains need not cost us much. They can be either yellow and white, or blue and white Liberty cretonne, made to the height of the dado rail, just to draw along the windows from top to bottom to exclude light and to hide the room from outsiders when it is lighted up, thus saving the great and useless expense of blinds, and they can be lined with some cheap material, or made double, and then, white ones being fixed as described later on, last a long time without washing, and can be either made of figured Madras, with a good deal of colour in it, at 4s. 6d. a yard, double width, or of fine muslin and guipure, which washes beautifully—a quality I have never discovered in the many Madras muslins that I have bought, because I could not resist their decorative qualities, though I was angry at my own weakness all the time.

Naturally I can lay down no really hard-and-fast lines for decorating a drawing-room, for so much depends on the style and shape of the chamber; and what I said of the morning-room applies here equally well. Still, a yellow and white room, made by using Pither's yellow and white 'berry' paper, with a dado of Collinson and Lock's '47' cretonne, with ivory paint, and yellow and white ceiling paper, and a blue carpet, makes a charming room; while one of the flowery, expensive papers, with a cretonne dado, is also safe to be charming too. In this case pink must be used in the ceiling, and the carpet should be either Maple's 'golden pine' or a very carefully chosen carpet in shades of sage-green.

As to the furniture of the drawing-room, that must be determined on and regulated simply by the amount of money we have to spend. If we have plenty we can purchase as many nice deep arm-chairs and small occasional chairs as we like—then it will only be a matter of taste; but if we are limited and have little to spend, we must go about our work circumspectly, and must not mind going into a great many shops before we finally obtain what will furnish our room nicely.

Here, again, the useful wicker chairs will come in, covered with pretty cretonnes, made in such a manner that they can have their coverings removed to be washed; and I should also once more advise one of the charming square sofas already described. I think I should adhere to velveteen for the covering, unless we can procure a gold thread tapestry sufficiently light and inexpensive for our purpose. Messrs. Maple were the best people to apply to for these goods, but lately they have not had the pretty ones of old days, change of fashion and need for novelty accounting for the absence of some of the best designs I have ever seen; but Liberty has some excellent tapestries now.

If the room have a bow-window, a cosy summer corner can be made by putting the sofa there, with a table in front or at the side, capable of holding books and plants; and these tables are, again, things that we must undoubtedly choose with a great deal of care, for there is nothing more annoying than a rickety table, or one that is knocked over easily, should the room be fuller than usual, or should we number an awkward friend among the members of our acquaintances.

I remember some years ago having to entertain such an individual in the days when I did not know as much as I do now about the fitness of things, and I really believe that unhappy man's sufferings gave me a lesson about tables I have never forgotten. I was always very fond of pretty things, and then had the mistaken idea that one could not have too many of them; so I fear that when we used to go in to dinner from the drawing-room, our walk resembled nothing so much as Mr. Dickens's celebrated description of the family whose rooms were so full that they had to 'take a walk among furniture' before they could get out of the room.

We were taking our walk among the furniture when the *contretemps* happened. My unfortunate acquaintance had fidgeted unhappily for some time, and he finally made a dart towards the lady he had to take in to dinner, knocking over the chair next him, and arriving at his destination with a fringed antimacassar neatly fastened to one of his coat-buttons. He then backed into a small table, on which stood some books and photographs, and only saved this, to send another spinning; this time smashing the whole concern, and depriving me of one of my pet flower-holders, the demolition of which I have never ceased to regret. But worse was to come: in one heroic effort to get away from the scene of the disaster he backed once more into a 'whatnot' full of china, and I draw a veil over my feelings and his, as the most merciful thing I can do.

Still, when next morning I stood among the ruins, like Marius among the ruins of Rome, I was honest enough to say, 'This is certainly my own fault,' and 'turning to,' as the maids say, I so rearranged that long and ugly room that when next I had a dinner party I was repaid a thousandfold for my exertions and sacrifices by the expression of relief on the countenances of the guests, who now saw themselves saved from the usual dangerous promenade among my belongings that had used to be their portion. Now fortunately we can purchase tables that are small and safe, and I think those which are made with double trays, or rather with one tray under the top, are perfectly safe. They are to be bought covered with stamped velveteen, or with the pretty stuffs that imitate Turkish saddle-bags, or with plush, but I prefer them made of plain dark wood, and either polished or else painted ivory, and the top covered with an ordinary cloth made from tapestry, or one of Burnett's charming serges edged with ball fringe; as, if plants in pots are placed upon them, drops of water are apt soon to spoil the covering, whereas serge will stand a good deal of water; although I am of opinion that plants should always be watered outside the room, on a balcony or in a garden if possible, as a little carelessness soon spoils one's things, and I have, alas! spoilt much by not enforcing this rule both on myself and others.

Another very good and useful table is the square ivory Queen Anne table, that has four square rails as an extra support to the legs. These are about 3*l*., and can be procured in different sizes, when, of course, the price alters too, and are extremely handy to hold the lamp for reading books, work, &c., and are large enough to write a note upon comfortably.

I am a great advocate for corners—that is to say, for giving the corners of the room an artistic look, and I also like to have my favourite winter corner close to the fireplace. Naturally, it would be intensely foolish if we all hankered after a corner. Still even then we could be accommodated, if we do not mind screening ourselves off from our fellows in a manner I must say I consider extremely ugly and silly.

It will hardly be believed that in a house I have heard of the mistress has erected a series of screens in her drawing-room, which resembles now nothing so much as a restaurant fitted up with boxes. Rather than suggest such a fearful idea I would abolish screens altogether; yet one round the back of the sofa is often a great comfort, and, judiciously arranged, makes the background for a very pretty corner.

But the mistress's corner can be arranged like this: put straight across the corner of the wall a small black table, made safe with the under-tray, and covered at the top with a Turkish antimacassar; this holds a plant in the daytime and the lamp at night, and is large enough to hold all the month's magazines, half on each side of the centrepiece; above this a black corner bracket for china, crowned by a big pot to hold grasses or bulrushes, can be hung on the wall; and in front of the table should stand a square stool, holding a large plant and pot, heavy enough to hold its own should any one come near enough to knock it over, were it too light. Then to the left of this, next the fireplace, put your own particular chair, leaving room for a stool of some kind, that is broad and low, and can hold your work-basket if you work, your favourite book, or your newspaper-stand with the paper-knife attached; and on the desk above and at the side of your chair hang a sabot for flowers, your favourite photographs, and any pet piece of china or ornaments you may fancy. One of mine consists of a mandarin's fan and case; the case is embroidered in silk, and gives a very pretty bit of colour, and the fan serves as a fire-screen should any one object to the cheerful blaze. Needless to add, I never use this screen myself.

On the other side of the fireplace I have a pair of brass bellows and a brass-handled brush, for I think an untidy hearth disturbs me more than anything else; and another Japanese fan, tied to a nail by a riband, which some of my friends find most useful when the fire is hot. Here, too, I have a really charming chair I bought at Liberty's. I think it was 14s. 6d., not more. It has rather a high back, and a rush seat, and as the front legs are taller than the other two, it just tilts back, and is most comfortable. I added a padded back cushion, tied on with tapes, which adds much to the effect, but none is required on the seat, as rushes make a very comfortable and easy support, and this chair is preferred by what is rudely called 'the master of the house,' my pet cat, to any other, and he is a gentleman who really knows what comfort is. He has made it his study, during a long and honourable life, so I think I am not wrong in quoting him as an authority.

While not emulating a good friend of mine, in whose house the putting on of coals partakes of the character of a protracted and arduous ceremony, I must say I dislike to see coals standing in a room, but the receptacles made for them in brass are so pretty now that they may almost be forgiven, though I would rather not see them in a drawing-room. However, if one is required, the brass baskets, *without* covers, are the best, and hold quite enough coals for the evening, indeed more than enough if the grate is as I described before, and moreover judiciously laid and managed. Brass fire-irons and dogs are a necessity, but then a little black poker, price 1s. 6d., called a 'pokerette' in the shops, and 'the curate' in the drawing-room, must supplement the brass one, or that will very soon be black and spoiled.

I do not like a rug laid down in front of the fire, for more reasons than one. I have known a little foot catch in it, and the owner precipitated with his poor little head on the hard fender; and it always is an assistance to a careless or dirty housemaid, who is thus served with a screen should she break one of the rules that should be enforced in every household, and proceed to clean her grate without first putting down the rough piece of material with which she should be furnished. She is obliged to do this should there be no rug, for then every mark would show, and she would not dare to put down black-lead in a *cracked* saucer, fire-irons, brushes, and a thin newspaper full of ashes, as I once discovered a girl doing in an apartment furnished with a wide rug, that hid this, as well as a multitude of other sins.

While being lived in and used, a drawing-room is and must be essentially a best room, and is invaluable as a teacher to the untidy or unmethodical mistress or servant. Fine manners are a necessity, and a certain amount of fine manners is maintained by use of a room that holds our dearest treasures, and sees little of the seamy side of life. It is on little things that our lives depend for comfort, and small habits, such as a changed dress for evening wear with a long skirt, to give the proper drawing-room air, the enforcement of the rule that slippers and cigars must never enter there, and a certain politeness maintained to each other in the best room, almost insensibly enforced by the very atmosphere of the chamber, will go a long way towards keeping up the mutual respect that husband and wife should have for each other, and which is a surer means of happiness than anything I know—than any amount of foolish terms of endearment, that are apt to be forgotten when the gloss of the honeymoon is rubbed off, and life becomes too full of anxieties and hurry for the old pet names.

Remember, please, I am not writing for votaries of fashion or for rich people, who could tell me doubtless a great many things I do not know, but for the ordinary educated middle-class girl who may never leave her country home until she is married, or may have had few opportunities of seeing the world, even in London; and she does require, I know full well, to be reminded that home should not excuse faded finery, down-at-heel shoes, or slovenliness of mind or body in either husband or wife, for nothing grows so easily as untidy habits or slovenly manners, and it is worth a little struggle to prevent oneself or one's friends deteriorating ever such a little bit.

The drawing-room would not be complete without a piano, and this is all too often a very ugly piece of furniture. I am glad to say white frames painted with beautiful flowers and designs are now being made, and these are easy to treat, but in ordinary rooms the usual cottage piano has to be thought of, and another corner can be made by placing the instrument across one side of the room in such a manner that the performer could see her audience. This naturally leaves the back of the piano exposed to view, and, as piano manufacturers still adhere to the red flannel or baize back, this is not a pretty object to contemplate. However, it is one that is easily changed, as it can be replaced by either a crewel-worked piece of art coloured serge, the useful and cheap Japanese leather paper, or else by a square of cretonne similar to that used for the curtains; but I prefer either the serge or paper to this. If the serge be worked with bulrushes and iris and grasses, or with long sprays of honeysuckle, the effect is charming. Then along the top can be placed a piece of serge, or felt or damask, worked too, and edged with an appropriate fringe, which thus makes an excellent shelf for odds and ends of china and bowls of flowers, as the top of the piano is seldom, if ever, opened by the ordinary piano player.

If a more careless arrangement be desired, a large square of drapery can be arranged gracefully over the back, securing it with small tintacks on the inside of the lid, or a large Japanese screen can be placed before it; but I think the best thing to do is to replace the baize back as suggested, not omitting to take out the crude red or green silk or elaborate carved wood front, and treat that as you treat the back.

I have seen a very pretty front to a piano made out of sage-green silk worked with rosebuds, or of turquoise-blue material worked in pale yellow campanulas, or yellow Scotch roses with their brown foliage. I have also seen a painted front put in, with dancing figures depicted on it; and, of course, all these arrangements are much to be preferred to the one supplied by the piano manufacturer, who is the only man, it seems to me, who resolutely refuses to march with the times, and makes no effort to improve the appearance of his manufactures.

The chair by the piano can be any pretty chair fancied by the owner. I have a very nice one in white wood, with the seat covered in Indian tapestry, which I gave a guinea for at Liberty's. A very good plan is to have an extra cushion, attached by ribbon to the side of the chair, for the use of any one who may prefer a higher seat than we may happen to care for. This should, of course, be made square, and be covered with the same material that is used for the chair, and does away with the necessity for a music stool with an adjustable seat—an article I cannot endure, as it always shakes, is most unsteady, and squeaks appallingly whenever there is to be a change in the weather. Another idea for a seat by the piano is to have a square ottoman, made to open. Two people can sit upon this to play duets; but I do not care for this very much, as there is no back, but in a small room it is of great use, as it holds a great deal of music, is cheap, and does not look badly if properly covered with a pretty material, nailed on, and adorned with a frill that serves a double purpose, being highly ornamental and hiding the opening of the box at the same time. Another receptacle for music can be made out of one of the small square black cupboards which I have spoken of before, and which serve as tables besides, if the top be covered with some sort of a cloth, and books and ornaments be scattered about too.

The grand piano, coffin-like as it undoubtedly is, is far more easily made into a decorative article of furniture, and while the bend in the structure makes a capital 'corner,' the whole thing can be admirably arranged if we commence by draping the entire end with some square of material, or, if we possess it, with a length of old brocade or an Indian shawl. The drapery is placed so that it hangs over the end and sides, and is secured in place by, first of all, a nice plant in a good pot, which keeps the cloth in place, and has no effect whatever on the tone of the piano. At the end I place Leech's collection of sketches, which we always call the 'long Punches,' in contradistinction to the bound volumes, and then any small things that I think look picturesque—not too many, nor any that cannot easily and comfortably be moved, should I have to entertain a pianist who wishes to imitate thunder, and cannot do so without having the lid opened widely. A good arrangement in the bend is a big palm in a brass pot on a black stand. These brass pots are to be procured at Hampton's, in Pall Mall East, but I fear they are very expensive. I have often looked and longed for one, but never dared purchase it, much as I hanker after such a possession—they are extremely decorative, and have a style of their own. Failing that, a nice square table with more plants and books, and a couple of low chairs, placed in a 'conversational' manner, are suitable, with another plant on a square stool placed in front of the table. This gives a very finished look to the piano, and I venture to state that when this is done the piano is not the first thing visitors see when they enter the room: indeed, I have once or twice been asked if I have a piano, so little in evidence is this instrument to any one who merely comes to make an ordinary call. Talking of calls reminds me, before we leave the drawing-room, to make a small protest about one of the most idiotic customs that still linger among us—that of making morning calls; and I should like to see a good deal of reform in this matter.

Formal visiting I never will or can go in for; and I have come to the conclusion that, if people are only known casually and in such a manner that to call on them is an effort, to make which we are braced up by the idea, and cherished with the hope, that the person one calls on, card-case in hand, will be out, life is too short for such nonsense, and that calling as per fashion ordained is more honoured in the breach than in the observance, and that for us ordinary folk, who have work to do in life, this fantastic waste of time can quite well be given up. I should much like to see, at the same time, more co-operation in our lives. I should like more freedom among us, less of the idea that an Englishman's house is his castle, and therefore I am always glad to note any step in the right direction, which is not followed when we set out in our best garments to make a round of calls.

Of course, people will say, 'If we do not make calls, we can neither extend our circle nor keep up our friendships,' but I really cannot see how cards conduce to either. That delightful institution of five-o'clock tea has done more for us, who cannot afford to give big entertainments, than a bushel of pasteboard; and I am convinced the idea of calls could be done away with altogether with very little trouble, and one way of doing this, especially in a small community, is to have one day, or even one evening, a week, or even a fortnight, when we are known to be at home and ready to see our friends.

I know some people scoff at the notion of an ordinary middle-class woman 'aping her betters,' and having her day at home; but the scoffers should reflect before they scoff, then, perhaps, they would alter their ideas. First of all, in a small household the servants can so manage their work that visitors on the day being expected, are no trouble at all. The fire would always be burning brightly in winter, the flowers and plants would be at their best in summer, and the mistress and her room together would be ready to see any one. I can speak from experience that my friends always turned up in shoals in dear hospitable Shortlands when I had my Thursdays, and came week after week to see me, secure of a cup of tea and a chat after a walk or drive; and I know how the winter sped along when I felt confident that So-and-so would be in any day of the week, and that I can 'turn into' this or that pleasant room any hour between 4 and 5.30, and find a welcome and a cup of tea ready for me, neither being in the least less warm because the previous Monday, and the Monday before that too maybe, my feet took me in precisely the same direction. In winter these informal gatherings are particularly pleasant, because I think the hours between the end of your drive or walk and dinner are occasionally a little depressing, and are not good preparation for the evening, which goes off much better if we have had a chat in the afternoon with a friend or two, which takes us out of our grooves and gives us something to talk about over the meal; while in summer, the fact that one is at home for certain on one day in the week brings friends from a distance to see us, and often causes impromptu tennis parties and little gatherings, all the pleasanter because they are informal and almost unexpected; while in these days of ostentation and glitter it is an excellent thing to know how to entertain well and cheaply, and see one's friends, without feeling each time we do so that we are so many steps nearer the Bankruptcy Court. If we contemplate seeing society in the way I have indicated above, a tea-table is a *sine quâ non* in our drawing-room. A very good sort of table is the rush and bamboo table, with little trays for cakes, that open and close, and therefore take up very little room in a chamber; there is a second tray under the top one where spare cups can be placed. And still another table is the useful little Sutherland table, that shuts up and stands modestly and unseen in a corner when not in use, and that is brought out in a moment, without fuss or trouble, and can be used for whist, chess, or any ordinary game; while a small nest of four narrow tables, adapted from an old Chippendale design, is an invaluable possession. Closed, the 'nest' takes up a very small space, and, opened out, the owner has four little tables to put about beside her guests, who thus are provided with places to put down their cups and plates upon, and are thus relieved of what is sometimes an intolerable nuisance.

The best five-o'clock teacloth is a fine white damask edged with torchon lace, and with a torchon lace insertion which washes beautifully, and this should be marked with a large monogram in scarlet thread. A really large, good monogram has an excellent effect. I purchased my cloths at Shoolbred's, who also procured me some one to work the monograms, as I am unfortunately no 'stitchist,' as Artemus Ward would say, and cannot sew one bit. But they are a little expensive. Still, if any one can work themselves, the cloths are only 5s. 6d.; the lace comes to about 3s. more; and then there is the monogram, which of course could be saved to any one who possesses cleverer fingers than have been given to me, but which are now worked for me at 1s. and 1s. 6d. each by a lady who thus is enabled to make a perceptible addition to her income, and who may be heard of at the Workers' Guild, 11 Kensington Square, W. Other tablecloths have red and blue borders; but I prefer the plain white with the monogram to any other. A nice bright copper kettle and a trivet should be always brought in with the tea, and a cosey should never be forgotten, while buns (home-made buns and scones are most excellent), biscuits, and bread and butter suffice for quite a large party of friends, and there is neither extra trouble nor fuss of any kind. Of course, teacups and saucers are of all sorts and conditions, but I think small blue and white ones on a china tray are the prettiest of all, and can generally be replaced should a misfortune happen to them; while Liberty's ornamental china cups and saucers are always pretty, and can invariably be matched.

No room is bearable without, or looks ugly with, plants and flowers, so I hope that these may always be found in the drawing-rooms, at least, of any of those who do me the favor to read, mark, and inwardly digest the pages of this little book.

CHAPTER X
CURTAINS, CARPETS, AND LIGHTING

Of course, in writing on the subject of curtains, we must begin first by saying that a great deal depends upon the shape and size of the windows, for all these particulars have to be carefully considered before we start on any expedition to inspect and buy our material for our draperies; for if a window be small or high up it requires far less management than the large bow-windows that take so much thought, and, alas! so much material too. Then, as there are French windows to be arranged for, and, in fact, square windows as well, we have to spend much time and thought over how we shall arrange, so as to suit all, before we cast our eyes over cretonnes, damasks, plushes, and the thousand and one materials, all more or less suited to the purpose for which they were designed.

The ordinary window, with the two sashes and the square frame, is very easily managed, even supposing that one has to keep out the neighbours' eyes as well as a certain amount of sunshine. The muslin curtains should be put up on rods like small stair-rods, fastened against the window frame top and bottom in such a way that they do not interfere with the free raising of the sash, which must open top and bottom; this arrangement—illustrated in my chapter on the dining-room—insures the curtains remaining in their place, and prevents them floating in and out on every dust-laden breeze that blows, while it leaves no long tail of draggled muslin to sweep the floor, and get torn and dirty almost before they have been up a week.

The best white curtains are undoubtedly made of soft clear muslin, edged and furthermore embellished by insertions of guipure lace—the insertion is put in a slip close to the edge, and washes beautifully—but those curtains, unless made at home, are undoubtedly expensive. Still, nothing looks like them, and if they are arranged on the rods in such a manner that the edges of the outside lace just touch, they form a complete screen, and yet hide nothing from the owner of the house, who can see from her windows comfortably without being spied over, and, being fixed, last clean really a very long time indeed. And then, if the thicker curtains are placed on a straight brass rod, as narrow as the weight they have to support will allow, no blinds are required, for the warm drapery draws straight over them, and either serves as a blind to keep out the light or a screen to keep out the draughts, and so does away with the expensive blind with its rollers, its cord eternally out of order, and its ugly effect from both inside and outside the house.

A good 'book' or Swiss 'mull' muslin costs about 10½d. a yard, the guipure edging and insertion about 1s. 6½d.; therefore the cost of these curtains is easily calculated by any one who measures her own windows and sees what length and quantity of material is required for them. Bedroom windows look extremely nice if treated in a similar manner in the French checked muslin, such as the *bonnes* use for their caps and aprons, and of which our Sunday summer frocks used to be made in our young days, and which costs 10½d. a yard. If this be used, the curtains must be edged with a two-inch goffered frill, which must invariably edge all the curtains that are not treated with lace edgings, for nothing looks worse than the hard line of a curtain that is neither frilled nor lace-trimmed.

Of the popularity of the soft and beautiful Madras muslins there is scarcely any necessity to speak, as it is now familiar to most of us; but despite its beauty and (in some cases) its cheapness, I must add a word of warning on the subject of Madras, especially addressed to our young friends with limited means, for the cheap sort of Madras does not wash satisfactorily, and should, therefore, be avoided by all those who have to study economy, and have not only to buy things, but to select them in such a manner that they shall last after their first visit to the wash-tub at the very least.

The cheap Madras washes into holes, and all the pretty colours vanish, and a limp rag returns to us instead of the charming curtains that gave such a style to the appearance of the outside of our house; and the expensive ones, too, are apt to 'run' in the washing, and are out of the purchasing power of any one whose means are really limited; for these cost from 6s. 9d. to 8s. 9d. a yard, and therefore become expensive items in our expenditure at once, although they contrast favourably with the fine lace and embroidered curtains sold ready to put up at 5l. or 6l. a pair, or at times even more than that. But ready-made curtains designed with large and marvellous patterns must not even enter a really artistic home. They mean nothing, can never be anything save vulgar and pretentious, and are therefore to be avoided; for if we are rich we can have the best Madras, the finest guipure and muslin; and if we are poor we can yet have our white muslin, either frilled or edged with guipure, as rich as our modest means will allow; or the valuable Mysore and artistic muslins at 9¾d. and 3¾d. a yard, which wash excellently if done at home—in water without soda and with a few drops of vinegar in to 'set the colours,' as the washerwomen say.

A bow-window, the orthodox suburban villa bow-window, is, I own, a very difficult subject to treat, but I have circumvented even that by an arrangement of curtains on rods managed as described above, and in the first-named window have two narrow white curtains meeting at the top of the window, and gradually sloping away until they are about five inches apart at the bottom; the wider centre sash is treated in the same manner with wider curtains, the plain edge of which meets the edge of the curtain that fits the narrow sash on both sides of the broader window; for the usual bow is made of a flat sash in the middle, between two narrow sashes that bow slightly; the muslin is 'taut', as sailors would say, and is always tidy, and by using these narrow *very* cheap rods all expensive fitted and formed poles and valances are done away with, and a most expensive and vexatious item in our expenditure completely swept off our schedule of payments to be made. The muslin curtains neatly up, a thicker rod can be fixed in three portions, each portion separate and distinct, for the heavier curtains. Those in any dining-room can be made of several materials. Shoolbred had a beautiful gold figured damask, double width, at 4*s.* 9*d.*, which looks like silk, though naturally it is nothing of the kind; this drapes beautifully and looks charming, as it falls into folds and never fades; it can be edged with a ball fringe to match, which adds a good deal to the expense, but looks better than anything else, or else by a frill, but this is a little heavy, as the material is thick. This material can be had in a beautiful pale blue and a good terracotta as well as in the yellow, but I have no experience of the wear of the two former colours, and therefore cannot tell whether they last as well and as satisfactorily as the yellow does. To make the window look really nice, you require one breadth hung down straight at the end of the first slip of window against the wall, edged all round the sides and bottom with ball fringe or the frill; then another breadth on the other side of the slip to pull halfway across the wider window to meet a third curtain hanging straight in the middle of the other division, and being met in its turn by a fourth, which, when undrawn, should hang straight against the wall in the same way that curtain number one does.

The artistic serges sold by Colbourne & Co., 82 Regent Street, at 1*s.* 11½*d.* a yard, and Stephen's Sicilienne damasks at 7*s.* 9*d.* a yard, are excellent curtain materials also, as are the stamped jutes and corduroy serges sold for this purpose by Mr. Smee.

But, whatever the material, in no case should the curtains be draped, or tied up or chained as if they were wild beasts, with great gold or brass chains (truly the very 'foolishest' things that were ever invented for the purpose), and they should never come below the window sill or the dado line, save and except in the case of a French window opening to a garden or conservatory, when the white drapery should be fixed on rods to the frame of the door, and the warmer curtains should be draped so as to keep out the draughts and be drawn readily; and this is done by sewing them to large rings that run easily on a brass pole, which must be as small and unobtrusive as possible; and when not in use the curtains must be drawn close to the wall and tied back, if wished, with Liberty soft silk handkerchiefs—the 3s. 6d. size makes two of these ties—in a colour to harmonise or contrast with that employed in the new curtains themselves. These curtains must be about an inch longer than the length from the pole to the floor, and must rather more than touch the floor, because a French window means a draught to one's toes, that can only be circumvented by longish curtains, and a thick mat, so placed as to be easily moved, should the window open into the room itself.

Roman sheetings are also excellent for curtains, and plush is the king of materials, if we could afford it; the shades of colour in the folds are perfect, and the tints in which plush is made are always lovely; but as we cannot afford that, we must turn our eyes away from such enchanting visions, and look out for a nice Mysore chintz for the drawing-room, which must be lined, to make it warmer and more durable, and trimmed with the goffered frill that always looks well in all washing materials; the frill need not be lined. For bedrooms, there is nothing better than the dark blue and white cretonne, the same both sides; or Burnett's excellent 'marguerite' cretonnes, in different colours, at 9½d. a yard; the dark blue and white need not be lined unless the bedroom receive the very early sun, when a lining is necessary if blinds be done without; but I should make the curtains double, as the material is as cheap as any lining procurable, and looks far better than any self-colour could possibly look. These cretonnes wash most beautifully, and begin at 9d. a yard. The chairs, frill to the mantel-board, eider-down, and any bookcase edges should all be finished with the same style of cretonne, though, of course, any other harmonious colour can be introduced to avoid too much sameness. The chair covers should be loose, and edged with a frill, as also should be the eider-down cover; this spoils any room if kept in its Turkey-patterned material, and should always be put into a cretonne washable cover, as much for beauty as for health. But these details must be kept for another chapter, as they do not enter into the great subject of curtains.

It may sound ridiculous, but I here state boldly that I can invariably make a more than shrewd guess of the character of the folks who inhabit a house by noticing what sort of ideas they have on the subject of draperies; and I may safely say that I have never been mistaken. The carefully and prettily and tidily arranged curtains tell me at once of the pleasant folk I shall find inside; just as surely as the dirty, untidy muslin or the gorgeously patterned, expensive, and pretentious curtains warn me against the slattern, or the vulgarian with whom I have nothing in common, should I ever have the bad fortune to have to enter behind those warning marks; while the soft Madras or delicate lace indicate an artistic mistress with whom I shall, I know, spend many pleasant hours. This being the case, do not wonder, dear readers, that I lay much stress and write at great length on this momentous subject, for it is one on which almost volumes could be written; for while the inside of your houses only speak to your friends and relations, the outside tells a great deal to strangers, and either repels or attracts, according to the manner in which you arrange your windows.

Fig. 16.

Unless your windows are very small, as in sketch 16, never be without white curtains of some kind, for if you are the house resembles some one who has forgotten her cuffs and collar or white frillings, but if they are like the sketch, you cannot do better than use Pither's old-gold-coloured, printed linen edged with ball fringe; this serves all purposes of blinds and curtains alike, and always looks artistic, while the windows are not obscured and stuffed up, as are those in most of our English houses.

And here let me say most emphatically that ordinary blinds are not necessary, and are never useful; if the house has very much sun, *inside* blinds are no use at all; the heat that makes most town houses unendurable is caused by the sun striking down on the glass of the window, and to obviate this the glass itself must be covered *outside*. Our summer is but a short one at best, but if we cannot bear the sun we must put up *outside* blinds, or hang grass mats over the glass outside; these are the only really necessary blinds; to say the least the others are unhealthy. The sun is the life-giver, after all, and he had better fade our curtains and our carpets than that the lack of his beams should fade our own and our children's cheeks! This, too, is another reason why we should never buy very expensive curtains or carpets; fortunately hardly any of the materials I have spoken of cost much, while Kidderminster squares—my favourite matting and rugs—or even stained floors and rugs, are all within the powers of the humblest of us.

I myself prefer matting for a dining-room at 1s. 6d. a yard, and covered here and there with rugs, put down where the greatest amount of traffic may be expected; but this is expensive, if set against the pretty carpets in art colours, made at Kidderminster, and sold by the yard at about 3s. 6d. a yard, the colours of which are extremely good. And if we cannot afford matting in the dining-room, a carpet that would go very well with the room would be shades of very faint sage-green, with dashes of terra-cotta in. But I much prefer the matting, and should always advise this for any one who could afford it, and yet could not afford the Oriental carpet that is, of course, the carpet for a dining-room. The rugs range from 7s. 6d., but these are Scinde rugs, and do not wear very well. Liberty, Maple, and Shoolbred have all an excellent choice, but I think Maple's rugs are the best for people with a small amount of money to spend; and there is this to consider about rugs, they can be shaken at least once a week and continually turned about, and when too shabby for downstairs they can be taken upstairs, finally dying an honourable death before the kitchen fire or by the bedsides of the maids. Still, much as I like matting, I must confess the total cost is more than three times the cost of a Kidderminster square, which in its turn can be taken up, shaken, and moved about, as, being square, there are no corners to consider, and no back and front and sides to think about either. But we must put carpet felt or paper-felt under our squares if we wish them to wear and to feel soft and pleasant under our feet; and it is as well to put down large sheets of brown paper before even the felt goes down. All this adds considerably to the wear of the carpet.

There is a curious habit in some parts of Canada of making a species of bed of hay under the carpet, and it gives a very pleasant feeling to any one walking thereon; of course soft, fine hay is chosen, and it is most carefully laid down, and evenly and tightly packed; and in a room on the basement floor, as so often rooms are situated in small suburban houses, it is a great comfort; it is very warm in winter and cool in summer, and if the hay-bed is made about twice a year, I believe it requires no further attention.

An old friend of mine who lived in poor circumstances in a stone-floor cottage in Dorsetshire, who had passed some years of her life in Canada, always stretched her carpet over such a bed, and I well remember how delightful her floor felt, and how she never suffered, as so many of her neighbours did, from rheumatism and other evils inseparable from the ordinary covering to a stone or brick floor. I have more than once recommended this in a basement kitchen or servants' sitting-room, and never without hearing that it was pronounced a great and unfailing success and source of comfort to the domestics.

If, however, a Kidderminster square is chosen, the boards for about two feet from the wainscot must be stained a good brown shade: if the boards are pretty good, and do not require stopping with putty to keep out the draughts, as so many of our suburban houses require 'stopping,' owing to the shrinking of the green wood used, alas! for the purposes of floors, doors, and windows, Edwin or Angelina can well manage this themselves. Whiteley keeps Ryland's stain ready prepared in a big tin jar, and with the right sort of brush this is soon put on; when dry it should be well and thoroughly polished with beeswax and turpentine, and if this is done weekly I am sure the floor will never require staining for many years; but if 'stopping' is necessary, the workmen employed can stain the floors too; for the extra charge will be but small, and it will save a back-ache, and insure the work being thoroughly and properly done.

These hints about carpets are perhaps a trifle prolix, but they will do for the whole of the house—of course varying the colours to suit the rooms, and being very careful in the selection of patterns. Mr. Morris has some of his very best designs manufactured in Kidderminster, so the cheap make of the mere carpet need not be sneered at; but we cannot afford Morris, much as we should like to do so, for his Kidderminsters are as costly as most people's Brussels; and if we are careful, we can get nearly as pretty patterns elsewhere at one fourth the cost, but we must be *very* careful, for there are some red carpets, some blue, and some a fearful nondescript hue, suggestive of the workhouse—I know not why—that would irretrievably and utterly spoil any room in which they were put; but there is a royal blue with paler blue flowers, or rather 'fan-like things,' that is perfect; this is, however, sold by the yard, and has to be made into a square, without a border, and just trimmed with a woollen fringe, which is procurable at Colbourne's, 82 Regent Street, and which wears magnificently: I have had one down now for three years in a room that experiences a great deal of traffic, and it is at the moment of writing as good as ever it was, and is admired by every one who comes in; and the sage-green carpet mentioned before is also quite safe to suit almost any room. This is also sold by the yard, and has to have a woollen fringe too.

If the house have bow-windows, an extra square of carpet, or else a Scinde rug at 7s. 6d., can be laid down there; there is not much 'traffic' in a bow-window, and the rugs look nicer than anything, and wear quite a reasonable time in such a locality, and these can be easily replaced. A piece of the carpet itself always looks out of place somehow, and spoils any room.

For a really good carpet, I like a fine Oriental carpet, with a good deal of white in it, or a Wilton, or velvet pile; but I always like something cheaper myself, as I do not like *old* carpets or old curtains. They must retain a certain amount of dust and dirt, and I therefore infinitely prefer either a good Kidderminster, or else the matting and rugs spoken of at first, which can be replaced when shabby without too great an effort for a moderate income. There are just one or two trifles that I should like to speak of here. Matting should be swept *one way* regularly, and by a proper matting brush. It can be washed with soap and a little water, and it has a wonderful way of never collecting dust that is marvellous. Oriental rugs and carpets should be swept *one* way only also; and the Kidderminster squares should be shaken often, but not continually swept; the shaking gets rid of the dirt, while sweeping wears them out much quicker than need be.

In connection with the carpets and curtains, we may just as well speak of the lighting of the sitting-rooms before passing away from them to the bedchambers. And here I must impress upon my readers never to have gas anywhere where they can avoid using it, and to pray heartily for that bright day to dawn when the electric light shall be within the reach of all, and when Mr. Swan tells us how to light our houses as perfectly as he has done his own; and I confess that when I recollect that charming abode, where fairies seem to superintend the lighting, so wonderfully is it managed, I feel consumed with rage and anger, to think that I was not born in a time when the electric light will be as much a matter of course as the present odious system of lighting by gas is; but as we are still unemancipated from the thraldom of gas, we must try to make the best of a bad job, and confine the enemy to where it can do least harm, and be of the most good at the same time.

An oil lamp in the hall is apt to give a gloomy impression to guests, and also is rather a difficult matter to manage. It is expensive, and is apt to get out of order at a critical moment; so I think gas must be adhered to here. A cathedral glass hanging lamp, square shape, and framed in brass, and fitted with an Argand burner, is as good a thing as one can possibly procure for gas, unless we select the more artistic beaten iron lamps sold by Strode and Co., of 48 Osnaburgh Street, W. The prices are about equal, I think, and quite a beautiful one can be bought for about 4*l*. It requires no cleaning beyond the ordinary cleaning, and gives a strong, steady light, the glass sides of the lantern or lamp presenting any flickering when the hall door is opened suddenly. I have occasionally seen a hall lighted from the sides, but I do not care for this, as it does not have the genial effect of the lighting from the top; but should this be preferred, a man at Whitechapel makes very charming side lanterns, of cathedral glass, that go round and almost cover in the gas bracket, thus preventing any danger of fire, and keeping away a very great deal of the heat and burnt atmosphere that make gas always so trying to any sensitive person. I think these lanterns are from 5s. to 10s. each, and they are, at all events, very artistic to look at.

Then there are beaten shields of brass, with the owner's initials on, from whence protrude the gas bracket, also in brass, and there are, furthermore, those delightful revivals of the old hammered iron trade that were to be seen in the Old London street at the Inventions, and the use of which would almost reconcile me to burning gas. These iron brackets and lamps are expensive, quite small brackets costing 1*l*. 12s.; but they are well worth the money if we have it to spend, because they are so nice to look at. In our sitting-rooms we should never for one moment allow ourselves to have gas. I always burn in a very large drawing-room two of Mortlock's blue and white china lamps fitted with duplex burners. At first, when the fiat went forth that gas was tabooed, those lamps were the bane of my life. I had a most excellent housemaid in those days, who did her work most beautifully, but only in her own way and in none other. True to my principles of non-interference, I had allowed her this way of hers, because it was as good a one as could be wished for; but when it came to suddenly cutting off her precious privilege of lighting up the gas and drawing the curtains, I soon saw that war was before me, and felt that now or never was I to maintain my right to my lamps, did I prefer them to what the gas company of the tiny town I then lived in facetiously called gas; but that was an awful smelling compound, which burned with a feeble and ghastly blue flame on weekdays, and which generally failed us altogether when Sunday meant gas in the church. Of course then we had comparatively to go without, as *that* gas would not be in church and our houses at the same time, and our lives bid fair to be & misery to us in the long December afternoons and evenings; when my good genius said 'Lamps,' and I then invested in those I still have, rejoiced to think we could see to read now, whether the gracious gas company deigned to allow us any gas (?) or no.

I had received full directions with the lamps, and knew exactly what to do with them. They were guaranteed not to smell, my one dread, and I was accordingly armed at every point to meet Emily's objections. She had work enough. Well, beyond cutting the wicks and refilling the brass cups, there was no addition; so she took them off with a flounce and a bang into her own particular sanctum, and looked like a walking volcano for the rest of the day. However, to make a long story short, those lamps were made to behave as if they were possessed by the very spirit of mischief. They smelt, they flared, they smoked, they sang a blood-curdling little song I feared meant explosions; but insisting on their being taken out of the room night after night and brought back until they did burn finally conquered Emily, and as she saw I meant to have my lamps she gave in, and they now never smell, and never give me a moment's trouble.

I mention all this to guide those young people who are apt to be treated as I was, and who, knowing paraffin *does smell*, may perhaps be inclined to give in and return to gas, because their servant declares she cannot manage the 'dratted thing.' The smell comes from some of the oil having been dropped on the brass part of the lamp, which gets heated, and, of course, smells abominably, and if the lamp be dull it is because the poor thing is clogged with oil and literally cannot manage to breathe; then drop the brass parts of the lamp, minus the wick, of course, into some clean water, and boil them as you would an egg over the fire. This loosens and gets away all the stale oil, which need never be there if the housemaid is really careful, and your lamp once more burns as brightly as ever it did. I use no screens over my lamps, as I put them behind me in such a manner that the light falls only on my book, and, of course, on the books and work of those who may also be in the room; but charming screens can be made by taking a sheet of tissue paper in such a manner in the centre that you can pass it rapidly up and down through your hands until it is a mass of crinkles and waves; then tear off the piece you have been holding and you have a pale pink wavy-looking screen that is charming, and costs the fraction of a farthing. The Germans also make beautiful lamp screens by cutting out scalloped pieces of tissue paper, on which are placed real leaves and coloured grasses. These are covered by another piece of tissue paper gummed lightly round the edges, and the effect of these when nicely arranged is really positively beautiful. About five of these scalloped pieces of tissue paper make one shade, and they are tied together with very narrow ribbon bows at the top, which allows of their being regulated to the size of the lamp. And yet another still more beautiful shade can be made by buying a wire frame made on purpose at Whiteley's, and covering all the divisions with thin blue silk, the palest shade possible. Each division should be covered in such a way that the stitches do not show. Round the edge sew a two-inch silk fringe, and arrange fluffy ruches of the silk down each rib and round the edge of the lamp-shade. This is not very expensive, and is the best shade possible. By the way, red and yellow shades should always be avoided; the first makes every one look like apoplectic fits, and the second as if jaundice were imminent; and don't ever buy the abominations of shades that are meant for owls' heads; they are monstrosities to be classed with the Mahdi notepaper and other vulgarisms of the day. Other nice occasional lamps are the very cheap brass lamps sold at 7s. 6d. and 10s. 6d. each. I do not think these good enough to read by, but they are most useful for ordinary use at dinner or to write a note by, and are also useful to put back on the buffets that do duty for sideboards in my dining-room, to give a little more light when we have extra folk to dinner, and I use my candelabra for lighting the larger table, but for all everyday use at table those brass lamps are quite enough, and, being easily lighted and kept clean, are really invaluable.

One is obliged to have gas in rooms where there are children, because candles and lamps are so easily knocked over, and it is useful, too, in bedrooms where a sudden light may be required, but it is a most unhealthy, destructive thing, and, as I said before, I look forward to Mr. Swan doing as much for us as he has done for himself.

If my readers—any of them—should doubt for one moment the truth of what I have said about the relative values of lamps and gas, let them for the next six months give the two things a fair trial in two separate rooms in the same house; let them look at the ceilings in those rooms, examine the picture-cords, and the relative cleanliness of the blinds and draperies, and let them—no; they, poor things, will need no examination. I was going to add, let them examine, too, their plants; but in one of those rooms there will be none left to examine, for they will be dead as surely as ever they were plants at all. Half the weary headaches and lassitude we have all felt at times come from this pernicious enemy; and there are few doctors whose first directions to an invalid's nurse do not contain emphatic orders to lower the gas and, in fact, to substitute candles for it as soon as possible; but if bedroom candles are used, they should never be allowed without a glass shield—sold, I think, by Messrs. Field and Co., the nightlight people. This insures that the carpets are free from being dropped upon by the wax or composite, and furthermore insures a certain amount of safety from fire, which is a vast consideration, for a draught, a floating curtain, and a bare unguarded candle may often result in a serious calamity, for, even if much damage by fire is not done, a serious fright may be given to some who are ill able to bear anything of the kind. Gas should never be in servants' bedrooms—the best of them cannot help burning it to waste; neither should they be allowed candles—they are careless, the very best of them; and I always provide my maidens with tiny paraffin lamps, costing 6d., which I can only buy in a Dorsetshire town (Messrs. A. and A. Drew, Wareham, Dorset, is the correct address)—even Whiteley doesn't keep them. These have a tiny brass cap that puts out the light, and are not in any way dangerous, because there is nothing to spill, the sponge and wick inside absorbing all the oil, and if they are knocked over they are so small the light pops out at once; yet there is light enough to dress by, if not to read novels in bed by, and the maids themselves prefer these small lamps to anything else.

In conclusion, remember that crystal A 1 oil, at 10d. the gallon, is the best, most economical oil to burn. It should be had in in a five-gallon tin, which fills up the small tins from whence the lamps are filled in their turn, which *must be filled by daylight*, and recollect also that china lamps are much the cleanest, and least likely to smell with the most careless housemaid, who must always be made to take her lamps out of the room over and over again; the mistress never *once* overlooking a smoking, dirty, or odoriferous lamp, until perfection is attained. That this is possible—ay, and easy—to obtain I have, I hope, demonstrated to all of my readers by the before-mentioned anecdote. If, however, the housemaid is really a good one, I should prefer to use Strode's beautiful copper and beaten iron lamps, with tinted glasses for shades; or else with pale blue silk shades, stretched between copper ribs that give a wonderfully artistic look to any room. Benson, who sells his wares at Smee's and Liberty's, designs perfect lamps also, and all these should be seen by the intending purchaser before finally deciding which to buy. Again I say, never do your shopping in a hurry: if you do, you are sure to see something you like better—in the next street may be, and, oh! agony, at half the price!

CHAPTER XI
BEDROOMS

At first the only upstairs rooms that will have to be furnished are Angelina's bedroom, Edwin's dressing-room, one spare room, and a room for the maid or maids, leaving any others until a nursery be required; for if our young people have only one servant it is quite impossible that they will be able to have a constant succession of folks staying in the house, and, therefore, one bedroom besides their own is all that should be prudently ready for occupation. I say 'prudently,' for few young housekeepers can resist at first the delights of showing off their houses and their presents to their less fortunate relations, and, in consequence, a stream of visitors is invited to pour into the house, to the detriment of anything like order, and to the dismay of the servant, who is most certainly right to grumble at all the extra work; and, by the way, I may mention here that to this same stream is due more than half the worry brides have at first with their domestics.

Also, the bedrooms should be kept very nice. This no one servant can do, unless she is considered and helped, and I should strongly advise Angelina not to be above making her own bed, even if she have a housemaid as well as a cook, for she and the housemaid together can shake it up and fold the blankets and sheets nicely and neatly, while the cook is clearing away breakfast, and interviewing the tradespeople downstairs, whose orders should be ready written out for them by the mistress, so that there should be no loitering at the back door, wasting time for both the cook and the men too. But before I go into the divers methods of bed-making, and speak of the beds themselves, I should like to describe one or two rooms, as far as paper and paint go, and give some idea of the colours I consider fittest for a bedroom. Formerly, anything in that way did for a room, where no one then seemed to remember we had to spend a good part of our lives, and where we had occasionally to be ill and miserable, and wanted as much help over our troubles as we could obtain from our surroundings; and who does not recollect the orthodox bedroom of her youth—the fearful paper, all blue roses and yellow lilies, or, what was worse still, the dreary drab and orange, or green upon green scrolls and foliage, that we used to contemplate with horror, wondering why such frightful papers were made! Then came the carpet, a threadbare monstrosity, with great sprawling green leaves and red blotches, 'made over,' as the Yankees say, from a first appearance in a drawing-room, where it had spent a long and honoured existence, and where its enormous design was not quite as much out of place as it was in the upper chambers. Indeed, the bedrooms, as a whole, seemed to be furnished, as regards a good many items, out of the cast-off raiment of the downstairs rooms; and curtains that had seen better days, and chairs too decrepit to be honourable company in the downstairs apartments, all crept up into the bedrooms, anything being good enough for a room where 'company' would not be expected to enter.

I myself remember a carpet that began life quite forty years ago, for it was over ten years old when I made its acquaintance in a country dining-room; it was drab, and was 'enlivened' with spots of brown, like enlarged ladybirds. It lived for twenty years in that room, covered in holland in the summer, and preserved from winter wear by the most appallingly frightful printed red and green 'felt square' I ever saw; it then was altered for the schoolroom, then went up into 'the girl's' bedroom, and still exists in strips beside the servants' beds, although the original owner of that fearful possession has been dead over twenty of those forty years; and when I consider the dirt and dust that has become a part and parcel of it, I am only thankful that our pretty cheap carpets do not last as carpets used to do, for I am sure such a possession cannot be healthy; though the present proud possessor points to the strips, as a proof of how much better things used to wear in her mother's days, than they do now, in these iconoclastic ones of ours.

I am afraid I am not an orthodox housekeeper, for I confess most frankly I do not want my things to wear for ever, certainly not my carpets and curtains, and that is one reason why I am so thankful for the present style of pretty light cretonnes, mattings, and Kidderminster carpets. They are so clean and bright, and enable us to have our bedrooms fresh, pleasant, and new, instead of making them up out of things that have seen their best days in another sphere; and as I want Angelina to recollect she may have to spend some little time in the bedroom occasionally, as years go by, I wish to impress upon her to remember all this in the arrangement of the house, and to be sure and buy only those colours that give her pleasure, and to have no jarring ugliness to fret her, and add in any measure to her time of illness and convalescence; for, as I have said before, no one knows how much we are affected insensibly by our surroundings, and how much our spirits are affected too by what we have to look at!

The first thing to recollect in choosing one's paper is that there should be nothing aggravating in it—no turns and twists that shall bother us as we lie in bed; no squares or triangles that flatly refuse to join; in fact, nothing special that can possibly worry us. I had once on one of my walls a charming paper of Japanese chrysanthemum design. It had little colour about it—only a faint pink flush, that just gave the idea of warmth without a glare. To give body to this, the dado was of Indian matting with a dado rail and wainscot paint of a good terra-cotta; the pink shade, not the brown. The ceiling was papered with a pale diaper-patterned terra-cotta paper, which was most pleasant to look at, and I had matting and rugs on the floor. A slight idea of this room can be obtained from the illustration on the previous page.

Fig. 17.—A corner in a bedroom, Gable-end, Shortlands.

The doors, mantelpiece, &c. were all painted to match, and the doors were panelled with terra-cotta chintz at 9*d*. a yard at Burnett's, and had brass fittings, which I bought at Maple's eleven years ago, and which have done service in two houses, and will go with me to a third, I hope, before long. On the mantelpiece I had a full flounce of blue and white Lahore cretonne, which is also used for covering the eider-down, and gave the necessary piece of blue colour there, which was repeated in the tiles at the back of the washing-stand, and on a big settee in one of the windows, which is a most useful possession, as it serves for a sofa, and opens wide to hold the dresses in. Maple keeps these box ottomans at about 2*l*. 10*s*., covered with odds and ends of cretonnes; to cover them with anything pretty costs a few shillings more, though, of course, occasionally the original covering may be pretty enough for use. Mine was hideous—great pink roses and green leaves, on a black ground; but for 10*s*. I made it quite a thing of beauty with blue and white cretonne, properly frilled, and I also added a big square frilled pillow, and a large drapery of gold thread tapestry, the same pattern I use for toilet-covers and tablecloths, over my two square cupboard-tables that serve to hold boots and odds and ends inside, and books, &c., on the top, thus answering a double purpose.

I think these small cupboards are really the most useful things I have ever invented, and so I will describe them fully, hoping other people may find them as satisfactory as I have done. When I was in Dorsetshire, I think I lived in the very awkwardest house in the whole county; and it was so badly arranged that to have a morning-room at all I was obliged to copy our French friends, and make what was a bedroom by night a charming sitting-room by day. But perhaps I ought not to grumble, as it was entirely due to this inconvenient house that I turned my mind more especially to making the most of every room I had; and as I had to stow away my belongings in pretty odds and ends, I thought of these small cupboards, and they have proved the greatest success.

They are made of deal, are about three feet high, and are quite square; they are painted some self-colour to match the room, and panelled with Japanese leather paper, and have one shelf inside; the handle is brass and so is the lock, and the hinges might be brass too if further decoration were required. They hold quite a quantity of things, and I cover them with a tapestry tablecloth, place a fern in a pot in the middle, and dot books and photographs about them just as one would on a table. I had them made by our own man, and I think they cost about 10s. or 12s., not more, and they are most useful, for they can be put anywhere, and are never in the way; and this obviates any necessity of the unsightly appearance of boots and shoes lying about the floor, while it allows of keeping some in reserve, for boots and shoes should never be bought and put on, but should be kept quite four months before taking them into wear, as they wear twice as long if this very simple precaution be taken.

The curtains to this room are short, as so often described, and are of the terra-cotta cretonne used to panel the doors, while loose muslin curtains that draw, of Liberty's yellow and white printed muslin, hang over the glass to keep off the eyes of 'over the way'; and as I had no blinds I supplemented these in summer by large dark blue serge curtains, at 1s. 11½d. a yard, which hang flat against the wall, and depend from very narrow brass rods at the top of the windows, the other curtains being only below the cathedral glass top windows (which are never shut winter or summer), and which, being opaque, require no permanent shading.

I may mention, by the way, that even in the bedrooms I should always remove the hideous china handles provided by the landlord and replace them with brass fittings. These are undoubtedly cheaper at Maple's than elsewhere, and cost, the brass finger-plates 1s. 10½d. each, and handles 1s. 11d. for two; brass bell-handles cost about 5s. 6d. each for downstairs, while very pretty brass rings are sold for about 2s. 6d. at Maple's, to be sewn on flat straps of plush, cretonne, or serge worked in some conventional design for bell-pulls; these are the nicest bell-pulls possible, and last years with care. All these fittings can be removed when the tenant leaves the house, only remember to carefully put away the china door-fittings yourself, or they will be mysteriously lost when you wish to replace them—a wasteful item that can be guarded against with just a little care. Especially also would I paper the bedroom ceilings with some cheap and pretty paper. Maple has an ideal bedroom ceiling at 4*d*. the piece in a peculiarly charming shade of blue, which is always pleasant to look at; and furthermore would I insist on a real dado, either of cretonne or matting, as this always keeps a room tidy and prevents the wall being spoiled, by the energetic manner in which the bed is always pushed into the wall, which is the housemaid's idea of placing it in position.

All Mr. Pither's papers are excellent for bedrooms, in either the 'berry' or the 'blossom' pattern; and the sage-green 'blossom,' with sage-green paint, a dado of sage-green marguerite cretonne, and terra-cotta ceiling papers and cretonnes, and ash furniture make an excellent bedroom; while the darkest blue 'berry,' with yellow and white cretonne dado and curtains, blue carpet and ceiling paper, and white, or rather cream, paint and furniture make another charming room; the flowery papers like old-fashioned chintzes in subdued colours, with either a chintz or matting dado, and ivory paint can furthermore be relied on to make a beautiful room. None of these decorations, by the way, is expensive really, and as the dados wear as long as the walls themselves they cannot be called a ruinous addition, and one is repaid for the outlay over and over again by knowing that nothing can harm one's walls; and as I have the walls sized behind the dado material, and have more than once taken down the dado to see if any dirt had crept behind, and found the wall as clean as the day when the dado was put up, I find the last objection to these dados done away with; for there are only two that have ever been made to me—viz. expense, and possible culture of dirt and creeping things.

And here, reminded of the enemies spoken of above, let me impress upon my readers never to buy bedroom furniture *at least* in sale-rooms. How can we know we are not buying infection, or how can we guarantee that we shall not become possessors of more than we have paid for? Therefore avoid sales, and go to some respectable firm and buy one or two good things, supplementing them later as money allows, and making shift for extras, as far as one can, until one can afford good solid furniture. In any case let the grate be seen to, and, if possible, buy one of Mr. Shuffery's slow-combustion stoves and pretty over-mantels, or at least have the stove. A bedroom fire is *not* waste or extravagance. I never believe firing is extravagance anywhere, and the slow-combustion stove will save its own cost in one month's consumption of coal; while a narrow strip of looking-glass about a foot wide, and enclosed in a painted deal frame, makes a pretty bedroom shelf; this can be supplemented by fans, brackets, and the ever-useful cheap and pretty chinas to be had of Gorringe.

Expensive as it doubtless is, I cannot see how Angelina is to do without something in the shape of a wardrobe, unless she is lucky enough to come across a little house already provided with cupboards. Some of the new houses, both at Bush Hill Park and at a queer, pretty little corner of the world called Brookgreen, Hammersmith (that I stumbled upon the other day, and was delighted with), have great receptacles that reminded me of the good days of old, when recesses in bedrooms were part of the house, and room-like cupboards were a portion of the structure; but I am compelled to confess that such conveniences are few and far between.

For example, most of the modern houses, and certainly one in which I once lived, have not one single attempt at one, and have not even deep recesses in which hooks and a curtain on a rod could be a substitute for a cupboard, and in consequence we were compelled to spend a small fortune on wardrobes. I purchased some very nice cheap ones at Maple's made out of deal, and painted a revolting drab colour, and also grained to imitate maple—bird's-eye maple. I only wish you could have heard the chorus of anger when these arrived home, you would all have been amused; but I said nothing, sent for my friend the painter, and gave them into his hands, and in a short time they returned, one painted a lovely sparrow's-egg blue, further embellished with Japanese leather panels and brass locks; the other an equally pretty shade of terra-cotta 'treated' very much in the same way. I am almost afraid to say how little these cost. One has a long glass in, and I think was 4*l.* 10*s.*, and the other 4*l.*; but they have ample accommodation, and are extremely pretty pieces of furniture, and match the dressing-tables, washing-stands, and chairs, of which more anon. These painted wardrobes can be embellished at home, if we use Aspinall's invaluable enamel paints, remembering that two coats of this make any old grained thing beautiful; all one has to do is to scrub the old paint well with strong soda-water, rubbing it down afterwards with glass-paper. All graining, by the way, can be treated like this, though naturally painters much prefer to add up a bill and insist on burning off all old paint. Should the graining be very thick, an application of 'Carson's detergent' is advisable; this costs 5*s.* at La Belle Sauvage Yard, London, E.C., and removes the old paint in flakes immediately—a much cheaper and far less offensive proceeding than the burning off of the paint so dear to the soul of the ordinary workman.

In my own room I must confess to greater extravagance, for I had a large dressing-table in light wood, and so fancied I must have all the rest to match, and in consequence I had to give 12*l*. or 14*l*. for my wardrobe. This I bought of Messrs. Hampton, in Pall Mall East, and better tradesmen I for one do not know. After I had had that wardrobe a few months the glass suddenly cracked straight across from no reason that I could discover, save from pure 'cussedness,' as the Yankees say. However, I wrote to the firm, telling them what had occurred, and they at once sent down an employé, who discovered a warp in the wood, and without a word or an atom of expense to me they removed the spoiled glass and door, and sent me a brand-new one—a perfectly fair thing to do, of course, as the fault was in the manufacture, but one very few people would have done, I venture to state, without acrimonious correspondence, and an attempt to charge at any rate. Why, only the other day I bought an umbrella at a shop I should love to 'name,' as they do in the House, and when it went into holes, real holes, in less than a month they declined altogether even to re-cover it, saying it had not had fair wear. It was not worth a fight, but that shop will now lose my custom, and I most certainly will never recommend it to any one. If tradesmen knew how far a little civility and courtesy went, some of them would, I am sure, imitate the noble conduct of the Messrs. Hampton.

My wardrobe has a deep drawer for hats, a place for hanging jackets, and plenty of shelves and other drawers for linen and dresses, and I could not do without it in the least, though, of course, it may be too dear for Angelina, in which case I must strongly recommend her to buy a cheap deal one and have it painted to match her room, putting on brass handles—the drop handles are the best and most decorative—and filling up any panels that there may be with Japanese paper, or tightly stretched cretonne, like that used for the hangings.

If Edwin be a clever carpenter, he can easily make a frame to simulate a wardrobe. The top can be formed of very tightly stretched holland (it does not show, and the glaze resists dirt and damp, I think, better than anything else), and the front can be hidden by a nice curtain—serge lined with holland would be best. The sides of the frame should have rings on, like picture rings, to fasten them to the flat surface of the wall, and can be painted. Edwin could put in some wide shelves, but these make-believe cupboards are best for hanging one's dresses and jackets in, as they will not stand much weight. A less costly thing even than this can be made with an arrangement of curtains, rods, and brackets, but the one suggested above should not cost 30*s*., curtain and all, would last years, and be removable from house to house, as no cupboard is.

The most valuable things I know, too, are Maple's box ottomans. No one makes them quite so cheaply as he does, and they are invaluable for ball-dresses, spare blankets, ordinary dresses—in fact, for anything; and, with a judicious arrangement of cushions, form sometimes an excellent substitute for a sofa. Though, if the room be large enough, I recommend Angelina to possess herself of what I always used to call 'a long chair,' which was originally a camp bedstead, is made of iron and sacking, lets down to a bed or rises up to an arm-chair, possesses an extra leg for a sofa, and finally has a long cushion, covered with cretonne or serge, that can be made to serve as a mattress if a spare bed is wanted in a hurry. I think this curious article of furniture costs 30s., and there is nothing like it for comfort. The sacking gives with one's weight, and never fatigues one, and it is even superior to a deck cane chair, which is very nice, but will creak and groan under one, and is apt to feel hard and ridgy after lying there for some time.

I do hope my readers will not think I am given to 'lying

Fig. 18.—Draped alcove for a bed.

down'; it is an action I scorn when I am well; but I know, alas! too well how necessary it is to be ready for an 'emergency,' and to know one has a place of refuge and rest if life grows too much for one, and one's headache is just a little too bad to bear without retiring into private life for a while. At first, of course, Angelina will have the house to herself, but that will not last—at least I hope for her sake it will not—and she will then be glad to have opportunities of resting for five or ten minutes, secure of safety from interruptions, and servants, and children, or visitors. Besides, when she is recovering after any illness there would be her sofa ready, and she would not be perpetually fretted and worried by seeing the room disorganised by the sudden introduction of a strange piece of furniture; the bringing in of which, and the bumping and banging inseparable from this same movement, often brings on a nervous attack, and fidgets her so much that she would rather be without it than witness the commotion caused by the moving.

If one's home has these little conveniences it adds immeasurably to one's comfort, and they are not costly; and here I may mention that I consider a screen indispensable too, for this can be moved to circumvent draughts or too much light, and can also be used to protect the patient from worry when the bed is made, &c.; things that always drive me distracted to witness, and that screened off cease to be, as far as I am concerned.

In most houses, too, the door opens confidingly on the only place where the bed can stand, and then a screen is invaluable; it hides the bed itself, and does not leave it exposed as it would were curtains used as a substitute. Curtains, too, are things I always disapprove of. I do not even like Mr. Arthur Smee's most excellent arrangement of wing-like brackets, to which curtains are attached, as I think people should have as much air as possible, and I see no more reason for curtaining a bed than there would be for curtaining one's chair or sofa. A screen insures privacy; curtains hide one's head only, and cannot possibly avoid being stuffy; if, however, the bare appearance of an uncurtained bed is objected to, the draped alcove sketched on the previous page will be found easy to arrange and very pretty indeed. This alcove is one of Messrs. Collinson and Lock's designs.

I have been very sorry to notice a very strong attempt made by those who ought to know better to revive that truly unhealthy and impossible thing in a properly managed house—the wooden bedstead. I hear that these detestable things are considered artistic—that to have a heap of feathers sunk into a carved oak box in the height of luxuriance and æstheticism, so I must beg my readers to carefully consider what a wooden bedstead means and used to mean.

It meant immense trouble with certain small animals that came there mysteriously with the clothes. It meant a taking to pieces, a scrubbing, and a putting together again continually; and, above all, it meant a bonfire were any person with an infectious disease to sleep upon it; and, in fact, I do not know one single thing in its favour, and yet folks in their craving after a false sensation of antiquity are actually thinking of going back to the wooden bedstead.

One of the worst and silliest things I know is to go back into the middle ages for those very articles that used to make our foremothers—I don't think our forefathers troubled much about their houses—miserable, and when I see tiny diamond panes of glass, for example, when invention has given us large sheets of glass through which light comes, and by throwing open which we can admit as much air as possible; or when I hear of the wooden bedsteads, I feel like a Philistine entirely, and long to uplift my testimony on the great superiority of this present nineteenth century of ours, when we are nothing if we are not sensible, and ought to know enough to make use of all the beauty of past days, while we reject unconditionally the futile, unhealthy nonsense that clings to them. Still, after this no one will be surprised to hear that I consider a brass or iron and brass bedstead a *sine quâ non*. Nothing is so clean, so cheerful-looking, and so healthy. There are no draperies to catch dust or to give the sleeper a headache, and, moreover, I never have a valance—never will allow one. Why should there be one? Not one single thing of any sort or description should be put under the bed, which, in a servant's room, or the room of an untidy person, serves as a regular hiding-place for boots, boxes, even soiled linen, and if there be nothing to hide there is no necessity that I can see for a valance. A brass and iron bedstead can be bought, full size, at Maple's for 3*l*. 10*s*., and, of course, very much handsomer ones can be procured; but plain beds are much the best, for they can be rubbed free from dust in a very few moments, and always look clean because they are so.

I do not think any one who has ever tried it can for one moment doubt that a spring mattress made entirely of finely woven chains is the very best and healthiest sort of bed that one can have, it never seems to get out of order, it is quickly made softer or harder by being wound up tighter or unwound, and, above all, it is easily kept clean, and is as easily disinfected, should any fever or other infectious disease attack the owner thereof.

I have had, and still possess, one of the old-fashioned spring beds that resemble very large mattresses, and, though this is extremely comfortable, it is not to be as highly recommended as a bed one can brush and know is quite clean, for it is covered with a tick, and has a mysterious internal arrangement of spiral springs that is apt at times to get out of order, and invariably groans and squeaks in an agonising way whenever one turns in bed, while the noise and motion are both very trying when one's nerves are a little unstrung and one is restless and cannot sleep. It is expensive to have it taken to pieces and cleaned, and the tick washed, which is not done half as often as it ought to be, because it is costly and tiresome. There are several sorts of chain-spring mattresses, and the 'Excelsior,' which is inexpensive, answers every purpose; but I personally much prefer a very fine woven chain, almost like chain-armour, which is expensive, but wears splendidly, and only requires a nice hair mattress over it to be complete. I always put over the chains themselves a square of brown holland, tied to each of the four corners of the bedstead. This should be washed twice, or even oftener, during the year, and it is also an excellent plan to put the nice new hair mattresses and pillows into neat brown holland pinafores, or cases; which can also be frequently washed in order to keep the ticks themselves clean as long as we possibly can. Unless this is done, the ticks become soiled and nasty-looking and shabby, because housemaids are but mortal, and will not remember to wash their hands and put on spotlessly clean aprons when they go up to make the beds. If brown holland is too dear, 'crash' serves every purpose, but the glaze on the holland resists dust better than anything, and insures cleanliness.

If people suffer very much from cold, I am luxurious enough to allow them a feather bed on the mattress. I always feel I am doing very wrong, and that it is a most unhealthy practice, though I have one myself, for in the winter, and indeed during most of the year, I hardly know what it is like to be even moderately warm in bed; but I still think I should be doing well were I to put away my feathers entirely, and only use the springs and the hair mattress, but I am not strong-minded enough, so, though I know feathers are unhealthy in every way, I still use them, believing that now I am too old to change my undoubtedly evil ways.

A brass and iron bedstead furnished with the spring mattress, nice hair mattress and bolster, and four pillows if a double, two if a single, bedstead, is the beau-ideal of a sleeping place for health, and should furthermore be provided with two under blankets—one in use, one in store in case of illness—and two good pairs of nice Witney blankets, and these should be marked in red wool with the date of purchase, initials, and number of the room to which they belong. If the four blankets are too much, those not in use should be very neatly folded under the mattress, thus insuring that they are always aired and ready for use. An eider-down quilt is also nice in winter, and should have an extra covering made from cretonne like the window curtains, or in a pretty contrast, edged all round with a two-inch goffered frill, and furnished with buttons and buttonholes, in order that it can be easily removed and sent to the wash.

Three pairs of sheets are the least that can be allowed to each bed; the top sheet of each pair should be frilled with Cash's patent frilling two inches and a half wide, and should have a large red monogram in the centre to look really well; these can be worked by Angelina, if she has clever fingers; and as it adds so very much to the appearance of the linen, I do hope where she can she will embellish her house-linen with nicely embroidered initials, repeating the same in the centre of the pillow-cases; which should be frilled and placed outside the bed during the day to look nice, the frilled cases being removed at night and replaced by plain ones, from motives of economy. Four plain pillow-cases for each pillow, and two or three frilled and embroidered ones for the top pillows, are the least that can be allowed when the linen is bought; for if Angelina have to stay in bed—and no doubt she will—a change from the plain pillow-case of night to the frilled one for day, and a removal of the plain counterpane for a pretty one, is as good almost as a change of room, and makes far more difference in one's feelings than can readily be believed. Now one especial word in Angelina's ear: I have never yet found in all my experience a servant who can really and truly be trusted to properly air the bed. Her first idea is to cover it up and get it made, and unless Angelina copies me I am quite certain she will find the bed stuffy and disagreeable, because it has not had time to get properly aired, and because it has been made up as soon almost as Angelina got out of it.

Now there is not one single thing that should be left on the bed once one is out of it. Do not be content with turning all the bed-clothes over the rail; see they are all pulled out from under the mattress, separated, and hung up, if possible. Then remove the pillows, and dot them about on chairs and sofas; hang up separately the under sheet and blanket where they will receive a current of air from the open window wet or dry; and then pull off the mattress, placing it as close to the window as it will go, which only takes about five minutes, as, of course, Edwin will help with the mattress, and then, when dressed, open all the windows possible. Leave the door wide open too, unless there are torrents of rain and a windy tempest going on; and I venture to remark that the bed will be all right and properly aired, even if Mary Jane rushes wildly upstairs from the breakfast table and sets to work at once.

May I also add: don't fold up your night attire! I used to be informed by my governess that no lady ever left her towels on the floor—as if any one wanted to—or went downstairs without neatly folding up her night-garment. Now this I will not do. It should be left to air with the beds, and should then be folded up, with the soft, woolly slippers in attendance, and put neatly into an embroidered case provided for it. How fussy and old-maidish all this seems, yet on these trifles depend so very much that I feel I really cannot say too much about them. It may seem silly of me here to tell most of my readers of things they may all do daily, just as they have their meals, but I know a great many women who never think of these items, and of course there may be a very great many others who just want to be given the same sort of little hints too; and as for the servants, I do not believe one exists who out of her own head would air a bed daily, and who does not regard such airing as a useless fad.

While we are on the subject of beds, I may mention that a matchbox, the boxes of Bryant and May's, painted with enamel paint, and embellished with a tiny picture, nailed to the wall just above one's head, is an excellent thing; and so is a bracket provided with either one of Mr. Drew's small paraffin lamps with a chimney, or else one of Field's candle-lamps, also with a glass shade; and that a bed pocket made out of a Japanese fan, covered with soft silk, and the pocket itself made of plush, and nailed within easy reach, is also very useful to hold a handkerchief or one's watch; and, furthermore, that great comfort is to be had from a table at one's bedside, on which can stand one's book or anything one may be likely to want in the night.

The counterpane of the bed should be one of these nice honeycomb quilts with a deep cotton fringe; in winter and summer both, the eider-down should be always on the bed ready for use, for some of our English summer nights are as cold and chilly as many of the autumn and winter ones; and very charming-looking day coverings for the beds can be bought for one guinea at Marshall and Snelgrove's, and are called Madras quilts. They have more substance than Madras muslin itself, and are ready trimmed with a neat fringe. Guipure and lace strips make nice quilts too, and very nice covers can be made of cretonne like the curtains edged by the pretty nine-inch goffered frill of which I am so fond; but if Angelina works, beautiful ones can be made from crash or workhouse sheeting, embroidered in scrolls and pomegranates in red chain stitch, a deep border of thicker work, also in a pomegranate pattern, forming an appropriate and very handsome finish to it. These quilts can be bought ready traced and begun at Francis's, Hanway Street, Oxford Street, W., at 30s.; they should be lined with sateen, and finished off by a wide border of furniture lace, turned over a band of sateen of any colour that will harmonise with the room itself.

A careful servant should brush under the bed daily to pick up any little bits of fluff or dust, and once a week, without fail, all the corners should be turned out and the room thoroughly cleaned. The floor, to be perfect, should be stained all over, polished and rubbed bright, and be furnished with nice rugs, which can be shaken daily, for nothing keeps so clean, and it is undoubtedly healthy, for, much as I like matting, and largely as I use it, it must fill up the corners entirely, and dust cannot help accumulating there, in a bedroom.

Furniture for the room itself could be had cheaply, did we know of any man willing to work under our orders, but this seems impossible.

I do not know if there are any trades-union rules among carpenters that prevent them working for themselves; but, if not, I am quite sure an honest mechanic could make a large fortune if only he set himself seriously to work, and would keep to reasonable prices.

Fig. 19.

Of course, skilled cabinet-making is one thing, and the sort of work I mean is another; but I am constrained to remark on this, because ordinary shops, even the very cheapest, charge such terrible prices for furniture, and I have had such useful things made from my own descriptions by a man in our own employ, that I am sure such a man near London would soon be of almost world-wide fame, and we should all have useful furniture, even if it were not of polished ash and oak, elegantly finished, and in exquisite style.

We should, of course, all prefer the very best furniture possible, if we could afford it; but, as we cannot, I should like to find a carpenter as good as my old one, who would work for himself and really give us honest work at honest prices.

There are some dressing-tables which I possess which this man made for 2*l*. 10*s*. out of strong, good deal. They have three very deep drawers each side and one in the middle, and underneath the top drawer in one case there is a rod to hold a curtain, and in the other there is a species of cupboard for boots. The curtain also hides boots, but I prefer the cupboard, as it is the tidiest, and has two divisions, one for shoes and one for boots. These were stained deal, but I soon had them painted, one turquoise blue, one terra-cotta, and added brass handles, and they are now not only useful but extremely pretty. The frames of the looking-glasses were painted to match, so that all was *en suite*.

There are, of course, many different sorts of dressing-tables, but I like mine at 2*l*. 10*s*. as much as any for use. My own happens to be much more expensive, because I had it, in the room I spoke of before, to serve for both a toilet-table and washing-stand in a confined space; but this came to about 9*l*., which is not so very much when one considers it was instead of two things. This has a very large glass in the centre, and drawers and recesses, which hold china odds and ends, and is very pretty too. The part that was used as a washing-stand is tiled, but now the tiles are covered, as I have at present plenty of room for another stand, and it no longer does double duty.

Mr. Smee has designed a charming table, and has given me the drawing, which is produced here. This is without exception the very best style of table for a small room, as the drawers are extremely deep, and would hold an immense quantity of things. The looking-glass is in the centre, the drawers extending as far back as they are in front, and the table is provided with two brackets to hold either china or flowers. This is painted any colour, and the handles are brass. In the very best quality the price is 6*l*. 18*s*., but it can be made cheaper, and Mr. Smee would no doubt tell any one who wrote to him how much cheaper it could be made. He has not told me exactly the lowest price, but it is an extremely charming piece of furniture, and it is as decorative as it is undoubtedly useful.

Then there are those truly abominable dressing-tables, the deal frame covered with muslin and lace and glazed calico, like the frock of a ballet-dancer, or else with some serge material that resembles nothing so much as a church altar; and that should never be used except in cases where the others really cannot be managed on the score of expense; but, as there are many nice sets of furniture to be bought for about 12*l*. 12*s*., I think, somehow, a dressing-table can be managed by Angelina that shall not serve as a dust-trap, a hiding hole for all sorts of débris, or an attraction for fire; for many a death has been caused by these flimsy petticoated things catching alight and flaring up in one moment.

I had one once which was rather a good possession, as it was in reality a deep square box. I believe it had once been an old wooden crib, retired from active service and covered with a lid; and although it was very useful, and held all my spare blankets, I never could bear the look of it, and it was finally shorn of its legs and turned into an ottoman with a chintz cover. But it is desperately heavy, and I never see it without feeling cross at its unalterable ugliness.

I never use the ordinary white toilet-cover; this is another of my pet detestations. I invariably have neat tapestry covers made to fit the tables &c., and edged with a ball fringe to match. I use, moreover, self-coloured felt and velveteen, also edged with furniture lace or fringe, and this I use also to cover the box pincushions that are in every room, and are invaluable for holding odds and ends, the gloves one has in wear, shoestrings, and so on. For these, a large-sized cigar box is an excellent foundation. This should be lined with wadding and glazed lining, the top carefully wadded too, and all the outside covered with lining; then cover it tightly with either plush, velveteen, or tapestry, and put fringe round in such a way that the opening is hidden. Very tidy folks tie these boxes together with ribbons. I do not; life is too short, and I find the fringe hides any gaps, and looks very nice too. The top part does for pins or one's brooches, though I prefer to keep my pins in a china Japanese dish, shaped like a fish, because I can't bear the pin-stuck look of a cushion; and I put my brooches away in their boxes, because they are apt to be knocked off and lost or bent, unless you are possessed of a maid or housemaid who is as careful as she ought to be, and yet somehow never is! The brushes and combs live in a middle drawer, the paper in which should be changed once a week, when the room is properly cleaned. They should never be placed on the toilet-cover, and, if there be no centre drawer, two cedar-wood trays covered with tapestry covers over pieces of washing stuff should be provided, to insure that they are not left on the toilet-covers, and that cleanliness is duly respected. In front of the toilet-table, however the room is covered, there should be an extra rug. Of course, if the carpet be new the first beauty of the carpet may be used if you like, but this I do not advise: first, because you may like to change your furniture—I love changing mine—and in this case you could not, because the carpet would be marked; and, secondly, because it is a pity to wear it out more in one place than another, which you could not avoid doing if you do not put a rug down in the place you use most. In the case of matting or staining a rug would be imperative, and I strongly recommend one for a carpet for the reasons mentioned above. Before we leave the dressing-table for the washing-stand, I should like to say a few words about the way to light it. Careful survey should be made of the room before the gas-brackets are put in, and, if possible, one should be so arranged as to bring the light over the centre of the glass.

In a big room a bracket each side is advisable. Long brass brackets should be used, which should be able to be moved either to the side or to the middle of the glass, bringing the light well over the top whenever it is possible, thus doing away at once with any necessity for candles and the attendant dangers. If candles are used they should be invariably protected with Price's candle guards; but once more I say, have one of Messrs. A. and A. Drew's perfect little 1s. 6d. lamps in every room. They are quite safe, and can be carried from room to room without the very smallest danger. They never smell, are lighted and put out in a moment, and are invaluable to any mother who pays domiciliary visits to her children, and puts down her light to tuck up or kiss the little sleepers, for she can place this lamp even in a draught and at the same time need not consider if a curtain is blowing close by, for if it did it could do no harm. They are useful even to the reader in bed, as they give sufficient light for that, although they do not come up to the excellent candle lamps recently invented, but which cost a guinea, as contrasted with our modest 1s. 6d., and have no protection for the flame, which, however, is far back in the lamp, and not easily reached. Another item must also be mentioned before we leave the toilet-table subject. Every scrap of hair should be collected by Angelina herself before she leaves the toilet-table, and be placed somewhere out of sight, to be burned by herself in the nearest fire. Avoid those terrible things called toilet-tidies, which make me shudder whenever I see them hanging up; but do not leave this item near a servant's hands: they cannot resist combing out the brush either into the washing basin or the toilet-pail. The drains become clogged—no one knows why, until that miserable creature the plumber has to be called in, when, after spoiling all that comes within his reach, he discovers the cause, and sends in a tremendous bill, all of which need never have happened had Angelina looked after this item herself. If the nursery fire be handy it can be disposed of every morning; if not, a little box could be kept in one corner of the dressing-table drawer, and the contents burned when the room is cleaned, which should be done with the very greatest regularity once a week, on a stated day, which should always be rigorously adhered to, and which, if properly done, minimises in a remarkable manner the discomfort and disagreeables of that abomination to the male mind, and to some female minds too—the spring clean. Whatever Angelina is, I do hope and trust she will duly appreciate her table-drawers, and not look upon them as a store-place for rubbish. She will, of course, have a store of gloves, handkerchiefs, and ribbons at first in her trousseau; and I most strongly advise her to keep in the toilet drawers the things she has in use, not her whole store. She should never allow herself more than three pairs of gloves in wear, one of which should be for evening wear, nor more than a dozen handkerchiefs in use; and she should never put away her gloves unmended or lacking buttons, nor allow a fortnight to pass without putting every drawer she possesses tidy, and seeing her handkerchiefs are correct in number. Tidiness and tidy habits are great helps to economy of time and money, and are therefore highly to be recommended for Angelina's consideration.

  There is nothing so expensive as a muddle; nothing so sure to unhinge the servants and make them cross, captious, and anxious to move on elsewhere. Keep straight and work is easy, because it is expected and looked out for; allow arrears to accumulate, and nothing is done.

And this also applies to the drawers in Angelina's own wardrobe. Unmended gloves, linen, or stockings should never for one moment be allowed, neither should one set of linen be taken into wear until the previous one is worn entirely out. This should be kept religiously, old linen being invaluable for burns (if it be *linen,* not *cotton*) or wounds, and to give away to the deserving poor who may be ill. Even in one's own illnesses old nightdresses are invaluable; as medicine, poultices, and constant and daily washing soon ruins one's nice new things. I am no advocate for hoarding, but I do know the value of old worn-out things, if only to have something to fall back upon if a friend comes in, to beg for Kitty Jones's ninth baby; or for old Mrs. Harris, in bed and suffering agonies from rheumatic fever, when rags and old flannel petticoats come in like a godsend for her use. If one's servants have good wages they do not need these things, and I do not think, in any case, they should be given old clothes: they come to look upon them as a right, and often enough one is prevented giving a far more deserving object some cast-off garments because one fancies that so-and-so will be offended; therefore I strongly advise Angelina to keep one especial ottoman or drawer to go to for her charities. I am sure she will find it a great help to her if she does so.

One of the palm-leafed baskets for soiled linen should be in every room; they are a little more expensive than the ordinary soiled linen baskets, but they stand three times the wear, and always look nice. Albeit this is an article I always put as much as possible in very humble retirement behind my cheval-glass, there is no choice in my mind between the palm-leaf and the wicker-work for wear, and I strongly recommend both the dark brown and the light-coloured ones; they are about 5s. 11d. each.

If Angelina can possibly afford it she should buy a cheval-glass; of course the long glass in the wardrobe shows one's dresses pretty well, but it cannot be moved about to suit the light like the cheval-glass can, neither does it ever somehow act quite in its place. I dress very hurriedly, for I have so little time generally for this operation. I am always doing something up to the last moment before I go out either for a drive or in the evening, so that I could not do without mine, and I have often been saved quite fearful *contretemps* by this faithful friend, which truthfully points out strings and skirts out of place, and has an unpleasant habit of suggesting that one's hair must be done again, by reflecting the back of one's head in a crude, and startling way, in the ordinary glass. Then it is of great use to visitors too, who may not have a long glass at all in the spare-room wardrobe, and are doubly thankful to find a cheval-glass there, lent of course out of Angelina's own room for the time being.

Another thing that I should like to speak of is the necessity of always having a clean brush and comb in the toilet drawer. A friend comes in unexpectedly to luncheon or dinner, and we are struck with dismay to find that it is the day before our own particular brushes are to be washed, and we have none fit to give her. If we always keep a 'company brush and comb' we need never be put to confusion as we otherwise should, for often, in dusty weather particularly, and especially if we drive much, our brushes look black almost after once using, and are not suitable to give a friend, without being really dirty.

This said washing of brushes is a vexed question. I have a friend who is so particular about hers that she never uses them more than once, and then has them washed rapidly in hot soapsuds. By holding the backs in her hand so that they do not touch the water, and thus only immersing the bristles, she gets them clean without spoiling them; they are dried in the fender, and she always has six brushes in use. Now, I think if we have three in use, and have them washed in routine, one a day, so as always to have one clean one ready for a friend, we shall do very well. And I think 5*s*. or 6*s*. ample to give for a brush; I have had some excellent ones from Whiteley's at 4*s*. 11*d*. and 4*s*. 6*d*. If we buy extravagantly dear brushes, we grudge their wear and tear and their numerous washings; but inexpensive ones can be kept cleaner, because we can more easily afford to buy new ones if we do not give too much at first. The old silver brushes at 5*l*., and beautiful ivory-backed ones at almost any price we like to give, are delightful to possess; but unless we can constantly renew the bristles, they soon get useless, and as we can't do that we must be content with ordinary ones; which same remark applies to combs. I like a black vulcanite at 1*s*. 9*d*. or 2*s*. better than any, for a comb is difficult to keep really nice, and one does not mind throwing a soiled or broken one away if one can easily and cheaply replace it.

Still, if Angelina should have beautiful brushes given to her in her collection of wedding gifts, I strongly counsel her to keep them by her for visiting and travelling, and to get other cheaper ones for every day; and this same remark applies to tortoiseshell combs. I like better things for visiting myself, and I am sure Angelina should keep her best brushes for this purpose. If the toilet-table is chosen with brackets, cut and scented flowers should never be allowed there. A few ferns and immortelles look nice, especially the pretty pink everlastings one can buy in the summer, but scented flowers are bad for a bedroom, though I much recommend a growing plant or two; they look nice, and are very healthy; but no flowers here even; a fern, a small palm, or the ubiquitous aspidistra being all to be preferred, because the leaves give out a healthy atmosphere, and are therefore useful as well as ornamental, while strongly scented blossoms poison the air and render it heavy and unfit for a sleeper to breathe.

Without going to the outrageous lengths some lovers of fresh air consider necessary, I strongly advise every one to try and sleep with some little bit of window open. I always do in summer with all that I can, in winter with one or two at the top only. The sudden change in temperature that makes this dangerous is guarded against by having an extra wrap handy on a chair, or thrown over the foot of the bed, which can be drawn up if the change becomes perceptible; but I am certain that two people in one room should never sleep with all the windows and doors shut, and I have never slept with mine closed, since I can recollect, without waking with a headache and a feeling of lassitude, though, of course, when I lived in London itself the noise was very trying, yet I became accustomed even to that; and I put down my singular immunity from colds to this habit of mine, and also to the open windows and doors that I always insist upon, and that for some part of the day always remain open, winter and summer, though the moment the sun goes, or rather begins to go, down, all windows, in the winter and autumn, should be rigorously closed, with the exception of about a quarter of an inch at the top.

But then, in connection with my open-air fad, I am a great advocate for good, jolly fires, and I do believe bedroom fires save a great amount of doctors' bills. Open your window a little, and have a fire, if you can possibly manage it, and I am sure you will all find a great difference in the expense. Of course this adds to the servant's work; but if she objects, equalise matters by helping her with the beds, and in dusting, and in a thousand-and-one little ways. I am sure you will not repent it.

Fig. 20.

Fires warm the whole house, take off the damp, raw feeling that is so trying in our English atmosphere, and give a cheerful feel and look that cannot be too highly esteemed. I would rather do without anything than a fire, and even in the height of summer the instant it rains I have my fires set going, with the windows open, not so much for the mere warmth of course, but to dry the atmosphere and prevent the house-walls from becoming chilled and damp and dangerous to health; while for three parts of the year they are emphatically a necessity, unless we want the doctor's gig or brougham to be always turning in at our front gate.

I could write pages about fires, I am so certain that in England nothing is saved by scrimping the coal, but I must not dwell upon this subject. I must pass on to the washing-stands, of which here are two drawings from Mr. Smee's designs, and which I consider the very perfection of stands. I prefer the larger one of the two, not because I could for one moment contemplate the odious notion of a double washing apparatus, but because the smaller one does not seem to me to have room for sponge-dish and all the etceteras one requires; but, of course, if the room were a small one, the single washing-stand would be best, because in that case space would be an object, and by placing a long painted shelf, or one of those nice little hanging sets of shelves, half cupboard, half bookcase, over it, we could obtain a place to put extra articles on. These washing-stands in the best materials come to 5*l*. 5*s*. each. The drawing, I think, will need but small explanation from me, as it will show exactly the proper style for a washing-stand; but I should like my readers to notice that the high-tiled back prevents the wall being spoiled, and does away with the idea of a 'splasher' being required, that the towels are to be hung on the round rails provided for them, and that the deep cupboards are especially to be commended, doing away as they do with any necessity for an extra piece of furniture, and they can also be used for bottles of medicine, Angelina's private duster, which she should keep in every room, cardboard boxes, and other trifles that are too useful to throw away and yet require to be hidden from sight.

Fig. 21.

There is no doubt in my mind that the Beaufort ware sold by Maple is the nicest and prettiest for bedroom use. It is pure white, and a most charming shape. The jug has a double lip, and the handles are in the centre, like a basket, simulating a twisted rope. The basin &c. have all handles and embellishments of the same rope-like design, and the cost is 17s. 6d. The ware is most excellent, and though much cheaper ware is, of course, to be procured, pretty blue and white sets being purchasable at 3s. 11½d., my white set exists triumphantly, after eleven years' wear and two moves, while I have bought more cheap sets for those all-devouring locusts the boys and the maids than I care to think about. I am convinced, therefore, that very cheap china for bedroom use is a mistake, for good ware stands rough usage much better, and therefore is cheaper in the end.

It is well, too, to buy the ware as much alike as possible for two or even three rooms, as nothing is so difficult to match as this. Before I became in the least *au fait* at these small contrivances that save so much, I had quite a regiment of ewerless basins and basinless ewers that had accumulated because I found it impossible to get them matched, and having them made was almost, nay quite, as costly as a new set. Of course, these were gradually used up, and not very gradually either, alas! by the servants; but they were ever so much too good for their heedless clutches, and I should have been saved a great deal had I had the sense to buy two sets alike, instead of exercising my taste by seeing how many different ones I could possess myself of.

Ware now is so extremely cheap that it is perhaps not of such vital consequence as it used to be to do this; still, as I had the other day to give 4s. for a jug to match a basin belonging to a set the whole of which cost only 5s., I think it is still worth mentioning, as it may save Angelina something, and every shilling is often a consideration to young beginners. The blue and white ware at about 5s. a set is good enough for any room, but, of course, Maple's white Beaufort ware is much prettier; and Mortlock, of Oxford Street, has or had some artistic pale blue, yellow, and red sets that would be lovely in a room that was furnished entirely in one of these colours. The soap-dish &c. are included in the cheap prices, but not a sponge dish. This should always be bought. Not only does it save the sponge from becoming sticky and unpleasant, but it saves the wall and floor from those detestable continuous dribbles of water that are the outcome of a sponge-basket, that may be all very well in theory, but is worse than useless in practice. A sponge-dish has all proper drainage, and may be more expensive at first, but, like a great many other expensive things, saves the whole of its cost in the long run.

The covers of the soap and toothbrush dishes should never be left on; the soap lasts ever so much longer than when it is shut up, and, of course, the veriest ignoramus knows the effect on one's toothbrush if it is kept covered over. I infinitely prefer to have a tall species of spill-holder or a rack for tooth and nail brushes, as this allows them to drain; and for servants' bedrooms one can buy iron things at 6½d. to hold the soap and two toothbrushes as well. These are not bad for schoolboys' rooms, as they are not ugly, but are not suitable for grown-up people's rooms, who are supposed reasonably to take care of their things; but with the Beaufort ware the ordinary dish for toothbrushes is sent, and is therefore used, but without the cover.

I always keep on my washing-stand one of Perry's invaluable sixpenny sticks of ink-eraser. I sometimes ink my fingers dreadfully, but nothing is too bad for Perry, whose delightful stick comes into use, and cleans away the stains directly. This, too, must not be put into confinement, as it becomes soft and melts away rapidly if it is.

For the tooth-water and glass, I most thoroughly recommend the charming little sets we buy at Douglas's glass-shop in Piccadilly. For 1s. 6d., 2s., and even less (I have bought a green set there for 9d.), one buys the prettiest possible glass jugs and glasses, and they are ever so much nicer than the old-fashioned glass water-bottles and tumblers; they are charming to look at, and far more easily kept clean. There are blue, red, green, and shades of opal; and the gas-globes should match. The best gas-globes are the tinted green globes, pinched in here and there in folds, which are 1s. 4½d. at Whiteley's, and 3s. and 4s. at any other shop—why, I don't know. The opal glasses are prettier, but then they are dearer. A dozen towels should be allowed to each washing-stand: four a week, or even three, are enough for most people. One big Turkish towel is indispensable for the bath, and a clean towel should be always on the second rail ready for the visitor, for whom we have already provided the hairbrush.

To every room should be apportioned a hot-water jug or can. There are none so good as the charming brass cans at 7s. 6d. The painted ones soon become shabby, and always smell of paint directly the hot water is put in; and not at all a bad plan is to have a brass label chained to the handle of the can, with the room's name on to which the can belongs. Cheaper brass cans can be had, but they hold less water, and as they have no cover the water very soon becomes cold. A larger oak-painted can should be provided for the housemaid. This she should use for refilling the ewers, and to bring larger quantities of water if a foot-bath is required in one's own room; but the foot-bath and also the slop-pails should be all of white china, and intense cleanliness should be insisted on, especially for the last-named articles, which never, even in the smallest establishment, should be made of anything save earthenware. These china ones cost 4s. 9d., and have a basket-work handle and a china cover. They should be scalded out every day with hot water and a little chloride of lime, chloride of lime being kept in any separate place, ready for use where there are any drains.

Before passing to the dressing-room, which should open, if possible, out of the bedroom, there are still one or two more trifles that can be mentioned in connection with it, as on trifles after all depend a great deal of our comfort, more especially in the upstairs department, and a sleepless night might often be prevented were some of the commonest precautions taken to insure rest.

One thing no dweller in the ordinary suburban residence should be without, and that is a wedge of wood attached to a brass chain to each window, ready to wedge the window closely together should a storm suddenly arise in the night. Who has not risen irate at the dismal rattling, and crammed in anything—toothbrush, comb, or what not—sacrificing often enough one or the other in one's rage at not being able in a moment to put a stop to this intolerable nuisance? Now a wedge ready to hand, nailed to the window by its chain, so that it cannot be lost or mislaid, obviates all this, and the window is secured at once and rest is insured simply by a little precaution and forethought. I believe that Whiteley keeps these wedges, but I used to buy mine of a clergyman in Dorset, who made them beautifully, and sold them in bunches in aid of the fund for restoring his church, and so popular were they that he made quite a nice little sum by their sale; but then Dorset is a very windy county, and I think the windows there rattle more than anywhere else.

Another thing should be secured, and that is a matchbox nailed to the wall, close by the bed, and the servant should be strictly forbidden ever to take the matches from one room to another; there should be a match-box *nailed on* in each room and in the passages, and Angelina should see herself that matches are never lacking there. I buy Bryant and May's boxes, but not their matches, as they are expensive, but I always have tiny boxes of Swedish matches at 5s. the gross, a gross lasting me considerably over a year; naturally I keep them locked in a store cupboard, in a room where there is sufficient warmth to keep them dry, and the maids have to ask me for them when they are required. When I used Bryant and May's matches and had them in as wanted from the grocer, I never spent less than 6d. and sometimes 1s. a week upon them, so I consider my present plan worth mentioning, for the save is really great, and in these small items much can be economised, if only one has a little knowledge and keeps one's eyes open. But the matchboxes and wedges must be nailed on, or else they will disappear in the same extraordinary way pins and hair-pins always contrive to do. Then, in bedrooms and sitting-rooms alike, I have the most delightful tiny brass hooks on which I hang a hearth-brush, for I have an immense dislike to an untidy and dirty hearth. As my old nurse used to say, 'These sort of things don't eat anything,' and a brush lasts five times as long if it have not to migrate from one room to another, and can instead have its own especial hook. You can buy ugly black hearth-brushes at 1s. 3d., but I always buy brass ones at 4s. 11½d. They last for years and years, and then can have new bristles added at the cost of 1s.; they look nice too, and are always to hand when wanted.

One of the principal things to remember all through these household arrangements surely is this: a place for everything, and everything in its place; time, temper, wear and tear of nerves, and servants being saved a thousand times over by this simple remedy. If the brush be in its place there is no need for Angelina to ring up tired Mary Jane to make a tidy hearth. The hot-water cans on their shelves in the bath-room, or in the pantry if there be no bath-room, allow of Angelina getting her own hot water if the maid be busy or out of the way, and so on through all the details of domesticity, which will only dovetail in a little house if this principle of tidiness and thought animates the mistress. And here let me beg that Angelina will resist with her might getting into the bad habit of putting her boots on and buttoning them on her nice cretonne chair covers. I mean the habit of putting the foot up on the chairs while she fastens the buttons. I once had a visitor staying with me who cut out a whole set of chair cushions in the month or six weeks she was with me; and I discovered she had brass tips to her heels, and these had cut out tiny holes all over the cushions, spoiling them utterly; all because she had acquired this very bad habit. If Angelina cannot button her boots without this action, she should take care never to put her heel on the chair; to keep to one for the process; and, if possible, to put down something, if only a scrap of paper, under the toe of the boot, which must soil the cushion, even if it do nothing worse.

I have in my time suffered so much from careless and inconsiderate visitors that I cannot help giving these little hints on which any newly married girl can act if she will. Example speaks louder than precept, and if Angelina scouts such actions herself, she influences her servants, and suggests to her visitors tidy habits, that may benefit her later on, if not on the first visit. I shall never forget one dreadful visitor I had—a visitor who was possessed of the damp, unpleasant hobby of searching in ditches and hedge-bottoms for clammy and awful things which she insisted on bringing home and investigating by the aid of a microscope. I should not have minded this one bit, if she had done it in a room we had, where the boys made messes, and that nothing could hurt; but I had just had my spare room done up, and the effect was so terrible I have never forgotten it to this day. It was such a pretty flowery room, too, that it deserves a word of description. The effect was purple and green, and the paper was guelder-roses and heliotrope—not at all a bad mixture of colour, remember, and one that lights up well; the paint was all the dull Japanese green varnished that is *not* arsenical; and that is very artistic, and by great good luck I found a charming French cretonne of the same style and almost the same pattern as the paper, and this I used as dado fixed with a dull green rail of 'scantling,' and as panels in the shutters and doors. I had a nice little brass bedstead, with a gold and white embroidered Liberty quilt trimmed round with ball fringe, and furniture, with gold, green, and blue and red tapestry covers on toilet, chest of drawers, and a new pincushion box covered with the same, and all trimmed with ball fringe. There was a nice new box-ottoman for hats and bonnets, a most useful possession for any one, especially if it be divided in two layers with a cheap tray, also covered with cretonne, new matting, and nice Liberty rugs on the floor, and several newly framed photographs on the walls; besides this there was a pretty table covered with plush, for a writing-table, duly furnished with blotter, inkstand, and wastepaper basket, &c.; a charming basket-chair, and two other chairs in pretty cretonnes, and odds and ends in the shape of ornaments. There were two gas brackets, so I did not have any candles in the room. I never have if I can help it; the servants are apt to light them and drop the grease about, so unless specially desired I never put candles anywhere, and I am more than thankful that in this case of which I am writing I did nothing of the kind, for my excellent housemaid came to me one morning when my friend was out 'bog-trotting'—or whatever the word for the occupation is—and, with a face of horror, begged me to come into the spare room before Mrs. W. returned, as she really did not know how she was going to get it straight again.

Shall I ever forget my anguish! On the bed, on the top of the new quilt, were spread specimens of all the nastinesses she had collected; on the brass rail and hanging on the dado, on nails stuck in for the purpose, and from most of the picture-nails, were mounted ghastlinesses on sheets of paper that were drying in a fine breeze coming straight into the room, laden with any amount of September damp and mist; the oil from the microscope lamp was on every chair and every table, and a perfect regiment of muddy boots and bedraggled skirts, cast about everywhere, spoke volumes of the extent of Mrs. W.'s wardrobe, and her ingenuity in filling up every hole and corner of that new and once pretty room.

And all this was caused just by a little lack of thought and care for other people's things, for, as I said before, we had, and generally have, a large unfurnished room, sacred to boys, where she could have done her worst and injured no one, for she might have nailed her nails and hung up specimens to her heart's content, and only pleased the legitimate owners of that chamber. I also forgot to mention that on the newly painted mantelpiece was a row of bottles full of dirty water, all of which either leaked or else had been put down there, wet from the ditches from which they had been filled, and to find room for them all my ornaments had been dislodged and were missing. We found them afterwards in bits, more or less, at the bottom of the ottoman, the top of which was spoiled by being used as a 'boot-rest' for Mrs. W. when she either wished to button or unbutton those articles of attire. When she had left me I simply had to do that room at the cost of 5*l*. or 6*l*., which I did not want, naturally, to spend, but my friend has never been to stay with me again, and she never will. I have told this long story, which I did not mean to go in for when I began my chapter, to point out to Angelina another caution. When 'things' are once nice and in order they require incessant care, if Angelina has been carelessly brought up, and if she has not acquired really nice habits; but if she avoids messing and is duly careful, her possessions will last her years, and give very little trouble. One more thing to remember is that, unless the door be provided with a curtain suspended from one of Maple's invaluable 7*s*. 9*d*. rods, nothing should induce Angelina to depend her dresses from crooks fixed into the doors. It spoils them, as they are exposed both to sun and dust, and the look of it is so unpleasantly suggestive of Bluebeard's wives that this is a habit that cannot, I think, be too strongly condemned. Besides, I remember dresses being torn and spoiled by being shut into doors and then taken down without seeing they are shut in; which is an argument against hanging them there at all, even covered with a curtain. Still, in a small house and with a large amount of clothing, a door is sometimes very 'handy' as an overflow wardrobe, and then a curtain arranged as suggested above is a *sine quâ non*.

One need not go to very much expense about bedroom chairs. Old worn-out drawing-room occasional chairs can be made beautiful for bedroom use by painting them blue to match the suite with Aspinall's hedge-sparrow's-egg blue enamel paint; particularly if one buys cushions, which are sold, I believe, both at Maple's and Whiteley's very cheaply, for about 1*s*. 2*d*. These should be re-covered with odds and ends of Liberty's Mysore cretonne; the yellow and white, blue and white, and terra-cotta and white being all admirable—with the particular shade of blue paint, I mean. The best bedroom chairs are these painted chairs, or else the black-framed Beaconsfield chairs, rush-seated, and also supplied with cushions in frilled cases, the cases being buttoned on so as to be easily removed for the wash, and the cushions supplied with tapes, so that they are fixed to the chairs, and neither move about when one is sitting upon them nor drop on when least expected.

There is no doubt that pictures should always be on a bedroom wall. Pictures and picture-frames are so cheap nowadays that some can generally be afforded even at first. Of course these gradually accumulate, and in years to come the walla will doubtless be decorated with photographs of the children at different stages; but Angelina's wedding photographs will be useful at first, and I cannot imagine a nicer wedding present than some of the exquisite photographs from the old masters that one buys ready framed at a shop close to Regent Circus, the name of which I have forgotten, but which is between the Circus and the meeting hall of the Salvation Army. These are not at all expensive; for 10s. and 15s. each quite large and most beautiful photographs can be obtained, and Angelina would have a vast amount of pleasure out of 10$l.$ spent judiciously on these lovely photographs for the adornment of her house, especially of her bedroom. These make admirable presents for young girls, who can none of them be taught too early to take a great pride in their bedrooms, and to accumulate there their own belongings in the way of pictures, books, and ornaments. I love to see a girl 'house-proud,' as the Germans say; and my own house, when I married first, was made habitable only because of the judicious manner in which my dear mother had impressed on me to take care of, and pride in, the many little sketches, engravings, and photographs I used to have given me. We were exceptionally lucky in that way, as of course we had a great many artistic friends; but still, all girls should remember they may have houses of their own, and always must have one room of their own, and should be taught to pride themselves on having pretty and artistic chambers sacred to their own use.

Naturally two sisters often have to occupy one room, but this need not alter the idea, and I would rather a girl cared for her room, and collected pictures, books, and china for that, than see her crave for ornaments and jewellery, which can give but very little pleasure as contrasted with pretty and delightfully artistic surroundings.

Angelina's task of making her bedroom pretty will be so much lightened if she has begun collecting treasures as soon as she was promoted to a room to herself, that I may, perhaps, be forgiven if I impress this fad of mine on all my readers, young and old; for mothers of growing daughters can perhaps benefit by an idea that may be useful to them, and of which it is just possible they may not have thought themselves; and I should let (as I do let) my daughter begin her collection as soon as she is old enough to value having her very own things, even to the sheets, pillow-cases, and towels, which she can embroider herself, and to a small collection of silver and china and pictures, added to, on birthdays and at Christmas, with an eye to a house of her own some day; or even a couple of rooms, when she may end an honoured career of 'old maidism,' made all the lighter and pleasanter by the store of pleasant memories secured to her by her possessions, which thus serve a double duty, and are both artistic and useful too.

If Angelina cannot afford pictures in any way, she can, no doubt, afford brackets. These are very cheap indeed in carved wood (which can be painted to match the room), would hold a scrap of blue and white china, and can be made even more decorative if surrounded by a 'trophy' or artistic arrangement of the ever-useful Japanese fans, one of which should be covered with silk and plush, and made into a bed-pocket for handkerchief, watch, or keys, although I like my watch in evidence, as then one sees exactly what time it is, and if it is the hour to rise, or to put out the gas, if one indulges, as I do, in the fascinating but wrong habit of reading in bed. I have a long bookcase in my room, as shown in the drawing on page 72, and this is full of bound magazines to fall back upon, should my own book be exhausted before I feel inclined to go to sleep. Even if the windows are open the serge curtains should be drawn, I think, unless one requires to get up very early, as I do not believe the brain ever really rests if there be much light in the room. That is another objection to blinds; they are never *dark enough*. The serge curtains are cheaper, and keep out the strongest sunlight there is.

I do not think what are generically known as 'short blinds' ever look nice in any bedroom. I can remember, however, when to have white curtains there to match, or in some measure go with those in the rest of the house, was considered the height of reckless extravagance, and a sure index of the bad financial position of the person who was sinful enough to indulge in them!

Of course if we live with opposite neighbours' eyes straight upon us we must cover our windows, or run the risk of being seen at our toilet; but even then we can curtain them by using the frequently advised double fixed rods, either covering the lower sash entirely with a full fluted blind of coloured Liberty muslin, or by draping the entire window—always the prettiest way of setting to work—with frilled muslin curtains meeting down the centre and almost covering the glass, at all events covering it completely if it be necessary to do so (see page 60). And now opinion on this subject has changed so much, we can afford to have our windows all look alike without exciting dismal prophecies from people who really know nothing at all about us.

Remember no house can possibly look pretty where white curtains are conspicuous by their absence, any more than a girl can look pretty if she has neither nice frilling or spotless collar and cuffs as a finish to her costume. And by white curtains I mean muslin curtains of almost any colour, with some white in them. Dark *thin* curtains are an abomination, I think. I once lived opposite some dark green muslin ones that made me always feel the owners were dirty people, although I knew quite well they were not. Muslin and guipure curtains, nicely made and fixed, are my pet curtains, and next to these come Liberty's printed muslins and cheap artistic muslins, though I have seen soft-hued silks used to great advantage in town houses; but this is, I should think, far too expensive for us, modest beginners as we are. White Madras muslin is not economical, as it cannot be said to wash well. It shrinks, pulls crooked, and generally loses all its colour in a most distressing manner the first, and always the second, time it pays a visit to the laundress, and if we cannot have guipure and muslin we must fall back on plain or printed muslin only. Cretonne curtains for a bedroom must invariably be lined if no blinds are used; and a very good thing to do in a very sunny room is to put an inner lining of very dark green twill inside the cretonne lining, so that it shall not show, thus insuring the darkness that I consider so necessary in a sleeping-room, the brain, as I said before, refusing absolutely to rest if much light comes across the eyes, and this is why a bed should never face the window, as this insures light of some sort falling on the face of the sleeper.

To sum up briefly, one's bedroom should be pretty, tasteful, and quiet, and should be as much thought about and kept as carefully as the grandest sitting-room we possess; and I may further mention, for those who cannot purchase Aspinall's enamel in hedge-sparrow's-egg blue, that a very decent substitute can be made from Prussian blue, middle Brunswick green, white lead, oil, and varnish, and just a little black paint or ochre to tone it all down. This must be mixed until the colour is precisely that of a hedge-sparrow's egg or very old turquoise, and is very troublesome to get right; therefore the above receipt will only be really of use to those of my colonial readers who may not be able to obtain Mr. Aspinall's invaluable enamels for home-decoration.

CHAPTER XII
DRESSING-ROOM

There is no doubt in my mind that the proper furniture for Edwin's dressing-room has not yet been evolved out of the inner consciousness of some enterprising and clever designer of dressing-tables and wardrobes. Of course there are plenty of so-called gentlemen's wardrobes, but I have never yet found one that was perfectly satisfactory, and if any one knows of one I should be very glad to hear from that happy creature.

I am quite sure gentlemen's coats should never be suspended from hooks, for if they are hung up there is always an unpleasant bulge in the collar, and it is impossible to keep the wretched things in shape; almost as impossible as it is to make a man look nice unless he has a valet to look after his clothes, brush them, fold them, and, in fact, turn him out respectably, with a neatly folded, clean umbrella and decent hat—that is to say, the ordinary male, who has business occupations, and gets up at the very last moment he can, to be able to snatch his breakfast and then catch his train.

I have, personally, no very expensive yearnings, but when I see one who shall be nameless in a coat that looks as if it had voyaged up the chimney and back, nether garments that, to put it mildly, have seen better days, and a hat that would disgrace the Sunday get-up of his own coachman, and hear that no one is to touch the venerable accumulation in a wardrobe upstairs, I do long for a good, strong-minded man-servant indoors who would see to his master's clothes, and insist on their being worn properly and treated decently.

This sounds like straying from the subject, but it really is not, for one unanswerable argument which puts a stop to a great deal of my eloquence is, 'If I had a decent place to keep my clothes in I should always look respectable.' Now, my readers shall give me their opinion as to the decency, or otherwise, of the accommodation afforded to this nameless individual.

In the first place, there is a charming-looking wardrobe in ash. The top is embellished by a ledge, on which artistic pottery is meant to stand, but where at this present moment repose a microscope, a lamp, very grimy and full of dreadful-looking oil that no one may touch, several dusty piles of lectures and reports of divers societies, and on the plain space below are at least five paper bandboxes, containing old and dilapidated hats, all more or less suggestive of Noah's ark and scarecrows; yet one and all far too precious to give away, and which no one dare touch, on pain of instant death.

One half of this wardrobe is lined with striped calico, against the dust, and is used for hanging up coats, dressing-gowns, &c., and where there is quite a crowd of the most hideous old coats, all too precious to part with—I can't think why—and then on the other side there is a deep space sacred to trousers, and three deep drawers besides, for shirts and under-garments of all kinds. Now this is actually not sufficient accommodation, and I have other drawers in the bedroom itself, where stores of summer or winter raiment, as the case may be, repose; and the dress things are also in yet another place; but I do think it is rather a mistake to have so much space for spoiling coats by hanging them up, and I am thinking of having shelves put in in that division, and seeing if that will be any good at all, though, as it is so much easier to hang up a coat than to fold it up, I much fear there will be strenuous opposition to that plan—at least at the first.

A wardrobe is a necessity in a dressing-room—unless one is lucky enough to find a good deep cupboard there already—and they can be bought at all prices. The one described above was about 10*l.*, and is certainly very pretty, but I am sure it is nothing like as useful or as well arranged as it ought to be, and I have one in the nursery, which is all drawers and shelves, that cost 4*l.* 10*s.*, and is hideous, which I am thinking of having painted turquoise blue, and adding brass handles and substituting this for the ash one, which can go nicely into the spare room, where it will no longer be desecrated with all sorts of débris being placed where pretty china is meant to go. There is one piece of furniture, invented by Mr. Watts, of Grafton Street, Tottenham Court Road, W., which is, however, perfect for a dressing-room, and therefore deserves more than a word of mention.

It is a combination of dressing-table and washing-stand that is simply invaluable. A long glass starts on the right-hand side from three drawers, with a place for brushes and combs, while on the left is ample space for washing, with a high tiled back, and a species of shelf to hold bottles, glasses, &c. There is also a deep space under the marble shelf on which the jug and basin stand, meant for boots, and covered in with a cretonne curtain on a brass rod, and is altogether as charming, artistic-looking, and useful a piece of furniture as any one would wish; it costs 6*l.* 10*s.* in stained deal, is beautifully made, and would not only be useful in a dressing-room, but in a young girl's room or any small place where there really is not sufficient accommodation for both washing-stand and toilet-table. I have narrow tapestry mats trimmed with ball fringe on the shelves, but I should not like to say how many have been wanted there, for men never can remember that wet sponges should be put in the sponge-dish and not on the new covers, or that brushes are best in the drawers intended for them, and not for sundry bits and scraps of paper, old soiled gloves, spoiled white ties, cartridges, fly-books, bits of gut, string, 'objects' for microscopes, and other nastinesses 'too numerous to mention,' as the auctioneers say when they have come to the end of their descriptive resources.

And, *apropos* of this, let me beg Angelina never to allow accumulations in either small or big drawers if she can possibly help it; nothing breeds moths or harbours dust like this, and I should advise her occasionally to brave Edwin's wrath, and turn out on her own account, if he is obdurate, and will keep every scrap and shred of rubbish that has ever come into his possession, because he cannot believe a time will not come when the possession of a few inches of paper, string, or catgut will be of paramount importance to him, and when a store of old clothes will stand between him and utter and entire destitution of raiment.

Now, without emulating a silly little friend of mine, who was only saved by the difference of a pot of snowdrops from bartering her bridegroom's best coat for a supply of flowers, with one of those engaging gentlemen who frequent the suburbs with a supply of blossoms, warranted to fade and die utterly within the space of twenty-four hours, I would strongly suggest a little dissimulation to Angelina, should Edwin prove the orthodox hoarder of old clothes that it appears to me, from judicious questioning, most men are.

Angelina should make a point of remembering the date of Edwin's coats, and should mark them in an invisible place (on the lining of the inside of the sleeve is the best) with the date of the purchase; and with this triumphant proof of her accuracy should she face and utterly confound Edwin when he meets her request for the coat to be given away, with the remark, '*That* coat! What can you be thinking of? I only bought it a month or two ago!' He is often so flabbergasted at learning the treasure is at least eighteen months old that he says no more, and allows Angelina to bear it off to gladden the heart of some old pensioner, on whose back it somehow looks so extremely well that Edwin cannot believe Angelina was right in her dates, and at every opportunity points out its excellent appearance on Jones or Styles as a proof of her reckless extravagance.

A little careful stealing from a husband who is an inveterate hoarder, and will not even succumb to the uncontradictable date, can be practised to advantage, and at the risk of exposing my own wickedness, and believing that a male eye rarely, if ever, falls upon my words of wisdom, I may tell

Angelina in the very strictest confidence how I have sometimes been driven to circumvent the nameless one spoken of before.

I have watched the gradual overflow of the wardrobe—ay, even on to the floor and the three chairs, and, biding my time, have neatly arranged the drawers, being quite sure I shall be asked immediately what I have done with all the precious things, missed the moment the dressing-room is entered. I disclose them arranged elsewhere, and after a week or two, when the gardener and the coachman's children have been scanned surreptitiously but eagerly to see if I have already given these valuable relics away, they become forgotten, or are only asked after occasionally; then, as time goes on, they are quite forgotten, and if asked for after three months cannot be found, as they are already doing duty elsewhere, under new and altered circumstances. Old boots it is almost impossible to get rid of without a positive battle, though how a man's happiness or welfare depends on knowing he has fourteen pairs of dreadful old boots under the kitchen dresser, to say nothing of as many more concealed in his own room and his dressing-room, is really more than I can understand, and must be one of those problems of life we are compelled to take as such, and leave for time to solve, if it possibly can.

I do not think it is of the very smallest use to give Edwin anything pretty of his 'very own,' as the children say, in his dressing-room. It is always a narrow, circumscribed spot, and brackets are apt to be knocked askew and their contents smashed, picture-glasses also coming in for similar hard treatment, while extra shelves for books are soon overloaded, and come rattling down in the dead of night, taking at least ten years off one's life with the awful fright received.

Therefore, if Edwin have a really nice wardrobe, a chair, and a dressing-table and washing-stand combined, as described previously, it is really all he wants, unless, of course, the room be a good size, when the walls can be decorated at will. Equally, of course, the wall-paper and the dado should match the bedroom, and here more than anywhere else should be the substantial dado of either cretonne or matting, as here the walls get mysterious knocks and indentations even more than they do in the passages and bedrooms.

If the bath has to be taken in the dressing-room—and sometimes even now old houses have not bath-rooms—the bath should stand on a large square of oilcloth, covered by a 'bath blanket.' This should be taken up and dried, and the oilcloth wiped carefully, as soon as the bath is emptied, or both will soon rot and be spoiled.

Very nice 'bath blankets' are made by taking the old-gold and dark brown blankets one buys of Mansergh and Sons, Lancaster, from 3*s.* to 11*s.* 6*d.* a pair, according to size, though those at 7*s.* a pair are the best size. A piece should be cut from one end to make the blanket square; and one of Francis's conventional designs should be ironed off in each corner, which is then worked over in either outline or a thick 'rope' or twisted chain-stitch, in double crewels, in about two or three colours. For instance, old gold looks well with the work in two shades of brown crewels, with a dash of dull blue; the brown blankets with golden crewels with, perhaps, a dash of red. But as it is rather difficult to get the design clearly on the rough, fuzzy blanket, an easier style is in cross-stitch. The canvas must be very coarse, and tacked to the blanket. An edging, as well as corners, looks nice, and the canvas threads must be pulled out afterwards. I think a big cross-stitch, monogram, or cypher looks nice. The edges of the blanket can be either button-holed over or hemmed with a line of cross-stitch defining the hem. These blankets are a great ornament to a bath or dressing-room, and are invaluable in any room where the bath must be taken in the room itself.

CHAPTER XIII
SPARE ROOMS

I think it is a most excellent plan to have the bedrooms on one floor of a house furnished as much as possible alike; that is to say, if economy be an object, and also if, as in several houses I know, the rooms open out either on a square landing or into a corridor that leads past them all.

Of course, the papers need not be alike, neither need they all have cretonne dados; but the paint should harmonise, and so should the wall-coverings, while the curtains and carpets should be identically the same; as if one have to move, or the cretonnes shrink in the wash, and the carpets become worn in patches, one thing can be made to supplement the other, and so a large outlay to replace old things—always the most worrying kind of outlay, I think—is avoided.

I have been constantly much entertained at seeing the shifts people have been put to to prevent things wearing out, but perhaps quite the most hideous thing seen in this way was a succession of extra bits of carpet edged all round with woolly black fringe to simulate mats, which were arranged on every spot on the carpet where especial wear could be expected, and these monstrosities were carefully put by each side of the bed, and in front of the looking-glass, washing-stand, and fireplace, with an especial tiny dab by the door. The consequence was that, when one was dressed for dinner in a long garment, all these mats were neatly rolled up in different corners of the room, and not only looked hideous, but were positively useless.

Now I see no use in preparing these species of save-alls in a room that is not always in use. If a thing be worn, then cover it; but I can't bear anything to be covered over to be saved. Better let all fade decently together, and do your patching out of a second carpet or a second material that has already done duty in another room. It is useless, I think, to cover handsome things; much better rub down the gorgeousness and subdue the splendour altogether, for nothing looks worse or, in my eyes, more atrociously vulgar than a room utterly unlike one's usual chamber, grandly prepared for the reception of 'company.' Once one's acquaintances and friends are given satin chairs to sit on, instead of the usual cretonne, they become bores to me at least, and, unless they can be satisfied to see me as I always am, I would rather they stayed away. There is always a stiffness and uncomfortableness in any gathering to entertain which we have felt it necessary to uncover our chairs.

In the same way let us in our upper chambers wear our things out equally. Splashers have become almost unknown since the invention of the high tiled-backed washing-stands, and so in another way mats have ceased to exist because bath-rooms are now almost universal possessions, and as most people—I will not say all—know how to behave themselves in one's house, there is no need even to put down the conventional square by the washing-stand that really was necessary when a washing-stand was one's only chance of properly performing one's ablutions.

Now most people have bath-rooms; but, if they have not, the bath can be prepared in the same way in the bedroom as described in our last chapter for the dressing-room.

I think every one who possibly can should possess something in the shape of a spare room, although, as I remarked in one of my former chapters, I have suffered so much from my visitors that I approach the subject feeling as if I at least could not have very much sympathy with it. And in no case will I advise any one to set apart for the use of the occasional visitor one of the best rooms in the house, as is far too often the case in those houses where the spare room should be either the nursery itself or a room for some of the children of the house! I have once or twice been literally so horrified at finding the room I should have at once given for the children set apart for visitors as a matter of course, and quite without a second thought, that I am compelled to speak rather more emphatically, perhaps, on this subject than I otherwise should do; but, after all, the house is the children's home, and for their sake I must beg attention from those who, as a matter of course, take the best rooms themselves, the second and third best for visitors, and then any rooms that may be over for the little ones, keeping the worst of all for 'the boys,' as if boys were raging beasts, to be put out of sight and hearing as far as ever the limits of the house would allow. Whilst recognising that a spare room is a necessary and pleasant thing, at once, so as to disarm criticism, I must ask my kind, good readers to ponder for a moment on what putting aside the very best room for one's friends means in an ordinary building where there are at the most three or four rooms on the floor above the 'reception' rooms, to use a house-agent's term, which said term means a great deal more than perhaps meets the eye at first.

It means keeping empty, perhaps, three parts of the year the brightest and most cheerful apartments, and it means relegating the children to inferior rooms, which, with a little taste and common-sense, can be made pretty, comfortable, and charming for your friends, who come presumably to see you, and not to spend the best part of their time in their bedrooms, for if they do they may just as well have stopped at home.

Now there is a great deal, to my mind, that can be written about the ethics of visiting that insensibly calls for attention, when we ponder over that problem of a spare room, and that may perhaps not be out of place, so I dwell for a few moments upon them before going into the decorative details of this particular chamber. One of the latest fads of social life is to do away with introductions at parties, and another is to ask people to stay with us, and, from the moment they enter our doors to the moment they leave them, to go on with our own occupations and engagements, exactly as if we had no friends staying with us; or rather as if we kept an hotel, and the comings in and goings out of our guests had no more to do with us than have those of the people staying in an inn to the people who keep it.

Perhaps the position and the luxurious comfort of the chamber prepared for their reception—half sitting-room, half bedroom as it is—suggests to the guest more than it is meant to do, and therefore should be altered before hospitality has ceased from the face of the earth and become a mere empty mockery.

I have often enough seen all sorts and descriptions of ideas for writing tables and other conveniences in a spare room, but of this I will have none; if I ask people to come and see me I want them to be with me, and not in their own rooms half the time; and letters can surely be written either in my company, or in the dining-room, should I be occupied in my own sanctum: while work of all sorts can be brought down after breakfast, when the members of the male sex have gone off to business, and there need be no reason for secluding oneself in one's bedroom to do one's mending.

I maintain that guests staying in one's house should be treated to what servants call company manners, and that we should make a difference for them, and try and make their visits pleasant to them, considering that they have come to us for a holiday; that leaving them to themselves, and going our own way while they go theirs, is distinctly averse to all the laws of old-fashioned and true hospitality; and that by making the spare room into a species of boudoir we appear to hint to them that we do not want them with us, except after dinner or for the afternoon drive, or really on any occasion when we can possibly do without them.

I should take as nice a room as I could for my guests after my children's convenience has been thought of—I like mine as near me as possible, and if possible on the same floor, with a schoolroom upstairs, a most invaluable possession in childish ailments, when change of room is wanted without any risks of draughts run by going downstairs—and though, of course, our proverbial bride and bridegroom will not have to think of all this for some years to come, I find I have had so many readers beside the bride for whom I meant to write this book that I cannot help being a little discursive for their sakes, the while I beg Angelina not to take the best room in the house for her guests, because she will hesitate so very much more, if she does, over dismantling the pretty room when the 'king comes' to his kingdom, and Miss or Master Baby arrives to rule the household with an iron rod.

Some of the charming painted suites of furniture are as nice as anything for the spare room, and take a great deal of raiment, and I strongly advise Angelina always to ask her guests if the boxes may be removed from the room. As soon as they are unpacked they can be put in the box-room until required, even if the visit is only for a few days, for a dirty travelling trunk can do a great deal of mischief, and, if put against the wall, has often enough ruined the paper, and dug holes in the plaster by being continually opened and shut as things were taken in and out. The paper and paint of the spare room should be a matter for great and careful consideration, too, and here I very strongly advise a dado of some kind or other. I always advise a dado in a bedroom of cretonne or matting, however the bed is placed, as nothing saves the walls so long from the tender mercies of the housemaid, and so keeps the room looking nice.

I heard of a bedroom in the country the other day that seemed to me the very ideal bedroom for a guest. The paint was white, and the paper was the very faintest possible shade of eau-de-Nil. There was a dado of eau-de-Nil and white chintz, with, I believe, a pattern of lilies-of-the-valley on, and the curtains were of the same. The bed had an eider-down quilt in green silk— rather extravagant this—and the furniture was all in white wood, with green and white mats &c. about. The effect in summer was simply perfect. I am, however, afraid in winter the effect would be too cold; but to be equally pleasant then, however, the cold effect could be obviated by putting pink cretonne curtains instead of the green chintz, and putting pink mats and a pink cover to the eider-down; but the pink must be very carefully chosen, and be either very faint or else almost terra-cotta, or it would look tawdry, I am sure.

The eider-down should always have a cover made of cretonne, like that used for the curtains, or else of a contrasting hue. The usual cover for an eider-down in turkey red would spoil any room, and as a motive of economy, if not of beauty, an extra cover is a very good thing; it makes the eider-down wear twice as long, and is able to be washed, a great advantage to anything that has to do with a bed.

There should always be four pillows and four or five good blankets to the spare-room bed, three pairs of sheets, the top one edged with Cash's patent frilling two inches wide, and a large red monogram on the centre of the top sheet, and at least twelve pillow-cases, with four extra ones frilled, and with monograms in the centre, which should be removed at bedtime and folded up. The counterpane should be a honeycomb one, with a deep fringe all round, and these are the only counterpanes that should be bought for real use. They always look very much better than any others, and look as well after they are washed as they do before. A Madras muslin quilt thrown over the bed in summer looks very nice; in winter the eider-down is all that is required, though I dare say I shall shock my readers by telling them that I never put away my eider-downs anywhere through the house in summer. I rarely find it warm enough at night, sleeping as I do with my windows open, to do without them.

If we can only afford one spare room, that room should have a double bed in, as often married folk would like to come to us for a night or two, and I have found it very awkward myself, never being able to take in any one, save a girl or a young man, because I personally have in my present house no such accommodation, and a small room does not matter for one night, if the bed be comfortable and large enough.

Maple's brass or black and brass bedsteads and 'Excelsior' mattresses are the most inexpensive bedsteads I know; a brass one should be chosen if one can afford this possibly, but a very nice black and brass one can be bought for 2*l*. 5*s*.; mattress ('Excelsior') at 2*l*. 9*s*.; hair mattress at 3*l*. 10*s*.; bolster at 17*s*. 6*d*., and good pillows at 5*s*. each. A room can be nicely and entirely furnished for 34*l*. 9*s*. 8*d*. in good furniture that will wear, though, of course, cheaper and less reliable furniture may be purchased. I actually hear that at Cardiff excellent suites of furniture in walnut can be bought for 12*l*., but I must believe these are simply veneered, and will fall to pieces at the least move or the smallest amount possible of wear and tear. There is no doubt that a great deal of thought has to be expended on a spare room, but there is not the smallest doubt that it ought to look as nice without (please forgive me for being insistent on this) suggesting a sitting-room, that our guests should feel at home in it at once. A flowery paper, like the old-fashioned chintzes, is bright and pleasant, but must not be too scrawly, or it will not be nice should sickness overtake our guest; but it should be lively and charming, and suggestive of pleasant thoughts, and then I am sure we shall be repaid by hearing our friends exclaim, 'Oh, what a sweet room! Why, I feel rested already.'

And now let me whisper one or two little sentences in Angelina's ear, suggested by what I have let slip above about possible sickness overtaking a guest, for very few people ever contemplate this side of the guest-chamber question.

It may be terribly bad for such a thing to happen in our new sweet room, but, however horrid it is for us, let us all recollect it is just one thousand times worse for the unfortunate 'sick and ill,' as the children say; for, in addition to his or her own pain and sufferings, he has the mental agony of knowing he has committed the one unpardonable sin, and that he has dared to fall sick in some one else's house, that he is some miles from his own doctor (and who believes, I should like to know, in any one's doctor except one's very own?), and that servants, hostess, and host are all vowing vengeance on him for his untoward behaviour.

But it is on such occasions as this that the hostess rises to the occasion, shows her real self, and demonstrates the true lengths to which a hospitable soul will go. She laughs his apologies to scorn, declares she loves nursing, and so manages that the convalescent blesses the hour when he fell ill under such tender handling, and in consequence improves twice as soon as he otherwise would have done, had he fretted and worried over the bother he was giving, and had he been shown plainly he was as great a nuisance as he undoubtedly is.

I am not writing on this subject 'without book,' as the saying is. Naturally we should all exclaim indignantly, We should all do our very best for any one who falls ill under our care; and you, most of you, smile at me, doubtless, for daring to insinuate you would not; but I know cases where, especially to relatives, the hostess's conduct was so chillingly all it ought to be, so freezingly polite, so intent on perpetually telling the unfortunate he was no trouble at all, in a martyr's voice, that disclosed all her words sought to conceal, that I must be forgiven if I say it needs real Christian charity, and the heart and temper of a saint, to show real hospitality when sickness happens; and it will not do any harm for any of us to contemplate circumstances in which we may all of us some day be placed.

One other special thing to remember as regards the spare room is that it must always be in such order that, if necessary, it can be ready for occupation in half an hour. I knew a most excellent housekeeper who, scarcely before the last box of her friend had been carried downstairs, had put her room into 'curl-papers' as it were, carefully banishing everything from the light of day until such times as it was necessary to prepare the chamber once more, with much ceremony, for a new-comer.

Now I much object to this sort of thing. When I have brought a pleasant visit to an end in a friend's house, it gives me a positive pang to see the pillows bereft of their cases and the bed of its sheets, and all covered over with a species of holland pinafore. I hate to see the toilet-covers taken off and folded up; and though this may be done when I am not there to see, it gives me such an unpleasant feeling that I never have the courage to put my spare room to bed; a room shrouded, gloomy, and unoccupied in a house always seeming to me like the unpleasant corpse of bygone pleasure, and as such to be strenuously avoided.

Then another reason, besides the mere sentimental one of disliking to see that one's visit is really over and done with, is that such a dismantling of the room often puts it out of one's power to entertain a sudden or unexpected guest, who comes down perhaps to dinner, and would be glad to spend the night, that may have turned out wet or cold, or that pleasantest of all pleasant visits, the Saturday to Monday sojourn, becomes impossible too, for it is not worth while to get the room ready for such a short time, when so much of Saturday would be taken up in airing the beds, and unpinning and putting up curtains, and shaking out toilet-covers, &c.

Now if the room be always straight, and requires nothing but the sheets on the bed, there is no trouble in the matter, and we are neither flurried ourselves nor allow our guests to be uncomfortably conscious that their arrival has made any difference to our domestic arrangements at all. I am quite sure, too, that it is a most excellent thing for most people to have some one staying in the house with them occasionally; much, secretly, as I dislike it myself, excusing myself to myself for my boorishness by saying my work prevents me being really able to entertain my visitors, still I never part with a guest without quite as secretly acknowledging that it has done us all an immense amount of good to be shaken out of our grooves—ay, even if our own special chair has been taken, and the newspapers read and the magazines cut before I have looked at them, another fad of mine, for, *entre nous*, nothing tries my otherwise angelic temper more than for some one to read out choice bits of news before I have seen them myself, or to read all the magazines before I have carefully gone over them, peeping at the pictures, and reading here and there a scrap, before settling down to them regularly one after the other.

One cannot help recognising these evil habits even in one's own self, and knowing that nothing makes a person more selfish, and therefore more unendurable, than to have no one to interfere with one's puerile little fancies and equally puerile little rules and regulations! In a small household rules and regulations that touch the servants, of course, must be simply 'Median and Persian,' or the house would never get along at all; but it puts no one out except ourselves, should we have to take the left side of the fireplace instead of the right, and it does us more good than I can say to have to control our small irritations at having our routine of life broken into, and to be shown that the world will not stop if we do go out in the morning instead of the afternoon, and that nothing appalling will happen should we be obliged to talk at breakfast, instead of, as usual, burying ourselves in our letters and our papers generally.

A constant supply of guests for the night, or on the Saturday-to-Monday principle, insures a constant change in our ideas and thoughts, and does away with that 'Englishman's house is his castle' notion that is so very pernicious, and that puts a stop to so much inexpensive and common-sense hospitality; while a new, cheerful face at the dinner-table relieves the strain of domesticity between husband and wife, and often insures a game of chess, or music, instead of the books and silence which would otherwise, perhaps, have been the order of the day.

Another thing also to recollect about the spare room, too, is, not to get into the habit of using the shelves and drawers in the wardrobe as a species of store-place. I know nothing more enraging than to be shown into a charming-looking room, with a beautiful great cupboard, and a gallant chest of drawers, that seem to promise us ample breathing-room for one's things, and to discover half the space we were so very gleefully looking forward to appropriating is already taken up by all sorts and conditions of household plenishing, or of last year's garments, or even the garments of the year before. I remember quite well once having such a receptacle turned out for me; and I saw carried away, the hostess's wedding dress and veil of some ten years back, all the long clothes and short clothes of the babies, small and great, several venerable opera-cloaks and fans, and, finally, a store of old linen put by against emergencies. You can all of you imagine what I endured. Not that I should have asked for this to be done, by the way, but the maid came in to take my boxes, and I was obliged to say I could not part with them, because if I did I should have nowhere to put my belongings. Of course this insured the shelves being cleared, with the uncomfortable result to me described above. I never dared ask what had become of all I had turned out, but I cut my visit short and went on somewhere else, I felt so unhappy at thinking of all the unfortunate garments bereft of their usual resting-place.

The spare room should be a cheerful, flowery-looking room, as, indeed, should all bedrooms if possible, and, if a sofa cannot be squeezed in, one of Maple's charming sofa-ottomans should be put there, and also an arm-chair and small table for books &c., for one's guests sometimes have headaches, and, especially if we live in town and have up our country cousins, require occasionally half an hour's rest after a long day's sight-seeing; or after the drive in the sleepy country air, if the cases are reversed, and we, in our turn, are country cousins entertaining our London friends with our own special sights and sounds.

No matter where the house is situated, every bedroom window should open at the top. This in London obviates a great many blacks flying in, as they do when the sash is thrown wide open at the bottom; an inch at the top seems to do more good than a yard anywhere else, and in the country prevents the deluges and spoiled paint and carpets caused by a sudden storm in the night, or, indeed, in the daytime, when the open window allows the tempest to enter bodily, as it were—unrecognised in the night, of course, unless one is awakened by any specially violent gust; and unseen by the housemaid in the day, who, whoever she may be, never seems to remember that such weather means that the windows should be immediately closed.

Every single thing belonging to the spare room should be religiously kept for its own use: the brass can for hot water, the palm-leaf soiled-linen basket, the little black cupboard for boots, which also serves as a table, the pin-trays, and the pincushion—all should never be allowed to stray away, and matches in a box nailed to the wall should also never be forgotten any more than the candles in their fixed stands, and the various little ornaments upon the mantelpiece, which should include a very regularly wound and most trustworthy clock.

If possible, I should have some pretty framed photographs on the wall, and, above all, a small bookcase, with a cupboard below for medicine and toilet bottles. I cannot bear the look of bottles standing about, and, besides that, medicine bottles are apt to be put down after the medicine is poured out, and sundry drops run down, and a sticky ring is left on the new toilet-cover as a reminder of one's guest, which is not as nice as one could wish. The medicine cupboard conveys a hint the most obtuse must take, and, as they only cost about 6s. 9d., are within the reach of almost every one. A few judiciously chosen amusing novels and good poetry can well be spared for the spare room, and often are of considerable service to guests who may not go about provided with their own literature. Reading often will lure back sleep, or pass away an hour profitably; and should we breakfast later or go to bed earlier than our guest is accustomed to at home, he takes a book and forgets he is waiting, and blesses instead of 'cusses' the difference in our household routine.

It seems to me even now that I have not said half as much on the mere relation of guest to host and hostess as I could have done, though I have hardly yet mentioned the word 'furniture,' so a few more hints may be dropped here. Never should any one be allowed to come to stay without the hostess herself seeing that a new nice square of soap is in the newly-washed soap-dish; that the towels are folded right, the water fresh and pure in the ewer, and also in the artistic jug, bought, if she be wise, at Douglas's, in Piccadilly, in tints to match the ewer; and making sure all is perfectly clean and in order. A small glass of flowers should stand on the toilet-table as a special greeting to one's friend, and all should suggest that personal thought and care has been given to the special shrine set apart for his or her reception.

I wonder who ever forgets their first visit from home, or who can cease to remember the sense of importance given to us, who once were brides, when our first guest arrived to stay with us, and inspect our new home, which we were then perfectly convinced was far prettier, neater, brighter, and more redolent of love and perfection than any place had ever been before, or could possibly be in the future. Ah! thank Heaven for memory! *Tout lasse, tout passe, tout casse*, but memory never dies; and if we in our first start in life have charming surroundings and pleasant homes, even if they only are of the simplest nature, as long as we live they are ours, and none can ever take them away from us.

Then another thing in the spare room to be particularly looked to is the arrangement for lighting it. Here gas is a *sine quâ non*. Candles are most dangerous; a careless guest drops the grease about, or maids cannot resist taking them about too, and more harm is done by candles in a house than almost anything else. At the same time, if gas be not laid on anywhere, the useful brass fixed brackets for candles are necessary; but they should be fixed one or two above the looking-glass, one above the bed, and one above the washing-stand, all the candles guarded by glass shields, and none loose, able to be carried about in a careless or heedless way. If there be no gas, a nightlight should always be provided, with a bracket for its reception, for there are some people who cannot sleep without a light, and nothing is so disagreeable as to have to ask for these little things, and to find that by making such a request we have upset the whole house; though, if a guest be thoughtful, and has these little fads, she should take nightlights &c. about with her. A quite model guest of mine the other day arrived with her own hot-water bottle. Could thoughtfulness go further than this?

If gas be in the house, there should always be a bracket as near the bed as possible. It cannot hurt any one to read in bed if there be no danger of setting the house on fire; and I am so fond of this pernicious habit, and feel so unhappy myself if I cannot indulge in it, that I always, if possible, make provision for my guests to read too, if they are 'so minded,' as the people in Dorsetshire always say.

So, before I describe one or two other arrangements of colours that might be tried in the spare room, I may mention two things that should never be lacking there. One is a clock; the other a list of the hours of the household and the postal arrangements—two things that will go some way to insure punctuality.

I could at once sit down and write a chapter all to itself on the inestimable blessings of punctuality, and the extreme rudeness of being unpunctual in the house of a friend.

In a small, or indeed in any ordinary, house, unpunctuality means disorder and waste of time, and, in consequence, of money. It means loss of temper both for mistress and servants, and it means throwing out all the little rules and routine on which so much depends. If a clock be provided in the spare room the two pet excuses, 'Oh! I forgot to wind my watch,' or 'My watch lost an hour in the night,' are done away with; while the hours of breakfast &c. contain a hint that cannot well be lost on the most obtuse person possible.

What does being late for breakfast mean? Let all lie-a-beds think over that problem, and if they cannot solve it for themselves, if they apply to me I will do so for them.

After all is said and done, I think blue and some shades of green (not arsenical shades—pray remember that) are the most restful colours for bedrooms, though terra-cotta can be used to great advantage in rooms where there is not much sun, and, while I like ivory paint if judiciously used with a brilliant paper, I cannot imagine anything more wretched than the little white bedroom old-time heroines used to rush up to, and cast themselves down in, when their lovers proved faithless and they wished to be alone. Nothing is colder-looking and more *un*restful than white, and I do not like for a bedroom these white-enamelled suites of furniture that one can buy. I much prefer them enamelled turquoise blue. Nothing is so pretty as this for a spare room, or the room set apart for the daughter of the house, except, of course, good ash furniture with brass fittings. This I should always have, were I able to afford it, in all my rooms, for I do not, and never shall, like dark woods or dark furniture in a bedroom, or indeed, as far as that goes, in any room, but a really good light wood is always pleasant to look at, and in consequence is to be preferred to enamelled furniture, which shines terribly somehow, and rather annoys me on the whole. I am now speaking about bedroom furniture not about drawing-room furniture, where the enamelled chairs and cabinets look charming and are all that they ought to be, but simply of the bedroom furniture I would have if one could afford it; but if one cannot afford really beautiful wood, I then much prefer to paint the things a charming colour, than to see common wood or the grained and stained horrors one used to be obliged to put up with, before Aspinall's came to our aid and suggested blue or white, instead of the yellow streaks that were our portion in those unhappy days.

Now here is, I consider, one of the prettiest rooms I have yet succeeded in doing. It has Maple's floral paper, a design that is just as pretty as ever it can be; the paint is all cream-coloured and 'flatted,' so that it washes just as a boarded floor does; there is a red and white matting dado, a dado rail painted cream-colour, and the cretonne, also Maple's, at 1s. 4½d. a yard, almost matches the paper, and looks really charming. The floral paper has a sort of flowery scroll all over it, and at first I was rather afraid it would turn out to be fidgety. I feared the flowers would run after each other over the walls, and refuse to be peaceable and quiet, but they are just what they ought to be, and never seem to move at all, while the cheerful effect of the blues, reds, and creams, that appear to make up the design without interfering with each other in the least, is really wonderful. I have had the ceiling papered with a very pretty blue and white paper, and on the walls I have a great many pictures, and have surrounded the dark over-mantel with Japanese fans and brackets, while the stove and mantelpiece came from Mr. Shuffery, and are, in consequence, all that they ought to be.

I have matting and rugs about the floor, and have light ash furniture, which I think looks better in a bedroom than anything else, and is to be preferred to all enamelled or painted suites, on which I fall back as a *pis aller*, when I cannot afford really good light wood, as I remarked before.

This would make a charming room for the best spare room, particularly if quilt and toilet-cover and pincushion box were covered with Russian embroideries in red and blue; in this case, the towels and sheets and pillow-cases should be worked with red and blue monograms too; in all cases should the towels be worked to match the pillow-cases. This does not take long, and at once gives an air of culture that nothing else does.

Perhaps a few words on the subject of a spare room set apart for bachelors would not be out of place; for young men, as a rule, are so careless that they require special legislating for. A quite charming and very cheap room can be made by using a delightful little blue and white paper sold by Messrs. Chappell and Payne, 11 Queen Street, Cheapside, at 10½d. a piece—it is 1,044; with this a dado of the willow-pattern cretonne could be used, and the paint could be all cream, or the grey-blue of the paper; the ceiling should be terra-cotta, and the floor should be stained, and some dhurries put about; the curtains could be dhurries too, or else terra-cotta 'Queen Anne' cretonne, sold by Burnett, and the furniture simply enamelled grey or terra-cotta. The hours of the household should be prominently displayed over the mantelpiece, while the gas should be placed near the bed to allow of reading, and no candles allowed, else may we run the risk of being burned in our beds; one of Drew's handy little 1s. 6d. lamps with shades being quite enough light should anything be forgotten downstairs, and it should be thought necessary to keep a light in a room, that we can carry about. Candles do an immense amount of damage, and are very costly: two excellent reasons why we should impress upon ourselves and our readers never to use them unless we cannot positively avoid doing so.

CHAPTER XIV
THE SERVANTS' ROOMS

Before I proceed to touch on the most important question of all, that of the nurseries, I will say a few words on the subject of the servants' bedrooms, for these are far too seldom seen by the mistress, who ought to have a regular time for visiting them, and for seeing that all the bedding and furniture generally is in a proper hygienic condition; for, notwithstanding the School Board and the amount of education given nowadays to the poorer classes, I am continually astonished at the careless disregard of the simplest rules of health and cleanliness shown by girls who ought to know a great deal better, and who will keep their kitchens &c. beautifully, yet will heedlessly allow their bedrooms to remain in a state that *ought* to disgrace a resident, nowadays, in Seven Dials.

In the first place, the ceilings of all servants' rooms should be whitewashed once a year, and the walls colour-washed, unless these are papered with the washable sanitary wall-papers that are really hygienic, and which would look well, and are rather nicer than the colour-wash, which is apt to come off on one's clothes; and the floor should be bare of all covering, and should simply have dhurries laid down by each bed, and by the washing-stands &c. Those wash splendidly, and always keep clean and nice, while the curtains at the window should be some cheap cretonne that would wash nicely, and draw and undraw easily, or else they will soon be rendered too shabby for use.

Each servant should have a separate bed, if possible, and that bed should be as comfortable as can be, without being unduly luxurious. The perfection of a bed for a servant, as for any one else, is the chain or wooden-lath mattress arrangement, with a good mattress on it, a pillow or two, and a bolster. No valances or curtains of any kind should be allowed, neither should their own boxes be kept in their rooms. One can give them locks and keys to their chests of drawers and wardrobes; but if their boxes are retained in the room, they cannot refrain somehow from hoarding all sorts of rubbish in them.

I should like myself to give each maid a really pretty room, but at present they are a little hopeless on this subject—as witness the smashed china and battered furniture that greets our alarmed sight at the inspection that should take place at least twice a year—but, alas! it is impossible. No sooner is the room put nice than something happens to destroy its beauty; and I really believe servants only feel happy if their rooms are allowed in some measure to resemble the homes of their youth, and to be merely places where they lie down to sleep as heavily as they can.

The simpler, therefore, a servant's room is furnished the better, and, if possible, a cupboard of some kind should be provided for them where they can hang up their dresses; this will enable them to keep them nice longer than they otherwise would were chairs or a hook on the door the only resting-place provided for the gowns. But, if this be impossible, a few hooks must supplement the chest of drawers, washing-stand, bedchair, and toilet-table with glass, which is all that is required in the room of a maid-servant, whose sheets, pillows, blankets, and other 'portable property' should all be marked with her name, and should be in her individual care as long as she is in your service—that is to say, that the property should be marked 'Cook,' 'Housemaid,' 'Parlourmaid,' &c.; this individualises each single thing, and makes the temporary owner responsible for it, and her alone. The sheets should be changed once in three weeks, also the pillow-cases, while three towels to each maid a week are none too much to allow them to use, do we desire them to be clean. If two or more servants share one room, the washstands and chests of drawers must be as many in number as the inmates of the room; this will save endless discussions and disagreeables, for after all maids are but mortal, and squabbles will arise out of small matters like these, which, ridiculous as they sound, are very often at the bottom of the troubles of those who are constantly changing their servants.

And, while we are on the subject of servants' rooms, I will just make a few remarks on this most intricate subject of domestic management, and will whisper what I really think is at the bottom of a good many of the troubles anent servants that undoubtedly exist. In the first place, mistresses are all too often like the parents of grown-up sons and daughters, who cannot remember that the curled and frilled darlings of the nurseries have become young men and women, and are exchanging the control of the schoolroom for the kindly advice that should never be out of place between parent and children, who, grow as tall as they will, can *never* be as old as those to whom they owe their existence. And inasmuch as parents all too often exercise this control when advice would be so much more in place, so do mistresses control and fret the maids, who would not fret at all were the silk chain, 'Don't you think?' used instead of the arbitrary command, 'I insist on the work being done as I order it.' Then, too, we are all apt to forget how dull the ordinary routine of a servant's life is. True, she has the joy of her morning gossip with the tradesman, and her few hours on Sunday; but that is not much for a young healthy girl, who appreciates pleasure as well as do our tennis-playing, ball-going daughters, and it is much better to try and give her some amusement oneself, instead of winking at the 'evenings out' and furtively stolen absences which most mistresses allow, because, otherwise, their maids would not stay. This can easily be done in these days by any one who lives in or near town; while even in the country there are always excursions to be made, or the county town to be visited, even if there are no picture-galleries or exhibitions as there are in London.

Besides which, servants like to know what is going on, even if they cannot go to things themselves. They fully appreciate being told of what one has seen oneself, and a cheerful account of a visit to London or to the theatre, &c., is as much appreciated by a maid as by the friends we regale with our experiences, who no doubt do not care for the account at all, and only wonder at our foolishness in wasting our time and money.

We have to face a great fact, also: in olden days our mothers as well as their maids were content with very much less than we are. They may have been, and no doubt were, much happier, but that is beside the question, more especially as we cannot return to the 'good old days' even if we would; but the fact remains the same. We have advanced, so have our servants; and when they can beat us at sums and geography, stand too much on our level to be thought of merely as the servants, who are to be content with anything we may choose to give them, and therefore must be treated in an entirely different manner to the old style.

Realise this, and domestic management is much simplified, because if we treat our maids just as we treat ourselves we shall find our trouble almost disappear. I invariably leave my maids a good deal to themselves about their work; and once they know what has to be done, I find it *is* done without my constantly being after them to see whether they have finished what I have told them to do or not; and it is well also to carefully consider what one's housekeeping bills ought to be once and for all, and if the books are less than that, praise the cook; if more, *at once* and firmly demonstrate that this is not right; but be prepared with your facts, and let her see that you really do understand your business, which is to carefully administer your income, and to see that no waste is allowed. It is impossible for one person to tell another what sum she ought to spend per week on her household, as one can only make a guess; individual tastes must be consulted, and people do not eat alike—for example, two or three people in my household never touch butter, one or two never use sugar or tea, and therefore what does for us does not do for the world at large; but for a household of ten persons, including washing, and allowing for a constant flow of visitors, the bills should never exceed 6*l*., and can very often be very much less. It is not well to 'allowance' servants, it is not a nice way of managing, and is no real save; honest servants do not require allowancing, and dishonest ones will not refrain from taking your property because they are only supposed to use just so much, on themselves.

To insure good servants, it is imperative that we should make real friends of those who live under our roof. We may be deceived once now and then; we may even be tricked and cheated, and be tempted to say in our haste that 'the poor in a loomp is bad'; but we must take courage and go on again, being quite sure that sooner or later we shall be rewarded by the love and care of one, if not more, of those who, while dwelling in our midst, too often are quite strangers to us, and are no more to us than the chairs on which we sit, and the tables at which we write.

How often, for example, do we understand the feelings with which a servant enters a new place? Do we recollect that she comes a stranger to strangers; that we have no idea of the hopes and fears, the thoughts and dreads, with which she enters our portals; that she is wondering whether we shall be distrustful or unkind or fairly sympathetic; and that she may spend her first night in tears by the side of a girl who was a complete stranger to her a few hours before, but with whom she will be obliged to spend most of her days and nights, whether she be nice or nasty, clean or the reverse?

We may not be able to save our new maid from this, but we can help her over a very 'tight place' if, when she arrives, we are at home to welcome her, to point out her place in the domestic routine, and to give her a few hints about those with whom she will have to live for the future.

If we had a guest coming among us on equal terms, free of all our pleasures and amusements, would not this be done? Much more, then, should we hold out a welcoming hand to those on whom so very much of our pleasure and comfort depend.

To know how much this is, we must, once now and then, be left without one of our staff—which is, of course, not a very extensive one, or those remarks would not apply. In an extensive staff the relations between mistress and maid are only represented by a housekeeper, who has all on her shoulders, and who must replace the missing maid in the household or do the necessary work herself.

Let, for example, our housemaid be laid aside by illness, or go home for one of her well-earned holidays, and straightway we are miserable. A thousand and one small omissions show us how much she remembered for us. And as we gaze at our dusty writing-table, our chair put in exactly the angle that most offends our eye, our breakfast-table laid in an unaccustomed manner, our letters put just where they never are in ordinary, we feel inclined to count the days that stretch unendingly, it seems to us, between now and her return to work, and we wonder what is before us when that 'young man' claims his bride, who, we are certain, cannot be half as much wanted by him as by us.

Or our cook may suddenly fall out of the ranks, and we get in temporary help. Oh dear! chaos then has most certainly come again. Butter flees, and is conspicuous for its vanishing powers; things have to be told in detail, and we have not succeeded in getting the 'help' into our ways before our own domestic comes back, to show us on what trifles depends the easy-going roll of the chariot wheels of life, that never seem to go so easily as after the jar occasioned by a temporary change of charioteer.

Looking back over a long stretch of life covered by many years of domestic duties, and calmly and dispassionately thinking over the mistakes—how many!—and the successes that have characterised it, I freely confess that when I have failed with our servants (and thankful am I to chronicle only two failures and one of these has since been redeemed by an early marriage), it has been entirely my own fault. A keener insight into character than I possess would have prevented our engaging a girl spoiled for us by a too careless mistress and a wicked master; and more judicious watchfulness would have saved a false step that, as it happened, was discovered in time, but not before the consequences were too apparent to be passed over, and which said false step was entirely due to the evil influence of a fellow-servant, from which we of course should have shielded her. We may accept it as an axiom that we cannot have nice, good servants unless we take the trouble of either training them ourselves, or get them from a mistress who has had an eye over the well-being of her maidens. It is impossible to obtain nice service from those who have never been taught how to serve, who come to us from careless or bad mistresses, and of whom we know no more than they do of us, and our likes and dislikes. If we, when requiring a servant, take the first, or even the second, that applies to us, not heeding where she was born, what her parents are, and knowing still less of her disposition, how can we expect success? We may be lucky enough to hit upon a good servant like this, but we very much doubt that it is likely we should. If mistresses have a large acquaintance it is possible to have a continual supply of good servants without applying to the registry offices; but they themselves must have as good a character as the required domestic, or else they will not be easily suited.

'As good a character, indeed! What is the world coming to?' says one indignant reader.

It is coming, we reply, to a better state of things—ay, even returning to the time when servants were of the household, and in consequence remained years in one place, when nowadays as many months are irksome to them.

Why? Because they like change. And so do we. Do we not go about from place to place, entertaining and being entertained, when the presence of a friend in the kitchen results in a reprimand and a pointing out of some duty, neglected, say we, that the friend may be entertained?

Are we never dull—we who have our music and our books? And are they never to be dull, whose work is always going on, and who have no relaxation unless we provide it for them?

We are no advocates for spoiling servants, any more than we should be for spoiling children, yet we are anxious that they should be happy; and that they may be happy it is necessary that we have a set of rules that must be kept, and that they should gradually learn that we wish to stand in the same relation to them, while they are in our house, as their parents would were they still in their care.

Rule the first is, that no young servant should be out alone after dark, giving reasons for this rule that are easily understood. Rule the second, that no one comes to the back door after a certain hour, because their friends are quite welcome to come to the front door, and once it is dark bad characters are about, and young girls are easily frightened; and rule the third, in which all the rest are comprehended, is that they must learn that we are always ready to hear all their hopes and fears, to help them choose their hats and dresses, to assist them in every way they wish, and to give them sympathy and kindness, which we will take from them in our turn should we be ill or in trouble.

How much more cheerfully will the cook help you to retrench if, instead of scolding about the waste, you ask her to help you to save what would otherwise be given or thrown away. And much more pleasantly will your housemaids help you when 'company comes,' if you tell them to look out for this or that celebrity, to listen if Miss Smith sings or if Mr. Brown plays; and how much they will do should you leave one or two of the pleasanter parts of preparing in their hands, preferring rather an ill-arranged flower vase than the idea that all the rough and none of the smooth falls to their share of the work. It will not hurt us to do a little dusting for once, or even to wash the china, and indeed it will do us good, for it will teach us how monotonous and wearisome is the work by which our 'maidens,' the dear old Dorset expression for our servants, earn their daily bread, but that ceases to have half its monotony and irksomeness should we help occasionally, when work is pressing, and there is more than usual to do. To have good and loving servants, then, it is necessary to have them tolerably young, to be firm, kind, and, above all, sympathetic, to know as much about their home life as is possible; and without telling them much, yet, when it is advisable, to take them into our confidence, secure in our turn of receiving sympathy, which is always precious, no matter from whom it is received.

Of course, this is not such an amusing life as the one lived by a mistress who is always enjoying herself, and thinking of little save her own garments, and the arrangement of the *menu* and that of the dinner-table, but it is a far more satisfactory one. We all have duties; it rests with ourselves whether or not we shall neglect them or do them. Still, if they are not done, if our servants turn out 'thieves, liars, and wretches,' as they were characterised by one female writer the other day, it were well to pause, and ask who should be blamed for such a dreadful state of things. Surely not those who come to us for training and care, but rather those who do nothing to earn the right to live, and who, taking but a low view of life, look upon it as a playground instead of regarding it as a field for work—a place where we can do as much good as in us lies.

Sympathy is the bond that binds men together—sympathy is the bond that should unite mistress and maid; on the lowest ground it is politic, on the highest it is ordained in a code of life given to all; and we shall none of us regret treating our servants well, for, speaking from experience, I can boldly state that, in trouble, sickness, and sorrow, one can rely implicitly for help on the maids whom we have trained ourselves, and whom we have treated exactly as we should wish them to treat us, and that I have found in a time when Fortune appeared to have turned her back on us, owing to matters on which we need not touch, that the servants stuck manfully to the ship, and did their best to help us weather a storm that, though sharp, was short, yet that might have stranded us hopelessly on a lee shore.

The only fault I cannot overcome at present is this bedroom question, and the breaking of the china &c. provided for their use, hence my advice about the simple furniture given to them; but I find daily improvement here, and I hope that the next generation will be able to give their servants pretty rooms as safely as they can at present give them healthy ones.

There is just one other point to touch upon, that of the meals of the kitchen. It is quite enough to allow an ordinary middle-class household good bread and butter, oatmeal porridge, and tea, coffee, or cocoa for breakfast; the kitchen dinner should be the same as the dining-room luncheon; tea might be supplemented by jam or an occasional home-made cake; and supper should be presumably bread and cheese, but any soup made from the receipts in the chapter on 'entertaining,' or odds and ends left at the late dinner, can be consumed if you can trust your cook; if you cannot, you must lay down a hard-and-fast rule of bread and cheese, and insist on its being kept, otherwise you will find yourselves in the case of a friend of mine, who went into her larder after an enormous dinner-party, expecting to find herself free from the necessity of ordering more food for at least a week, and discovered it empty, swept, and garnished, because, the cook informed her, they always had for their suppers any little thing 'as was' left over.

Never be afraid to praise your servants, as one lady is I know of, for fear they may think she cannot do without them: we *can't* do without them—why should we pretend we can? They are far more likely to remain where they are appreciated and cared for than where they know they are only looked upon as so much necessary furniture; and do not be afraid to blame them, emulating another friend of mine, who saw her servant reading her letters at her desk, and stepped out of the room unobserved because she shrank from the disagreeable but emphatically necessary task of telling the maid of her odious and dishonourable fault; but say straight out to the delinquent servant herself what you have in your mind against her, never sending the message by another servant, nor nagging, but remarking firmly what you have to say yourself in such a way that she cannot avoid perceiving you mean emphatically what you say.

Let your maids have good books to read, and let them see newspapers, but do not keep a kitchen bookshelf. This they distrust at once, and look out for their own literature, which is generally pernicious; but if you yourself have read a good story, recommend it to them, and talk to them about it. You can always get a servant to read proper books by taking care to read them yourself, and by letting them see you are sharing your literature with them; even if they spoil or soil the book, books are cheap, and they had better do this than soil their minds by the rubbish they might buy, revolting naturally against 'Lizzy, or a Parlourmaid's Duties, described in a story,' or 'Grace, or How to Clean Silver,' or the similar charming works which one generally finds in the houses of those who keep 'kitchen bookshelves,' regardless of the fact that Ouida and other exquisite feminine novelists are the favourite food of the drawing-room, and that they could not read one page of the 'books' themselves provided for the maid's entertainment.

If you have a garden, encourage the servants to walk and sit and work in it; and, above all, take interest in their clothes, lend them patterns, and, in fact, do all in your power to raise them to your station. The lower classes, thanks to education, are rapidly climbing; they will rise whether we like it or not, and we had better, on the lowest grounds, assist them to share the place they will take and push us from, should they find we are antagonistic and jealous instead of helpful and sympathising.

I have had twenty years' experience of household management. I have had three cooks in the time, and have never had a maid give me 'warning'; and though, no doubt, some day I shall find servants a 'bother,' because they will get married, and I cannot expect to keep mine all their lives, I think my twenty years of success entitle me to lay down the law on the subject of the management of one's maids just a little. But, lest my readers should tire of the subject, I will pass on to the nurseries, which, after all, are much more interesting to the young housekeeper.

CHAPTER XV
THE NURSERIES

There are several things of course to be considered in the first choice of a nursery, and, unfortunately, in far too many cases economy has to be considered even before what is really and actually good for a child's health. 'Economy: how I dislike that word!' remarked a plaintive friend, actually of the sterner sex, and how I agree with him only my own soul knows; but economy is a stern, a hard fact, and above all has it to be considered when expenses begin to advance by 'leaps and bounds,' and Edwin regards the future, across the berceaunette, most dolefully; and thinking over school bills and doctors' bills, much in the distance yet, but steadily advancing towards him, begins to wonder how two hands are to do it all, and whether he had not better at once look up all the papers he can possess himself of that relate to State emigration. It is hard for me to keep the 'juste milieu,' for I am really possessed by the idea of good nurseries; and when I recollect how much money is wasted on keeping up appearances, and also in retaining that 'spare room,' I almost feel inclined to throw prudence to the winds, and declare that two good nurseries are as imperative for one child as I believe in my heart they are. And, really, even in the orthodox suburban villa, with its four or five bedrooms, this accommodation can be found, if only Angelina uses her senses, and really desires to do her best for her little ones. But this is not always the case, I am sorry to say, and there is no doubt that in most houses the position of the nurseries is a subject of very small interest. So long as it is tolerably out of the way, and, in fact, 'far from humanity's reach,' most parents are quite satisfied, and ask little else than that their ears may not be assaulted by cries, and their china shaken to its very foundations by little feet rushing and jumping overhead in a way that is undoubtedly trying to the nerves, but is very delightful to those who see in such noises ample evidence of the health and good spirits of the small folk who are making them.

Perhaps, however, the 'demon builder,' the cause of so very many of our domestic woes and worries, is as much to blame as the people who take the houses he runs up for us. Still, demand creates supply, and I cannot help thinking that, if the British matron insisted on nurseries as well as the regulation 'three reception-rooms' of the house-agents' lists, in time we should be provided with large airy chambers, as much a matter of course as the bath-room of recent years, that, once conspicuous by its absence, in now a *sine quâ non* in even tiny houses built for clerks, and rented at about 30*l*. a year.

I am very much divided in in my mind as to the manner in which to write this chapter, as I cannot determine whether to describe an ideal nursery—the nursery in which we were all brought up—or the orthodox nursery, made out of the worst bedroom in the house, the one farthest away from the sitting-rooms, and where nothing is considered save how to prevent any visitors' ears being assailed with shouts, and their nerves tried by sudden bangs immediately overhead. I am not in the least exaggerating when I say that, especially in London, the very top rooms in a tall house are those set aside for the little ones, Pass along any of our most fashionable squares and thoroughfares, and look up at the windows. Where are the necessary bars placed that denote the nurseries? Why, at the highest windows of all. My readers can notice this for themselves, and can say whether I am right or wrong. And how often do we not find an excellent spare room in a house where two, or perhaps even more, children are stuffed into one room that is day and night nursery combined, while half the year the best chamber is kept empty, sacred to an occasional guest, whose presence should never be courted at all in a house not large enough to allow of there being two nurseries for the children's own use. I am the very last person in the world to make children into miniature tyrants; I do not allow mine to engross the conversation or to be in evidence at all hours of the day. They do not behave as if they were grown up at an early age, neither do they go out to luncheon or tea perpetually, thus becoming *blasé* before their time. They are frankly children, and are treated as such, and I feel it rather necessary to say this at the outset, for fear my readers may feel constrained to write and tell me (after what I have said above) I have fallen into the prevailing error of the day, and make my children a nuisance to themselves and every one else by spoiling them; for, despite the usual position of the nursery, there is no doubt that children will soon cease to exist at all, and will become grown-up men and women before they have changed their teeth.

Despite the position of the nurseries, did I say? Nay, surely rather should I write because of the position of the nurseries, which are so far off that the mother scarcely ever climbs up to them, and in consequence has her children downstairs with her in and out of season, until they gradually absorb the grown-up atmosphere and become little prigs who care nothing for a romp, and object to going into the country for the summer because the country is so very dull, and have their own opinions, pretty freely expressed too, about their clothes and the cooking at their own or their friends' houses.

I feel I may perhaps be accused of being hard on the child of the period, but I confess openly the child of the period is my pet detestation—poor little soul!—not because of its personality as a child, but because it is such a painful subject for contemplation. I cannot bear to see poor innocent babies dressed out to imitate old pictures, with long skirts sweeping the ground, because they are picturesque, with bare arms and wide lace collars, and manners to match; who go out perpetually to luncheon and tea-parties, and who, do they happen to be passably good-looking, are worshipped by a crowd of foolish women until the conversation is engrossed by the child, who very soon becomes an intolerable nuisance; who cannot play because of its absurd skirt, and will grow up the useless, affected, selfish, ball-loving girl that is the terror of every mother who recognises that life has duties as well as pleasures, and hopes that her daughters will do some good work in a world where the harvest is indeed plenteous and the labourers few.

To have good and healthy children it is positively necessary to have good and healthy nurseries, and as soon as Angelina becomes the proud possessor of her first baby she should seriously and soberly consider the great nursery question. Of course she will have thought of it before the tyrant arrives, but so much depends on different small things that she will not seriously and definitely determine what to do until she sees what her nurse is like, and whether she is to have the baby at night or to hand it over to somebody else.

I could write pages about people's first babies, poor little things! What experiments are tried on them in the way of hygienic and stupid clothes, the patent foods, the ghastly tins of milk, and the fearful medicines! I do not believe one young mother exists who has not her own special theories about babies, and who does not scorn proudly the experience so freely offered her by her mother, who has brought up a family, and may therefore be supposed to know something of children, or by her numerous friends who have all made a more or less successful effort in the same direction. And, between ourselves, I have often wondered how any first child ever grows up, so wonderful are the trials it goes through, so marvellous are the plans tried, to insure that perfection that each Angelina in turn thinks lies latent in the small red squalling person that makes such a remarkable change in all the household arrangements all at once.

The first danger that assails Angelina when baby arrives is that Edwin's life shall be made a burden to him because all his little comforts are forgotten, the hours of meals altered, and Angelina herself is off upstairs every two minutes, because the dear infant is howling, or because she fancies he is howling. Even so, the nurse should be capable of quelling the rage, unassisted by her mistress, or she is not worth her wages, and had better go.

I hope I shall not be considered hard-hearted if I tell Angelina quite in confidence, that, if she can depend upon her cow, baby becomes a pleasure instead of a nuisance, if he or she and the cow are introduced at a very early stage of his or her career. In these days of ours few women are strong enough or have sufficient leisure to give themselves up entirely to the infant's convenience; and I maintain that a woman has as much right to consider herself and her health, and her duties to her husband, society at large, and her own house, as to give herself up body and soul to a baby, who thrives as well on the bottle, if properly looked after, as on anything else.

I know quite well that by saying this I may lay myself open to all sorts of medical opinions, and I am sure to be told I am disgracing my sex. But, as I have done all through my book, I am speaking from experience, and only on subjects of which I have personal knowledge.

For had I not beautiful theories too when my eldest daughter arrived on the scene? We were living in one of the dullest, stupidest, nastiest little country towns in the world in those days, and there were few claims of society on me then. I had no particular occupations, and I was going to devote my energies to that poor child. I did. She howled remorselessly morning, noon, and night. The doctor, my dear old doctor, old-fashioned, too, in his notions, said my ways were correct, and he could not make out her shrieks at all. I confess I have struggled with her until I have wept with exhaustion, and at last a blessing in the shape of a good nurse arrived, and solved the mystery. The unfortunate infant was starved, and her shrieks were shrieks of hunger. She was introduced to a particularly nice Alderney cow; and from that day to this her cries ceased, and she has grown and thrived, and become an almost grown-up member of society, and a decidedly healthy one.

Despite my experience with Muriel, I honestly attempted to 'do my duty' with the two next; there were no shrieks this time, but there were all sorts of other things, and the cow had soon to be called into requisition; and my two youngest children, who are stronger and far less liable to small ailments and colds than the other three, never had anything else, and were as good and prosperous a pair of babies and children as one may wish to see, for after No. 3 had proved to me my theories were very beautiful as theories, but rather unworkable in practice, I gave them up, trusted a great deal to my good nurse, and clung to the cow. Naturally, Londoners are at the mercy of their milkman, but the Alderney Dairy, for example, possesses a conscience and good milk; and no one will ever convince me that milk out of tins can ever come up to the fresh, nice, clean milk given by a properly managed and constituted cow; and, of course, in the country one has one's own cows and sees exactly what is going on, and knows one has the same milk, until the child is old enough to bear the change.

The great things for young children are quiet and regularity, and these are insured by having good nurseries and a good nurse. The nurse chosen for a first baby should never be less than twenty-five. Your young nurses are the most fearful mistakes for young mothers; they do not understand handling or dressing a baby, and they send off for the doctor at every moment, when an older woman would have the sense to know what to do, thus spending on the physician what would have paid good wages over and over again. They think of nothing save their own pleasure and amusement, and have no real love either for the child, who wearies them, or for the mistress, who, tired of their incapacity, is continually scolding without making any real change in the conduct, that is bad because the girl lacks what can only be given her by age, and a much longer experience than she can ever possibly possess. A perfect nurse is often obtained from a friend's nursery where she has lived for some time as second nurse in a good establishment. She should have some four or five years' character, and when found should be clung to, until Angelina's nursery is transformed into the 'girls'' sitting-room, when nurse has often become so precious she stays on and on until transferred to the nursery of the first girl who is married and requires her help. What a comfort such a woman is to all in the house no one save the happy mistress can ever know! She is delightful in sickness and trouble, 'her' children are her first thought, their trials and joys are hers, and she helps, as only a good nurse can, the overworked mother should any special trials come, that are made bearable only because some one else shares them too.

But the perfect nurse presupposes the perfect nursery, and, as all young mothers should strive for the first at all events, so I do not see why I should not take it for granted that the baby is considered more than an occasional visitor, and describe at once how a nursery ought to be furnished and decorated, because I do not believe any child ought to be in the room in the day in which he *and his nurse* have slept all night; nor that a child should sleep all night in a room where his nurse has had her meals all day, and where he has been most of the twelve waking hours; any more than I consider a child's day nursery should be his mother's sitting-room, where visitors come, and all sorts of irregularities are practised in the way of draughts, heat, light, &c., that should never be allowed.

The day nursery should be as roomy a room as can be had, and the window should be able to be opened top and bottom; no blinds should be allowed, but the nice muslin and serge, or rather cretonne, curtains should be arranged here as elsewhere, to temper the light and make the room look cheerful and pretty.

Cheerfulness and prettiness should be the twin guardian angels of Angelina's nurseries; a bright paper of either a faint pink or blue should be on the walls with a scarcely perceptible pattern; there should be a cretonne dado with a painted rail; and all the paint should be varnished to allow of its being frequently washed. That the cretonne dado cannot be washed does not matter one bit; it can be brushed frequently, and it always looks tidy, and defies the kickings of little feet and the pickings of small fingers, that so soon make chaos in the very smart rooms, unless particular care is taken that the children shall respect these rooms in a way they can easily be taught to do with very little trouble. I most successfully cured a young person of five, whose depredations were something awful, by making him pay up all his available cash towards a new paper. I never had to complain again, for he seemed to realise very quickly that if mischief cost money it was not worth the candle, and had better be given up.

But with a cretonne dado half the temptation to tear tempting morsels off corners is done away with, and the rail keeps off chairs from the paper, and gives a reason for the short-frilled curtains, that are in no one's way and are never trailing on the ground, a trap for the unwary and a regular home for dust. The ceiling should be whitewashed, and should be done at least once every two years (it should really be done every spring); and if a little blue is put into the wash one gets a hint of colour, and does away with the utter ugliness and glare of the orthodox ceiling, which is always trying, and, in my eyes, spoils any house.

The floor should be stained two feet from the wall, wiped every day with a damp cloth to take up all the dust and fluff, and polished every Saturday regularly with beeswax and turpentine, the clean smell of which is always so nice and wholesome, I think, and makes a house pleasant at once; but before the staining is done great care should be taken, to see that the boards are planed, and that no splinters are in evidence, and that any gaps that there may be are properly stopped to keep out the draughts, then the staining may safely be done. A nice square of Kidderminster can then be chosen, and put down over the warm carpet felt, without which a thin carpet does not do for a nursery, because of itself it is not warm enough.

The walls and paint being of a pink, like the pink, say, of the inside of a rose, or of the lighter shade of coral, with no distinct and distracting pattern on the wall, a pretty flowery cretonne could be chosen for the dado and window curtains. I have seen one in a pale green shade, with fluffy balls of guelder-roses on, and groups of pinks which would be perfect; but this was so long ago that I fear it could not be had now, though, of course, others equally pretty are sure to be easily procurable. The doors where this cretonne was used were painted with the same flowers, which were also to be found on the cupboard doors, with small bright English birds poised here and there among them. It had a most cheerful effect, and a baby who lived there used to be contented for a long time by himself if he could only lie and 'talk' to the birds and flowers in a curious language all his very own.

But, if a blue room is preferred to the pink, that can be managed very cheaply, for I have lately discovered an almost perfect blue and white paper, sold by Pither and Co., of Mortimer Street, that is all it should be for a day nursery. The colour is clear and clean, and the pattern cheerful without fussily calling attention to itself, while its cheapness, 1s. a piece, would allow of its being renewed every now and then should it become shabby, and the paint can be blue, and a blue and white cretonne to harmonise with it can be had at Burnett's for 9½d. a yard. It has a sort of pattern of daisies overlapping each other on it, and is very pretty indeed. The rail should be painted blue, and no little fingers can do any harm to this, while it would take years to make the cretonne dirty, if it be brushed now and then and occasionally cleaned with dry bread. The curtains to the windows can be made of the same cretonne lined and frilled, and would do away with the necessity of blinds if made as I so often recommend; and this would be really a great economy in any nursery, for I know well how often tassels are torn off and spoiled, the blind-cords broken, and the springs rendered quite unworkable, not only by the children, but by the under-nurses, who can never learn that a blind does not require the putting forth of immense strength to make it move; and will not realise that both bells and blinds answer to gentle handling as well as to the fiercer tug, which often enough brings the blind down on one's head, and leaves the bell hanging out with its neck broken.

If we use the blue arrangement we could panel the doors and cupboards with cretonne, which always looks nice, and makes a wonderful difference at once in the look of a room.

If there are proper recesses by the fireplaces these should at once be utilised for cupboards, flush to the wall, so that no little heads can be banged against those cruel corners. These cupboards are most useful. The lower shelves can be used for rubbish—the delicious rubbish that is so much nicer than expensive toys; and the upper shelves can be used for the work in hand and better toys, kept for Sundays and holidays and those grand occasions when nursery company comes, and visitors may arrive who have no imaginativeness, or only see old bits of wood once sacred to cotton, shankless buttons, fir-cones, and scraps of silk and paper, where other bolder folk perceive strings of diamonds and pearls, and libraries of fairies, and wardrobes sacred to unknown but much-beloved friends; whose houses are the fir-cones, and who dress themselves magnificently in sweepings begged from the maid, or even from that proud lady, the dressmaker, whose occasional visits, with her 'own machine,' are something to look forward to by any small mother who has an army of dolls, and very little indeed to clothe them in.

Who amongst us cannot remember the intense bliss of our nursery cupboard, the delicious joy of having one place all our own, where we could hoard unchecked those thousand and one trifles that no drawing-room could be expected to give house-room to—where even nurse did not interfere, because our rubbish (rubbish, indeed!) kept us so delightfully quiet? Ay, and who amongst us who does recollect this can grudge a day nursery to even one child who requires it—all the more because it is a solitary little girl, and can make its own companions out of trifles, when otherwise its mother would be making it grown-up before its time, by never leaving it alone for a moment to those devices and play that keep it a child, and don't allow it to grow up an 'old person' almost before it can stand steadily on its fat legs?

Given the blessed refuge of a nursery, with its appealing cupboard, and very little other furniture is required. A nice solid round table, with (please don't faint, all ye æsthetic folk) oilcloth sewn strongly over it as a cover, because then no tablecloth is needed, save at meals, and there are no draperies to be caught hold of; and because this rubs clean every morning, because nothing stains it, and even milk can be washed off; a comfortable deep chair for nurse, low enough for her to hold baby comfortably and easily; a chair for each child, and one for company; and a delightful sofa, and nothing more is really required.

Why a sofa, say you? Because no one who has not one in a nursery can know how invaluable such a possession is. Children have often tiny ailments that are not bad enough for bed, and bed should never be resorted to in the daytime unless positively necessary. An aching head, a 'stuffy' cold, all these are much more bearable if a broad cosy sofa is available, while an occasional rest for a growing child is a great thing always to be able to secure; a child, recollect, who ever complains of being 'so tired' being a child that requires watching, *not* coddling, and to whom that sofa may prove little else but salvation.

This need not cost much either, for the beau-ideal of a nursery sofa is one that no fashionable person would look at now; it stands square on its feet, has a high square back and arms, no springs, only two big square cushions, and has some pillows of soft feathers, to mitigate the severity of the details, which—O shades of all my long-lost youth!—were the best things I ever had in all my life for ammunition, either at the sacking of a town or the defence of some Scottish castle; when, arrayed in a broad plaid sash brought back from Scotland by some one who knew how I adored the 'Days of Bruce,' and other works of the kind, the very names of which I have forgotten, I became in a moment Sir William Wallace himself, and was happier then, I dare say, than I have ever been since.

For there is another aspect to the nursery sofa that is not to be despised, besides its great use in illness or fatigue; it is a never-failing source of inspiration for regularly good games—it is a fortress, a whole city, a ship at sea, an elephant—in fact, anything any one likes to imagine it is. The broad square cushions are rafts to put off to sea in when the ship itself is destroyed; they are fire-escapes or desert islands, or icebergs at will; while no one who has not had them can possibly tell the joy it is to throw the soft pillows about, when nurse has put away the ornaments on the chimneypiece, and retired with her chair and her baby into the next room, where she is near enough to check unseemly revels, and yet not too near to come in for a share of the fray, which waxes fast and furious when the sofa and all its capabilities are fully appreciated, and where the coverings are warranted not to hurt.

I could write pages both about the nursery cupboards and the sofa, but will mercifully refrain, because I have other things to say about the furnishing of the walls, and the emphatic necessity of a high guard for the fire fastened into the wall, so that it cannot be taken, as we took ours once, for the gratings before a lion in an imaginary 'Zoo,' also furnished by the sofa; while we have also to consider the night apartment, for naturally the perfect nursery of which I would like to think we were all possessed has its night apartment leading out of it. This should be painted and papered *en suite* with the day room, and have very dark serge curtains to draw over the windows, so that all light may be excluded, thus enabling the sense of darkness and quiet to be obtained that is so very necessary for a small child. I do not think I have mentioned what I should like to impress very much on my readers, that on no account, *on no pretext whatever*, should that most pernicious gas be allowed in any nursery, either day or night. There is nothing more harmful for small lungs than the vitiated atmosphere caused by gas, nothing worse for small brains and eyes than the glitter and harsh glare of the gas, that a servant invariably turns up to its height, and very often drags down, regardless that an escape of gas is pouring out of the top of the outraged chandelier or bracket. There is no reason, either, why gas should be allowed; a good duplex lamp gives quite sufficient light to work by, and must be kept clean, or it will smell and also give out no light at all, and all danger is done away with if it be set well in the centre of the nursery table, which has, remember, no cloth to drag off suddenly, and which should stand square against the wall, or in a recess by the fire when not actually in use for nursery meals. Or a really strong, good bracket, painted the colour of the wall, just high enough to be out of the reach of little hands, might be provided on purpose for the lamp, and the nurse could either have a wicker-work table provided for her, or could put her wicker-work covered basket on a chair by her side, and sit close under her lamp to work; or it might even stand on the mantelpiece on a broad shelf, where also it would be equally well out of the little folks' way. You have nothing to do, as I said in one of my former chapters, but to notice the effect gas has on plants, and then notice how these same plants live on and flourish without gas, to understand that my theory about the unhealthiness of gas is a right one; and I think all will agree with me in saying that directly one is ill one recognises for oneself how disturbing gas is, and the first demand of a restless invalid is to have the gas put out, and a candle given instead. I shall never forget one case of illness I once had the unpleasantness of seeing. The wife, who had constituted herself nurse, and who knew about as much of nursing as an ordinary cat would, asked me to look in on the invalid and see what I thought of him. I went into the dressing-room, and even there the evil was apparent. A hot gust of air met me, and, to my horror, I saw no less than three gas jets, in a small room, flaring away, because the lady wanted plenty of light, and thought it would cheer the restless, fevered creature whose uneasy head was tossing on the pillow, and whose wild eyes looked in vain for relief; so out went all that gas, the windows were opened at the top, two wax candles, provided with shades, were lighted, and in less than an hour the room became cool, and the poor man was asleep for the first time for—I had almost written days; and it was certainly days since he had had any deep or restful sleep at all.

    I do not think, even, when we are grown up, we at all realise the necessity or even the possibility of complete rest; but a baby does, poor little thing, and is very often never allowed to have it. There is no sense of peace in most houses, and I want dreadfully to impress upon all my readers that they must 'seek peace and ensue it' for their children, if they utterly refuse to do it for themselves, and, therefore, the nursery should be quiet, and should even be a haven of rest to the mother herself, when she is overdone with her unpaid-for, never-ceasing work; and where she has her especial chair and footstool, and where she comes not only to see the babies, but to have the quiet, confidential talk with nurse, who should be able to have confidence reposed in her; or she is most certainly not fit for her place, which, if it be not a confidential one in the very highest sense of the word, is positively nothing at all.

The night nursery should, of course, have a fireplace and a ventilator. The fire should not be a matter of course, unless the room is far from the day nursery, when a fire should be lighted in cold weather as a matter of course. A room for children should never be overheated in any way; but no one should fall into the foolish idea that a fireless bedroom is hardening, and a fire makes people tender, for it does nothing of the sort; it simply makes life bearable to the chilly, and prevents all those dreadful lung troubles that used to be the scourge of so many English families, but that since the almost entire disappearance of those foolish, wicked low frocks and short sleeves in our nurseries, and the appearance of more fires, have well nigh been stamped out; and will be stamped out entirely when the Queen, so sensible in all other ways, puts a stop to the order she has given about low dresses, and recognises that people can be quite as full dressed with their clothes on as they are almost stripped to the waist and exposed, in the most delicate part of the human frame, to the bitter winds from which we English people are never entirely free.

I hope I shall not be considered a hopeless faddist with my theories; but at all events I have common-sense on my side, and most people who think at all will, I am sure, see that I am right in all I say, and that I speak from experience; and as a baby's education begins quite as soon as the mite is washed and dressed for the first time, I may be forgiven, perhaps, if I insist on peace, quiet, rest, proper clothes, and absence of gas, even as soon as a nursery is required at all. Of course for the first few weeks the baby does not require a room all to itself, but it should be ready for it, for sometimes it is just as well that it should go into its own premises, thus giving its mother time and quiet to be restored to her proper state of health again, which I do not think she is allowed to do when she is wearied by hearing the infant howl when it is dressed, and when she may be aroused any moment, even from most necessary sleep, by the small tyrant, who cannot be relied on for anything in certainty—at all events, at that early stage. If the nursery has been properly aired and got ready for the baby, and a nurse engaged to come on after the monthly nurse leaves, there is no reason why the baby should not go there whenever his mother wants to get rid of him; and I maintain that often far too much is sacrificed for the infant, who, in his turn, suffers from too much kindness and consideration, and who does not require half the fuss and trouble he causes in a house where he is a first arrival, and, in consequence, is something too precious and amusing—and, in fact, is almost treated like a phenomenon, or at least like a very precious fragile new toy.

Now, a baby is nothing of the kind, and here, then, common-sense must act as a supplementary nurse, and come to the rescue. She must firmly insist on the small person becoming used from the very first to take his rest in his own berceaunette. She may look aside should the frilled pillow be warmed, because, despite the flannel on the head, a cold pillow is always an unpleasant surprise, and one promptly resented by a baby; but she must insist on his neither being cuddled up by his mother nor allowed to sleep with the nurse, just as much as she must frown on his going to sleep with a full bottle (like a drunkard) by his side, because if he does he will wake a little and suck, and then sleep a little more, and so on, getting neither sleep nor food in a manner that can possibly be of the smallest use to him.

And now I should like to say a few words—*for ladies only, please*—about the great necessity of having everything down to the nurseries, or nursery, ready before the young person expected makes his *début* in a troublesome world. I have been astounded often by the manner in which young matrons put off making the most necessary preparations, until often enough, just at the last, the expectant mother sets to all in a hurry to do what should have been done ages before—wearies and agitates herself to death almost in her endeavours to make up for lost time, and very often causes such a state of things that danger to herself ensues; and at the best great trouble is caused, simply because she would not listen to other people, and be a little beforehand with the world.

Do you know, I quite secretly think some of these young ladies believe, that if no encouragement is given to the baby in the way of having a pretty room and nice wardrobe ready for it, it may not, after all, arrive in the world at all, and that this is the reason why so much is left to do until very much too late; but though I dare say it is very hard to realise that an infant can really and truly come to the small, perfect house, where such an event has never happened before, I can assure you all that, once it has given a hint of its intentions, its arrival is only a matter of time, and that come it most undoubtedly and certainly will, and therefore, under these circumstances, it is much better to be ready for its arrival, and not have to distract yourself and others at a critical time, by telling a strange nurse fetched in a hurry where she may be able to borrow clothes that should have been ready months before; or to know things are not aired, or that there is not a room where nurse and baby can retire safely when you want to be quite quiet; or to have half an hour's talk either with your husband or your familiar friends who are admitted to your room, where thus you can have the freedom from supervision for a short time; or the perfect rest I for one can never have with a nurse and baby perpetually in evidence.

But all too often one is compelled to have the infant in one's room because of the absurd way in which our houses are arranged, and I do wish architects and builders (to return to another old grievance, like the gas subject) would consult a jury of matrons, even if they will not consult their wives alone, before they set to work to give us any more houses, for really they are one and all ignorant of the commonest principles of their art as regarded from a purely feminine point of view. Why won't they recollect that one or two rooms should lead out of each other? Why won't they remember nurseries are wanted in most houses? and why will they not arrange their plans with a memory of some of the most common events of domestic life? If they did, the first floors of most habitations would be very different to what they are now, and domestic life would be much easier. I can only hope that the conscientious male, whose eye of course ceased to fall on this page when he read the warning words *For ladies only*, will take up the thread of my discourse where it ceased to be private, and will read, mark, and inwardly digest as much of this last paragraph of mine as he possibly can.

Of course, one of the first things to be provided is a bed for the small infant, as from the very earliest dawn of its existence there is no doubt in my mind that it ought to be taught to sleep in its own cot, and that without any of the pernicious petting, patting, and putting to sleep that mothers and nurses are so fond of, and that brings about its own revenges in the forming speedily of a most unruly tyrant, who promptly makes their lives a burden to them, refusing to go to his slumbers without an attendant nymph.

People fondly imagine that babies do not know in the least what their caretakers do until they are, at the smallest computation, three months old, and have begun, in nursery parlance, to 'take notice.' Now, let any one who has ever seen an infant taken by some one who is ignorant of its ways contrast the picture with that of this same baby taken by a 'past mistress' of the art, and they will at once understand what I mean when I declare solemnly that a child is never too small, too tiny, to feel and know whether it has to deal with some one who knows its ways, and means it to be brought up decently and properly, or with a well-meaning idiot, who allows herself to be conquered and enslaved by a long clothes slobberer, who the more it is given in to the more it immediately exacts from its worshippers.

To hear some people with a baby is really quite enough to make one forswear a nursery for ever; the talk, the abject drivel, that is poured out like incense before it, the foolish petting, and the silly humouring, all being as vexatious to listen to as it is bad for the child itself, the 'pigeon English' provided for its entertainment often resulting in the baby talk that makes the ordinary two-year-old a perfect terror to any one who entertains it with conversation; while the sense of super-importance given to it in its cradle makes it a tyrant for the rest of its young life, until it goes to school or mixes with other people, and is intensely miserable because then, and then only, is it taught its real worth in the world.

Therefore, on every ground, it is better to begin at the very beginning and continue as one means to go on, and so I strongly advise the berceaunette to be ready with the nursery, and that the first sleep be taken in that sheltered spot.

There are a variety of these articles, but to my mind only one to be recommended, and that is the delightful hammock berceaunette to be obtained of Mrs. S. B. Garrard, in Westbourne Grove, and these have such a world-wide reputation now that I suppose all the world knows of them, and therefore no description is necessary; but for fear there may be folks who have not seen them, I may mention that the bed portion is quilted and hung on four strong legs, exactly like a hammock is hung, and that curtains are arranged in such a way that the light can be excluded without at the same time unduly excluding a proper amount of fresh air.

There are innumerable ways of trimming and making these berceaunettes. I have seen the hammock portion of quilted satin and silk and sateens of all colours, covered with fine muslins and trimmed real lace; but, honestly, even if we could afford such vanities as these, I do not consider them suitable for a small baby, who should never have any garments that cannot be properly washed constantly, and should not have any belongings that cannot share the same fate; and I have discovered that nothing looks, wears, and washes so well as plain white or figured cambric, edged with torchon lace; the hammock part made of cambric too, washable by any good nurse; and curtains tied back with old-gold-coloured ribbons, bows of which can be used as decorations, whenever this may be considered necessary. Terra-cotta ribbons look nice too, but I prefer the old gold to anything else, and it is newer than the everlasting pink or blue, which was all our foremothers ever halted between; though a sweet arrangement of palest pink, palest blue, and butter colour looks very French and uncommon. The only objection I have ever had made to me about these hammock berceaunettes is that they are easily knocked over. Well, all I can say is that I have never known them to be knocked over, while I have seen a 'good old-fashioned' wicker-work cradle, with the deep hood and flowery chintz, daisy-fringed flounces, of our own infancy, prostrated by some one knocking against and displacing one of the chairs, on two of which it was always necessary to place it, and this catastrophe has occurred to my certain knowledge more than once. The basket, which is such a necessary addition to baby's trousseau, should match the berceaunette; and these too can be purchased of the hammock kind, and fold flat in a box for travelling. But before we describe this and speak of the contents we must complete our sketch of the bed, which would be incomplete without just a word about the necessary bedding.

One light hair mattress goes into the hammock part with a nice piece of blanket, and then, instead of the universal mackintosh sheet, we always have a thick piece of what country people call 'blanket sheeting'; it is not a blanket nor yet a sheet, but something between the two, and invaluable for nursery use, as it can be washed daily—of course three or four pieces should be in use—and is quite as useful as mackintosh without being in the least bit unhealthy. Small pillows, very soft, and shaped in to the neck, are sold with the berceaunettes, and these should be provided with very fine cotton pillow-cases, edged with a tiny cambric frill—linen is too cold—and the cotton, if fine enough, gives no chill, and yet does not scrub the tender skin; the sheet should be for appearance only at first, and should be simply a piece of cotton or longcloth frilled, and tacked on the blanket, and folded over to look nice, but only, as I said before, for appearance' sake, for the warmth of the blankets is most important for the infant, and should be supplemented by a miniature eider-down quilt in a washing cover of figured cambric edged with torchon, and, if fancied, embellished in its turn with some pretty bows.

Another thing: though I would always have an infant kept as quiet as possible, utterly and strenuously forbidding long railway journeys, much changing of nurseries, much seeing of company, I yet do say that to some noises the baby must be early accustomed. I have been in young married people's households where the magic words, 'Oh, if you please, mum, nurse says baby is asleep, have brought about a state of things that reminds one of the Sleeping Beauty's palace. The canary bird is hustled under an antimacassar, the piano is closed, and conversation is carried on in whispers, until a shrill cry sets us free from bondage and the spell is removed. In such a household Edwin's song has been brought to an abrupt conclusion, his cheery whistle announcing his home-coming received with chill reprimand, and we have gone about the passages on tiptoe, echoing in our souls Edwin's hasty but understandable mutter of 'Confound baby!' which is a sentiment which should be on no one's lips for one moment, of course.

Now if, when the young person first arrives, he is taught his proper place in the economy of the household, we shall have none of this. Precious, perfect, and beautiful as no doubt he is, the world is full of others just exactly like him, and while we all of us, I hope, recognise and believe in the serious and solemn side of maternity, while we know and feel that here is an immortal soul committed to our charge to train in the best way possible—for time and for eternity too, if we can—I do maintain that the lives of the parents are to be considered too, and that Edwin and Angelina have no right to sink themselves and their identity in that terrible middle-class 'pa' and 'ma' which seems to swallow, like some all-devouring serpent, the prettinesses and good taste of so many of our young married people, and that causes more unhappiness, I venture to state, than almost anything else.

The cry of an infant is soon interpreted by his nurse, who easily discriminates between hunger and temper, and the shrieks of temper must be stopped at once, or else our lives will be made a burden to us. How often have the untamed shrieks of children embittered my existence! and I am sure hundreds of people have suffered as I do. Now, unless something really has happened, I go so far as to say children can fall and hurt themselves without announcing the fact to the neighbours. I always make my own children try and exercise self-control, and the small troubles that are the fate of all cease to be the terror of the household when little ones bear them manfully, and have their wounds dressed without roaring all the time, and the wounds cease to be terrible to the children themselves, and pain becomes bearable, if the sufferer sees that there is nothing so serious after all, and that nothing terrible results from it; but this training must begin at the very beginning—it cannot begin too early. Children must learn that they can help their elders, who have so much an their shoulders already, and babies must be taught to be decent members of society, so will their coming be a pleasure, and not the torment and upsetting it all too often is in a household.

With a first baby the danger of this is always immense, and Angelina requires almost superhuman courage to prevent it being otherwise. It is a temptation to her to give herself airs to her friends, and to snub her own and Edwin's mothers, who, having brought up children, may be presumed to know something about the subject, and to make Edwin's life a burden to him too; while some Edwins are worse than their wives, and insist on dragging the poor child out of its bed at all seasons of the day and night to exhibit it, being, of course, bitterly indignant when the infant resents such treatment, and becomes crabbed and puny and miserable in consequence.

Therefore I consider I can hardly say too much or repeat too often the axiom that both bed and nursery should be ready for the baby, and that from the first he should be accustomed to both in that perfect house which shall be built some day when my ship comes home, and I have time to learn to draw. The nurseries shall lead past dressing-room and bath-room from the mother's bedroom itself—that is to say, that the bedroom shall have all this leading out of it, and that the night nursery shall be so close to the mother's room that she can reach it at once should she desire to do so, while the children, when old enough, should run in and out when they like—a bolt being shot, of course, when dressing goes on—and shall feel that they and their parents are always within touch of each other.

Here would, of course, come in once more the need of training, but why should children rise at early dawn, and make grown-up people's lives a burden to them? They will not if properly trained, and this training becomes possible when the nurseries are on the same floor as their mother's room, though a good big room can and *should* be had in our perfect house for tournaments, steeplechases, and theatrical performances when the elders begin to grow up and learn duly how to amuse themselves, while it is not necessary for Angelina to be always in and out of her nurseries, worrying her nurse to death, when our prize arrangement is possible, because she will be near enough to know nothing goes wrong; which, if she be sharp and acute, she will discover quite quickly enough for herself from the looks of the children and the general atmosphere without always 'poking about,' as the servants call it, to see how matters are. But all this must be begun at the beginning, and with No. 1, if she wishes to be really happy; therefore she should be quite sure of her monthly nurse, and be ready with her facts at her fingers' ends for this worthy, who, like every one else nowadays, has so improved in her ways and manners as to be a real comfort and pleasure, and can teach Angelina lessons of patience, neatness, and excellent management that will be worth a Jew's eye if she is lucky enough to get a good nurse; but forewarned is forearmed, and so let the berceaunette be ready, and let Angelina insist on this being used if she wishes to have peace in her nursery after the monthly nurse has departed, and the ordinary routine of life begins once more.

But, before I touch upon the subject of the monthly nurse, I want to impress upon my readers that, though the nursery is undoubtedly a kingdom, where the children can do pretty much as they like providing they do not get into mischief, and that they remember that, being ladies and gentlemen in embryo, they must behave as 'sich,' they yet must look upon the nursery as a lesson-ground, where good seed can be sown, and one of the first lessons to teach any one, child or small maid, is to be gentle and quiet. I never could understand why children cannot be happy without yelling at the top of their voices, and servants without stamping about in heavy boots, slamming doors, and shouting to each other; and one of the first things I always impress on all my household is that loud shrieks and strident voices are not allowed from any one. I have actually had my life rendered a burden to me sometimes by neighbours' offspring, whose one end and aim in life seemed to me to see who could scream loudest (I don't mean cry, by the way, but simply yell at the top of their voices, for the pleasure of hearing them, I suppose); and remembering that we as children never were allowed to indulge in a pastime that would have seriously impaired our father's powers of working—that we were perfectly happy, although we were not permitted to shriek—I have had none of this elegant amusement in my nursery, and we have found ourselves extremely comfortable without it; and this same discipline of gentleness and quiet is also valuable in keeping a room nice and being able to have pretty things in it.

Why should children be destructive and untidy? A good nurse soon sees they are not, and by giving the dear things nice surroundings you do your best to insure nice tastes, though, of course, some untidy, tasteless ancestor may crop out suddenly and utterly confound all one's theories, by giving us a child who will not learn the proper colours to harmonise with each other, the while he or she puts boots on the beds, and leaves a room looking as if hay had just been made therein.

But with children, as with everything else, one can but do one's best and utmost for them, never relaxing one's care and trouble—and one can do no more. They are sure to come right in the end somehow, although we cannot quite see how. And so, regardless of the ravages of boys and small maids, I go on making my house pretty, and hope by silent example to do yet more than I have already done towards humanising both of these riotous elements in one's household; for boys should not be the tyrants they undoubtedly are, and should learn easily that things have a right to respect as well as people.

I am a great advocate for the silent teaching, too, of really good pictures on the nursery walls. I do not like the idea of any rubbish being good enough for there, any crudely coloured, badly designed Christmas number atrocity being pinned up with pins or small nails, and called 'pretty, pretty' to some baby, who, I am thankful to say, not unseldom pulls it down and soon reduces it to the end it so richly deserves. Often a good picture is full of teaching to a thoughtful child. Excellent photographs can now be bought very cheaply, and some etchings are not too dear, but all should be carefully selected, either for the lesson or pleasant story they tell, for no one knows how much early impressions do for children, save those who vividly remember the small things that influenced themselves in their extreme youth, and are thus enabled to use their experience for their own or other people's children; a lovely photograph of moonlight on the sea, for example, having given me personally more pleasure as a child, than any amount of dolls ever did, although I was heartily attached to them, and loved them as few children do now in these highly educated days of ours.

Why, I remember we had quite a serious revolt in our schoolroom once, over this very picture subject. We as children were exceptionally lucky in our surroundings, and our schoolroom was hung with really good engravings of excellent pictures, many of them proofs of Sir Edwin Landseer's, while many of our father's works were there too, at which we were never tired of looking. I don't think any one, save an artist's children, could ever feel towards these said engravings quite as we did, for, being in a good many of them at all sorts of stages, we felt really the proprietorship in them that only the author is supposed to feel, while we were never tired of remembering the odds and ends of stories connected with the progress of each picture; and made other histories, too, for ourselves out of the motionless creatures that we were once, but out of whose knowledge we had so quickly grown: and then to hear that all these sources of our inspiration were to be torn from us, and what for? why, because in an educational frenzy maps were supposed to be better for us, and more in keeping in the schoolroom; and therefore our beloved pictures were to be put elsewhere to give place, forsooth, to glazed monstrosities, the very colours of which, crude greens and pinks and yellows, were enough to cause an æsthetic fever; although in those days æstheticism was a thing unknown, undescribed too, in any dictionary!

But an appeal to a higher power brought the pictures back, and the maps were rolled up above them, and only allowed to fall over them at such times as they were required to show their ugly faces to us in a geography lesson; a subject I have detested, I am sorry to say, simply because, I verily believe, of the rage we were in when we heard our dear pictures were to be taken from us!

I cannot help digressing, dear readers, when I think how happy children may be, and how miserable they are too often made by their over-kind, very foolish parents. We were let alone a great deal as children, mercifully, and taught that if we wanted amusement we must find it in ourselves; and I can never be too thankful for an education that has enabled me, with only a small cessation, to be happy always in my own company, without the everlasting craving for information as to 'What shall I do?' If we used to make this most aggravating inquiry, we did not do it twice, and soon discovered that we could make occupations for ourselves without driving our elders nearly mad in the process. Children cannot too early learn to amuse themselves, and therefore great care should be taken by parents that they have the means for this, the while the children do not know much care is taken, and are shown—what children are so seldom shown nowadays—that they are not the head and front of the household, and that something is due to the bread-winners and managers of the establishment, as well as to themselves.

I am sure good pictures are, therefore, or ought to be, indispensable in all nurseries, while the moment a child is old enough to inhabit a separate room, he or she should be encouraged to the utmost to begin to care for the surroundings, and to carefully collect pretty things around them, for in after life each thing so collected will be as a link to a precious past, and serve to remind them of happy times, that may influence their whole life if properly remembered and looked back upon. This is another hint for parents, especially for young parents. A child's mind is a curious thing (or at least mine was, and I am speaking, as I always speak, from actual experience), and receives certain memories in the shape of pictures. My memory always seems to me like a room hung round with paintings, and I recollect each incident of my life as one remembers a picture one has once seen and never forgotten. I have but to think for a moment, and I see—don't faint, please, I was only three; I am not quite a Methuselah, though it will sound like it—I see the Duke of Wellington riding along with bowed shoulders, and putting his hand, or rather his fingers, up to his hat every few seconds in answer to every one's respectful bows. I see flash by from our play-place on 'the leads'—the best play-place in the world; now, alas! no more—the royal carriage with four grey horses and the scarlet-jacketed riders, and I see the Queen in a hideous plaid-flounced frock and large bonnet, and the Prince Consort, and two big boys, drive by to look at some one's pictures in our neighbourhood; and I remember seeing two 'Bloomers,' followed by jeering boys, turn round the corner by our house, and remember quite well how sorry I felt for the stupid women, although I had profound contempt for their louder assertions of women's rights. Now I remember a great deal more than this, of course, but I mention these three things to illustrate what I mean about the pictures memory can paint; and to show that it is a parent's duty to provide the children with such mental pictures as shall always be a pleasure and, if possible, a profit to contemplate. Let the children see in reason all they possibly can. You can influence a child's present, but, once it is grown up, you cannot touch its future. You can see your children have a pleasant series of pictures connected with their childhood at any rate, and by making your child observe, and by showing it pleasant things, you will give it a richer store of wealth than anything else could do. Whenever we went out with our mother she always did this. 'Remember,' she said to me, 'that you have seen the Duke of Wellington,' and, though I was three only, I have never forgotten him. Look at that beautiful colour; see yonder field of wheat; look at the sea. No preaching here—but somehow the words stay by one, and insensibly one learns to notice, and from this pass to the possession of mental treasures nothing takes from us.

But we must have a certain amount of enterprise, and never, never neglect an opportunity, and we must see all we can, either as children or grown-up people. Why, I have known people go to the seaside for six weeks, and sit on the beach, morning after morning, because every one else did, regardless of the fact that all round the place itself lay lovely scenery and marvellously interesting country, into which they actually had not the energy to penetrate. Think of the opportunities wasted by them—the opportunities we all waste if we allow a day to pass by while we shut our eyes and will not see for ourselves the new things that come every morning for the observant ones among us! And do not let your children exist ignorant of the thousand and one throbbing historical events by which they are surrounded. Better spend your money on showing them good pictures, beautiful scenery, celebrated men and places, than on aimless gaiety, idiotic balls, and smart clothes and expensive food; and above all let them have a bright, happy childhood among charming surroundings. Believe me, you will give them a better inheritance than if you had fed them and dressed them luxuriously, and had laid up a large fortune for them.

Let beauty and simplicity, honesty and frankness, be your guide in your nurseries, and then you will not have very much trouble with your children.

CHAPTER XVI
IN RETIREMENT

There comes a time in most households when the mistress has perforce to contemplate an enforced retirement from public life; and I wish to impress upon all those who may be in a similar plight that the time will pass much more quickly and agreeably if the room selected for the temporary prison is made as pretty, convenient, and as unlike the orthodox sick-room as can be managed.

Naturally these times are looked forward to with dread by all young wives. They are fully convinced that they must die, and in fact make themselves perfectly wretched and miserable because of their ignorance, and of their not unnatural dislike to speak of their dreads and fears; and though, of course, I can only lightly touch on these matters in a book which I trust may be widely used and read, I want to whisper a few words to reassure all those who may be contemplating the arrival of No. 1. If girls are brought up in a proper, healthy manner, if they do not rush about from ball to party or from one excitement to the other, if they realise their condition, and dress and rest themselves properly beforehand, in nine cases out of ten the illness, being a natural one, has no attendant dangers, and should therefore be looked upon in an entirely different manner than it is at present. There is a most excellent little book published by Messrs. Churchill, and written by Dr. Chevasse, which all young wives should procure. It is called 'Advice to a Wife,' and is a really necessary possession. This can be supplemented later by 'Advice to a Mother' (same author and publisher); and, possessed of these books, any young matron can manage herself most successfully without the constant harassment of continually seeing the doctor. But, besides the purely medical aspect of the case, there are matters that can and must be arranged early, and by the expectant mother herself alone; and one of these, and the most important of all, is undoubtedly the choice of the nurse, who should be engaged as early as possible, for most good nurses are secured as soon as it is probable their services will be required later on. And as, to my mind, a good nurse is 'all the battle,' this once secured the worst is over, and Angelina may contemplate the future, if not with absolute calmness, at all events with a brave and trustful heart. I do not think too much stress can be laid upon this looking after a nurse. And though girls may indeed congratulate themselves on their position to-day as regards the orthodox monthly nurse, as contrasted with their mothers' and grandmothers' accounts of all they suffered at the hands of the old-time Mrs. Gamp, with whose vagaries we are all so familiar, still great care must be exercised in the choice, as nothing is so important, especially for No. 1, as to have a really good, kind woman in the nurse, and one who will neither unduly coddle the patient nor allow her to do rash things, of which she will most certainly repent unto her dying day; and I should like to implore any one who is contemplating the arrival of King Baby not to trust entirely to the doctor's recommendation, but to rely for once, at least, on her mother's advice, and to employ some one who is personally known to some member of the family.

I have known, and still know, a nurse who is simply perfect. She is of no use to the general public, as 'her ladies' keep her well employed among themselves and their friends, but I shall write a little about her here, as a guide to those who may be likely to require some one in a similar capacity.

But before I do this let me say a few words about the extreme folly, from my point of view, of engaging what is called a lady-nurse. 'She is so companionable, so delightful, so much nicer than any mere working woman can possibly be,' say those who have friends they wish to find places for; but I must declare I have never, in all my large experience, found them in the very least bit satisfactory or of the very least use practically.

As a theory they are all they ought to be; but in practice they are a most dismal failure! They will keep the room pretty with flowers, and will forget to remove them at night; and they will do what I may term the decorative parts of nursing, leaving all the more practical ones to any of the already overworked servants who can be pressed into the service, and who of course resent this immensely, and generally give warning at a most inconvenient time; but I have really found them do very little besides this!

Thinking of my good nurse causes me to remember other things in connection with these events, on which I will touch for one moment; the while I maintain strenuously that, as a rule, not half enough loving thought is bestowed upon the mother, who, I insist, should be the first object of every one's care until she has been for at least a fortnight over her trouble; and I trace a good deal of my own nervous irritability and ill-health to the fact that after my last baby arrived I had an enormous quantity of small worries that the presence in the house of a careful guard would have obviated, and to the fact that wearisome details of an illness of a relative were carried to me as usual, and I had to see to matters that should never have been even whispered about before me, but the arrangement of all of which was left entirely to me; and the only rest I obtained during all that weary time was literally snatched for me, from the jaws of all those who are accustomed to depend on me, by nurse, who was my one bright gleam of hope, and to whose never-failing energy and thoughtfulness I always look back most gratefully and thankfully.

Speaking as I do from experience only, perhaps I may be forgiven if I repeat myself, and beg for far more consideration for the mother than she ever gets. I hope I shall not be considered a monster if I whisper quite low that I do not believe a new baby is anything but a profound nuisance to its relations at the very first. It howls when peace is required, it demands unceasing attention, and it is thrust into Angelina's arms, and she has to admire it and adore it at the risk of being thought most unnatural, when she really is rather resenting the intrusion, and requires at least a week to reconcile herself to her new fate. My nurse never allows *her* baby to be a torment. Somehow she has such a pleasant way with her that babies cannot be a trouble where she is. She turns them out always as if they had just come out of a band-box, and one never realises a baby can be unpleasant so long as she has the dressing of them, and the seeing to them generally; but then she is so very methodical, so clean, so bright, so cheerful, that somehow I find, when I come to write down her method, I cannot remember so much what she did as how she did it, and that I cannot recall her routine of work half as easily as I can each detail of her neat form and *jolly* face, and the perfect joy it was to me to have about me a woman who never fussed, never kept me waiting, always did to-day what she did yesterday at the same time, and, above all, presented me with a nice bright-looking baby to look at just when that infant was wanted, and not at inopportune moments, or just at the special moment when she would have been a worry.

And oh, what a contrast she was to the good old-fashioned nurse who came to me with No. 1! who had a routine and who kept to it, and who regarded all new ideas and thoughts as dangerous and 'flying in the face of Providence,' yet who was goodness and trustworthiness itself; but she was too old to learn that people differ, and what is one man's meat is another man's poison, and so made my life a burden to me because she could not understand that I was really and truly different in my tastes and likings to most of her other ladies, who loved to be fed constantly and be as constantly 'waited on' and looked after, while all I required was to be let alone in peace and quiet and fed rather less than most people. Still she was a dragon of watchfulness, and kept away all those small bothers which men can never refrain from bringing to their wives, regardless that at such times the smallest worry becomes gigantic, and assumes proportions that would be ludicrous, were they not really and truly very real; and have real effects too on the nerves and temper of the unfortunate invalid. And here let me say sternly, and as forcibly as I can, that the life of the ordinary house-mother has never been properly appreciated by the male sex; and, if at no other time can we obtain consideration and thought, it is imperative that for at least three weeks after the arrival of a baby the wife should have mental as well as bodily rest, and that she should be absolutely shielded from all domestic cares and worries. And every husband should be taught by the doctor and nurse combined that there is real and great need for the wife to be carefully kept from *little* worries and bothers, until she has regained her usual balance of health, and is able to hear with more equanimity of the death of some dear friend, maybe, than she was a few weeks before; to simply be told that cook had had a soldier to tea; and that there had been so much butter used in the kitchen that the Bankruptcy Court is in the near future.

Husbands are far too apt to say and think that the life of a woman is a mere giddy whirl of frocks and gaiety, that all the time he is 'toiling in the City,' or doing the equivalent of that in some other walk in life, she is airily fluttering from flower to flower, extracting all the sweetness she can out of it, and bitterly resents it should she be tired in the evening, or require a little lively talk, instead of hours of contemplation of a sleeping countenance, at which perchance she looks sadly, and wonders if she ever really did think it so good-looking, as she seems to remember she once did, in some far-off existence long since dead. But have men the smallest idea of what a never-ceasing, uninteresting work a woman's far too often is? Men never can be acquainted with or realise—bless them!—the thousand worries a woman knows all too well; the abject fears for her children that always haunt her, the dread that Tommy's whine may mean scarlet fever, or that Trixy's temper indicates measles; the impatience with which she would fain greet the daily details of food and drink, and which she has to smother; the sordid arrangements with butcher and baker, and the endless trouble she has to keep the house nice, the children well, and the expenses down to the lowest sum she can possibly manage with, and all this is done within the walls of one house. A man's work takes him far afield; he rubs his intellect against those of hundreds of other people daily. He goes to his 'toil' through amusing streets which always vary, and he has the grand excitement of being paid for his 'toil,' while the ordinary woman works on and on ceaselessly without pay, sometimes without thanks; and handicapped by indifferent health and nervous dread for her babies that no man—no *man*, I repeat, with a fine accent of scorn on the noun—can ever comprehend, much less appreciate in the least; gets through an amount of real positive labour, an account of which might astonish the husband, but which he would most certainly not believe in were it written out in plain words for his perusal, and placed before him. Of course, I am not writing about the 'upper ten,' about whose domestic arrangements I know nothing, and which, judging from the papers, are not always as successful as they might be. Here, no doubt, ladies spend their days in the 'fluttering' spoken of above, and may not earn their keep—to put the matter a little coarsely—but we ordinary folk cannot do much fluttering, even if we would; and I can but hope that men will realise what a woman's work means for the future, and will take care she is really nursed and guarded, in a manner the husband alone can see is done, at a time when the brain should be allowed to rest, as well as the rest of the body.

A man cannot realise that a woman ever can have ambition—that she can sicken at the dusters and pudding-cloths that are supposed to be her proper occupation, that she does sometimes feel even a little bit better educated or cleverer than the clever creature who makes the money; and if only I can get one of the male sex to believe that we do sometimes want a little of his freedom, a little of his powers of money-making, a little of his ability to take a holiday unhaunted by never-ceasing dreads and fears of what awful ends the children are coming to at home in our absence, I shall not have lived in vain, particularly if at the same time he takes the double burden on his own shoulders, when his wife has presented him with a small son or daughter, and takes care that not even a whisper of the cook's wickedness passes the bedroom door, until Materfamilias is able to bring her mind to bear upon a matter that can, no doubt, be explained as soon as the feminine intellect grapples with it.

And one more very serious word for the last on this subject: let Edwin bear in mind that much more care is needed with No. 5 or No. 6 than was ever bestowed at the time when No. 1 put the house in a stir, and altered all the domestic arrangements. Angelina is not so young as she was, dear soul; she is very tired. She is quite sure such a numerous family must bring her to the workhouse, and unless Edwin is goodness itself he may so depress and harass his wife by his depression that she may slip out of his fingers altogether, and leave him to himself, that most utterly to be pitied person on earth, a widower with young children, to find out what he has lost, and to realise all too late what he might have saved, had he remembered how desperately hard women do work, and how unending and never-ceasing is their toil; which has dulness as a background and utter sameness as a rule, as a drawback to its being satisfactorily performed.

Once let the nurse be secured for as early a date as one can conveniently do with her, there are the small garments to be seen to. These consist of very fine lawn shirts (12), long flannels (6 for day, of fine Welsh flannel; 4

for night, of rather a thicker quality), fine long-cloth petticoats (6), monthly gowns of cambric and trimmed with muslin embroideries on the bodices only (8), and nightgowns (8); besides this 4 head-flannels will be required, and a large flannel shawl to wrap the child in as it is taken from room to room; about six dozen large Russian diapers and six good flannel pilches. Three or four pairs of tiny woollen shoes complete the outfit, which may furthermore have added to it four good robes; but these I strongly advise no one to buy until it is time to talk about the christening, for relatives often present the baby with smart frocks; and as they are really worn very little, and cost a great deal of money, are not necessary, especially in the country, where really nice monthly gowns are good enough for any baby; and the smart robes tempt young mothers to adopt the pernicious custom of low necks and short sleeves, making these even shorter by tying them up on the small shoulders with gay ribbons, that soon find their way into the little mouths. Even in smart low-necked frocks I always had a species of long-sleeved, extra high bodice tacked; for, apart from the appearance of the small skinny arms and necks of most young babies, I consider it suicidal of any mother to condemn her children to a style of dress that is about as unsuitable to our climate as anything well can be. I should put even a tiny baby into a high fine flannel vest. I always make the long flannel barra-coats with three pleats in the bodices back and front, and line the stay bodices with flannel, thus reducing the chance of colds greatly; and I live in hopes of seeing in a very short time the total disappearance of low dresses everywhere; for to my mind this is a custom as foolish and indecent as any we still retain from our savage ancestors. Besides the clothes enumerated above, four or five strips of flannel about six inches wide, herring-boned each side, and about eighteen inches long, will be required, and six swathes to roll round the infant and give support to the back; this, new-fashioned doctors try to dispense with, but from long experience I am convinced these binders are a most important portion of a young baby's attire.

The basket should contain a complete set of baby's things ready aired, and furthermore a skein of whitey-brown thread, a *new* pair of scissors, a pot of cold cream, pins, safety pins, and some old pieces of linen; and the young mother will do wisely if she has the long pieces of Russian diaper used as hand-towels for some three or four months before taking them for the baby, as this softens them and makes them much better for the nurse's use. All these things should be in readiness quite two months before they are required, and should be placed, with a large mackintosh sheet, two old blankets, and three coarse 'blanket-sheets,' where, should they be required in a hurry, they can be found at once. Attention to these particulars and directions saves fuss and worry and often prevents danger.

These matters seen to, the young wife may now turn her mind to the arrangement of her own chamber, which she should do her very best to make as pretty as she can; or she should carefully look at the rooms at her disposal and see which will be the nicest and most cheerful for her to occupy; for there is really no need, unless we like, for the event to take place in the room usually occupied, and, if preferred, a pretty room might be got ready beforehand; but, if this be impossible, at least all the washing and toilet apparatus might depart, and some tables and low pretty chairs and a sofa, books and plants, replace the washing-stand and toilet-table, that can be relegated to another room until Angelina is herself again. Taking into consideration that, as an enterprising advertiser remarks, one half one's time is spent in one's bedroom, we cannot possibly take too much care about them to have them nice and pretty; for I am convinced one comes down to one's day's work far better tempered from a pretty and convenient room, than one does from an ugly, inconvenient place, where we have worn ourselves out in hunting for our properties, or been worried by contemplating hideous papers and draperies, and ugly conventional walls without pictures or decoration of any kind; while if one has to be ill, and, what is more, has to contemplate a long period of convalescence in one spot, one cannot too carefully select one's surroundings, for there is no doubt that one's mind acts insensibly on one's body, and that one's convalescence is a great deal more advanced or retarded, as the case may be, than we think for by our surroundings; therefore, I am sure we shall not be wasting our time if we think a good deal about the arrangement of a room where the young mother will have to spend at least three weeks, and where she will remain a much more willing prisoner, if she is not harassed and worried by a bedroom where she cannot have any of her usual surroundings, and where the bedroom aspect of the chamber predominates over everything else, so preventing any visitors to her, save of the most intimate and personal kind possible. I do hope that the queer notion that nurse ought to sleep in the room with her patient has almost, if not quite, died out. I never could make out why this was considered necessary, unless in very severe cases, where sitting up is thought of consequence; and even then (though it sounds Irish I can't help saying it) the nurse could take her rest in another room, leaving some one else to sit up in turn; for I know nothing more truly irritating than to see a second bed in the room, and to feel the eternal presence of a stranger, who might just as well be snugly resting in the adjacent dressing-room, where she could be reached quite as well by ringing a small bell, that could stand on the table by the side of the bed, as she is by a call from the patient, whose voice is sure to be none of the strongest.

I have often marvelled at the way people bear these small worries, and never turn their minds towards relieving themselves of them. I suppose we are most of us too conventional, and cannot get out of our grooves easily, but I am quite sure from experience that no one requires a nurse during the night in an ordinary case, and that one's comfort is mightily increased by seeing her depart into the dressing-room, with or without the baby, as fires or other matters are arranged, and to know she will not return until the next morning unless she has been rung for; and then her departure leaves room for far more decoration than would otherwise be possible, for, if the house is conveniently built, and the dressing-rooms or nurseries are near enough to be available, I should turn out all the bedroomy furniture into other rooms, and replace this with some of the sitting-room furniture, only retaining the bed, which in its turn can retire behind a screen when the sofa, is taken to, and convalescence has really and truly begun.

To do this satisfactorily, the bed must be specially thought about, and should be provided with an extra lot of frilled and monogramed pillow-cases; these are removed at night, and their presence, and that of a nice piece of linen, frilled and worked too, and fashioned in such a way that it appears like a frilled sheet, in the morning, is almost as good as a complete change of linen, without any bustle. The eider-down should be removed, and placed in another room to be aired, and the bed should be covered with one of the beautiful embroidered quilts which should be in every one's possession.

These quilts are copies of old work done by our grandmothers; or else are embroidered in the red and blue 'Russian-work,' and are lined with a coloured sateen or Bolton sheeting; they can be edged with lace, worked with coloured threads to match, or by a band of the sateen over which a coarse lace is turned; these quilts make any couch ornamental at once. Of course the toilet-covers must correspond, and the towels should be marked in similar colours, and should in some measure repeat the prevailing tints of the bedroom itself, which is not complete without both books and growing plants in pots, nor without some convenient light. A good lamp can be placed on a bracket, if gas is disliked; or a good bracket lamp in beaten iron can be fixed in the wall just above the bed, or to one side thereof; and great comfort is found from either a wall-pocket made from a Japanese fan and plush, or a big bag of plush strung from the brass end of the bed, to contain one's handkerchief, keys, pencil, letters from the post, and the odds and ends that will accumulate, and, furthermore, will lose themselves in a most peculiar and aggravating manner, unless one has a distinct place to put them in from whence they cannot possibly stray; while I again repeat that no 'bedroomy' atmosphere must be allowed, and that every medicine bottle, towel, basin, sponge, &c., must be taken away out of the room the moment they are done with, and that the sick-room must be looked upon for the time being as much as possible in the light of a sitting-room, where friends can come, and where life can go on smoothly and pleasantly, without being reminded every five minutes that one is laid aside, and unable to feel or look pleasant and like oneself. I wonder, too, if other people know how useful a good heliotrope shade is for one's dressing-gown, and the short flannel jacket that should be one's day attire until the dressing-gown can be put on and one can lie on the sofa? These dressing-jackets, or more properly 'bed-gowns,' are simply invaluable—in winter especially, when one's arms do get so cold in the ordinary nightdress, and when the dressing-gown proper is a distinct nuisance; and they should be wadded, and of fine heliotrope cashmere with a soft fall, and frill of either torchon or yak lace, and are most becoming to any one. The arms should be lined with wadding too; and, in fact, they are just what one requires before one gets up, as they save the dressing-gown from the inevitable crushing that is its portion if we wear it in bed, while we have the required warmth over the chest, which would not otherwise be ours, for reading or writing or using one's arms at all always disturbs the bedclothes in a most tiresome manner, which does not trouble us when we are possessed of the proper short jacket.

The bother I have had, too, to find a really comfortable way of reading in bed. How one's book does flop over just when one doesn't wish it to, and how tired one does get of holding it! And I have now discovered that the only way is to have a couple of cushions or pillows, and to shake them into a good position oneself, finally resting the volume luxuriously upon them.

Then, too, remember always to have some *fresh* sweet flowers in your room all day, and if your dinner leaves an odour of food behind it, burn two of the joss-sticks sold at the Baker Street Bazaar at 6*d*. a packet—those make your room at once like an Eastern palace, and are simply delightful; and insist mildly but forcibly on your windows being opened whenever the sun shines, and in the dressing-room when it doesn't; for there is, I am convinced after long experience, nothing like fresh air for any and every one; and though I have been perpetually told I should catch my death of cold at such times, I have never had a suspicion of one, and am remarkably free from this tiresome ailment.

Summer babies must be legislated for rather differently to winter ones; they must be washed and dressed out of their mother's room for one thing, as they always require the fire, that would be cruelty itself in the bedroom. They can often be taken out earlier, and are much easier to manage. Still, I think all these details can be safely left to the nurse, who should always be engaged for two months certain, and for three if you know your woman and can afford it; for until a baby is three months old it flourishes far better in the care of the monthly nurse than in that of even one's own nurse, who has grown a little 'rusty' in her knowledge of infants most likely, and who can never be as *au fait* with them as is any one who has a constant succession of these tiny creatures always under her care.

It is imperative in the case of a first baby that the monthly nurse remains until the stationary nurse arrives, so that she can find out if she has really been trained in nice ways, and can really handle a baby. She can tell at once if she knows what she is about, and, if she does not, can at once put her right, and tell her the 'ways' the child has been used to.

A general rule should be the daily bath in tepid water, using a high standing bath in a wooden case; the child is washed all over quickly on the nurse's lap; protected by a large flannel apron, with a soft sponge, and the best soap to be found; it is then floated gently into the bath, and the water merrily and quickly dashed over the limbs, while the nurse talks brightly and cheerfully to it; after about three or four minutes of this it is taken out, and dried rapidly with an extremely soft towel, powdered all over in every tiny crease and fold of fat, its flannel binder is sewn on again, and its garments arranged with the flannel petticoat and shirt tacked together, put on very swiftly; it should then be fed and put into its bed warm, and there it should stop until time for feeding again, when it can be taken out for an airing in the garden, or in some sheltered spot according to the time of year and the means at command.

Regularity, quiet, and its own nurseries and nurse are the things to keep a baby well and make it grow up strong; and for this one must depend partly on one's nurse, who should be a superior woman, possessed of the real religion which caused the little maid who was converted to sweep *under* the door-mats, a duty she had not fulfilled before she saw the error of her ways, and not a humbug, who would insist on leaving an ailing or sick infant because it was her night for church or chapel; but she must be a real friend too, and be treated as such, if we wish to have peace and a well-ordered household, for in these hurrying days of ours we must depend a good deal on our nurses if we are to keep bright and strong, and be companions to our husbands, and later on to the boys and girls, who will require so much more from us than the mere infant, whose well-being we must, of course, superintend and legislate for ceaselessly, but for whom we need not turn ourselves into domestic animals merely, incapable of aught, because of our slavedom to the baby, who in nine cases out of ten does far better with a really good nurse than it can with us.

I may, of course, have been exceptionally lucky with my nurse, and, judging from what I hear of other people's experiences, I suppose I must have been; but during all my many years of being dependent on them I have never had one selfish woman in my house, nor one who would not at any moment sacrifice her own interests and comforts to mine. I cannot account for this any more than I can account for other people's miseries; but I honestly say here that I never cease to wonder at the cries that rend the air about the wickedness of domestics, for I have never found one who has not honestly and *according to her lights* done her best to help me on my way; and I owe more than I can say now to my friends in the kitchen, who will do anything to save me trouble, and will when I am busy, as I generally am, do all in their power to assist me; while no words of mine could express the unselfish care given by my nurses both to me and the children during years that are past now, I hope for ever, but that, while they lasted, would have driven a bad or selfish woman away from us. Real, true, good friends are, I am sure, far more often found among what we call the 'lower classes' than in those ranks from whence we generally take our acquaintances! Of course, this is all digression, but yet it really does relate to the nursery after all, for there, if anywhere in her household, must our bride look for her helpmate; and this should be all arranged and thought out with the help of the monthly nurse in the time of retirement, for this first arrival changes all the household arrangements entirely, and in such a manner that the greatest tact and care is necessary to readjust the establishment, or else misery and discomfort will be rampant, in the once happy and well-managed home.

Above all, let the young wife remember that her baby and her experience are not either wonderful or unique; that she only possesses what millions of women possess and know of; and let her rely just a little on her own mother, who may have old-fashioned notions, but who has brought her up successfully, and so doubtless has that best of all gifts, experience, to hand on to her daughter, who cannot do better than listen to her; the while she recovers her strength, keeps calm, and does her best to get well, and looks out for all the assistance she can obtain from her nurse, and further on from her own experience of what her children are.

Just one other thing: it is absolutely necessary in legislating for our children to remember what they are likely to inherit in the way of *tendencies*.

We have long ceased to regard either the souls or the brains of our children as strictly new and original compositions, as clean white paper over which we and time can write exactly what we wish; for science has taught us all about 'heredity,' and convinced us that we are all of us bundles of odds and ends, or scraps of this grandparent, with curious 'sports' of that uncle or aunt suddenly cropping up; and so, if we remember tendencies to consumption, or fevers, or gout, or, in fact, anything that we or our forefathers have shown a tendency for, we shall be able to manage our children much better than we otherwise should; for those children who are constantly 'catching' things, or meeting with accidents because of the brittleness of bone, or careless heedlessness inherited from some ancestor, must be more carefully watched and looked after than those who, coming of a healthy, splendidly constituted stock, are rarely ill, and only require water, air, and a pure, good diet to grow up splendid specimens of humanity, enjoying their lives thoroughly, and fully appreciating every day they live.

Heredity is a great, a most important fact; and if only this could be taught in schools, if young men and women would recognise the wickedness of cousins marrying, and of passing on sickly or vicious tendencies to their children, we should look forward more and more hopefully to a future, when health should be demonstrated as the best possession a man can have—the best inheritance he can demand of his parents; for health means happiness and beauty and pleasure, and without health we cannot be either happy, good-tempered, or prosperous, or succeed in a world where life is one constant procession of beauty and surpassing interest, to those whose hearts are in the right place, and whose pure, wholesome blood courses vigorously through the veins and arteries of the whole body.

CHAPTER XVII
THE SCHOOLROOM

In the selection of the schoolroom there are several things to be thought of; but if the nursery be done away with, and there should be no upstairs sitting-room, I strongly advise the schoolroom being on the bedroom floor. This is often a most useful institution, for sometimes it serves as a refuge to invalids who are well enough to leave their bedrooms, but not well enough to run the risks of draught on the stairs, while the children are out of the way of visitors, and are not always running up and down the passages in a distracting and untidy manner.

Let me urge on all mothers of families to cling to either a day nursery or a schoolroom until the children are really too old to be glad of some place where they can do actually and positively as they like; that is to say, of course, unless they like to behave like savages, but this rarely happens in a household where the little ones have been accustomed to nice surroundings, and to be treated like human beings from their cradles.

It is most important that children should be let a great deal alone, and to insure this it is perfectly necessary that some room should be set apart for their use entirely, furnished in such a way that one is not constantly obliged to be saying 'Don't do this' and 'Don't do that,' and yet in a manner that shall foster every nice taste and encourage every good habit possible; and great care should be also taken to insure sufficient sunshine, for sunshine is life and health, and a dark and sunless room often fosters a dark and sunless nature.

I should strongly advise the floor of the schoolroom to be covered with Indian matting, if expense be no object, with rugs about at intervals: this is always clean and fresh, and can be changed often. Next to Indian matting comes the stained edge to the floor so often recommended, with the nice square of Kidderminster carpet laid down over carpet felt, and edged with a woollen fringe; the best carpets of this particular make are called 'three-ply,' and are sold by the yard, and are infinitely superior in every way to the 'squares' sold ready made in different sizes, and edged by a border, which is generally far too large a pattern to look nice. The carpets sold by the yard are much better designs and colours, and wear three times as long as the cheaper makes; but under *no* circumstances should the schoolroom be the refuge for half-worn costly carpets, which want wearing out, and yet are too shabby for the downstairs apartments. These had far better be got rid of in some sale; for an old carpet is nothing but a dust-bin on a small scale, and can never be fresh enough to pat in a room where there are children.

The walls could be covered with one of the washable sanitary papers, if one can be procured in a sufficiently pretty pattern; but it is emphatically necessary that the walls should have a real dado, either of oilcloth painted some good artistic shade—four coats are necessary to eliminate the pattern—of cretonne, or matting, which would be best of all. This keeps the lower part of the wall tidy always; and if the sanitary paper can be obtained in a self-colour, the plainness of this can be done away with by a good selection of pictures, than which nothing is more necessary in a schoolroom; and the children had far better be plainly dressed and fed than have bad pictures provided for them, or ugly drawings only relating to their work.

In these days of cheap art there is no reason why we should be without pictures of some kind everywhere, and they should be chosen carefully, either for their beauty or for the lesson they teach. Having a positive horror of gambling, horse-racing, or betting in any shape or form myself, I cannot regard any house satisfactorily furnished without autotypes of my father's pictures of 'The Road to Ruin.' These admirable pictures have pointed a moral over and over again in my house, and will, I hope, point many another; for the children are always ready to look at them and make out for themselves the dismal o'er-true tale. If, however, these pictures should be objected to, I should advise autotypes of some of Sir Joshua's lovely child-pictures, Leader's 'At evening time it shall be light,' 'Chill October,' any of the etchings after Burton Barber's amusing dog-pictures, and those equally entertaining fox-terrier sketches of Mr. Yates Carrington, Waller's 'The Day of Reckoning,' and, in fact, any of the beautiful etchings done of late years, and that average 5*l.* each; these purchases being infinitely more necessary in a house where there are children than diamonds or plate or smart furniture and expensive decorations, and should be bought, as soon as ever they can be afforded, by any householder who really has the welfare of his family at heart.

The ceiling should be papered in some bright blue and white paper, and should have a good ventilator somewhere in the centre. No gas should be allowed, and light should be furnished by two good hanging lamps conveniently placed; while each child who is old enough to do its work after tea in the winter should have its own shaded Queen's reading lamp, and should be taught to keep it clean and bright for itself; thus the servants would not be troubled on this subject unduly, though, should there be a schoolroom maid, she could take the lamps under her charge with the rest of the schoolroom belongings.

There should be two good cupboards in the room, which could be placed in the recesses on each side of the fireplace, should there be any; these could be simply made with shelves in the recesses and with wooden doors to fasten over them; these could be painted some self-colour to match the prevailing colour of the room, and the panels could be filled in either with the ever-useful Japanese leather paper, or be embellished by Mrs. McClelland's clever brush with studies of some lovely flowers; brass handles should be added, and while one cupboard should be set apart for the governess and the schoolroom books, the other should be so arranged that, if possible, each child should have its own shelf. The top of these cupboards could form an excellent receptacle for toys and games, while some of the hanging bookshelves spoken of before could supplement the shelves should there not be room for the extra books. The windows must open top and bottom, and should have short muslin and cretonne curtains; no blinds, of course, but, should the situation be as sunny as it ought to be, outside blinds should be provided, and, furthermore, window-boxes for flowers should never be wanting; the children learn a great deal looking after them, and lessons are far less trying on a hot day if the room is kept cool by sun-blinds, while what air there is blows in over a sweet scent caused perhaps by that best of all mixtures, mignonette and ten-week stocks.

Great care must be taken in selecting the proper tables and chairs; these latter must be wide and comfortable, and the table *must* be solid and stand on good strong legs while lessons go on. I strongly advise the tablecloth to be removed for fear of accidents with ink, and if oilcloth is sewn over the top this is not as tiresome to write on as is a deal surface, and though it may not look petty it is decidedly clean and remarkably useful, and can be covered with the cloth when lessons are over. Footstools should never be wanting, and a good broad window-seat, that could be made to open and hold books &c., is very useful also, as it will contain a great many odds and ends; while no schoolroom could be complete in my eyes without kittens and puppies, the training and care of which are often of the greatest service to the young masters and mistresses, who, teaching their pets obedience and good behaviour, insensibly learn quite as much as they are themselves teaching.

Though I maintain that education of a certain kind is begun the moment a baby learns to cry for what it wants, and that, no matter how small a child is, it is never too small to be taught obedience, of course its real education begins when it learns its letters. I could read at two, and have read ever since, never being able to be happy without a book or paper; and I am of opinion that the sooner a child can pick up its letters the better, for the moment it can read it is independent, and can amuse itself without always hankering after companionship and entertainment. The best way to teach a child to read is to give it a small wooden frame, made in compartments, and a box of red and black letters; these it picks up one by one, and soon learns to slip them into the frame, making small words. From this it passes easily to a book, and becomes master of a store of amusement that will last all its life; while the governess should be asked to read aloud as much as she can to the children, taking care, of course, to select good and amusing stories, the while she does not bore them with a too forcibly impressed moral tag at the end.

One cannot, of course, lay down any hard-and-fast rules for other people's children, and can only, after all, give very general hints as to schoolroom arrangements and management, for each household is so different that what suits one family is not of much use to another. Still there are general hints on education that may be of assistance to those who may be about to set up a schoolroom, and, though I feel rather diffident about speaking as much about myself as I must, I think I must tell just a little more of the way in which I have managed that most important part of the establishment.

To begin with: great cleanliness, order, regularity, and punctuality must be insisted on and maintained by the dining-room example. The children's breakfast should be at eight, and should consist, if possible, of oatmeal porridge every other day, followed by either an egg, bacon, or some fish. I say advisedly 'if possible,' for some children cannot touch porridge; and though I am no advocate for pampering appetite, and scorn rich and elaborate cooking, which in England all too often engulfs the money that would buy pictures or allow of excursions and travel, I do protest most solemnly against the petty tyranny of making children eat food that is actually and positively nauseous to them: and, furthermore, without consulting the child, and so making him unduly of consequence in his own eyes, it is imperative that a judicious parent should notice likes and dislikes, and so legislate that something should be provided that all the children can eat; and no breakfast should pass without fruit of some kind being provided. Children crave for fruit and sweet things, and a careful parent gives enough, without allowing the excess that is so harmful, and that only occurs in families, as a rule, where sweets are ignored, and fruit handed round as a rarity after the conclusion of a large and expensive meal.

In winter lessons could be from nine until twelve, when the walk should be taken, or some games indulged in. Luncheon should be at one, and should far oftener include fish or chicken than it usually does. Tea, with jam or cake, should be at five, and each child should be encouraged to have milk and a biscuit before it goes to bed. A few pure sweets should be given always after luncheon, and no punishment should ever be inflicted through the appetite. This makes food too prominent a matter in the small mind, and I have always found a few stern and forcible words of more effect than any punishment could be after the first struggle for authority, which invariably occurs once in the lifetime of every child. In two or three cases in my own schoolroom one whipping has been found quite sufficient; while two of the children have never required anything more serious than an early retirement for reflection in bed, and a few serious sentences that were to the purpose, and did not go beyond it. I am quite aware that in these days it is considered abominable even to suggest a child shall be 'smacked,' but in the case of deliberate obstinacy or unbridled howling there is nothing else for it, and, this once done, trouble ceases—the child has found its master, and then there is peace.

I am so convinced that if one has a happy childhood one's whole life is sweetened by it, no matter whatever happens afterwards, that I cannot impress too much upon my readers the absolute necessity of securing this, at any rate, for their boys and girls. This, however, is not to be had by dressing them finely, and dragging them about from drawing-room to drawing-room, from late party to late party, or by pampering them and considering them until one cannot call the house one's own, neither does it consist in leaving them to themselves altogether. Apparently, children should be left greatly to themselves, but much in the same manner that—I speak in all sincerity—a higher Power manages us and our affairs. Let the free-will be there, but let the guiding hand, unseen though it should be, never be lacking, and we shall find the children happy and good, because they are surrounded with clean good air, and are brought up in an atmosphere absolutely free from taint of any kind.

The instant the schoolroom is started, that instant both mothers and fathers should become in a measure omniscient and omnipresent; and, above all, they should remember the clear sight and hearing of the children, and should, furthermore, recollect that what they say and do means a great deal more now than it ever did. Let them see their own lives are full of interest, and are of good aim and intent, and they will find example is greater than precept, and that they have succeeded by unconscious example where everything else would have failed.

Of course, it is absolutely necessary that all girls should learn to sew, to cook, and to play the piano; and all boys should have some way of employing their fingers, and no household should be complete without its hospital box; into this the girls can collect all the frocks and petticoats they can make, while the boys can make scrapbooks, paint pictures with watercolours over prints from 'Punch' or the 'Illustrated London News,' or cut out ships or wooden dolls; and while they are doing this they could be read to from Scott, Dickens, Thackeray, or Miss Yonge—a strange mixture, may be, but to those four writers the world can never be grateful enough, try hard as it may, while the schoolroom contingent brought up on these splendid people's brains will be worth a hundred of the present-day children, fostered on such idle rubbish as Rider Haggard produces, and others that shall be nameless. And here let me beg and pray the parents to make a stand for Dickens and Thackeray, even if they will not for the other two authors of whom I have spoken. Dickens has become neglected, I know, and Oxford undergraduates, taking to Thackeray late, fall asleep over 'Esmond' and 'The Virginians'; but let these books be in the schoolroom, and boys and girls take to them naturally, like ducks take to water, and are at once made happier by them than they can be by anything else.

Sewing must be learned by girls, because they never know how they may be placed; but, once learnt, I trust no girl may be condemned to sew because it is feminine, for unless she really and truly likes the occupation—and most women do—there is no greater cruelty possible to inflict on a young girl than to make her sew when her fingers are itching to draw, practise, or even write a book. Never prevent her doing this; the greatest happiness I have ever had is when I can get perfect peace and quiet and take my pen in hand, and, even if I never succeed in making a name for myself and startling a world that is over-full of writers already, I can never feel I have lost the time I have spent in writing, for then I have been perfectly contented, and then for me the world has ceased to be—outside Nature—beloved Nature!—and my desk. And then, harming no one, I trust, and helping just a few, I have passed away entirely from all worries incidental to the life of any woman who marries, and has children and a household always on her mind, and have ceased to think of anything save the work on hand at the moment. Girls must learn also to cook, because thus they become mistress of all the details of the household expenditure; and they must learn music, because they can be useful either to accompany songs and glees, or to play dance-music to the little ones; but if no distinct taste is shown, hours should not be wasted on an accomplishment that is most useless, save and except as a mere background, unless decided talent is displayed, when, of course, music should be encouraged as much as possible, for nothing keeps a household more together than does music, and if the boys and girls can only play and sing together there is small difficulty about finding them occupation and keeping them happy at home.

I am always sorry that the power to make music and the capacity for enjoying games were left out of my composition, and in consequence are conspicuous by their absence from our household; but reading has taken their place, and not one of us is unhappy as long as books are to be had; but one tires sometimes of this, and I could wish heartily we all loved games or went in for music, for these tastes are most excellent safeguards against *ennui* and the craving for excitement and going about that all modern folks seem to possess.

Now one word about Sunday in the schoolroom, and we will pass on to other matters. Whatever you do, never let Sunday be a day of dulness and penance, but make it as bright and happy as you can. Let the household rise as early as on a weekday, be regular at some bright, good service, and make it altogether a bright and pleasant day; let the children see the 'Graphic' and 'Illustrated London News,' and read their ordinary books. If a book is fit for a weekday it is fit for Sunday. Dine early, because the servants want a little rest, and as a culminating treat have a nice supper about eight, and let the children share it. Don't tease them with strict rules and sad faces, but let them learn on this day to appreciate rest and to learn something of a higher life, that need not be kept for Sunday alone, but that one has more time to think of on Sunday than on any other day of the week.

I do not myself like to see tennis played or boating or driving for pleasure indulged in, simply, I think, because of old-time prejudice, and because of the noise made or the work given to one's coachman and horses; but logically there is not half as much harm in these pursuits as there is in the spiteful gossip so many people indulge in after church, or the wasted hours spent in sleep after a heavy dinner eaten under protest and grumbled at everlastingly; and I would much rather my boys played tennis than that they lounged about smoking and sleeping, or wasted their time reading the 'Sporting Times,' and longing after their far less harmful rackets. But I at present can manage without this, and prefer to do so, for at present inspecting the animals and wandering about the garden with them seems to suffice, while newspapers and books come in on wet days; while we are all so busy during the week, that the holiday comes as a blessed oasis for which we are all truly thankful. And the children love the illustrated papers—a storehouse of knowledge no parent should be without; and the money spent on them is never wasted, though an Englishman, as a rule, will grudge a few shillings a week for papers, while he never hesitates for a moment to spend double the amount on his dinner, or on that Moloch of English households, the tobacconist.

Above all encourage your own and your children's friends to come in to tea and talk on Sunday afternoons. This gives no work to the servants, and always makes a nice break. The tea can be set ready before the maids go out, and if many cups are wanted they can be washed up early; and any guest should be made welcome, and sometimes asked to remain for the early supper, which, being cold, and prepared on Saturday, is again of no trouble to the maids. I am very fond of Sunday visitors, and as few English houses open their doors, especially in the country and more distant suburbs, on that day, visitors are often glad to drop in when they can be sure of a welcome and a cup of tea.

Tea in the schoolroom is often, too, a very good institution, for thus the governess sees a little more of life, and acts as hostess; and each child should have its own cup and saucer and plate. This is a great safeguard against breakages, for if one is smashed it must be spoken of at once, and extra cups can be kept for the visitors; but all should be different, so that any breakage may be seen at once, as generally the schoolroom-maid is but young, and apt to conceal any small depredations among the crockery. Now the two great difficulties in a schoolroom are the governess and the schoolroom-maid, and infinite care must be taken in the selection of both. Of course the governess is the first care, and, though she should be mistress in the schoolroom, she yet must only be a viceroy, and must act for the mother entirely, and not at all on her own responsibility unless she is expressly desired to do so. No governess should be engaged who cannot be in some measure a companion to the mother, to whom and with whom she should be in perfect accord; for there are endless ways in which the governess can save a mother of a household, does she make herself really pleasant, if only in conveying the children to the dentist—a necessary business, but one that need not harrow the mother's feelings if the governess is as good and useful as she ought to be; for the governess does not feel, as a mother does, that all her teeth are being taken out bodily the moment Tommy opens his mouth for inspection, and endures none of the vicarious pangs that make any fanciful mother's life a burden to her, even though nothing happens. The governess must be healthy, strong-minded, good-tempered, and, above all, must have some nice hobbies, and be fond of teaching them; then the schoolroom will indeed be the heart of the house, and will send out a series of healthy, happy children into the great world. Make the governess one with the household; let your interests be hers, the children for the time being a mutual possession. Take any amount of trouble to procure a really nice girl of a good family, and then you may breathe freely; while if the schoolroom-maid comes young too, and is carefully trained, you will then have a perfectly managed schoolroom, and feel you can rest awhile should you desire it, secure that your place is well filled by a competent minister, who will rule in your place until you return both well and wisely.

Never discuss your governess either with or before the children, and take care that her life is as much as possible a fac-simile of yours. Let her have books and papers and share in any gaiety that is going; and above all try and make her think that she becomes part of the family, should she really stay some time with you, and that your interest in her will last as long as life itself. I can imagine nothing more wicked than to cast off old governesses or servants, and to decline to keep those who have helped us so much, and in a manner no amount of money will repay.

The schoolroom would not be complete in my eyes without just a few sentences on the subject of the children's dress. This would, in the case of the girls, consist of good warm underclothing; in two sets of combination garments, one in wool, the other in long-cloth; a stay-bodice—never stays on any pretext whatever—made of ribbed material, on which a flannel skirt should be sewn in winter; then another skirt, also sewn on a bodice; and finally that invaluable costume, the 'smock-frock,' the skirt trimmed with three rows of tucks, the sleeves full, and the full bodice drawn in with either a loose band or a soft sash of Liberty silk. From the day a baby is put into short clothes until the girl of fifteen becomes too lanky for such a plain dress, there is no other costume as suitable for all times of the year. In summer very thin cashmere is enough, with perhaps a soft silk handkerchief underneath for outdoor wear; in winter a long coat of cashmere and soft cap make admirable outdoor garments, and are put on in a very few moments, while all Liberty's soft silks and cashmeres are warm without an undue amount of weight, and are all of such lovely colours that no one thinks of the plainness of the material used for a moment. Until girls are fifteen they should always wear pinafores of some kind. I use a very large white diaper pinafore tied with Liberty sashes, and they should furthermore have shoes with straps and low wide heels; while for boys nothing is so sensible as the much-copied Jack Tar suit, with its serge trousers and wide loose shirts, though I personally prefer the Scotch kilt; the sailor suits are soon shabby and generally untidy, while the kilts always look well, wear for ever almost, and there are no knees either of stockings or trousers always giving out and requiring to be mended every moment or so. After the kilts boys can take to jackets and trousers, which in perfection can only be bought of Swears and Wells, Regent Street, W., whose charges are, of course, rather awful to contemplate, but whose clothes undoubtedly outwear three suits of any one else's; and I speak from the experience of my three boys, for whom I have often tried to go elsewhere, but have always had to return to Swears, for nowhere else can I buy things that to a certain extent will defy the rough usage given to them. The sailor suits can be bought best of Redfern, at Cowes, in the Isle of Wight; the kilts of Swears also.

To conclude: the eye of the mother should really never be taken from the children, as long as they are growing. Weak backs should be detected at once, and allowed to rest on a proper sofa and carefully bathed with salt water; weak ankles should be treated the same; cuts should be dressed with calendula and soft rags; a supply of both and of sticking-plaster should be in every schoolroom cupboard. Camphor is also a good thing to keep ready; it stops many an incipient cold. A good supply of fruit and jam and fresh air and regular exercise stop many an illness and save many a doctor's bill, and, in fact, a doctor should indeed rarely be required nowadays in a house where mother, governess, and nurse really know their business and really look after the children; for, unless in real illness, doctors seldom are of any use in a schoolroom, and only add up accounts that are really accounts of the mother's ignorance or selfishness or neglect.

Naturally, when children inherit disease—and that people who inherit diseases or are related should marry is nothing more or less than a crime in my eyes, and should be to the world at large—or are susceptible by inheritance to colds, fevers, &c., the above does not apply; then skilled attention is necessary, and in real cases of need a doctor should be consulted as early as possible; but all girls, and indeed boys, should be taught always something about themselves and their formation, and they should learn early those marvellous, unchangeable laws of health which, once broken, render not only themselves but future generations miserable and wretched for ever; but, of course, great care must be taken here, as indeed everywhere else, to keep the *via media*, else will the children become self-conscious prigs, always anxious about themselves and their well-being.

CHAPTER XVIII
BOYS AND GIRLS

There is yet a more critical time for the parents, I think, than even the schoolroom time, and that is, first of all, when the boys go off to school; and, secondly, when we have to realise that the small nursery toddlers are grown up, and really as capable of taking care of themselves as we are ourselves. Let me speak of the boys first, as, after all, that terrible wrench is the worst experience of all, and one, I hope most truly and sincerely, which will be saved for future mothers, and that before many years have passed; for I maintain, and always shall maintain most strenuously, that there never was a worse system of education than the general education that present-day lads must go through, or be entirely different to the rest of the male sex, though even that would be a good thing in my eyes, for I cannot allow that the male half of the world is so good or so perfect at present that it cannot be improved, neither can I allow that the result of education as at present given is in any way as perfect as it might be; and as an example of what I mean it would be well to consider, I think, why the return of the boys from school is as the letting loose of a horde of barbarians on a peaceful land; and why, after the first week at all events, the urchins cease to be regarded as returned angels, and one and all are spoken of as 'those dreadful boys.'

As an example of what I mean, I may speak of one household where the girls are gently ruled and delicately brought up by their dead mother's bridesmaid, who gave up her own one chance of wedded happiness because of her most romantic attachment to her girlhood friend, and who, when father and mother died within a few years of each other, leaving a young and turbulent household to 'Aunt Mary and Providence,' came to live among the children, loving them all, but instinctively looking upon the boys as just one remove from wild animals.

At least the preparations for their return from Rugby would suggest as much, for in the big country-house drawing-room the beautiful Indian carpet is rolled up and replaced by a time-worn drugget, the little brother's best hat and coat are relegated from the hall to Aunt Mary's own room, covers are put on everything that can be covered, and lace curtains are moved; and, in fact, when prepared for the holidays, the whole house appears as if ready to stand a heavy and protracted siege.

Even the garden and greenhouses are rigorously locked; wire shades and iron hurdles protect tender seedlings and grass edges; the head gardener wears a countenance of mingled dread and determination; and in the stables nothing is left get-at-able save the boys' own ponies, a venerable 'four-wheel,' and sundry odds and ends of ancient harness, which no one could hurt because its condition is quite hopeless already.

And in a town house, when the holidays are within appreciable distance, over and over again have I not seen similar preparations, though on a smaller scale? Have I not noted how nurse puts away the children's best toys; how the girls in the schoolroom, aided by their agitated governess, conceal all their beloved possessions, and train their pets to 'lie low,' as 'Brer Fox' would say? Does not Paterfamilias rehearse a long code of laws, all to be enforced, he says, the moment the boys come home? And is not Materfamilias, after all, the only creature in the whole establishment who has not one *arrière pensèe*, and who finds nothing in the least to spoil the rapture of the return of those who have never for one moment been out of her thoughts since the last time she saw them off, through her tears, on their return to Dr. Swishey's academy for young gentlemen?

Ah, the boys little know what they cause that tender soul to suffer when an extra hour's cricket excuses them for forgetting their weekly letter home; how the omission makes her turn pale when a sudden ring at the bell comes, lest it should be a telegram summoning her to the bedside of the dear things, who are most likely rioting in the playground at the very moment; and how she is only withheld by dread of ridicule and the largeness of the railway fare from rushing off at once to see for herself that all is well; and she has to content herself with writing a loving letter of expostulation, doubtless characterised as 'a jaw,' and thrown aside half read through.

And when they are at home under her own roof she naturally looks forward to peace, at all events, and safety from dreads and fears such as these; but, poor soul, she soon finds out her mistake.

Her days are spent in wondering where the boys have gone to, in painfully concealing the marks of their ravages in library and staircase and hall from the paternal eye, and in propitiating the outraged schoolroom and nursery establishments, who do not see, as she does, that the fact of its being holiday time accounts for all, and that all should be forgiven those who are only at home for so short a period in the year.

But even mother begins to tire of acting as a buffer between her sons and her husband and the other members of the family. And by the time cook has given warning—heedless that she is the only woman who can cook the dinner to suit the master—because Reggie will melt lead in her spoons or playfully drop gunpowder in the fire, or because some pounds of butter mysteriously disappeared and followers were hinted at—though the state of her saucepans and George's trouser pockets pointed out that toffee, not the policeman, was at the bottom of the loss—Materfamilias finds herself wondering how Dr. Swishey manages to look so well at the end of the term, and begins to think that perhaps after all she will not be quite as sorry as usual when the cab comes round and the boys go off, leaving her free to go out to dinner without dreading to see flames issuing out of the drawing-room windows when the carriage turns the corner of the Square on her return home, or fearing a summons from the festive board to bid her go back at once because one or other of the boys has done something dreadful either to himself or some other member of the family.

Now, granted that this is not an isolated case—and, judging from a large personal experience of 'other folks' children,' I venture boldly to state that this is the rule and not the exception—I as boldly remark that the present manner of dealing with the *genus homo* as expressed in the schoolboy is entirely a wrong one, and, waxing bolder yet, I say that the grown-up youth evolved from such an education as most lads obtain nowadays is so emphatically unsatisfactory that I am quite sure some radical change should be made in the way we bring up our boys.

Born into a home where their sisters are sheltered and cared for until they leave it for one of their own, from their very birth they are treated in an entirely different manner. As little mites they govern the house, because they are of the superior sex, and they are finally sent away from home into the great world of school, where, neither by age nor experience, can they be in the least fitted for the warfare, or enabled by careful and judicious training to hold their own, or to choose between the good and evil that is so freely offered them there. Small boys are herded with big ones, who alternately bully and confide in them; tender and sentimental fancies are derided; and the word 'manly' is made to express ferocity, cruelty, uncleanness, and a thousand and one awful things that, when we discover our children are aware of, we wonder feebly when and how they have acquired their knowledge.

What wonder the return of the boys is dreaded, when they come as strangers into a home where God placed them for the careful training, the unceasing supervision, of body and mind? How can a boy join in and make part of a circle that for half or even three parts of the year is complete without him? How can he respect and appreciate laws and routine that are entirely different to all he has been accustomed to more than two thirds of his time? And how can he help being spoiled, selfish, and tyrannical, when the very shortness of his residence under the home-roof is made an excuse for pampering him and making every one, man, woman, and child, give way to him, because, poor dear lad, he is only at home for the holidays, while the others are always there?

There is no doubt in my mind that boys ought to go more into the world and see more of human nature than girls need do; but with all my strength I would maintain that the ordinary boarding-school plan is a great and hideous mistake. By all means let them go to school all day; but let them at night return home, where the mother's eye can see how they are, and how they progress with their lessons, and to insure them that best of all feeling for any one—the certain knowledge that home is home to them in the fullest sense of the word; and that, far from being outsiders or honoured guests, feared as well as honoured, they are part and parcel of the family, and bound to give and take, sharing the rough with the smooth, and helping in every way they can to aid the weaker vessels of the family, and becoming gentlemen in the widest sense of the word.

Of course, parents who keep their boys at home have little time for rest, and cannot be incessantly in the very middle of society's whirl; but is any price too large to pay for the souls of our children—any sacrifice too great to insure that one's boys are to the fullest degree given the benefit of our knowledge and our shielding care? And shall we not be repaid for anything it may cost us in the wear-and-tear of our brain-power if, instead of the stage-door-haunting, toothpick-gnawing 'masher' of the present day, we rear a race of manly, God-fearing, home-loving youths, who may restore the age of chivalry and the strong, pure, tender-hearted men that were once England's boast?

Like most problems presented to our minds as we go through the world, there are here other sides to contemplate beyond the one we have just attempted to sketch. For there are homes where the boy's one chance of salvation is given by a good training at school; where the vanity of the mother and the evil example of the father are worse than anything else can possibly be; and where the atmosphere is so pernicious that an honest and true-hearted schoolmaster dreads to send his pupils home, for they may once more acquire habits that he is only just beginning really to eradicate. There are also intensely weak and foolish parents who, not able to refuse themselves any gratification, cannot debar their children from having their own way, and who, not having been trained themselves, cannot train others; and there are yet others who send off their children to rid themselves of the clear-eyed tormentors who ask such tiresome questions, and will follow the example of their parents, not content to be put off with the trite remark that grown-up folks can do and say things little people would be severely punished and reprimanded for doing and saying.

Still, notwithstanding these sides to the picture, we can boldly state that if boys were invariably part of a household, if their parents accept their responsibilities and see they have no right to pay some careless person—any one, in fact, who wants to make money by teaching—to take their responsibilities off their hands, we should very soon have a different state of things as regards the male sex as a whole; and at all events we should cease to dread the holidays and speak of our sons as 'those dreadful boys.'

But the selfishness of the ordinary parent, and the cupidity of the orthodox schoolmaster, whose real profits are made from the boarders, and who, therefore, discourages to the best of his power the idea of home-boarders, are twin giants in the way of those who only ask to be allowed to bring up their own children in their own way, and I can but look forward and hope for other mothers all that I have only been able to demand for myself in part, and that a very small part of all I would have wished for the boys, who, once given over to school, only return for good for a few moments, as it were, on their way to the real battle of life, which soon engulfs them entirely, and so we never really have our boys our own, nor are allowed to train them for ourselves at a time when we alone should be able to do it satisfactorily, because we alone should understand them best and know what they inherit mentally and bodily; in fact, the nursery and schoolroom once passed through, we have lost our children, and have only now to think how we can make home happy for them until they leave us for their own homes, which will depend on our early training whether they are happy ones or not.

And indeed one of the most abstruse of all our numerous domestic problems is shadowed forth in the words 'quite grown-up,' for there are few fathers and mothers who realise, it seems to me, that their children have actually passed through nursery and schoolroom, and are in deed and truth quite grown-up, and in consequence of this the domestic relations become strained, and home ceases to be the pleasant retreat it used to be from the throng and turmoils of the outside world.

There are most certainly households where the relations are more than strained, where open hostility replaces the old-time affection, and from whence sons rush to 'the bad,' and daughters marry the first man that asks them, simply because they wish for freedom and to be able to do as they like.

Naturally, they often enough discover they have exchanged King Log for King Stork, and wish themselves at home once more over and over again; but that such cases are not only possible, but are continually occurring around us, seems to me so sad, that I should like to say a few words on the subject of 'The Proper Relations between Parents and Children,' hoping in some measure to propose a solution to the problem.

In the first place, we are in some measure suffering from the rebound that has taken place when the severe bonds that bound our parents were removed. They suffered themselves so greatly from the petty tyrannies that were considered the right thing in their youth, that, in desiring to save their children from similar misery, they have gone to the other extreme, and allowed such laxity of manner that children rule the house, as in America, and barely condescend in their grown-up stage to consult their parents at all about their engagements, their occupations, or even their friendships or their marriages.

Surely there is a medium between the discipline that enforced silence on the child until all originality was crushed out of him, that thought severe strictures on the dress and personal appearance of one's daughters the sole way of checking vanity, and that refused confidence because it was lowering oneself from the awful height occupied by a parent, and that which is conspicuous by its absence, and that results in an independent race of young people, who respect nothing, and are certainly not going to make an exception in the case of their father and mother, who are either ready to go as great lengths as their children, or else suddenly assert an authority that only exists in their own imaginations, and that causes a turmoil because opposition is as unexpected as it is arbitrary.

If we would have authority we must have it from the very beginning, and I am old-fashioned enough myself to be a great believer in the nursery and nursery frocks for very little children. I am always angry, I confess, when I see a small lady of four or five dressed up to the eyes in a fantastic frock designed to attract attention to the tiny wearer, of which she is all too conscious, and carried about from this luncheon to that tea, to the weariness of herself and all who are not connected with her; and indeed do well to be angry, for did not she, as one of those specimens, refuse to go into the country because she found it so extremely dull; and also because I know it is from such a bringing-up as this that we obtain the emancipated female or the fast girl, who thinks of nothing but 'dress' and 'the service,' and which results, all too often, in making home miserable for the elder folk, who only see in the pretty child a plaything flattering to their vanity, and do not recognise the fact that, much sooner than we expect it, she in her turn will be quite grown-up.

The nursery stage should emphatically be a time for shabby clothes and dolls and noise, and for healthy natural play. The midday meal should be the only one taken with the mother, who, however, should make a point of knowing all about the others, and should also contrive to be often in the nursery, and have the children with her for not less than an hour or two a day.

To insure happiness with a grown-up family these tiny beginnings should be well studied. The mother's influence should be so much felt, and so indispensable to the house, that when withdrawn for a while it should indeed be something more than missed. But familiarity in early childhood breeds contempt in youth; and it is well known that a child who is always with grown-up people never knows what childishness is, and never becomes as healthy-minded as one who has had a little wholesome neglect from society and from perpetual supervision of its elders.

When we as parents begin to see the children growing up, we should, I maintain, then carefully see that our own immediate friends are those whose society and conversation can do our girls no harm. When I have occasionally heard talk that has brought blushes to my cheeks at my mature age, and seen the young girls not only listening but joining in it, I have almost been tempted to declare my girls shall never go into society at all; but as I know this is impossible, I have made up my mind whose houses they shall go to, reserving to myself the right to tell them boldly why such and such a one is not a desirable acquaintance.

Then, too, their own friends, made at school or at the homes of mutual acquaintances, should be welcomed emphatically whenever they like to come. I remember too well feeling much aggrieved at not being able to ask an occasional friend to tea to refuse this privilege. But if the friends become too numerous, it is easy to point out that either you cannot afford such indiscriminate visiting, or to restrict the number of visitors to a certain number; only let it be understood that their friends are always welcome in moderation, and that, though you are delighted to see them, you do not expect them thrown on your hands for entertainment, and that you assume the right to point out to your children the desirability or the reverse of any of their acquaintances, and that you expect them to give due weight to your opinion.

It is more than necessary, in my mind, to keep perpetually before one's children that the home into which they were born is their inheritance that nothing can take from them. And by this I do not mean that I consider a parent bound to provide fortunes for either sons or daughters. I have too often seen the great harm of this to advocate it for one moment; but that they should always not only be welcome there, but claim as a right the shelter and counsel and affection that are their due, no matter what they have done or how grievously they have sinned. For *no* cause should a father or mother refuse to see their own child, and they should a thousand times more never allow the unmarried daughter to feel herself a burden, whose food and shelter are grudged her, any more than they should continually hint that marriage is a woman's only destiny, refusing to the girls the ample education lavished on the sons, and so depriving them of every means of making their own living.

But grown-up daughters, in my eyes, are a most precious possession, if properly brought up. They at last take some of the heavy burdens a mother has always to bear alone off her shoulders; and if she be moderately intelligent, and has intelligently brought up the girls, there is no reason why they should not be a thousand times more valuable in her eyes than they were as pretty babies and engaging little girls.

But then we must remember that they are grown-up, that they have an opinion more or less valuable, and that they have idiosyncrasies to be respected, the while they respect ours, remembering our position towards them, our fuller experience, and our affectionate care for them. As long as the parents live, they should be master and mistress in the house; but the children should be as viceroys, helping their parents in every way that they can in their social duties and in the routine of the house. It is trying, we know, to have the piano going and billiard-balls rolling when we want to read Jones's speech on Home Rule, or Gladstone's latest statements; but it is far more trying not to know where one's children are, and to feel they are happier anywhere else than in their own homes.

It is their home as much as it is ours, and it will be home indeed if by judicious training in their youth we have made friends of our children, if we have given them our confidence, our affection, and our best days, and have not become strangers to them by being perpetually in society when they were as perpetually sent to school; the while we have not become too familiar, and make them old before their time, by taking them with us to gatherings in smart frocks when they ought to have been disreputably shabby in pinafores in the nursery. Then we shall discover that our grown-up sons and daughters are not so many cuckoos pushing us out of the old nest, but intelligent friends and companions—all the more delightful to us because they are quite grown-up.

CHAPTER XIX
ENTERTAINING ONE'S FRIENDS

In a small house entertaining one's friends is too often a most arduous and tiresome business, because we will one and all of us attempt to do a great deal too much, and appear to be able to afford all kinds of luxuries that we cannot possibly manage, and I strongly advise any young bride with small means and a smaller *ménage* to confine herself entirely to afternoon teas, which require no waiting and cost extremely little, and to refuse on her part to go out to large dinners, which she cannot return, and for which she can neither afford the necessary dress, gloves, flowers, nor cabs, asking her friends to invite her to simpler entertainments boldly, and giving her reasons, which, of course, will be received kindly and in good faith by her friends. I am convinced that this absurd striving after society is at the bottom of the falseness of most of our English entertainments, and I trust some day to see 'parties' on a much broader and more satisfactory basis than they are at present, and I therefore beg all young householders to pause before they begin the same old round of costly gaiety, and to consider if they at least cannot bring about a better state of things. I have often in different houses seen with amazement how invitations are issued, and wondered if I am the only person who is thus taken behind the scenes and shown how hollow such invitations often are. Surely I must be, or else the great crushes I read of would never come off, and the dinners I hear about would lack guests, for I have rarely heard invitations talked over without listening to some such conversation as this: 'Ask the Joneses, Gertrude.' 'Oh no, mother! she *is* such a dowdy, and their last garden party was maddening.' 'I can't help it, my dear. I went to their party, and we must pay them back. And then there are the Brownes; don't forget the *e*—ridiculous creatures! It's astonishing how some people creep up and others go down.' 'And he is dreadful, mother;' and, in fact, I could go on for pages, while other pages could be occupied with descriptions of how the invitation is received at the Joneses' and the Brownes', who all go expecting to be bored or starved, and who return home to comment spitefully on an entertainment which, if successful, carries in their minds the donors half-way to the Bankruptcy Court, and, if a failure, is the cause of a good deal of violent abuse and unkind sneers levelled at their hosts. And then the conversation at these entertainments: 'Have you seen the So-and-so's lately?' 'Oh no; they never go anywhere now. Didn't you hear about her and So-and-so?' But really, when it comes to the talk I overhear at balls, dinners, at-homes, or in the Park, I lose my temper, and so will turn at once to other matters altogether.

Afternoon teas, tennis-parties, and little dinners are all possible to the young housekeeper, but the little dinners to be inexpensive must be in the winter, and for them I have written out half a dozen menus which may be of use in the ordinary household, with the ordinary plain cook of the period, whose wages are about 20*l*. These will be found at the end of the chapter, but to insure even such a modest dinner as one of these makes being a success the mistress must see herself that her glass and silver are spotless, the table well laid, and the flowers charmingly arranged by herself.

The very last fashion (which, however, may change next week, but is worth mentioning because of its simpleness and sense) for table arrangements is to have no dessert whatever on the table, which has a piece of embroidery in the centre of the cloth, and then in the middle of this place a large flat wide-open wicker basket, which you should cover entirely with moss; border it with ivy or berberis leaves, and stand any flowers you may be able to procure in such a way that they appear growing; low groups of flowers are arranged in vases all over the table with growing ferns in pots, and, in fact, the table is made to look as much like a bank of flowers as possible. Candles with shades to match the prevailing hue of the flowers should stand on the table, and the dessert should be handed round after dinner, and should consist of one dish of good fruit and one of French sweetmeats, thus simplifying matters very much indeed.

Flowers should never be mixed; daffodils and brown leaves look lovely together, so do scarlet geraniums and white azaleas, pink azaleas, and brown leaves; wisteria and laburnum, Maréchal Niel roses and lilacs, are all good contrasts, but clumps of yellow tulips, or narcissi or roses, all one colour, are undoubtedly more fashionable than even the small contrasts just spoken of, while Salviati glass is beautiful on a table, and the specimen glasses of that make hold flowers far better than anything else: and should flowers be scarce the centrepiece could be all brown ivy and mosses and evergreens, with just a few flowers in the Salviati glasses only.

But neither food nor flowers, nor, indeed, anything else, will make a party successful if the mistress does not make a good hostess, and exert herself to see her quests are happy. She should take care the right people meet, and nothing should induce her to refrain from introducing her guests; this is a most ridiculous practice, and is simply laziness. A hostess is bound to see all her guests are amused, and this can only be done by personally noticing who is talking to whom, and whether all the people present have some one with whom to converse.

This absence of introductions makes conversation almost a lost art, and has made the ordinary 'society' nothing more or less than a bore and a trouble; while, as the ambition of most people is to know more folks than their neighbours and to go to more balls in one night than our foremothers used to see in their lifetimes, entertaining has become a farce and bids fair to die of its own immensity.

Therefore, as these are undoubtedly hard times, and many people are not 'entertaining' at all because they cannot now afford to outdo their neighbours, let me beg any young beginner to start well and simply, confining herself to those friends she really wishes to see, and to giving parties that are not above her modest means, and that do not entail hiring extra help, who smash her crockery and cost a month's wages for a few hours' work, and agitate her so by their vagaries that she cannot talk sensibly to her neighbour; and let her furthermore ask people sometimes who cannot ask her again, but who can talk amusingly, and she will, I am sure, have much more out of her little dinners than most people do out of a whole London season's fatigue and expense, both of which often ruin the health and the future of many a girl, who traces back to the severe 'pleasures' of town the lassitude and suffering that render the latter half of a woman's life all too often hours of suffering and sorrow; for she has used up in the year or two of her girlhood all the strength and health that should have sustained her all through her days, and repents at leisure the stupidity and culpable weakness of the mother who allowed her to sacrifice the possessions for a lifetime in a few months.

To enable our young housekeeper to manage so that her housekeeping bills will not overwhelm her after one of her little dinners, I have appended to each of the menus the exact cost of each, and I strongly advise any one to whom economy is an object to use New Zealand lamb or mutton. If properly warmed through and gently thawed close to the fire before putting it down to roast, the meat is simply delicious and as good as the best English; but it must be treated carefully, or else it will not be nice, but when properly thawed no one can tell it from English meat, and I think housekeepers would be a little astonished if they knew how often the 'best English' meat of the butcher's book was really and truly the New Zealand meat they speak of with such horror.

Menu No. I.

White Soup.

Soles, Sauce Maître d'hôtel.

Stuffed Pigeons.

Roast Beef, Yorkshire Pudding.

Wild Duck.

Mince Pies.

French Pancakes.

Cauliflower au gratin.

Dessert.

White Soup.—A quart and a pint of milk, a dozen fine potatoes, piece of butter size of a walnut, two onions, salt and pepper to taste. *Simmer* all together for two hours, then rub through fine hair sieve, add two tablespoonfuls of sago, and bring all gradually to a boil. Serve very hot, with dice of bread fried. Cost of soup for six persons, 1s.

Fried Soles.—A fine pair at 3s. Garnish with lemon and parsley, fry in *lard*; serve with melted butter, with fine chopped parsley in, flavoured with lemon. Cost, 3s. 6d.

Stuffed Pigeons.—Three pigeons at 10d. each. Bone them; make a stuffing of thyme, parsley, crumbs of bread, small piece of ham, a couple of mushrooms, one egg, salt and pepper to taste; chop altogether and mix with egg; stuff pigeons and sew them up; put them into a saucepan, with a small piece of bacon and any stock that may be in the digester. Stew for half an hour, take them out, divide them into neat portions, and put them in a hot dish ready for serving. Add a teaspoonful of flour mixed with water to thicken the gravy they are stewed in, and strain it through a sieve on the pigeons; then serve. *Outside* cost, 3s. 6d.

Rolled Ribs of Beef.—Six pounds, the bones from which can be used for stock for the gravy for the pigeons. The beef is rolled by the butcher ready for roasting. Serve with horse-radish neatly arranged about it, mashed potatoes, stewed celery; and Yorkshire pudding—half a pint of milk, six large tablespoonfuls of flour, three eggs, and a tablespoonful of salt. Put the flour into a basin with the salt, and stir gradually to this enough milk to make it into a stiff batter; when quite smooth add the rest of the milk, and the eggs well beaten; beat well together, and then pour into a shallow tin which has been rubbed with beef dripping; bake an hour in the oven, and then put under the meat for half an hour. Meat, 6 lbs. of New Zealand at 10d., 5s.; pudding, 6d.; vegetables, 1s.—6s. 6d.

Wild Duck, 4s. 6d.—Plainly roasted; served with cayenne pepper, lemons cut in halves, and fried potatoes. 5s.

Mince Pies.—Make some good puff paste by allowing one pound of butter to each pound of flour; line small patty pans and bake; fill with mincemeat (which can be bought ready-made and excellent for 10*d.* a jar, which is sufficient for a dozen pies), cover with thin paste, and put into a brisk oven for twenty-five minutes; serve with sifted sugar over them.

French Pancakes.—Take two eggs, and their weight in sugar, flour, and butter; mix well together; add quarter of a teacupful of milk; mix well together; bake in saucer for twenty minutes, filling each saucer only half full; take out; spread small quantity of jam, then fold over; dust sifted sugar over the top, and serve very hot. Cost, 8*d.*

Cauliflower au gratin.—Fine cauliflower nicely boiled; then grate a quarter of a pound of cheese over it, and place small atoms of butter about the top of it; add a little cayenne and salt to taste; put in the oven to brown, and serve very hot. Cost altogether, about 8*d.*

Complete cost of dinner.—Soup, 1*s.*; fish, 3*s.* 6*d.*; entrée, 3*s.* 6*d.*; beef, 6*s.* 6*d.*; game, 5*s.*; mince pies, 1*s.* 6*d.*; pancakes, 8*d.*; cheese, 8*d.*—1*l.* 2*s.* 4*d.*

Menu No. II

Clear Soup.
Turbot, Lobster Sauce.
Cutlets à la Réforme.
Turkey, Stuffed Chestnuts.
Teal.
Éclairs.
Pears in Jelly.
Prince Albert's Pudding.
Cheese Fondu.
Dessert.

Clear Soup.—Sixpennyworth of bones, three carrots, three onions, sprig of thyme, two sprigs of parsley, one blade of mace, a dozen peppercorns, head of celery. Simmer whole day in three quarts of water, let it stand all night, remove fat in the morning, boil it again next day, let it come to boiling point, throw in the whites and shells of two eggs, whip it altogether when it boils, remove from fire, then skim it, and pass it through a jelly-bag; put a little macedoine in the bottom of a hot tureen and pour soup over, add a glass of sherry and serve. Outside cost, 1*s.*

Half a Turbot.—Tinned lobster, cut in dice, put into melted butter, and flavoured with anchovy. Turbot, about 3s.; sauce, 9d.

Cutlets à la Réforme.—Three pounds of the loin of pork cut into cutlets and fried; make about a gill of melted butter, add to it two tablespoonfuls of the liquor from a bottle of piccalilly and six or eight pieces of the pickle cut small. When very hot put on your dish, arrange cutlets in round, and put the pickle-sauce in the middle. Outside cost, 3s.

Small Turkey.—Stuffed with ordinary stuffing, with about two dozen chestnuts boiled soft and added to the stuffing, sausages, bread-sauce, Brussels sprouts, mashed potatoes. Turkey, 6s.; stuffing &c., 2s. more; outside cost, 8s.

Three teal at 1s. each, plainly roasted, and sent in on slices of toast; lemons and cayenne pepper. 3s. 6d.

Eclairs.—Bought at any confectioner's at 2d. each. 1s.

Pears in Jelly.—Six stewing pears, 2 oz. sugar, 2 oz. butter, one pint water, half an ounce gelatine soaked in water; stew the pears until they are soft, turn out into a basin, and add the gelatine when hot; place pears when *comparatively* cold round buttered mould, pour in syrup, turn out when set, serve cold. 8d.

Prince Albert's Pudding.—Quarter of a pound of bread-crumbs, quarter of a pound of butter, 2 oz. sugar, two tablespoonfuls of raspberry jam, two eggs, mixed thoroughly, placed in mould, and boiled for two hours and a half; serve hot with sifted sugar over. Outside cost, 1s.

Cheese Fondu.—Two eggs, the weight of one in Cheddar cheese, the weight of one in butter; pepper and salt to taste, separate the yolks from the whites of the eggs, beat the former in a basin, and grate the cheese, break the butter into small pieces, add it to the other ingredients with pepper and salt, beat all together thoroughly, well whisk the whites of the eggs, stir them lightly in, and bake the fondu in a small cake tin, which should be only half filled, as the cheese will rise very much; pin a napkin round the tin and serve very hot and quickly, as if allowed to stand long it would be quite spoiled. Average cost, 5d.

Soup, 1s.; fish, 3s. 9d.; cutlets, 3s.; turkey, 6s.; teal, 3s. 6d.; éclairs, 1s.; pears, 8d.; pudding, 1s.—cheese, 5d.—1l. 0s. 4d.

Menu No. III.

Hare Soup.
Filleted Soles à la Maître d'hôtel.

Mutton Cutlets.
Sirloin of Beef.
Ptarmigan.
Peaches, whipped cream.
Cabinet Pudding.
Toasted Cheese.
Dessert.

Hare Soup.—Sprig of thyme, sprig of parsley, three onions, three carrots, two turnips, one head celery, twelve peppercorns, half a dozen cloves, three quarts of water, sixpennyworth of bones, a small hare cut up into joints; simmer all together for about three hours. Take out the meat of the hare and put bones back. Keep the soup simmering the whole day, set aside at night; skim off fat next morning. When wanted thicken with one tablespoonful of flour mixed with a little of the stock; put in meat, rub all through sieve into a *hot* tureen; serve with dice of fried bread. Cost, 5s.

Soles.—Three small soles, filleted, plain boiled, each piece rolled and placed on a small skewer, which is removed when the fish is sent to table, served covered with sauce made as follows:—Half a pint of milk, tablespoonful of flour, mixed to smooth paste with a little milk, piece of butter size of walnut, salt and pepper to taste, two teaspoonfuls of parsley, teaspoonful of lemon juice. Average cost, 2s. 9d.

Mutton Cutlets.—Two pounds best end of the neck of mutton (New Zealand, 6½d. per lb.) cut thin, egged and bread-crumbed, fried in boiling lard to a light brown, arranged in a crown with fried parsley in centre, fried in same lard. 1s. 6d.

Six pounds of the sirloin, at 10d., nicely roasted, and sent to table garnished with horse-radish, Brussels sprouts, and fried potatoes; Yorkshire pudding, as per receipt in menu. 6s. 6d., outside cost.

Ptarmigan.—Plainly roasted, sent in on to toast, basted *well* with dripping, or else they are very dry, bread-sauce, with a very little cayenne pepper added, mashed potatoes. About 4s.

Tin of American peaches, sweetened to taste, arranged round cream, sixpennyworth whipped well, any whites of eggs can be added; flavour with four drops essence of vanilla; the cream must be heaped up in the centre of the peaches. Tin of peaches, 10½d.; cream, 6d.; extras, 3d. Average cost, 1s. 7½d.

Cabinet Pudding.—Four sponge-cakes, 2 oz. raisins, currants, and sultanas mixed, small piece of lemon-peel, nutmeg to taste, two eggs, sufficient milk to soak cakes, 1 oz. sugar, teacupful of milk, in which the two eggs should be beaten and poured over the sponge-cakes; set all to soak for an hour; place the currants &c. first in a buttered mould, then slices of sponge-cake, then more currants, and then sponge-cakes, until the mould is three parts full; then mix eggs, milk, sugar, and nutmeg all together, beat well, pour it over the pudding, set it for an hour to swell, then tie tightly down, boil for two hours and a half; serve very hot with melted butter poured over, flavoured with two tablespoonfuls of brandy and a little sugar. 9d.

Toasted Cheese.—Grate a quarter of a pound of cheese on lightly toasted bread, pepper and salt to taste, tiny piece of butter on each square; put in the oven for a few moments to melt cheese, add cayenne, serve very hot. Cost about 9d.

Soup, 5s.; fish, 2s. 9d.; cutlets, 1s. 6d.; beef, 6s. 6d.; ptarmigan, 4s.; peaches, 1s. 7½d.; pudding, 9d.; cheese, 9d.—1l. 2s. 10½d.

Menu No. IV.

Carrot Soup.
Cutlets of Cod. Anchovy Sauce.
Curried Kidneys.
Rolled Loin of Mutton, stuffed.
Boiled Pheasant, Celery Sauce.
Plum Pudding, Brandy Sauce.
Chocolate Cream.
Cheese Soufflés.
Dessert.

Carrot Soup.—Three pints of stock, made of threepennyworth of bones cracked, and put in about two quarts of water; add three carrots, three onions, and a head of celery, a little thyme and parsley. Simmer the whole day; allow the fat to rise during the night, removing every scrap of it the next morning, when proceed as follows:—Put two onions and one turnip into the stock and simmer for three hours; then scrape and cut thin six large carrots; strain the soup on them, and stew altogether until soft enough to pass through a hair sieve; then boil all together once more, and add seasoning to taste; add cayenne. The soup should be red, and about the consistency of pease soup. Serve hot with fried dice of bread. Outside cost, 1s.

Cutlets of Cod.—About 4 lbs. of cod, at 4d., cut into large cutlets; fry them, having previously covered them with egg and bread-crumbs. Serve with plain melted butter, flavoured nicely with anchovy. Cost, 1s. 8d.

Curried Kidneys.—Three nice-sized kidneys, cut and skinned and put into any stock; one apple, one onion. Thicken all with a teaspoonful of flour and a teaspoonful of curry powder; small piece of butter, pepper, and salt. Stew for half an hour; add plain boiled rice, carefully done, and serve very hot. Average cost, 10*d*.

Six pounds of loin of mutton at 9*d*. a pound—New Zealand, bone, and then prepare a stuffing with thyme, parsley, bread-crumbs, and about 2 oz. of suet, all chopped very fine; add salt and pepper to taste, mix with one egg. Put this thickly inside the mutton; roll it, and secure with skewers. Serve with currant jelly (3½*d*. a pot), mashed potatoes, and nice cauliflower. Outside cost, 6*s*.

Boiled Pheasant.—One quite sufficient for six people, plain boiled, and covered with celery sauce, made as follows:—Half a pint of milk, two teaspoonfuls of flour mixed to a smooth paste with a little milk. Stew one head of celery in the milk until tender, then add a piece of butter size of a walnut, and pepper and salt to taste. Pass all through fine sieve into a hot tureen, and then serve. Pheasant, 2*s*. 6*d*.; sauce, 6*d*.

Plum Pudding.—Three-quarters of a pound of raisins, ¾ lb. of currants, ¼ lb. of mixed peel, ¼ lb. and half a ¼ lb. of bread-crumbs, same quantity of suet, four eggs, half a wineglassful of brandy. Stone and cut the raisins in halves, do not chop them; wash and dry the currants, and mince the suet finely; cut the candied peel into thin slices and grate the bread very fine. Mix these dry ingredients well, then moisten with the eggs (which should be well beaten) and the brandy; stir well, and press the pudding into a buttered mould, tie it down tightly with a floured cloth, and boil for five or six hours. Cost, 2*s*. Special sauce.—Two ounces of butter beaten to a cream, 2 oz. of sugar, three parts of a glass of sherry and brandy mixed, beaten all together to a stiff paste. Cost, 10*d*.

Chocolate Cream.—One and a half ounce of grated chocolate, 2 oz. of sugar, ¾ of a pint of cream, ¾ oz. of Nelson's gelatine, and the yolks of three eggs. (N.B.—If the whites of the eggs are added to the cream, and all well mixed, less cream can be used.) Beat the yolks of the eggs well, put them in a basin with the grated chocolate, the sugar, and rather more than half the cream, stir all together, pour into a jug, set jug in a saucepan of boiling water, and stir all one way until the mixture thickens, but do not allow it to boil, or it will curdle; strain all into a basin, stir in the gelatine and the other portion of cream, which should be well whipped; then pour into a mould which has been previously oiled with the very purest salad oil; turn out when cold. Outside cost, 2*s*.

Cheese Soufflés.—Quarter of a pound of cheese grated, two tablespoonfuls of flour, piece of butter size of walnut, two eggs, half a teacupful of milk, cayenne and salt to taste; mix well together, and put in a saucepan over fire for about five minutes, stirring all the time to prevent burning; drop a tablespoonful of the mixture into buttered patty-pans; put in a steamer until set; then take them out and put on a sieve to cool; cover with egg and bread-crumb, and fry in boiling lard; serve hot. Cost, about 8*d*. Half this quantity sufficient for six people.

Cost of Dinner.—Soup, 1*s*.; fish, 1*s*. 8*d*.; curried kidneys, 10*d*.; meat, 6*s*.; game, 3*s*.; pudding and sauce, 2*s*. 10*d*.; cream, 2*s*.; cheese, 4*d*.—17*s*. 9*d*.

MENU No. V.

Mulligatawny Soup.
Cod and Oyster Sauce.
Croquettes of Chicken.
Leg of Mutton à la Bretonne.
Pheasants.
Méringues à la crême.
Turrets.
Cheese Straws.
Dessert.

Mulligatawny Soup.—Three pints of stock, made by taking threepennyworth of bones, breaking them small, and putting them to simmer on one side of the fire for the whole of the day before it is required, with three carrots, three onions, one head of celery, and one clove, and a small piece of bacon; stand all night in larder; remove fat next morning. Boil a rabbit, cut it in dice, and fry; then add it, with a small amount of lemon juice and two tablespoonfuls of curry powder mixed smooth with stock separately, to the stock. Serve very hot, with plain boiled rice on separate dish. Cost of soup, 2*s*. 4*d*.—rabbit, 1*s*. 6*d*.; bones, 3*d*.; vegetables, 3*d*.; rice, 1*d*.; bacon, 1*d*.; curry powder, 2*d*.

Three pounds of cod at 6*d*. a pound, plain boiled; eight oysters cut in half for sauce, which is made of the liquor of the oysters; teacupful of milk, piece of butter size of walnut, salt, and two teaspoonfuls of flour. Cod, 1*s*. 6*d*.; oysters, 8*d*.; milk, butter, &c., 3*d*.—2*s*. 5*d*.

Croquettes of Chicken.—Take the two legs of a nicely cooked chicken (the bones of which can be added to those for soup); mince the meat small, then pound smooth in a mortar. Make a sauce with a piece of butter size of a walnut, one onion chopped fine and browned, and half a teacupful of milk; when at boiling point add one teaspoonful of flour, mixed smooth with milk, salt, and pepper to taste, add the yolks of two eggs, then put in the chicken and stir all together until thoroughly mixed, remove from fire; when cold make up the mixture into croquettes, cover with egg and bread-crumbs, and fry in dripping from leg of mutton; serve very hot garnished with parsley. Any remains of cold chicken will do for this dish. Portion of chicken, 9*d*.; eggs (3), 2½*d*., sometimes 3*d*.; total cost, 1*s*. 2½*d*.

Leg of Mutton à la Bretonne.—Choose a leg of Welsh mutton about 6 lbs. in weight, get four cloves of garlic, make an incision with the point of a knife in four different parts round the knuckle and place the garlic in it, hang it up for a day or two, and then roast it for an hour and a half. Take a quart of French haricots and place them in a saucepan with half a gallon of water. Add salt, half an ounce of butter, and set them to simmer until tender, when the liquor must be poured into a basin. Keep the haricots hot, peel and cut two large onions into thin slices, put some of the fat from the dripping-pan into the fryingpan, put in the onions, and fry a light brown. Add them to the haricots, with the fat &c. that the mutton has produced in roasting, season with salt and pepper, toss them about a little, and serve very hot on a large dish on which the mutton is put, garnished with a frill. Serve with mashed potatoes, Brussels sprouts, currant jelly. Cost, with best Welsh mutton, 8*s*.; with New Zealand, *just as good*, 5*s*.

Roasted Pheasant, 2*s*. 6*d*.—Plainly and nicely roasted, sent in on a bed of bread-crumbs made from crusts and pieces of bread dried in the oven and rolled small with the rolling-pin. Potatoes plainly boiled and rubbed through a sieve, with a very small piece of butter. 2*s*. 9*d*.

Méringues.—Use the three whites of the eggs the yolks of which you have used for the croquettes; whisk them to a stiff froth, and with a wooden spoon stir in quickly a quarter and half a quarter of a pound of white sifted sugar. Put some boards in the oven thick enough to prevent the bottom of the méringues from acquiring too much colour. Cut some strips of paper about two inches wide, put this on the board, and drop a tablespoonful at a time of the mixture on paper, giving them as nearly as possible the shape of an egg, keeping each méringue about two inches apart. Strew over some sifted sugar, and bake in a moderate oven for half an hour. As soon as they begin to colour remove them; take each slip of paper by the two ends and turn it gently on the table, and with a small spoon take out the soft part. Spread some clean paper, turn the méringues upside down, and put them into the oven to harden; then fill with whipped cream just flavoured with vanilla and sweetened with sugar; put two halves together and serve. Threepennyworth of cream is *quite* enough for six people, so this dish would cost about 4*d.*, as the eggs were charged for in the croquettes. 4*d.*

Turret Puddings.—Take two eggs, add their weight in flour, sugar, and butter; beat the eggs thoroughly first, then add sugar and flour and the butter melted; beat all together to a cream; fill small tins, bake for twenty minutes; add sauce, made from milk, two teaspoonfuls of flour, and a tablespoonful of brandy; serve hot. Outside cost, 1*s.*

Cheese Straws.—Two ounces of butter, 2 oz. of flour, 2 oz. of breadcrumbs, 2 oz. of cheese grated, half a small saltspoon of mixed salt and cayenne; mix all together to a paste, and roll it out a quarter of an inch in thickness; cut it into narrow strips, lay them on a sheet of paper, and bake for a few minutes; arrange them in a pyramid on a napkin, and serve hot. Cost, 6*d.*

General cost of dinner.—Soup, 2*s.* 4*d.*; fish, 2*s.* 5*d.*; entrée, 1*s.* 2½*d.*; mutton, 8*s.*; game, 2*s.* 9*d.*; sweets (2), 1*s.* 4*d.*; cheese, 6*d.*—18*s.* 6½*d.* Very excellent thick cream can be had from the Gloucester Dairy Company, Gloucester, who send 16 oz. for 1*s.* postage paid. This is invaluable for méringues. The Gloucester Dairy Company's little Gloucester cheeses for 2*s.* 6*d.* are also very useful for dinner-parties.

Menu No. VI.

Almond Soup.
Salmon, Caper Sauce.
Beef Olives.
Grilled Mushrooms.
Saddle of Mutton.
Widgeon.
Tipsy Cake.
College Pudding.
Apple Jelly.
Macaroni Cheese.
Dessert.

White Soup.—Two pounds of veal, two quarts of water, one onion, quarter of a pint of cream, an ounce of butter, two dozen sweet almonds pounded to paste, salt and cayenne pepper to taste. Boil the veal, water, and onion slowly all the previous day, take off all the fat, strain, add other ingredients, thicken with one pennyworth of arrowroot, and serve very hot. 2*s.* 10*d.*

Salmon.—Three pounds, nicely boiled, plain melted butter; add a small amount of liquor from a bottle of capers, a teaspoonful of the capers chopped fine, and half a teaspoonful of lemon juice. Fish, 7s. 6d.; sauce, 6d.

Beef Olives.—One pound of beefsteak, cut in squares about three inches and half an inch thick, chopped thyme and parsley, pepper and salt sprinkled over the beef, roll each piece, place on small skewer, stew in stock for an hour, thicken stock with a little flour and butter, pour over the olives, and serve very hot. 1s. 2d.

Grilled Mushrooms.—Wipe a dozen mushrooms carefully, place on tin in front of fire with a small piece of butter, salt and pepper to taste on each, have ready twelve little pieces of toasted bread, and when done put a mushroom on each piece; serve very hot. Outside cost, 2s. 6d.

Small Saddle of Mutton (about 8 lbs.).—Currant jelly, potatoes put through sieve after well boiling, stewed celery covered with melted butter, currant jelly. Outside cost of all, 10s.

Widgeon.—Plainly roasted, sent in very hot with their own gravy, lemon juice, and cayenne; potato shavings—potatoes to be cut in thin strips, fried a light brown in boiling lard, then placed on blotting paper to remove grease, placed in *hot* vegetable dish and served. 3s.

Tipsy Cake.—Take a sixpenny Madeira cake, cut it in three rounds, spread the rounds with raspberry jam, scoop out the middle of the top slices, soak it in a quarter of a pint of sherry until tender; fill up centre with preserved fruit, and cover with whipped cream. Outside cost, 2s.

College Pudding.—Butter a shape, stick it all round with split raisins, line with brown cut from a sally lunn, cut the rest in slices, and put it with a few ratifias and macaroons into the mould; beat two eggs in enough milk to cover the pudding; add a tablespoonful of sugar, cover it with a buttered paper and a cloth; boil it for an hour. Cost, 1s.

Apple Shape.—Two pounds of apples, boiled to a pulp in half a teacupful of water, juice of one lemon, two ounces of sugar, half an ounce of gelatine, soaked in quarter of a pint of water; mix well together, and rub together through a hair sieve whilst hot; butter a mould, pour in, leave until cold. Serve with custard made as follows:—Quarter of a pint of milk, one egg, teaspoonful of corn-flour, sugar to taste; bring the milk to boiling point, and add other ingredients; stir until thick, remove from fire, set to cool; when cold pour it over the shape. 10d.

Macaroni Cheese.—Quarter of a pound of macaroni, two ounces of butter, three ounces of Cheddar cheese, pepper and salt to taste, half a pint of milk, one pint of water, bread-crumbs. Boil the macaroni until tender in the milk and water, sprinkle cheese and some of the butter among it, then season with the pepper, and cover all with finely grated bread-crumbs. Warm the rest of the butter and pour it over the bread-crumbs; brown it before a fire, and serve very hot. Cost, 9*d*.

Soup, 2*s*. 10*d*.; fish, 8*s*.; beef olives, 1*s*. 2*d*.; mushrooms, 2*s*. 6*d*.; mutton, 10*s*.; widgeon, 3*s*.; sweets, 3*s*. 10*d*.; cheese, 10*d*. Total cost, 1*l*. 12*s*. 2*d*.

I think the receipts given above would form the nucleus for any amount of moderate entertainment, but I may speak of two capital books which would assist any young housekeeper, and which have done me so much good I should be ungrateful not to mention them. One is Mrs. de Salis's 'Entrées à la Mode,' published by Longmans at 1*s*. 6*d*., and the other is Mrs. Beeton's 'Household Management,' a 7*s*. 6*d*. book, but one no mistress of a household should ever think of being without.

Though naturally invalids' cooking does not come in properly when one should be thinking of nothing but pleasant matters, cooking reminds me of a valuable piece of information given to me by a friend, and at the risk of being called to order I must just give one hint in regard to beef-tea, the making of which is often very wasteful and tiring to an invalid's patience, and which can be made most successfully by taking a nice juicy beefsteak and cutting off all the superfluous fat; then this should be salted and peppered to taste, and floured on both sides; then the bottom of a stew-pan should be covered with just enough water to keep the meat from sticking, and the meat should be allowed to stew by the side of the fire from one hour and a quarter, according to size. The gravy is excellent rich beef-tea, while the steak itself is beautifully tender and fit to be sent to table. One or two allspice berries put in with the meat give a flavour of wine, and thus we have good pleasant beef-tea for an invalid and luncheon for ourselves, with none of the waste that often accompanies the making of what is all too often a tasteless, greasy, and disagreeable compound.

Another dish for a convalescent is made by treating a chop in the same way as a steak as regards the pepper, salt, and flour. It is then put on a plate with a tablespoonful of water, covered with another plate exactly the same size, and put into a slow oven for more than an hour. When cooked, the top plate should be turned down to the bottom, so the chop is hot to the last, and has not been disturbed, and is so tender and thoroughly cooked it does not need masticating, and it is also so nice that many clergymen are glad to find this ready for them after leaving church, instead of the orthodox cold supper. It literally cooks itself, and is therefore no trouble on Sundays; while for a country doctor, whose hours are uncertain, and who all too often subsists on either sodden or scorched-up food, it is a perfect dish, and should be recollected by all those good housewives who are often enough at their wits' end to find something nice for the bread-winner when he returns home after a long and fatiguing drive over country roads and open moors.

So, that I may not be utterly condemned for dragging in my invalids, I will just mention that a very nice dish for a small evening party is made by simply grating raw chestnuts up very finely into a dish, and covering them thickly with whipped cream, sweetened and flavoured to taste; while tins of American peaches, placed in a deep dish and sweetened to taste and covered with good whipped cream, are also things most useful to the country housewife, who is often called upon to provide a good *extra* dish in a hurry, despite her distance from shops and the impossibility of getting anything decent in her village; while Edwards' desiccated soup is an excellent 'standby' in any country house, for with its aid soup is always forthcoming; and with soup and a pretty-looking sweet the simplest dinner may be made to pass off with sufficient *éclat* to satisfy a guest who may have been cajoled into sharing pot-luck, despite the fact that the nearest butcher is four miles off and that it is not the game season—a species of entertaining most trying to any one, especially in the country, but which even there can be faced with equanimity if we have sense, a few tinned provisions in our store-cupboards, and a cook who does not become flurried and who has her stockpot always going. A very good dinner can be extemporised by adding some of Edwards' desiccated soup to the ordinary soup; a side-dish can be made from poached eggs on spinach, from tinned lobsters made into cutlets, from any remains of cold meat made into croquettes; while pancakes and tinned peaches and cream add sufficient variety to whatever had been prepared for the late dinner, which can be furthermore supplemented and helped out by some of the cooked cheese prepared in one of the ways given in the menu receipts; but a welcome must be forthcoming too, else no amount of dinner will make the unexpected guest feel as if he were being entertained.

One last hint: always, unless you live in London, keep two or three new toothbrushes and a clean brush and comb in the house; then, should your guest be willing to remain until the next morning unexpectedly, you will even be ready for that emergency, and will not have one tiny flaw left to be found in your simple but most complete system of entertaining.

CHAPTER XX
THE SUMMING-UP

I have been so continually asked what is the very smallest possible sum of money that will suffice to furnish a little house for a young couple beginning life, that I have drawn up from actual bills a short schedule of the cost of furnishing the ordinary villa residence in the suburbs. But to this must be added quite another 50*l*. should the householder have literally every single thing to buy; for in this special house, as will be seen from the list, several rather important items were already procured, and wedding presents made a great and perceptible difference in the appearance of the modest *ménage*, as is fortunately generally the case with all young couples starting in life, who, if they are wise, will only purchase necessaries at first, saving their money until they are actually married, and know not only what their friends have given them, but also what the house itself really requires. There is no doubt, if this be done, the following will suffice at first; and on 150*l*. the house will not only look nice but artistic too.

Dining-room.

Bought of		£	s.	d.
A. and R. Smee	Six oak-framed rush-seated chairs at 25s.	7	10	0
Maple	Mahogany table	3	5	0
"	Kidderminster square carpet	1	17	6
Burnett	Felt for curtains	1	4	9
Whiteley	Fender	0	7	6
"	Fireirons	0	9	6
		£14	14	3

There were two deep cupboards in this special room, which rendered the purchase of a sideboard unnecessary; if one be imperative, I recommend the purchase of Maple's 'Vicarage' suite of furniture at 20*l*. It is both pretty and good, I *hear*; I have not actual personal experience of it.

Drawing-room.

Bought of		£	s.	d.
Shoolbred	Two squares of carpet	3	15	0
Maple	Sofa and pillows, covered velveteen	9	2	6
Whiteley	Fenders	1	5	6
"	Fireirons	0	15	0
Smee	Walnut octagonal table	5	0	0
"	Stuffed arm-chair	5	18	0
"	Sutherland table	2	0	0
"	Low chair	0	16	6
"	Arm-chair in rush &c.	1	2	6
"	Walnut and rush easy chair	2	5	0
Whiteley	Two low basket chairs	1	0	0
"	Cushions made at home	0	12	0
Burnett	Cretonne for curtains &c.	1	10	0
Holroyd and Barker	Muslin for second curtains	0	10	6
		£35	12	6

I strongly advise in addition to this one of Messrs. Trübner's excellent revolving bookcases, of which a drawing was made in my dining-room sketch. I consider no lover of books should be without one of these invaluable bookcases.

Best Bedroom.

Bought of		£	s.	d.
Maple	Black and brass bedstead	3	5	0
"	Excelsior spring mattress	2	9	0
"	Hair mattress	3	10	0
"	Bolster	0	17	6
"	Four pillows (5s. each)	1	0	0
Smee	Washing-stand	5	5	0
"	Dressing-table and glass	5	5	0
Maple	Kidderminster square	1	14	0
Smee	Two pretty chairs (5s.)	0	10	0
Maple	Box ottoman	2	15	0
Smee	Chest of drawers	6	10	0
Burnett	Cretonne for curtains	0	15	0

Smee	Muslin for ditto (4½d.)	0	6	0
Whiteley	Fender	0	4	3
"	Fireirons	0	3	11
		£34	9	8

Ware was in the possession of the young people, but a nice set can be bought for 7s. 6d., and even a little less; glass jug and glass for 1s. 6d., at Douglas's, the artistic glass-shop in Piccadilly.

Dressing-Room.

Bought of		£	s.	d.
Treloar	Rug on floor	0	12	0
Whiteley	Bath	1	1	0
Watts	Dressing-table and washing-stand combined	6	5	0
Maple	Wardrobe	5	0	0
"	Set of ware &c.	0	8	6
		£13	6	6

Spare Room.

Bought of		£	s.	d.
Maple	Five-foot bedstead	2	5	0
"	Excelsior mattress	2	9	0
"	Hair mattress	3	10	0
"	Bolster and pillows (4)	1	17	6
Smee	Washing-stand	5	5	0
"	Dressing-table and glass, very deep drawers	5	5	0
"	Two chairs (5s.)	0	10	0
"	Chest of drawers	4	10	0
Burnett	Cretonne for curtains	0	15	0
Smee	Muslin ""	0	6	0
Treloar	Kidderminster square	1	1	0
Whiteley	Fender	0	4	3
"	Fireirons	0	3	11
"	Set of ware	0	5	0
		£28	6	8

Servant's Room (one Maid).

Bought of		£	s.	d.
Maple	Japanned bedstead	0	13	6
"	Palliasse	0	6	9
"	Mattress	0	10	0
"	Bolster and pillow	0	9	0
"	Dressing-table	0	4	9
"	Toilet-glass	0	5	0
"	Set of ware	0	3	9
"	Chair	0	2	0
"	Washing-stand	0	5	0
"	Dhurries for bedside	0	3	10
		£4	5	1

Staircase.

Bought of		£	s.	d.
Shoolbred	Kalmuc stair-carpet	2	15	0
Maple	Umbrella-stand	0	12	0
"	Hooks and rails for hats	0	15	0
		£4	2	0

Kitchen.

(Whiteley for all.)

	£	s.	d.
Deal Table	1	1	6
Two Chairs (3s. 9d.)	0	7	6
Three cups and saucers (2¾d.)	0	0	8¼
Three plates (2¼d.)	0	0	6¾
One bread-and-butter plate	0	2	4¾
Two bowls	0	0	4½
Set of jugs	0	1	6
Bread-pan	0	1	6½
Four brown jars	0	2	11
Two pie-dishes	0	1	1½
Hot-water jug	0	2	6
Slop-pail	0	4	9

Knife-tray	0	1	6
Egg-whisk	0	0	7½
Fish-slice	0	0	10½
Mincing-knife	0	1	4½
Sugar-tin	0	2	3
Weights and scales	0	8	11
Pestle and mortar	0	3	3
Copper kettle	0	7	3
Two wire covers	0	1	3½
Sweep's brush for stove	0	1	1½
Two stove-brushes	0	3	4
Banister brush	0	2	0
Scrubbing-brushes	0	1	3½
Broom	0	2	11
Carpet-broom	0	2	11
Knifeboard	0	1	1½
Two plate-brushes	0	1	9½
Plate-polisher	0	1	6½
Salt-box	0	1	3½
Leather	0	1	1½
Housemaid's box	0	2	3½
One fork-tin	0	0	6½
Colander	0	1	4½
Spice-box	0	1	11½
Cake-tin	0	0	7½
Tart-tins	0	0	5¾
Patty-pans	0	0	6½
Meat-saw	0	1	11½
Meat-chopper	0	1	11½
Coalscuttle	0	4	6
Coal-hammer	0	0	10¾
Coal-shovel	0	2	3
Toast-fork	0	0	6½
Pepper-box	0	0	4¾
Tea-tray	0	1	11½

Paste jagger	0	1	11½
Two flat irons	0	1	9½
Pail	0	1	4½
Brass water-jug	0	5	6
Japanned can	0	5	11
Two saucepans	0	9	6
One saucepan	0	2	3
One saucepan	0	1	9½
'Digester'	0	12	0
Basting-ladle	0	0	11½
Two tin moulds	0	3	6
Oval fryingpan	0	1	2½
Gridiron	0	1	9½
Fish-kettle	0	3	11
Tea-kettle	0	4	11
Knives	0	0	8¾
Dustpan	0	0	10¾
Bread-grater	0	0	7¾
Gravy-strainer	0	1	0½
Flour-dredger	0	0	7¾
Pasteboard	0	1	11½
Rolling-pin	0	1	9½
Steps	0	5	3
Set of dinner ware	1	1	0
Set of tea-ware	0	12	6
	£11	2	1½

Summary of all.

	£	s.	d.
Dining-room	14	14	3
Two drawing-rooms	35	12	0
Best bedroom	34	9	8
Spare room	28	6	8
Servant's room	4	5	1
Staircase	4	2	0
Kitchen things	11	2	1½

Dressing-room	13	6	6
	£145	18	3½

Besides this we spent about 5*l*. on blankets and odds and ends; but all house linen was given, and several other things. However, the above will demonstrate how it is possible to furnish a small house on 150*l*., and have for this good, well-made furniture that will wear, and is not mere cheap rubbish stuck together to sell, and not meant to last.

To manage this satisfactorily it is necessary to keep one's eyes open and know precisely where to buy everything, for locality makes an enormous difference, and different shops have always some one thing cheaper than any other establishment; and while Whiteley will ask 1*s*. 4½*d*. for the glass globes that cost 3*s*. 6*d*. at Shoolbred's, Shoolbred will sell for 3*s*. 6*d*. a brass can that costs 4*s*. 6*d*. or 5*s*. everywhere else. To furnish cheaply and satisfactorily, therefore, one's eyes must be kept open, and one must know exactly where to go for everything. And I may mention here, as a short and succinct guide, that cretonnes are cheaper and better at Burnett's, King Street, Covent Garden, and at Colbourne's, 82 Regent Street, than anywhere else; that Maple's Oriental rugs and carpets, matting, wall-papers, and brasses are also the cheapest in the market. Wicker chairs are to be had at Colbourne's for 31*s*. 9*d*., painted any colour with Aspinall's enamel, and cushioned and covered with cretonne or printed linen; that artistic and beautiful draperies are to ha procured at Liberty's and Collinson and Lock's, whose dearer cretonnes are unsurpassed; that Mr. Arthur Smee's furniture is the best and most artistic, in my opinion, in London; that Stephens, 326 Regent Street, has the best and cheapest Turkish embroidered antimacassars, and also possesses some beautiful and inexpensive materials for curtains—notably a cheap brocade that is made in exquisite colours and called Sicilian damask; that the brass rods and ends for windows are to be had cheaper of Whiteley and Colbourne than anywhere else, and are quite as good as the more expensive makes; artistic pottery is to be had of Mr. Elliott, 18 Queen's Road, Bayswater; cheap chairs of Messrs. Harding Bros., Beaconsfield, Bucks; and for all gas-fittings I strongly recommend Mr. Strode, 48 Osnaburgh Street, Regent's Park, N.W. I have tried all these firms for years, and am speaking of them from experience entirely.

It may not be out of place in my last chapter to mention the exact cost of setting up and keeping a carriage; for by the time my readers have come as far on their life's journey as I have, they may reasonably expect to have the great comfort and luxury of a modest equipage of their own, than which there is no greater blessing in the world, and which I would rather cling to than anything else I possess, and which really does not cost half as much as the constant hiring of flys and driving in cabs which are so dear to the heart of the orthodox British matron, who goes on her weary round of society gaieties which she does not really enjoy, little thinking how much happier she would be spending her money in a thousand different ways.

But one must keep one's carriage with common-sense, like everything else, and must not be under the thumb of one's coachman, who must not be allowed for one moment to buy his own corn &c., as no class receives higher percentages than does the coachman who is allowed his own sweet will in matters appertaining to the stable. A widow lady who cannot well battle with tradesmen herself had much better apply to some good firm like Withers and Co., of Oxford Street, who for a certain sum a year, which varies according to the style of horse and man desired, will provide everything, down to a safe place for the carriages, which can be left unhesitatingly in their charge. But for a couple who desire to set up their carriage and do not quite know how to do it, I think the following will be sufficient guide for them:—

Estimated Cost of setting up one Horse and a Carriage.

	£	s.	d.
Good horse (should be bought in the country if possible)	50	0	0
Set of good single harness (Stores)	7	0	0
Brushes, leathers, sponges, &c. (Shoolbred)	2	0	0
Rugs, rollers, &c. (Shoolbred)	3	0	0
Brougham or victoria (Holland and Holland)	175	0	0
Coachman's livery (Goodall and Graham, Conduit Street)	10	11	0
Boots—less discount (Thierry, Regent Street)	3	0	0
Stable suit (Goodall and Graham)	3	0	0
Mackintosh (Goodall and Graham)	1	10	0
Mackintosh rug (Whiteley)	1	10	0
Mats (Holland and Holland)	1	10	0
Carriage rugs (Swears and Wells)	3	0	0
	£261	1	6

Of course the carriage need not cost as much; but, if possible, a new carriage is to be preferred to a second-hand one. Still, at Holland and Holland's, Oxford Street, W., one can often, especially at the end of the season, pick up a second-hand carriage very cheaply, and at such a place as this one can be sure that no rubbish is being bought; but sales should be avoided, as should advertisements, and if a second-hand carriage is necessary I strongly advise intending purchasers to go to Holland and Holland and ask them to keep their eyes open, remembering, likewise, that at the end of the season one is far more likely to do a good stroke of business in this way than at any other time of the year. In our climate, if only one carriage can be kept, a brougham is to be preferred to any other; this makes one independent of weather entirely, and one's garments do not become as dusty and spoiled as they invariably do in an open vehicle. Once the carriage is purchased, we have to consider the cost of keeping it up, which, of course, varies considerably in every locality, but I think the account given below strikes the average, and allows the outside cost of everything. Of course, very often the rent of the stables is covered in the rent of the house, which includes also a place for the coachman.

Estimated Cost of keeping one Horse and Carriage.

	£	s.	d.
Coachman's wages (from 23s. to 25s., say)	62	8	0
Livery	13	0	0
Corn, straw, hay, &c.	40	0	0
Shoeing	3	0	0
Repairs &c.	26	0	0
Rent of stable &c.	20	0	0
	£164	8	0

'Repairs &c.' include 'depreciation,' which is calculated on 20 per cent. of estimated value of whole, less livery, otherwise provided for. Of course, a second horse could be added for about 40*l*. a year more, good double harness being procurable at from 18*l*. to 20*l*.

Passing from the carriage to dwell for a moment on the great dress question, which is a most serious one in these days of ours, I find I can really lay down no laws on this subject, but I strongly advise all young brides who cannot afford a maid to learn dressmaking for themselves, or to search out some place where, for a reasonable cost, the renovating of dresses and simple making can be carried on for her, or else she will soon find herself in difficulties. Her under-linen in her trousseau should last her ten or twelve years at least, and with ordinary care her trousseau dresses should, with judicious management, last her quite two years; this gets over the worst part of one's life as regards pecuniary bothers, as a rule; but the less she can spend on dress the better, always allowing herself enough to look nice and be tidy on. A man can dress himself well on 30*l.* a year, and a woman can do likewise on 50*l.*, but this requires, in both cases, the most careful management, while the average cost of a child is from 10*l.* to 15*l.* Women with small means will do much better if they confine themselves to one colour, and would look much nicer at a far less cost if they would only purchase things to match; but English people, as a rule, only buy things because they like them, never considering whether they possess already any garment at home with which the new possession will harmonise or agree entirely. Brown and red are good colours for winter nowadays when so many people have seal-skins; greys are good shades for summer, the ever-useful serge and washing silks looking always delightfully cool and ladylike.

Our book, now rapidly coming to a conclusion, would not be complete without one word about the 'garret'—otherwise the box-room—which, all too often, is a storehouse for all sorts and conditions of rubbish, put up there in a desperate hope that, sooner or later, the odds and ends will come in usefully. There cannot be a greater mistake than hoarding, and I strongly advise my readers never to allow this to be done. If one's clothes when worn out are not fit for one's poorer friends, I suggest some respectable dealer should be applied to, and that they should be sold. I am aware this sounds an awful proposition to most people, but how rarely are our dresses suitable for those who would wear cast-off raiment? while, if we sell them, we can give the money in charity, or buy pictures or flowers for our rooms. Still, if this should be repugnant to the feelings of my readers, they can always send all their rubbish to the Kilburn Orphanage of Mercy, the good sisters there being able to use to the veriest fragment all they receive, and which does then immediate good.

Let the box-room or garret be thoroughly turned out and investigated once every three months; keep there all pieces of paper similar to the papers on your walls for mending purposes, and any travelling trunks or boxes that may be wanted; but do not accumulate rubbish of any kind. Even sentimental rubbish should be destroyed at once; when we die it will be done by hands which are not as tender as ours are, and no good is done by hoarding all sorts and kinds of letters and flowers, or even babies' first shoes. They may mean life itself to us; they will be nothing but the veriest rubbish to our successors.

Standing as it were in the garret, our long work of revising and writing this book at last drawing to a conclusion, and feeling sad, as one always feels when parting with an occupation that has been on one's mind for many a month, I should like to say a few words on that saddest of all subjects, a death in the house—only a few words; but a house that has never known a death is indeed an almost impossible thing to contemplate, and so our record would not be complete without this. Thank Heaven, we look out with brighter eyes on the other country than did our ancestors, but we have still many customs to leave off, many others we could adopt with benefit from the relics of past days.

I would advocate great cheerfulness about our dead. They should never be left alone, and candles and bright flowers should fill the room; where, had I my way, the blessed sunshine should stream in always, gloom should be discouraged, and the service with its music and the coloured pall should suggest not our grief but the gain of those who, even to the agnostic of the period, appear at rest, and can most certainly never weary or hunger any more; while to us who hope to look beyond these shadows their happiness should overshadow our grief entirely. Still, whichever way we look on the silence that surrounds our little life, there are certain things that I would urge on the survivors. Let all the personal linen and garments of the dead friend be at once sent to Kilburn, or to Miss Hinton's, A. F. D. Society, 4 York Place, Clifton. These garments are distributed at once among the families of poor clergymen, and so immediately benefit a most deserving class. Do not permit any hoarding (I once knew a whole valuable wardrobeful of clothes consumed by the moth, because the widow's feelings did not allow of the garments being disturbed, though they were not too acute to prevent her becoming engaged to be married before the year was out); and, above all, burn all letters that may be left *unread*; this will save endless mischief, and should be done at once. No one knows who may be the next to depart and be no more seen, and so this should not be delayed any longer than is possible.

It is far better to do these things at once. If we close the room in which our beloved have passed away, and think time will enable us to face the task with more boldness, we shall find we are grievously mistaken; the longer we put it off the worse it will be, and we shall not forget them any quicker because their own possessions have been given to those who can benefit by them. Each thing in life should always be in use; hoarding of any kind in a garret is useless, and wicked too.

And now I have come to the last hint, I think, I have to give my young householders. Of course, the subject is practically inexhaustible, and enlarges itself for one every day we live; but I have given you all my own experience up to the present date, and if it should save one young couple the mistakes I made in my first start in life, or give them the help I should have been so glad of myself twenty years ago, I shall feel I have not spent my time in vain; while let no one despise the homely subject, for it is our first duty in life to try and make our homes so bright and beautiful and pleasant that they may shed radiance on all in their immediate neighbourhood, setting the example that is worth so very much precept, and be like good deeds, 'shining like a candle in this naughty world.' Let love, beauty, carefulness, and economy rule your lives, O young householders! and then you will find that life is the most interesting thing possible, and is always, to the very last day of it, well worth the trouble of living.

INDEX

A,B,C,D,E,F,G,H,I,J,K,L,M,N,O,P,Q,R,S,T,U,V,W,Y

Absurd arrangement of our houses,
Account book, leaf from an,
Accounts,
A. F. D. Society, Miss Hinton's,
Afternoon teas,
Airing bedroom,
— beds,
— nursery,
'Allowancing' servants,
American cloth,
Angelina's bedroom,
— private duster,
— wardrobe,
Antimacassars,
— Stephens',
— Turkish,
A place for everything,
Apple shape,
Arm-chair,
Arm-chairs, Colbourne's,
— tapestry for covering, Maple's,
Arsenic in wall-paper,
Art and the bitter lot of the poor,
— colours,
— furniture,
Artistic corners,
Aspinall's paint,

Babies, baths for,
— clothing,
— cow's milk for,
— garments,
— special theories about,

Babies, their berceaunettes,
Baby-talk, stupid,
Back of piano exposed, remedy for,
Baker Street vases,
Bamboo brackets (Liberty's, and at Baker Street Bazaar),
Basket chairs,
Baskets for soiled linen, palm-leaved,
Bath and bath blankets,
Beaconsfield chairs,
Beaufort ware,
Beautiful things, making them common,
Bed airing,
— gowns,
— making,
— pocket,
Bedroom brackets,
— carpet,
— chairs,
— cupboards,
— curtains,
— door fittings,
— match-boxes,
— paper,
— — colour for,
— screen,
— ware,
— windows, muslin for,
— — too many,
Bedrooms,
— colour for,
— papering ceilings of,
Beds for servants,
Bedside, table near,
Bedstead, brass or iron, the best,
— wooden,
Beef, cold,
— olives,
Beer,
Beginning housekeeping,
Bellows for dining-room,
Benson's lamps,

Berceaunettes,
'Berry' paper,
Bills, regular payment of,
Biscuit-box,
Black-lead,
Blankets, Witney,
Blinds and their rollers, doing away with,
Blue and white paper for bachelor's spare room, Chappel & Payne's,
Boarding-school plan a mistake,
Bohemian ware,
Boiled rabbit,
Bolton sheeting,
Bookcase, bedroom,
— velveteen cover,
Bookcases, revolving American,
Books for spare rooms,
Boudoir, spare room made into,
Bow-windowed villas, window-seats in,
Bow-windows, curtains for,
Box ottomans for bedrooms,
— — — — Maple's,
— — — hats and bonnets,
— pincushions,
— room,
Brackets,
Brandy the one spirituous liquor that should be kept in a house,
Brass brush for dining-room,
— door handles best,
— fire-irons,
— fittings for bedroom doors, Maple's,
— headed nails,
— kettle,
Brass pots,
— pots for palms, Hampton's,
Bread,
— brown,
— knives, Mappin & Webb's,
— price of,
— stands,
— wasted,
Bread-pan with cover,

Breakfast,
— table,
— — gloomy,
— — punctuality,
Brewers,
Bromley,
Brooks, Shirley,
Brougham, cost of,
Brushes and combs,
Brushing under beds,
Buckland, Frank,
Burnett, address of,
Burnett's 'Marguerite' cretonne curtains,
— serges,
Bush Hill Park,
Butchers,
Butter, cost of,
Buyers of bottles, rags, &c.,

Cabinet pudding,
Cabinets,
— made by Smee,
'Calls,' doing away with,
Canadian custom respecting carpets,
Candle shields,
Candlesticks, Liberty's,
Carbolic acid,
Careless housemaid,
— servants,
Carlyle, Mr. and Mrs.,
Carpentry, amateur,
Carpet designs, Mr. Morris's,
— for drawing-room,
— royal blue, Colbourne's,
Carpets,
— hints about,
— Oriental,
— Wilton,
Carriage, cost of keeping a,
— rugs, rollers, &c., cost of,
Carrot soup,

Carson's 'detergent,'
Cauliflower *au gratin*,
Centre-piece,
Chairs, bedroom,
— dining-room,
— embellished by carvings,
— Harding Bros.',
— Liberty's,
— New Zealand pine, for dining-room,
— (rush-seated, black-framed) for dining-room,
— Smee's,
Chambers, large, airy,
Chappel & Payne, address of,
Charming chair for drawing-room (rush-seated),
Checked muslin for bedroom windows,
Cheerful surroundings,
Cheese fondus,
— soufflés,
— straws,
Cheval glass,
Chickens,
Child of the period, the,
Children and inherited tendencies,
— amusing themselves,
— authors for,
— collecting pretty things around them,
— destructive and untidy,
— diet for,
— grown-up,
— helping their elders,
— hour for rising,
— hours for studying,
— importance of quiet and regularity for,
— — — sunshine for,
— punishing,
— spoiling them,
— teaching them self-control,
— the home they were born in,
Children's breakfast,
— dress,
— education,

Chimneys,
China, Crown, Derby, and Worcester,
— gilt on,
China, Minton's ivy-patterned,
— Oriental,
— real,
Chippendale chairs,
— furniture,
Chocolate cream,
Choosing rooms,
Cigars in drawing-room,
Clean brush and comb in toilet drawer,
Clear soup,
Clock, necessity for, in spare rooms,
Clocks, Oetzmann's,
Coachman's livery, cost of,
Coats hanging in rooms,
Coffee,
— cost of,
Colbourne, Messrs, address of,
College pudding,
Colours for bedrooms,
Combination dressing-table and washing-stand, Watts's,
Common sense,
'Confound baby!',
Conservatory, tiny,
Cook, overburdened,
— thoughtful,
Cooks, 'experienced,'
Cost of dinner,
Cottage piano,
Counterpanes,
Cradles,
Credit, nothing so dear as,
Cretonne,
— curtain,
— on mantelpiece,
Croquettes of chickens,
Cruet-stands,
Cupboards forgotten,
— small,

Curried kidneys,
Curtain, bedroom,
— rods, bedroom,
— — Maple's,
Curtains,
— *v.* screens,
Cutlets *à la réforme*,
— of cod,

Dado, Collison and Lock's,
— in dining-room,
— in drawing-room,
— leather paper for,
Dado rail, Maple's,
— Treloar's,
Damasks, Stephens' 'Sicilienne,'
Day nursery,
Deal dressing-tables,
Decorating drawing-room,
'Demon builder,' the,
Dessert service, Hewett's,
— — Mortlock's,
'Digesters,'
Dining-room,
— mantelpiece,
— walls,
Dining-rooms, orthodox,
Dinner, complete cost of,
— service, best,
— sets, Mortlock's,
— waggons,
Disagreeable details,
Dishes,
Disinfectants,
Doctors' bills,
Domestic problems,
'Do nothing in a hurry,'
Door front,
— — brass stand behind,
— — double curtains for,
Double tray tables,

Dr. Chevasse,
— — books by, for young mothers,
Drain disinfectant,
Drainage,
Drains,
— time for seeing to,
Draped alcove, Collison & Lock's design,
Drawing-room,
— blue wooden mantelpiece for,
— carpet, Colbourne's,
— — Maple's,
— — Shoolbred's,
— — Smee's,
— — Treloar's,
— colour for,
— curtains,
— essentially a best room,
— mistress's corner,
— tea-table for,
Dress and personal appearance of daughters,
— cost of, for man and wife,
Dress, wife's,
Dressing jackets invaluable,
— gown,
— room,
— table and washing-stand combined,
— tables, price of,
— — should not be dust-traps,
— — Smee's,
Drugget, hard-wearing, Pither's,
Dulwich,
Duplex burners,
Dustbin,
— not a necessity,
Dusters,
Dust-sheets for furniture,
Dyeing, Pullar's,

Eclairs,
Edwin's dressing room,
— — substantial dado for,

Eider-down quilts,
Eggs,
Electric light,
'Eligible residences,'
Elliot, Mr.,
— — address of,
Enamel paints,
Enfield,
'Excelsior' mattresses for spare rooms,
— spring mattress,
Exhibiting baby, danger of,

Fashion and folly,
Feather beds,
Ferns and immortelles for toilet-table,
Field & Co.'s candle shields,
Finchley,
Finger-glasses,
Fire-keeping, recipe for,
Fireplaces,
— misplaced,
Fires, benefit from, in winter and summer,
— in bedrooms, benefit of,
First babies,
— — washing them,
Fish,
— contracts for,
Fish Market, Central,
— markets,
Fittings,
Five o'clock tea,
Flannel pilches,
Flock papers,
Floor (bedroom), staining all over,
Floral paper for spare room,
— — Maple's,
Flour,
Flowers in bedrooms,
Foot-baths,
Footstools for dining-room,
— — morning-room, Whiteley's and Shoolbred's,

Forest Hill,
Formal visiting,
Fowl,
French pancakes,
— parents,
— windows and curtains,
Fresh air,
— flowers in sick-room,
Friezes,
— Mrs. McClelland's,
Frilling for sheets, Cash's,
Fruit,
Frying-pans,
Furnishing, schedule of cost of,
Furniture, fearful expense of,

Garden, small,
Gardening,
Garrard, Mrs. S. B. (beds, &c., for infants),
Garret,
— regular investigation of,
Gas, best for spare rooms,
— effect of, on plants,
— fittings, Strode's,
— in bedrooms, evil of,
— — rooms where there are children, necessity for,
— — sitting-rooms,
— *v*. paraffine,
Gentlemen's wardrobes,
German lamp screens,
Gilt legs to chairs,
Glass,
— best,
Glass cloths,
Glasses and bottles, coloured, Douglas & Co.'s,
Going off to school,
Good hostess,
— monthly nurses all the battle,
— servants, insuring them,
Gossip, spiteful,
Governess,

'Graining,' a barbarism,
Grand piano,
— — made a decorative piece of furniture,
Grate, wasteful,
Grates, Barnard's,
Green water,
Gridirons,
Grilled mushrooms,
Groceries,
Grown-up daughters,
— families,
Guests, making them comfortable,
Guipure lace for curtains,

Hall,
— candlesticks,
— ceilings papered,
— flooring,
— gas-lamps,
— lighted from the sides,
— — — — top,
— oil lamp unsuited for,
Halls, stone,
Happy childhood,
Harding Bros., address of,
Hare soup,
Harness for carriage, price of,
Hassan and Co.'s chickens,
Healthy children,
Heavy mahogany,
Hewett's bazaar,
— dessert services,
Hoarding in garrets,
— old clothes,
Honest mechanic, prospect for an,
Honeycomb quilts,
Horse, price of, for carriage,
Hot-water cans for bedrooms,
— dishes,
House decoration and the landlord,
— — Collison & Lock's,

— — Morris's,
— — Smee's,
— hunting,
— inspection, preliminary,
— rent,
Household books,
— economy,
— servants, young girls as,
Housekeeping bills,
Housemaid's duties,
— pantry,
House-mother, life of, not appreciated,

Ideal and real nurseries,
Indian matting for schoolroom floors,
— tapestry, Liberty's,
Infant and nurse,
Infants, knowingness of,
Informal gatherings,
Inherited tendencies,
Ink-erasers for hand cleaning (Perry's),
Inkstands purchased at Baker Street Bazaar,
Invalids, cooking for,
Inventions Exhibition,
Iron brackets and lamps,

Jack Tar suit,
Jackets and trousers for boys,
Japanese fan,
— — for fireside,
— leather paper,
— — — for the hall,
— paper for wardrobe panels,
— screen for piano,
Joss-sticks,
Judicious watchfulness regarding servants,
Jugs and pots, Elliot's,
Jury of matrons,

Kidderminster squares,
Kilburn Orphanage,

Kitchen arrangements,
— capabilities of,
Kitchen ceilings, annual white-washing of,
— dado in,
— dinner,
— dismal,
— grates skimped,
— — smells from,
— management,
— passages,
— position of,
— staircase a cause of worry,
— underground,
— utensils,
— wash-tub not needed for,
Kitcheners, Steel & Garland's,
Koffee Kanns, Ashe's,
Kurd rugs,
Kyrle Society,

Ladies' chamber in retirement,
Lahore cretonne,
Lamp brackets,
— screens, German,
— — selecting colour of,
Lamps, beaten iron,
— Benson's,
— brass,
— china,
— duplex, for nursery,
— glass hanging,
— Mortlock's,
— paraffine, Drew's,
— Smee's,
— Strode's,
Landing, the,
Landseer, Sir Edwin,
Leases and structural repairs,
Legs of mutton,
— — — à la Bretonne,
Lemon pudding,

Liberty's cretonnes,
— sashes,
— silk handkerchiefs,
— — — for curtains,
— tapestries,
Lighting bedrooms,
— of sitting-rooms,
Linen marking,
— old-gold colour printed, Pither's,
Linoleum mat for dining-room,
London markets,
— north side of,
Lordship Lane,
Low frocks and short sleeves for children, disappearance of,
Luncheon,
— hour (orthodox) for young wives,

Macaroni cheese,
Madras muslin,
Mahogany sideboard, old,
Making a bedroom pretty,
Managing servants,
Mantelpieces, cheap wooden, Shuffery's,
Maple,
Maple's bedsteads,
— box ottomans,
— Golden Pine carpet,
Marble mantelpiece, white,
Marguerite cretonnes, Burnett's,
Mats,
Matting for dining-room,
— price of,
— sweeping in one way,
— Treloar's,
Mattresses, cases for,
Mayfair, tiny hovels in,
McClelland, Mrs.,
Meal odours in rooms,
Meals and money,
Meat, 'best English,' often New Zealand,
— New Zealand,

— price of,
Medical attendance,
Menus, cost of,
Meringues,
Midday meal,
Middle-class parents,
Milk,
Milkmen, Londoners at the mercy of,
Mince pies,
Minton's china,
Monograms on cloths,
Monthly nurse,
Moreen curtains,
— damask,
Morning-room, books and magazines for,
— chairs,
Morning-room decoration,
— desk for,
— embellishing door-panels of,
— no gas in,
— paper for, Smee's,
— sage-green paper for,
— sofa,
— stand for papers,
— under care of housemaid,
— work-table,
Morocco, dull brown,
Morris, Mr.,
Mortlock's china,
— — lamps,
— ware,
Mulligatawny soup,
Music, receptacle for,
Muslin curtains,
Muslins, Liberty's,
Mutton cutlets,
Mysore chintz, Liberty's,
— muslin,

Neck of mutton,
Nevill's hot-water bread,

New babies, making ready for,
— baby a profound nuisance,
Night garments,
— — embroidered case for,
— nursery,
— — management of fire in,
Nurseries,
— bright paper for,
— cretonne, dado, and painted rail for,
— gas in,
— good duplex lamp for,
— pictures on walls of,
— position of,
— strong guard for fires in,
— two in a house,
— *v.* spare rooms,
Nursery a children's kingdom,
— blue and white paper for,
— ceiling,
— chair for each child in,
— choice of a,
— cretonne cleaned with dry bread,
Nursery cupboards,
— doors,
— floor,
— furnishing the walls of,
— made out of worst bedroom,
— sofa,
— table,
— walls,
Nursing,

Occasional visitor,
Oetzmann,
Oilcloth, cheap,
— for walls,
— resembling old mosaic,
Old London lamps,
— night-dresses invaluable,
Oriental carpets for dining-room,
— — Smee's, for drawing-room,

— rugs and carpets, sweeping them one way,
— — for hall,
Our dead,
Ovens, cleansing,

Painted suites of furniture,
Painting,
— spare rooms,
Palm-leaved baskets for soiled linen,
Panelled drawing-room,
Panes, of glass, tiny,
Pantry, housemaid's,
Paper for day nursery, Pither's,
— stand,
Papering,
Pears in jelly,
Penge,
Persian and Turkey carpets,
Personal expenses, wife's,
Petty tyrannies,
Pheasant, boiled,
— roasted,
Photographs for bedrooms, where to buy,
— — nursery,
Piano back, draping,
— chair,
— drapery for back,
Piano, drawing-room,
— front,
— grand,
— stool unendurable,
Picture rail, Maple's,
— teaching for children,
Pictures for bedrooms,
— hooks for,
— in schoolroom,
Pigeons, stuffed,
Pinafores,
Pincushions,
Pither, address of,
Pither's papers,

— printed linen,
Plain cook, wages of,
Plantation coffee,
Plants and flowers for rooms,
Plates,
Plum pudding,
Plumber, &c.,
Pokerette,
'Portable property,' servants',
Pretence of wealth,
Pretty room for each servant,
Prince Albert's pudding,
Printed muslin, Liberty's,
Professional decorator,
Ptarmigan,
Purchasing furniture,
Putting the feet on chairs,

Queen Anne cretonne (terra cotta),
— — table,
— — tables, Oetzmann's,
Quilts, cretonne covering for,
— eider-down,
— Francis's,

Rabbits, buying them,
Reading in bed,
Rebecca jars,
— — Elliot's,
Reception-rooms, the regulation,
Recipes for menus,
Rents less out of London,
Rest, necessity of complete,
Returning from school,
Ribs of beef,
Rice pudding,
Rider Haggard,
Rolled ribs of beef,
Roman sheeting for curtains,
Room for children, heating properly,
Rooms, appropriation of,

Round tables,
Rugs, good,
— in front of fires, danger from,
Rush *v.* bamboo table,
Russian diapers,
— embroideries,
Rylands' stain for floors,

Saddle of mutton, small,
Salmon,
Salt-cellars,
— Doulton's,
Salviati glass,
— ware,
Sanitary papers for children's schoolroom,
Sanitas in saucers,
Satin chairs,
Saucepans,
— cleaning them,
— number of,
— Whiteley's,
School training for boys,
Schoolboys, dealing with,
Schoolmaster, orthodox,
Schoolroom ceiling,
— dresses,
— Indian matting for,
— Kidderminster carpet for,
— maid,
— papering walls of,
— position of, in house,
— tables and chairs,
Schoolrooms,
Scinde rugs,
— — price of,
Screens,
— in bedrooms,
Scullery,
— ceiling,
— walls,
Second-hand carriages,

— — where sold,
Selfishness of parents,
Separate beds for servants,
Serge curtains,
Serges, Burnett's,
— Colbourne & Co.'s,
Servants,
— apartments,
— bedrooms,
— clothes of,
— encouraging them to walk and work in the garden,
— feelings of new,
— giving them good books to read,
— harassing them,
— pretty furniture for,
— wasteful,
Sets of bedroom furniture, price of,
Settees (bamboo), Liberty's, for the hall,
Sewing for girls,
Sheets, bed,
Shelves for morning-room,
— recesses for,
Sheraton furniture,
Shoolbred,
Shoolbred's curtains,
Shop specialties,
Shopping, judicious,
Short blinds in bedrooms,
Side lanterns,
Sideboards,
Sink,
— regular flushing of,
Sinks, disinfecting,
Sitting-room and workroom for servants,
Sketches, Mrs. McClelland's,
Slamming doors,
Sleeping with window open,
Slop-pails,
Slovenly manners,
Small girls,
— house, price of furnishing,

— infant, bed for,
Smuts and blacks,
Soap,
Sofa-ottomans for spare rooms,
Sofas,
— covering for,
— Maple's,
— nursery,
— striped curtains for,
— substitute for,
Soles, boiled,
— fried,
Soup from bones and vegetables,
Soups, excellent,
Spare glass and china,
— room beds,
— — floor,
— — furniture,
— — — cost of,
— — readiness for occupation,
Spring mattress best for beds,
Squabbles about money,
Square black cupboards, receptacles for music,
— ottoman for piano,
Stained floors,
Stair carpets,
Staircases,
Stamped velveteen,
Stephens, address of,
Stores,
Straight backed chairs, Smee's,
Strange nurse,
Strode, address of,
Strode's iron lamps,
Suburban clay,
Suburbs of London,
Sugar,
— price of,
Summer babies,
Sunday in the schoolroom,
Sunday's supper,

Sundries,
Sunless rooms,
Sunshine, first necessity of,
Sutherland table for drawing-room,
Swiss 'mull' muslin, cost of,

Table drawers, bedroom,
Tablecloths,
Tables, Chippendale design,
— rickety,
Tapestry, drawing-room,
— imitation,
— tablecloth,
— toilet covers,
Tea after dinner odious,
— cost of,
— in the schoolroom,
Tea cloth, five o'clock,
Tea-table in drawing-room,
Tea-things in morning-room,
Teetotallers,
Temporary 'help' for cook,
Tennis,
— parties, afternoon,
Terra-cotta chintz for bedroom doors, Burnett's,
— paper,
Third room to sit in,
Tiled hearth,
Toasted cheese,
Tobacco,
Toilet covers,
— drawers,
— 'tidies' to be avoided,
Tooth-brushes,
Tooth water-glasses,
Treatment of servants,
Treloar,
Treloar's matting,
Trübner & Co.,
Tumblers,
Turbot, half a,

Turkey carpets,
— small,
Turret puddings,

Umbrella stands,
— — Maple's,
Umbrellas, wet,
Unhealthiness of gas,
Unpunctuality, effects of,
Upholsters,
Upholstering chairs,

Varnished wall-paper,
Vases,
Vegetable dishes,
Visiting, ethics of,

Wall-paper,
Wall-papers, E. Pither's,
Wardrobe, Edwin's dressing-room,
— making, amateur,
Wardrobes,
— Hampton's,
Washable papers,
Washing brushes,
— — Whiteley's,
— cost of,
Washing stand,
Waste-paper bags,
Water-bottles,
Watts, Mr., address of,
Wedding finery, excessive display of,
White curtains,
— soup,
Whiteley,
Wicker chairs for drawing-room,
Widgeon,
Wild duck,
Window-blinds,
Windows,
— cathedral glass top,

— open at the top,
Window wedges,
Winter babies,
Withers & Co., address of,
Witney blankets,
Women architects,
Wooden bedsteads,
— mantelpieces,
Woollen tapestry,
Worrying the nurse to death,
Writing-desk for the dining-room,

Yorkshire pudding,
Young couples,
— — decoration of house for,
— — management of house for,
— nurses a mistake,